CRUSADE

EXILE BOOK 3

CRUSADE

EXILE BOOK 3

GLYNN STEWART

FAOLAN'S PEN
PUBLISHING
faolanspen.com

This edition published in 2019 by:

Faolan's Pen Publishing Inc.

22 King St. S, Suite 300

Waterloo, Ontario

N2J 1N8 Canada

ISBN-13: 978-1-988035-94-9 (print) | 978-1-988035-95-6 (epub)

A record of this book is available from Library and Archives Canada.

Printed in the United States of America

1 2 3 4 5 6 7 8 9 10

First edition

First printing: December 2019

Illustration © 2019 Tom Edwards

TomEdwardsDesign.com

Faolan's Pen Publishing logo is a trademark of Faolan's Pen Publishing Inc.

Read more books from Glynn Stewart at faolanspen.com

1

―――――――

"Get ThreeHeart on the com," Admiral Isaac Lestroud barked. "We need those cruisers in closer, coordinating their fire with Oohoon's ships."

The small black man's words were only half of his order. As Captain Aloysius Connor calmly took over control of the flag deck's communications system, Isaac's hands were flying through the three-dimensional representation of his fleet.

Lord of Seven Stars ThreeHeart was the commander of the Skree-Skree portion of his fleet. Those eight strike cruisers weren't going to make or break this battle, but they'd be a *lot* more effective if the Skree-Skree ships were supporting Oohoon's two battlecruisers.

Isaac finished positioning the icons in his hologram and flipped them to his operations officer.

"I've got it," Connor replied. "The Vistans are holding their flank just fine. It's our new friends who are stepping on each other's tails."

Most of the ships in Isaac's fleet were almost identical. The Vistans, rescuees from a shattered world who were now humanity's strongest allies in this corner of the galaxy, had the most experience adapting human technology to their physiologies.

Oohoon's people, the Tohnbohn, had been inducted into the

alliance eighteen months ago. They'd received a pair of battlecruisers built by Isaac's home Republic of Exilium to anchor their fleet and would be commissioning their first home-built battlecruisers soon.

The Skree-Skree were a far more recent addition and the reason why the fleet was *here*. The genocidal AIs known as the Rogue Matrices had tried to terraform the Skree-Skree homeworld six months earlier.

One of Isaac's battle groups had been close enough to stop that and recruit the aliens to his new alliance, but the attack had led them here. This system was ten light-years from the Skree-Skree System and was just *crawling* with robots.

"Our not-so-friendly robots picked up on the lack of coordination," Isaac told Connor as he studied the screen. Ten of the Matrix combat platforms were now charging directly at Oohoon's battlecruisers. Unlike *his* ships, they went from zero to ten percent of lightspeed in the blink of an eye.

"ThreeHeart got your call," Connor replied. "The Matrices are going to...ow."

The Skree-Skree were scavengers and ambush predators. The name the humans had hung on them was the sound that their entire language sounded like, and they very much reminded Isaac of a rat crossed with a hunchbacked monkey.

ThreeHeart moved his ships into position as ordered, yes...but he waited a critical ten seconds to do so with *purpose*, his ships' particle-cannon turrets hammering into the flanks of a group of Matrices with their attention locked on Oohoon's apparently vulnerable battle-cruisers.

"Keep Swimmer-Under-Sunlight-Skies informed," Isaac said calmly. "Then order Vice Admiral Anderson to swing towards Oohoon with *Dante* and her escorts. If the Matrices want to stick their robotic feelers in a guillotine, lets chop them off."

There were only twenty combat platforms in the fleet facing him, even backed up by about sixty smaller units. He had six battlecruisers and thirty-two strike cruisers to face them, a fleet that was requiring *another* recalibration of his mental math for warfare.

The problem, of course, was that this was only the outer security element. There were at *least* as many ships orbiting their actual prey.

Deeper in the system was the massive sphere of the Regional Construction Matrix, an AI dedicated to transforming worlds in sixty systems to the standards set by its builders.

An AI that had lost the protocol that prevented it from terraforming worlds with people living on them.

———

DANTE WAS the oldest surviving battlecruiser of the Republic of Exilium, rebuilt at one point from the wreckage of the two ships that had come with the Exiles on their seventy-thousand-light-year voyage from the Terran Confederacy.

Since then, she'd been the testbed for every technology the Exiles had bought from or been given by first the Matrices and then the ragged survivors of the AIs' Assini builders. Every technology inside Isaac's flagship, *Vigil*, had been first tested in *Dante*.

Even *Vigil* was now obsolete, "merely" equal to the four battlecruisers the Republic had given the Vistans and the Tohnbohn. More powerful warships had been built and were on their way to Isaac, but his fastest ships only moved at two hundred and fifty-six times the speed of light.

And as *Dante* and her four strike-cruiser escorts slammed fire into the Rogue Matrix formation flank, they were just over a hundred light-years from home.

"Swimmer-Under-Sunlight-Skies suggests that his ships and *Vigil* advance on the remainder of the formation," Lieutenant Commander Ursula Bayer reported. She was the communications officer on his staff, the most junior of the handful of officers supporting Isaac.

She might be junior, but the dark-haired, stocky officer was proving *very* good at assessing what did and didn't need to be given to the Admiral.

"VK," Isaac barked at thin air. "Assess?"

Specialty Matrix XR-13-9-D-VK was a human-modified "child" of a Matrix AI that had entered service with the Republic of Exilium. It acted as a backup to the battlecruiser's executive officer but was also available to the Admiral for tactical queries.

"Three battlecruisers and eighteen strike cruisers should suffice to deal with the units not caught in their attempt to take advantage of our momentary weakness," the AI replied. "Most likely reaction will be for them to attempt to withdraw. We will not be able to match their velocity for almost eleven minutes after they commence a retreat, and will lose weapons range."

"That's what I thought," Isaac agreed. The light and heavy particle cannons that made most of his force's weaponry had an effective range of about two light-seconds. His ships could accelerate *fast*, but they couldn't match the Matrices' reactionless engines.

They could go a lot faster than the Matrices in the long run, as he reminded his techs every time they wanted to install reactionless drives on his ships.

"Inform the Third-Among-Singers that he is to hold position for now," Isaac ordered. He studied his display. The second group of combat platforms were lurking at the edge of their range, trading mostly-useless laser fire with *Vigil* and her Vistan sisters. The group that had tried to savage Oohoon's cruisers was now slipping out of the trap in pieces, but he was still looking at twelve or more combat platforms that would fall back on the main force.

"Get me Captain Alstairs," he continued. "We can take these bastards, but the last thing I want is to face them backed up by the RCM itself. It's time for a show."

VIGIL MIGHT NO LONGER BE the most advanced ship of Isaac Lestroud's Exilium Space Fleet, but she was still his personal flagship and had the most experienced crew in the ESF. No other crew could have pulled off what he needed them to.

In a moment of apparent misreading of the data, the battlecruiser zigged *into* the path of one of the gamma-ray lasers the Matrices were firing at his fleet. The beam hit *something*, and oxygen and other volatiles blazed into space as the battlecruiser lurched beneath the Admiral.

The screens on Isaac's own chair told him the truth: *Vigil* was still fully functional, though they'd just expended ten percent of her supply of oxygen and other gases in the tank they'd put in the line of fire.

The main display, however, showed him that Captain Cameron Alstairs had potentially missed his calling as a thespian. *Vigil*'s acceleration had cut by over half, and she was using what was left to try and hide behind the ten strike cruisers still escorting her.

Even the toughest units in this fight could only take a handful of hits before being knocked out of it. The extreme range was the only thing keeping either fleet intact…but *Vigil*'s current course was blood in the water, and the Matrices *knew* Isaac's ship by now. *Vigil* had left a trail of broken and shattered Matrix warships across a dozen systems already.

The Matrices went for it. Forty AI warships flung themselves forward, trying to close with the "crippled" battlecruiser. They did it well, picking up the scattered survivors of their other wing and coordinating their ECM to cover their approach, but they'd fallen into his trap.

"And…now," Isaac murmured.

Vigil flipped back over her escorts to bring her main weapons to bear. The battlecruiser was just under half a kilometer long, looking like nothing so much as an arrow with a ring in front of the "fletching" of her engines.

The long arrowhead supported light particle-cannon turrets that matched her main heavy particle cannon for range, and all of those beams fired at once.

Like the Matrices, *Vigil* had been built with gamma-ray lasers. Hers had been upgraded with technology from the Matrices' builders, and they had over twice the striking power of his enemy's weapons.

All of the Tohnbohn and Vistan battlecruisers were exact clones of *Vigil*, though they lacked the human-mod Matrix AI. *Dante* was a bit more of a mess, lacking the main particle cannon but having even heavier lasers.

Combined with thirty-two strike cruisers, Isaac's fleet commanded an unimaginable amount of firepower, and the Matrices had gone for his bait…letting him bring *all* of it to bear inside their most effective ranges.

The hologram in front of him lit up with brilliant lines marking the assortment of energy weapons in play. The Matrix ships could take hits from most of his weapons...but his ships could take hits from their weapons, too.

It was a massacre—but luring the robots into effective range of his fleet had also got *them* into effective range.

"*Lastborn* has been hit," Connor reported as the Skree-Skree strike cruiser got herself caught in the line of fire from the combat platforms. "...*Lastborn* is gone."

Isaac nodded silently. The Skree-Skree ship wasn't the only one. *Macduff* was one of his own, and the strike cruiser was reeling out of the line, spewing volatiles in every direction. Escape pods started to blast clear of the ship...and then her matter-conversion core went critical.

"Last Matrix units just punched out," Isaac's operations officer reported softly as the violent sun of *Macduff*'s death lit up their screen. "None of the combat platforms escaped."

The Matrices used a very different FTL from the modified Alcubierre warp engine his people used. The tachyon-punch transition was nearly instantaneous across a vast range, but it was also lethal to organics and caused severe degradation to the holographic memory systems used by the Matrices.

"We've brought the Regional Matrix to bay," Isaac said aloud. "I don't care about recon units anymore. I need damage reports from the fleet as soon as possible—and we need shuttles out searching for our survivors."

One of the Vistan strike cruisers was gone too. Three ships—barely two hundred people, with the amount of automation the Republic was building into their vessels now—wasn't much against twenty Matrix combat platforms in the grand scheme of things.

But there were barely more than four million humans in Exilium, the leftovers of a rebellion that First Admiral Adrienne Gallant had crushed. And since Isaac Lestroud had once been Isaac *Gallant*, the First Admiral's only son, he couldn't avoid feeling responsible for every last one of them.

His allies might come from more-intact species—the Tohnbohn and

Skree-Skree even still had their own homeworlds, despite the Matrices —but that didn't mean their lives were worth less.

"VK?" he asked aloud.

"Admiral." The AI was technically always paying attention, but the Matrices serving in the Republic fleet were learning to provide some degree of privacy now.

"How's our link with Twenty-Five?" Isaac asked.

"We have a full telemetry hookup with ZDX-175-25," VK confirmed. "They have confirmed all ships are standing by to punch into the system on your order."

VK was editorializing, Isaac knew. Their allied Combat Coordination Matrices—the AIs that ran the Matrix combat platforms—were *far* too happy that Regional Construction Matrix XR-13-9 and the Assini had finally made it possible for them to fight their genocidal cousins.

They didn't take waiting very well, even when they *understood* the plan.

"Twenty-Five knows the plan," Isaac reiterated his thought aloud. "They hold until I give the order."

"If the situation becomes critical enough, I cannot guarantee that our Combat Coordination friends will hold," VK warned him. The AIs that worked with humans got more human in many ways, Isaac was realizing. VK and their siblings might be cousins to ZDX-175-25, but their loyalties were *very* clear.

"If the situation is that critical, VK, I doubt I'll mind," he admitted to the computer. "Twenty-Five is not an idiot, after all. Just very focused."

"Sir, I have that damage report," Connor reported as he stepped up to the side of Isaac's seat. "It could have been a lot worse, but…"

"It can always be worse," Isaac replied, bringing up the data on the screens attached to his seat arms. The big holographic display in front of him was showing the main tactical display, allowing everyone on the flag bridge to keep a careful eye on their target.

Isaac had been a battle group commander for the Terran Confederacy for years before he'd joined the rebellion against his mother and been exiled. He'd commanded the Exilium Space Fleet since then, and had been in charge of an allied fleet fighting the Matrices since the fall of the Vistan homeworld three years before.

He knew how to read between the lines of the official reports he was being given.

"Inform Captain Tremaine and Captain Sanders they are to pull their ships back to the rendezvous point," he told Connor. "Neither *Romeo* nor *Horatio* is combat-capable." He needed two future strike cruisers more than he needed two half-crippled strike cruisers today.

He continued down the list.

"Tell ThreeHeart his people don't lie as well as they think they do," he continued. "*Dancer* and *Forlorn* are to fall back with *Romeo* and *Horatio*. *Shaaaaa* is to do the same, as is *Frozen Memory*."

Shaaaaa was a Tohnbohn strike cruiser…but *Frozen Memory* was one of his Vistan *battlecruisers* and he was going to miss her.

"Swimmer-Under-Sunlit-Skies had a note attached to the report that said he was expecting that," Connor said with a chuckle. "Translation was funky, it always is with those guys, but something along the lines of 'this report is dark-water-beast-crap.'"

The Vistans had two mouths and hearing sensitive enough to allow for echolocation, which made their language mostly incomprehensible and utterly unpronounceable to humans. The translation programs in *Vigil*'s computers were working overtime these days.

At least the Matrices could translate their own communications.

"Let's get those ships out of here," Isaac ordered. "That brings us down to five battlecruisers and thirty-one strike cruisers. It should be enough."

The massive icon at the center of the holographic display mocked him. His people had never fought one of the Regional Construction Matrices before. The AI on that spherical ship was in charge of the Construction—terraforming—operations across dozens of worlds. It had already Constructed dozens of worlds.

It had tried to Construct Vista, a process that had killed nine-tenths of the planet's population before they could be evacuated to the nearest world where the Construction process was complete, now known as Refuge. It had tried to Construct the Skree-Skree homeworld.

Isaac's scouts suggested that this particular RCM was responsible for the deaths of at least seven intelligent species before it had encountered the Republic and the Republic's allies.

That ended today. His thirty-six ships might not be enough to punch through the eighty warships around the RCM, let alone deal with the six-kilometer black sphere of the RCM's primary hull, but he had to try.

If nothing else, well…that his fleet didn't look like enough was the *point*.

2

―――――

"SOMETHING ABOUT THIS STINKS," Connor noted several minutes later. Their damaged ships had vanished into warp, heading back to a rendezvous point almost half a light-year away.

"Other than the fact that we're advancing on an artificially intelligent starship almost six kilometers across?" Isaac asked. His remaining ships were holding a perfect formation, with four-ship escort boxes around each battlecruiser and the extra cruisers spread out into wings that expanded their lines of fire.

Even the Matrices had stopped firing missiles, he noted. Adrienne Gallant's engineers back in the Confederacy had been professional paranoids and had built in an AI-operated failsafe to activate a warship's defenses against cee-fractional objects.

Those same failsafes were present on every ship in his fleet and had proven, again and again, that they were capable of engaging even the Matrices' reactionless missiles traveling at point nine nine cee.

Vigil and *Dante* now carried the K-sequence AIs, and those Matrix-descended systems were *far* more capable than the Republic's original Confederacy-built AIs. Even the strike cruisers, which still lacked full Matrix offshoots, had far more capable AIs than had been available to the Republic four years earlier, when they'd first been designed.

Nothing in Isaac's fleet even carried missiles. The Matrices were just as effective at shooting them down. Even a single one of the recon nodes that served as destroyer escorts for the Matrices could absorb every missile the Republic could build. The RCM…well, they had only a limited idea what it had for weapons or defenses.

"Well, yes, we're charging willy-nilly at the largest starship we've ever seen," Connor agreed. "A ship we know nothing about, at that."

"We know what XR-13-9 has for defenses," Isaac pointed out. "Which represented a huge leap of trust on their part."

It was amazing what rescuing the last survivors of an AI's creator race could do for that AI's opinion of you.

"We do, which is why this stinks," Connor replied. "Where are the fortresses, Isaac? Where are the mines, the missile platforms, the multi-shot gamma-ray laser satellites? Where are all the fixed defenses we *know* the Matrices can build—but that XR carefully didn't tell us how many they'd built around themselves?"

Isaac looked at the hologram.

"Not here," he said slowly. "Alstairs!"

"Admiral?" the Captain replied instantly.

"Full spread of sensor drones, right at that big bastard," Isaac ordered. "If there's something up with it, I want to know."

"You don't think they're hiding the defenses?" his operations officer asked.

Isaac gestured at the screen. "There's nothing but empty space between us and the gas giant they're orbiting. That they weren't punching out was already feeling wrong, but you're right.

"*If* that's the RCM, then all of the defenses are missing."

"You think it's a decoy?" Alstairs asked as dozens of new green icons materialized on the hologram. Unlike the capital ships, the drones did have reactionless drives—and being only somewhat larger than Matrix missiles, they moved at eighty percent of the speed of light.

"It might be an ECM screen, in which case I'm wondering what the other jaw of the trap is," Isaac replied. "But everything *says* that it's a six-kilometer Matrix ship, and the only six-kilometer Matrix ship anyone knows about is a Regional Construction Matrix."

"It could have built another one," Connor suggested.

"It could have," Isaac agreed. "But budding off a new AI of that scale is a massive project. Just building D and dumping most of Thirteen-Nine's memory into them ate up enough resources for multiple combat platforms."

Or so XR-13-9-D, the direct bud from XR-13-9 that was the patriarch of all of the K-series AIs, had said. If Isaac was going to start mistrusting D again, he was in *real* trouble.

"The hull alone of an RCM is at least an eighteen-month project," VK interjected into the conversation. "Building a Matrix Core of sufficient size to hold the full capabilities of a Regional Construction Matrix would take at least twice that."

"Drones show she's there," Alstairs reported. "The buggers are just as trigger-happy as always."

They were thirty minutes from range and rapidly approaching the point of no return. Isaac had to make the call and his gut said something was wrong…but that it wasn't wrong *enough* to counter everything he'd put together.

"We continue the advance," he said calmly. "Make sure the subcommanders know we think there might be something wrong here, but the truth is that it can't be *more* dangerous than an RCM."

All three of his subordinate flotilla leaders had different ranks. Swimmer-Under-Sunlit-Skies was the Third-Among-Singers of the Guardian Star-Choir of Refuge. ThreeHeart was one of three Lords of Seven Stars among the Skree-Skree's Sworn Guardians.

Oohoon was…well, Oohoon. The Tohnbohn didn't really go in for titles or ranks as humans understood them. Someday, Isaac would work out how their society was organized, but for now, Oohoon was in command of their ships. That had to be enough.

Sub-commander covered all his bases, though. People knew who he meant.

"What if they took an RCM hull and packed it full of guns?" Connor asked softly. "Our Matrices built *Interceptor*, but we haven't seen much in terms of variation in the Rogues' line of battle."

"Protocol *should* resist that level of resource application toward combat units," VK replied. "But…the RCMs, especially, are not entirely bound by protocols outside the Core Protocols."

"And we all know what happened to the Core Protocols," Isaac observed. Those had, after all, included prohibitions against harming sentients. Repeated tachyon punches had turned those sections of the Rogue's code, at least, into swiss cheese.

"So, we could be looking at, what, a Matrix dreadnought?" Connor asked.

"If we are, we need to know," the Admiral replied grimly. "And if we are, I still think the plan will work. Let's see what they do when we cross the point of no return."

He smiled coldly.

"If they *don't* do what I expect, that does suggest that ship is not a Regional Construction Matrix, after all."

"WELL, THAT'S DEFINITELY AN ANSWER," VK concluded, the AI seeing the same data as the humans without needing to study the holographic presentation.

"Agreed."

Isaac's answer echoed in the quiet of the flag deck. His battlecruisers and strike cruisers were advancing on the Matrix position, and the Matrices had finally responded. The combat platforms, recon and security nodes, and recon nodes were all ships he'd expected to come out at him. Those were the subordinate Matrices the Rogues used as warships.

He hadn't been expecting the big ship to come out to meet him. They'd "known" that was the Regional Construction Matrix, which meant that it would either run or hang back while its defenders counterattacked.

His battle plan had hinged on the Rogue Matrices doing one of those things. He hadn't expected the big ship to sortie with the smaller AI warships.

"All right, VK. Give me an estimate," Isaac ordered. "If that thing is a dreadnought built on an RCM hull chassis, how bad are we looking at?"

"We have no basis to expect new weapons systems on Rogue ships," the AI replied. "They're limited to the same pulse gun, gamma-ray laser and reactionless missile arsenal as the rest of the unmodified Matrices.

"Given the mass and hull surface available, however…my calculations suggest approximately twenty times the armament of a combat platform."

"So, over a hundred grasers, thousands of pulse guns and an insane number of missiles," Connor concluded. "With that many launchers, could they actually get missiles through?"

"Negative. Our own pulse-gun armament is sufficient to deal with a functionally infinite number of incoming missiles," VK replied confidently.

Isaac said nothing, his hands already flying across his controls as the tactical crew drew in the usual engagement spheres. Range was mostly limited by the ability to hit with lightspeed or near-lightspeed energy weapons. Even using tachyon com–equipped drones to provide real-time targeting data, accuracy dropped off to nearly nothing at about half a million kilometers.

Across the entirety of both fleets, only the battlecruisers actually carried weapons that could land heavy hits beyond that range. Their heavy particle cannons could hurt a combat platform at half again that range, as could *Valiant* and *Dante's* high-gamma-frequency lasers.

"Effective range is in ten minutes," Connor reported. "Your orders, Admiral?"

They were already past the point of no return. They were too close to the gas giant the Rogues had been orbiting to bring up their warp drives safely, and they had too much velocity to reverse course and escape the Matrices and their reactionless point one cee drives.

"If the situation was worse, we could risk warping out," Isaac noted softly. "But this is still doable, I think. Get me Twenty-Five."

———

THE MATRIX DREADNOUGHT was clearly calculating that the allies had identified it for what it was by now. Its core AI also decided that it had *enough* grasers that a low hit probability was entirely acceptable.

The computers calmly drew the gamma-ray lasers in on the hologram as thin red lines. Dozens of them. *Hundreds.* There were sixty AI warships approaching Isaac's fleet, and there were a *lot* of energy weapons on board those ships.

"Hits along the line, but they don't have the energy to breach the armor," Connor reported. "Maybe half a dozen hits, but that's a *lot* of fire."

"All battlecruisers, target the dreadnought," Isaac said calmly. "It's a big target. We're going to ring their damn bell. *Fire.*"

Four heavy particle cannons, eight gamma-ray lasers and four high-gamma-frequency lasers fired at one target. Over half of the beams struck home, a six-kilometer-wide target easier to hit than anything else in play.

"I've got vaporized armor and that's it," VK told them. "No breaches, no critical system damage. The range is too long for the amount of armor on that beast."

"It'll have to do," Isaac said. "All ships to reverse thrust, maintain beams on target and focus fire on the dreadnought until I order differently. Standard range?"

"Now," Connor half-whispered.

The occasional hits were starting to become more common, and they were hitting with real force now. New icons flickered across Isaac's fleet as armor plating shattered under the fire and damage reports trickled in.

"Dreadnought continues to absorb our fire," the AI said. "We're punching through now, but it has a lot of mass. We've knocked a couple of grasers out, that's all. She's going to rotate to protect them."

"Do it," Isaac murmured. More icons marked the dreadnought as multiple systems went down on the target.

"She's down at least ten grasers…she is rotating," Connor ordered.

"Execute Mousetrap," Isaac snapped. "All ships, break off, target the combat platforms."

The dreadnought was now ZDX-175-25's problem. The plan had

been for *their* Matrices, Matrices that had kept the prohibitions against killing and were phenomenally angry at their cousins who hadn't, to ambush and destroy the RCM.

Now a modified version of that plan came into effect. Fifteen combat platforms accompanied by thirty recon nodes tachyon-punched into the star system, three hundred thousand kilometers behind the dreadnought.

The need to pull ships all the way back to Exilium, almost a hundred light-years away from the Skree-Skree home system, had limited the ability of the ESF to fully upgrade its ships. Any Matrix unit was capable of self-replication—which meant they were also capable of self-*upgrading*.

The forty-five friendly Matrix warships weren't carrying grasers. Aided by the survivors of their creators, the Assini, they'd upgraded their energy weapons to *zettahertz* lasers.

Those beams were capable of punching through the armor the Rogue Matrix dreadnought carried at over seven hundred thousand kilometers. At three hundred thousand kilometers, they tore through the entire dreadnought like it was made of tissue paper.

The rest of the fleet focused on the combat platforms, hammering the ships with particle cannons and lasers as they closed. The dreadnought didn't die easily either, and grasers lashed Isaac's fleet, sending new red icons cascading across his displays.

"Dreadnought is down," VK reported. "Power signatures are disrupted, conversion cores are—"

The dreadnought disappeared as her matter-conversion power systems destabilized into tiny suns.

"*Iago* is gone," Connor reported. "*Macbeth* and *Othello* have taken critical damage and we've lost another of ThreeHeart's cruisers. Sir, we can't—"

"We take them," Isaac cut him off. He'd known when he had chosen not to break off that it was going to cost. "As few get away as we can manage."

The Matrices could replace AI cores faster than he could replace crews, but at this point, the allies could replace *ships* faster than a single Regional Construction Matrix could.

"Hammer them," he ordered grimly. The holographic display announced the loss of another Vistan strike cruiser, eighty people they'd rescued from the death of their world only to lead to their deaths here.

Two of his allied combat platforms blew apart as well…and then it was over.

"Estimate six combat platforms and eighteen lesser nodes escaped," VK reported. "The rest have been destroyed. Along with the dreadnought."

Isaac exhaled. His focus was always on the other list.

He'd once thought *Othello* was a cursed ship, but she was still there. So was *Macbeth*, but the damage codes suggested that wasn't going to last.

Including *Iago*, six more strike cruisers had been lost finishing the job. None of his battlecruisers were undamaged. His own Matrices had lost three combat platforms and five recon nodes.

And they hadn't stopped the Regional Construction Matrix.

"All ships to form up on the debris field and deploy shuttles for search and rescue," Isaac ordered, forcing his voice to level calm.

"Sub-commanders are invited aboard *Vigil* for operational discussions in two hours. I want full damage reports and supply status for every vessel by then. Can we manage that, Connor?"

"Priority is S&R, I assume?" his operations officer asked, his voice shaken.

"Exactly.

"I'll make it all happen."

"Thank you, Aloysius."

3

———————

THE DETAILED DAMAGE reports weren't any better than the estimates and high-level reports Isaac had received as the battle ended. He'd lost fewer ships than he'd dared hope, but nine strike cruisers and eight Matrix warships was still a lot of dead people and AIs.

Worse, he'd fought the battle he'd been expecting to…but his intended target hadn't been anywhere near this system. He flipped through the astrographic charts as he waited in the conference room.

The three-dimensional map he had filling the room stretched from Exilium on one end, the Constructed World he and his fellow Exiles had colonized on arrival, to their current location at the other. The Skree-Skree home system was ten light-years away on a not-quite-direct line to Exilium.

The Tohnbohn's Bohon System was twenty light-years away but "up" from that direct line, putting them ninety-two light-years from Exilium.

Vista was in the Hearthfire System, thirty-six light-years from their current position and "down", putting it seventy light-years from Exilium. Refuge was the same distance from Exilium and thirty-four light-years from here.

Every warp drive ship in his fleet could travel at two hundred and fifty-six times the speed of light—the Matrices were even faster. With Matrix- and Assini-augmented construction facilities, they'd built the new strike cruisers quickly enough that the older ships with slower drives were only used for home defense now.

Exilium was building a lot of battlecruisers and strike cruisers now. Crewing them was a nightmare, which was the main reason he had the allies he did. They were building their own ships, but the arsenal of this alliance was humanity's manufactories in their tiny colony.

"Your guests are here, Admiral," one of the Marine guards told him.

"Send them all in," he ordered.

Vice Admiral Lauretta Giannovi was first. She'd hitched her wagon to his rising star in the military of the Terran Confederacy a long time before. When he'd risen to command a battle group in his mother's fleet, Lauretta Giannovi had commanded his battlecruiser flagship.

She'd followed him into rebellion and remained the second-ranked officer of the Exilium Space Fleet. She was a tall and dark-skinned woman, pale only in comparison to him, and they traded nods as she took her seat across from him.

Giannovi was the only other human in the room. The senior Republic officer after Isaac himself, she acted as the sub-commander for the Republic contingent while he commanded the entire fleet.

He knew Swimmer-Under-Sunlit-Skies relatively well. The Vistan had served as gunnery officer on the flagship of Sings-Over-Darkened-Waters, the leader of their defensive militia, when the Matrices had arrived to Construct their world.

He'd skyrocketed in rank since then, an inevitable consequence of being competent in an explosively expanding military facing a battle for the very existence of their species.

Swimmer looked like a large, squat frog, with massive expanses of darker skin along his neck and head that acted as sonar receivers. He had both gills and mouths on either side of his neck as well, and his breathing through his gills created an echoing series of chirps that allowed him to "see" the world. The bulbous eyes on the top of a Vistan's head were all but useless.

Lord of Seven Stars ThreeHeart followed the Vistan. The two aliens were both roughly the same height, barely a hundred and sixty centimeters tall, but ThreeHeart was both skinnier and more hunched over than the amphibious Vistan. The Skree-Skree looked very rodent-like to human eyes, with a long tail and a body that permanently leaned forward.

Of course, where a rodent would have had fur, a Skree-Skree had light blue feathers and a beak instead of a muzzle. The rapid-fire chirping of their language was almost as impossible for a human to understand as the two-mouthed speech of a Vistan.

Last, as Isaac had come to expect, was Oohoon. The Tohnbohn was a large creature, nearly the size of the horse-like Assini whose pacifism kept them a *long* way from this mission, wrapped in a heavy shell. They had eight stubby legs emerging from the bottom of the shell that moved them along, and four long and delicate arms that could emerge from anywhere around the shell.

Similarly, they had four "heads" that were really just stalks with two eyes on them. The Tohnbohn's mouth and vocal organs were concealed and protected inside the shell, the echo helping create an almost whalesong-esque tone to their language.

Oohoon started speaking, and it took a moment for the computerized translator in Isaac's ear to catch up with the soft, slow song.

"Will Twenty-Five be joining us?"

"I have linked in, Eminence Oohoon," ZDX-175-25's mechanized voice sounded in the room. The Tohnbohn had a translator inside their shell that would be giving them a translated version of Twenty-Five's words.

"My remotes are currently busy engaging in analysis of the Rogue dreadnought," Twenty-Five continued. "I believe that was a higher priority than having a physical presence at this meeting."

ThreeHeart's rapid-fired chirps and squeaks answered.

"I agree. Rescue of our injured and assessment of that vessel are highest priority," the Skree-Skree fleet commander noted when the translator caught up. "I am concerned that such a ship may be on its way to my own world to complete what they once began!"

"I'm concerned that ships like it are headed to all of our worlds,"

Isaac admitted, which struck all of the others silent. "VK, Twenty-Five. How many of these things might our Rogue have built?"

"It is difficult to be certain," Twenty-Five replied. "This vessel is in neither our databanks nor the databanks from *Shezarim*."

Shezarim had been the Assini evacuation ship that Isaac and his people had ended up rescuing. So far as anyone could tell, the five thousand or so Assini on that ship were the last survivors of their race —a scouting expedition had been sent to their home system, but *Shezarim* had barely escaped ahead of a world-killing solar flare.

The ship had carried a full database of everything the Assini had developed since unleashing the Matrices on the galaxy. It was that database that had seen Isaac's ships and the Matrices upgraded—and that had underwritten the construction of the *new* battlecruisers currently on their way from Exilium.

"But it is based on the hull structure in our databanks for the Regional Construction Matrix," VK said. "That requires eighteen months to construct. Presuming they are using a somewhat upgraded combat platform AI rather than a full RCM, and that the vessel is lacking the internal storage and shipyards of an RCM, the weapons and engines could take another eight to ten months."

"So, they started building these after we kicked their asses at Vista," Isaac concluded. "That explains why they didn't come back before the evacuation was done."

"The number of these dreadnoughts available to the Matrix is limited but unknown," Twenty-Five concluded. "Standard protocols would indicate that a minimum of three be constructed—one to carry out the first counterstrike and two to provide the doubled-strength follow-up if that failed."

"Except we were lured into a trap," Swimmer-Under-Sunlit-Skies said. "We once again forgot that our enemy, while mechanical, is intelligent."

"The situation is more complicated than that, Third-Among-Singers," Isaac replied. "All of our intelligence was quite certain that the Regional Construction Matrix was here. The data lined up and our initial scouts saw the dreadnought, which was built to appear to be an RCM."

He shook his head.

"For our intelligence to bring us here with the level of certainty we had, I think our enemy has been leading us on this chase for at least six months. Perhaps a year. We know they will protect the Regional Matrix at any price.

"Everything they have done for the last year led up to this. I don't know if they expected the dreadnought to win or if they expected us to think we'd killed the Regional Matrix when we took it down. In either case, they've been setting us up for a while."

"We will need to review all of our thoughts and divinations for that time," Oohoon stated. "Our enemy is clever. The fault does not rest on us, Swimmer-Under-Sunlit-Skies."

Isaac waved a hand at the holographic presentation. Swimmer couldn't see it, but there was also a speaker in the room, creating the right series of chirps for the Vistan to get the same three-dimensional image as the rest of the sub-commanders.

"Oohoon touches on a key point," he admitted. "We need to reassess our assumptions and re-scout systems we've previously ignored. That will take time and deployment of lighter ships."

"Most of that should be carried out by our recon nodes," Twenty-Five offered. "Our ships are much faster than the rest of the alliance's."

"They'd also kill any of the rest of us who came along," Giannovi muttered. "But Twenty-Five is right, Admiral. That's a task for the recon nodes. What do we do with the rest of the fleet?"

Isaac tapped a command, swapping out the astrographic map with a listing of the damage reports.

"*Spring Dream* is probably the least damaged ship in the fleet," he noted, highlighting the Vistan battlecruiser flagship. "Left to her own devices, she could be back up to full capacity in two or three weeks."

Vigil was only a few days behind her. *Macbeth*, on the other hand, was going to have to be towed into warp.

"We need to rest and repair, and many of our ships are not in a state to carry out their own repairs," he continued.

"The yards we have assembled in Skree-Skree are due to complete their battlecruisers in a few days," ThreeHeart squeaked. "If we bring the fleet there, those yards can see to our repairs as quickly as possible."

Short of scattering the fleet to half a dozen systems, some of them months of travel away, Isaac saw no better option. He was glad the Skree-Skree had suggested it himself, though. That meant Isaac wasn't *asking* the aliens to take on the task of repairing the entire fleet.

"If your people are willing, that is the optimal solution," he agreed. "We have further reinforcements already on the way from Exilium and Vista. Oohoon—I will need to make contact with the Great Ones and see if they can spare more ships.

"We missed our enemy. The next time we find them, they'll have more of these dreadnoughts with them," he concluded grimly. "We need to be ready for that."

The four *Fortitude*-class battlecruisers on their way from Exilium would go a long way toward that. They were the culmination of everything Isaac's one-eyed wizard of a tech genius could pull out of the Matrix and Assini files.

"Your Great Voice," Oohoon replied, their words slow as always. "She also said she might have more allies for us soon."

That could only be Amelie Lestroud, Isaac knew. The former President of Exilium had been the leader of the rebellion that had ended in the humans being exiled out there. She'd been the ambassador to both the Skree-Skree and the Oohoon.

It was a job that made sure no one tried to go to the old boss to override the new boss—and one that Isaac had approved of for personal reasons. It was, after all, generally a good thing to have your wife *with* you instead of six months' travel away!

"That is what she hopes," he agreed. "We won't know for sure until Amelie makes contact. We only know that we have *found* another new species. We don't know what they're like just yet."

Having his wife nearby was good. So was having a supremely competent partner who could forge interstellar multispecies treaties and bring new allies into the fight.

It just meant that sometimes he had to let her go do things even *he* thought were insanely dangerous!

4

Amelie Lestroud knew perfectly well that she had no place on the bridge of a battlecruiser anywhere near a potential conflict. She also knew perfectly well that Captain Chantel Holmwood would never have dreamed of throwing her tall blonde ex-President out of anywhere on the ship.

Holmwood was a perfectly competent officer, one of the unlucky destroyer Captains who'd come on their seventy-thousand-light-year voyage after being declared a risk in the wake of Amelie's revolution. Faced, however, with her boss's wife, her former President, her nation's current Ambassador Plenipotentiary *and* her nation's Foreign Minister, well…

Amelie had chosen to take her august personage, which contained *all* of those ranks and titles, to an observation deck and avoid overwhelming the woman in charge of her transport. It was bad enough, in her studied opinion, that President Emilia Nyong'o had insisted that the Foreign Minister travel aboard a battlecruiser!

Watchtower had the misfortune of being already half-built when the technological windfalls of Exilium's alliances had arrived. Some upgrades had been shoehorned in as she was built, but she'd never gone in for the full refits of her older sisters and hadn't been built from the ground up like her younger sisters.

She was probably the closest thing left to the original *Vigilance*-class designs, though she at least had the AI core that the "export" battle-cruisers lacked.

"WK," Amelie called *Watchtower*'s K-sequence AI aloud as she looked at the armored paneling that closed the observation deck from the disturbing view of the warp. "Can you mirror the main bridge hologram down here for me? I'd appreciate a running update on the situation as well, if you can spare the cycles."

WK, at least, had a *little* bit less of the hero worship most of her husband's fleet had for her.

"Of course," the AI confirmed instantly. The observation deck was mostly empty space by design, with a transparent roof to look out into the deep when the shutters could be safely opened. The holoprojectors that Amelie had noted as she came in were more than capable of duplicating the main tactical display.

"Maintaining updates for you won't be a problem, Minister Lestroud."

"Thank you," she told the computer, glancing over at her companion as he shook his head.

The stocky man had a good thirty years on her, which meant that he was creeping near the end of his first century. Ten years earlier, Roger Faulkner had been a senior minister in the government of the Terran Confederacy, serving First Admiral Adrienne Gallant. He'd been a key part of her plan for an orderly transition of power.

His betrayal had resulted in him being beaten to the edge of death before Gallant had intervened personally to save his life—and then packed him off to the far end of the galaxy. He limped and one of his eyes was an obvious cybernetic replacement, but he was still damn useful.

"Still feels weird to have one of them aboard our ship," Faulkner told her. "Even four years ago, I'm not sure any of us would have trusted the Matrices that much."

"We know a lot more about them now than we did four years ago," Amelie pointed out as she studied the holographic display.

"Hell, the Matrices we work with know more about themselves than they did four years ago. And the K-sequence AIs aren't…really Matrices."

Faulkner waved off her point.

"I know," he agreed. "I don't pretend to understand the lecture of just what D did to create the new cores for them, but I accept that they're different and loyal. Still weird to have the ship talk to me."

Amelie snorted.

"How about being important enough that we're dedicating an entire battlecruiser to hauling you around?" she asked. "*That* one is taking some getting used to."

The automation level of the new ships, most obviously presented by WK itself, meant that the Exilium Space Fleet could maintain almost three times the ships they'd once planned for. That was still only eight battlecruisers and thirty-two strike cruisers, but that was a *hell* of a fleet.

That one of those eight ships was acting as Amelie Lestroud's personal chariot wasn't something she was entirely comfortable with. The display she was studying showed that she'd won at least half the argument, though.

Only two of the four ships accompanying *Watchtower* were strike cruisers. The other two were freighters, hauling both supplies and munitions for the three warships and a carefully curated selection of tech and machinery for potential gifts for their hopefully new allies.

"We will exit warped space in just over one minute, Minister," WK informed her. "Do you need a link to Captain Holmwood?"

Amelie chuckled softly.

"I suspect, WK, that it will be *very* obvious when I need a link to the good Captain," she told the AI. "For now, it's bad enough that I'm eavesdropping. I have no intention of getting in her way."

"Understood, Minister."

The Republic of Exilium's Foreign Minister chuckled and picked her drink up as she watched the timer tick down. She remembered what warp travel had been like before the advances of Lyle Reinhardt and the research and development infrastructure they'd built in Exilium. She'd barely been able to force herself to eat and drink in warp then—and there'd been a six-month trip to Exilium after they'd been kicked through the wormhole to this end of the galaxy.

The new drives were *much* smoother. The Confederacy had never seen a need to focus on them—but Adrienne Gallant had made sure that the Exiles didn't have the Confederacy's wormhole technology. She'd handed the Exiles *everything* else, from black research projects to brutally honest internal histories of Gallant's coup, but she'd seen the Confederacy's wormhole technology neatly excised from it all.

There were days Amelie hated Adrienne Gallant for that over anything else. A wormhole generator would have allowed Exilium to get aid to the Vistan refugees in *hours*, not months. The platforms the Confederacy had used to tie their star systems together had been able to generate wormholes across hundreds of light-years.

Instead, they were limited to warp drives that could move them at two hundred and fifty-six times the speed of light—and Amelie had to be grateful for them.

The alternative, after all, was what the Assini had done: tachyon punch–equipped AI ships and massive sublight vessels. That hadn't ended well for that people, either. Less than five thousand of them survived, a tiny colony on an isolated island on Exilium.

Even now, the Assini's impact loomed large on the galaxy. Those five thousand people might be few and terrified, but they had been some of the most elite researchers the race possessed and they were *determined* to help undo the damage they'd caused.

"Warp exit," WK's melodious voice announced. "Updating tactical display as we pick up information."

The AI paused and the hologram solidified in front of Amelie.

"Initial reports from the recon nodes appear unchanged," they continued. "No planets are missing or have changed orbits, which suggests the Matrices haven't made it here yet."

Amelie concealed a wince. The K-sequence AIs' sense of humor… left much to be desired.

The system wouldn't have required much work on the part of the Construction Matrices. A large rocky world, probably twice the size of Earth, was right in the middle of the liquid-water zone. Its axial tilt looked like it would give them vicious seasons, but the planet was otherwise habitable.

Two more rocks were closer to the F-sequence star, and a fourth orbited at the edge of the system, outside three small gas giants and an average asteroid belt.

The habitable planet was the focus of Amelie's attention and *Watchtower*'s sensors. She was looking for what the Matrix recon nodes had reported…and there it was.

Six large stations orbited around the planet's equator, each almost twice *Watchtower*'s half-kilometer length. As more data came in, it was clear that each of the six stations was linked to a space elevator attached to the surface.

More stations hung around them, but those kilometer-wide anchors alone probably represented a massive industrial capacity. Small ships danced around the planet and the rest of the system, too.

"Scans suggest cloudscoop operations on the inner gas giant and mining operations in the asteroid belt," WK reported. "Commander Riker notes an interesting lack, however."

"Which is?" Amelie prodded.

"There are no large shipyards in the system," the AI told her. "Most of the apparently civilian shipping could have been built here, but there is nothing here that would allow for the construction of large vessels such as the recon nodes detected."

"I'm not seeing any warships yet," she pointed out. "I'm not disregarding the recon nodes' data just yet."

"I don't think anyone is," Faulkner murmured. "But if the recon nodes were reporting seven-hundred-meter warships, I think they saw seven-hundred-meter warships. If we don't see them here, that suggests the same thing as the lack of shipyards."

"The ships weren't from here," Amelie agreed.

"Tactical and I have confirmed a ship-basing facility on the habitable planet's moon," WK noted, flashing a new set of icons on that planetoid. "It appears to be home to a small force of gunships notably larger than our shuttles."

"Show me," she ordered.

It was a series of extremely long-range images, but the telescopes and scanners in play were *very* good. She could read the military iconography on the display by now and she nodded slowly as the details filled in.

There was no way they could estimate the ships' capabilities, but they were twelve meters wide by fifty meters long and clearly designed to launch from a low-gravity base.

"Numbers?" she asked. It wasn't really *her* job to account for that, but it was useful for her to know.

"Thirty visible, hangars and accessways suggest at least that many again concealed," WK said. "Certainty of at least sixty, fifty percent probability of one hundred twenty."

"When will we see them seeing us?" Faulkner asked, the aide watching the hologram with a somewhat horrified fascination.

"We emerged five light-minutes from the planet. Light from our arrival will reach them in two minutes. We will see their response in seven."

"Has Holmwood deployed recon drones yet?" Amelie asked.

"No, Minister. The doctrine she's operating under says to conceal as much of our abilities as possible," WK reminded her.

"Fair. But still…the recon nodes reported at least two *big* ships. Where are they?"

Her tablet buzzed. The military people on the ship had their personal computers tattooed into their left forearms, but she'd never quite gone that far. *Tablet* covered a vast variety of options, even with Exilium's limited consumer industry, but Amelie's own was roughly the size of her thumb, a stick she could put down on any surface to project a holographic keyboard and screen. It would respond to voice commands in carry mode but was most useful when you were sitting down somewhere.

"That's Captain Holmwood," she said without checking. No one else would be trying to contact her right now. "WK, get me that holo-link to the bridge, please."

Her hologram of the star system shifted slightly to make space for a holographic image of *Watchtower*'s command dais and the plumply petite uniformed woman sitting in it.

"Your Eminence," Holmwood greeted her.

"We've been over this, Captain," Amelie replied. "*Minister* will do when you don't think you can use my name."

The smaller and younger woman nodded.

"Minister, then," Holmwood said. "We have completed our initial scans of the system, and the warships detected by the recon nodes are either absent or hiding. Either way, we don't believe they were built here."

"Which means they came from somewhere else and may have left for there," Amelie concluded. "Do you think they're hiding?"

"If they detected the recon nodes and have any idea what the Matrices are, I can't see them having stripped the system of defenses," the ESF Captain told her. "The recon nodes saw the ships sortie towards them, so we can assume they were detected."

"So, they're playing clever buggers." Amelie shook her head. "Pull all of the communications data you can get from the local networks and dump it to my people. We need time and raw data to build a translator."

"Do you want us to move in closer?" Holmwood asked, probably the question she'd commed about in the first place.

"No," Amelie decided aloud. "Let's maintain our current separation from the planet. Any chance they can sneak up on us?"

"Not without tachyon-punching or something else I don't know about, Minister," the Captain replied. "Even then, they'd have to get damn close to be a threat, and nothing I'm seeing suggests that kind of tech level."

"We're only seeing civilian tech and a planetary defense force," Amelie pointed out. "Keep your eyes open and keep me informed, but for now, we wait and try to process a translation protocol."

"Understood, Minister Lestroud!"

———

WHEN THE ALERT jerked Amelie from her sleep, her computer stubbornly insisted it had been eight hours since they'd arrived in the system and four hours since she'd gone to sleep. She was quite sure that was wrong, because there was no way she'd been asleep for more than maybe two minutes.

Regardless of how awake she felt, duty called. The advantage of having WK aboard was that she didn't need to put on enough clothes to talk to a human to get updated, either.

"WK, what's going on?" she asked. "That's a battle stations alert."

"Yes, Minister," the AI confirmed. "May I take control of your quarters' display?"

"Do it," she ordered, pulling clothes out of the closet to dress as rapidly as she could. The Ambassador Plenipotentiary of the Republic of Exilium needed to be composed and unruffled, no matter what.

At least when meeting with other humans. WK wasn't, as she understood it, continuously consciously aware of everything going on in the ship—but there was certainly no way to pretend that the AI wasn't fully aware of just how fragile the masks humanity's officers and leaders put on were.

The wall display lit up, adding a wonderful distorting light effect to her clothes selection as she dressed.

"When the locals became aware of our presence, they launched sixty gunships from the moon base," WK laid out. "Those gunships never left orbit of the planet. Currently, Captain Holmwood estimates that they are no threat to your escort even if they were to sortie against us in numbers.

"Twenty-one minutes and thirty-two seconds ago, several sensor anomalies were flagged in the asteroid belt. Commander Riker, as officer of the watch, ordered a more detailed analysis, including directed active sensors."

Watchtower's tactical officer had to have been feeling nervous if he'd ordered that. Blasting a chunk of the locals' space with high-powered radar wasn't exactly a *friendly* gesture, after all.

"By the time we had feedback from the active sensors, it was clear what we were looking at, and Commander Riker woke up Captain Holmwood, who triggered the battle stations alert when our contacts moved out."

The display was zooming in on the contacts as WK spoke, highlighting eighteen ships heading toward *Watchtower*.

Two were the big ships that had sortied against the recon nodes. Seven hundred meters long and three hundred meters wide, they looked like nothing so much as a dagger with two curved blades.

Six were smaller ships, closer to the strike cruisers Exilium was now building. Those were built along a similar design to the bigger ships but lacking the forked forward half. The single-bladed curved-dagger design was also applied to the ten smallest ships, each slightly smaller than the destroyers the Terran Confederacy had built.

Practice at picking out Isaac's formations helped her ID that there were two groups in the fleet heading her way. One of the big ships had four mid-sized escorts and six smaller escorts, while the other had two mid-sized and four small escorts.

She tugged her jacket into place over her blouse and shook her head.

"Any coms from them yet? A first-contact package or anything of the sort?" she asked.

"Nothing," WK told her. "They left the asteroid belt and are accelerating in our direction. If we don't maneuver to evade or engage, they will reach our standard weapons range in about an hour and forty-five minutes."

They were slower to accelerate than Amelie's ships. Even her freighters could dance circles around the local warships if she gave the word.

"Captain Holmwood is asking me to check if you're awake," the AI asked. "May I connect her?"

"Give me ten seconds to get out of my bedroom, WK," Amelie told them with a chuckle. She was as unruffled as she could be, but her bedroom was most definitely *not*.

"Connect her once I'm in the office," she continued as she opened the door to her room.

It was time to *really* get to work.

5

—————

"Minister Lestroud, I think we are rapidly approaching the point where this becomes a political decision," Captain Holmwood said the moment Amelie opened a channel from her office. The Captain clearly subscribed to the same theory on letting people see her out of sorts as Amelie did and was in full combat uniform despite having also been woken in the middle of the night.

"What is the situation looking like, Captain?" Amelie asked.

"We don't know what they're armed with, but their acceleration is below what we'd expect for any ship that could go toe-to-toe with a *Vigilance* or our two *Romeos*," Holmwood noted. "If it comes down to it, I'm comfortable with our ability to at least cover our own retreat.

"However, my understanding is that if we open fire, we've already failed the mission. I still hesitate to let them get the first shot—and running away isn't going to help our future prospects."

"We don't have a translation protocol yet," Amelie told the officer. "There's less civilian communication than I'd have expected for the scale of the system's industry. WK tells me we're looking at around a hundred minutes to contact?"

"Until we're likely to hit, yes," Holmwood confirm. "Our particle cannon might be able to make an impact at longer range, but I'm assuming they have comparable defenses to the Confederacy prior to our Exile."

That was probably a generous assumption, but Amelie was only so familiar with weapons technology.

"I can't guarantee we'll be able to talk to them in the next hour and a half," she told the Captain. "But I think the best way to make sure we're at least moving in that direction is for us to make the first move."

"You want us to send over our first-contact package?" Holmwood asked. "It's been updated with the Matrices' help, but it's still…"

"Not perfect," Amelie agreed. "But if they have a half a brain, that package is pretty clearly an attempt to communicate. I'm not going to have you shoot at these people if I can possibly avoid it, but we need to talk to them."

She shook her head.

"Without some form of back-and-forth, we have no basis to assume they're on anything except an attack run, and I won't order you to take the first hit, Captain. There aren't enough of us humans out here for that."

There were small contingents from humanity's various allied races aboard *Watchtower*, but it would be the battlecruiser's human crew that would bear the brunt of any fighting.

"We'll send the transmission immediately, Minister," Holmwood promised. "Would you care to join us on the bridge? The next hour or so are going to very much be your show."

Amelie had to agree. She didn't have much of a place on the bridge of a warship, but talking to these people was her job. The best place to do that and to see the results of her efforts was from the battlecruiser's bridge.

"I'll be there as quickly as I can," she told Holmwood. "Keep me informed."

"Yes, Minister."

"Any response or change in their approach profile?" Amelie asked as she entered the bridge.

"Nothing yet, Minister," Commander Alex Heathers reported. The communications officer's console was closest to the door she'd entered through and the redheaded woman and her team were buried in their consoles. "No major progress on the translation, either. We're at least six or seven hours away from being able to talk to anyone."

"It could be worse, I suppose," Holmwood muttered as Amelie reached the command dais. There were several observer chairs scattered across the bridge, but one was right next to the Captain's seat.

"The system could have been wiped out by the Matrices between the recon and our arrival?" Amelie asked. "That would definitely count."

The Captain winced.

"Or they could be a serious threat to us," Holmwood noted. "We've got a pretty solid scan on their energy signatures now. Power plants are fusion across the board. No conversion cores, so they have nowhere near our power budgets. Definitely no warp ring, which raises the question of where they came from and how they got here."

"Each of those ships out-masses *Watchtower* by, what, fifty percent?" Amelie asked. "I know we have the tech edge, Captain, but quantity has a quality all its own, doesn't it?"

"And *Mercutio* alone produces more power than both of their battle groups," Holmwood pointed out. "Power generation isn't everything, sure, but it means I can be confident we have more powerful weapons across the board. If the Matrices can't hit me with their missiles, I'm not worried about these guys' birds."

"Fair," Amelie conceded. The Captain was the expert, after all. She might feel that Holmwood was being overly optimistic, but the woman seemed to have reasons for her assessment.

"They received the first-contact package ten minutes ago," Holmwood said. "I'd have expected them to do *something* by now."

"Unfortunately, I have to agree with you on breaking off," Amelie replied. "Moving away would give them more time, but it could easily be taken as a sign of weakness." She sighed. "It's your discretion, Captain. I suggest we send the first-contact protocol again."

"Understood." Holmwood gestured to Heathers, then turned her attention back to the big holodisplay as the com officer set to work. "If they keep coming, I need to do *something*, Minister," she murmured.

"I don't expect us to take their best hit and smile," Amelie responded. "We have *time*, Captain." She shook her head, looking at the oncoming set of warships. They were in the locals' territory, so she could understand paranoia, but she was at least *trying* to talk to them.

"Spend some of that time working up a plan for warning shots," she finally told the Captain. "I don't want to kill anyone—if it comes down to that, we get out of Dodge ASAP—but I want a plan for getting them to back off while being clear we *don't* want to fight them."

"That's...not an easy set of parameters," Holmwood answered slowly. "But I think we can do it."

"I leave it in your hands, Captain," Amelie said. "And I hope that these people talk to us before it becomes necessary. It's their system, yes, but since *we* aren't being aggressive, you'd think they'd at least *talk* to us."

The ESF Captain scoffed softly.

"Would we?" Holmwood asked.

———

WATCHING the local defense fleet accelerate toward them, Amelie had to admit that the Matrices' influence in their prior first contacts had spoiled them. With both the Vistans and the Skree-Skree, the Republic's ships had arrived while the Matrices were trying to transform their homeworlds.

The Tohnbohn were steady and methodical by nature. If someone wanted to talk to them, they were going to wait and see what they had to say—and while the Matrices might not have been in the Tohnbohn's system yet, the big shelled aliens had known about the machines, and potential allies had been met with joy.

These people had to be at least *aware* of the Matrices—if you had interstellar travel, you almost certainly had good enough telescopes to see planets being moved into place and having their atmosphere changed.

"Contacts are at five light-seconds and closing," Riker reported.

The tension on *Watchtower*'s bridge could have been cut with a knife.

"Send the first-contact package again," Amelie ordered. "Perhaps third time will be the charm. If it isn't..." She shook her head.

"Captain, you are cleared to fire your warning shots at the one-million-kilometer mark," she told Holmwood.

"If the locals cross the seven-hundred-thousand-kilometer mark without making contact or adjusting from an attack course, get the hell out of here," she continued. "Do whatever is necessary to cover the safe retreat of the transports."

"Understood, Minister," Holmwood replied.

This might be Amelie Lestroud's mission, but Captain Holmwood commanded their little flotilla. If the delegation's ships were in danger, Amelie was no longer in command and she knew it.

To her surprise, she didn't think they were in danger. Someone over there was playing games.

"WK, if they had missiles based on what we've seen of their drive tech, what would their effective range be?" she asked.

"Assuming similar design protocols to the Terran Confederacy, their missiles would have a range in this geometry of just over two million kilometers." The AI paused. "They would be no threat to us."

"But they wouldn't know that," Amelie concluded. "If they were planning on firing first, Captain, they'd have already opened fire. The idiots are playing chicken. Dominance games."

It was almost...human.

"Two minutes before they cross the one-million-kilometer mark," Holmwood said. "If they want to play dominance games, how do we play? Would obliterating one of their battleships end the game?"

"Breathe, Captain," Amelie ordered. She understood the other woman's frustration. "Stand by for your warning shots. Either they'll divert before then, or that should make the point."

She hesitated.

"Does your warning shot use the main gun?" she asked.

"Grasers only," Holmwood replied. "Our secondaries and the strike cruisers' primaries. Should I...?"

"No," Amelie said. "That's exactly what I was hoping you'd say, Captain. You're well ahead of me."

The petite Captain smiled grimly.

"I was a Confederacy officer, Minister," she pointed out. "Paranoia and hiding your cards came with the territory." She shook her head at the hologram.

"I like the ESF *much* better," Holmwood concluded. "Warning shots in sixty seconds. Contacts have not changed course."

"It's your call, Captain Holmwood," Amelie said. "Fire at your discretion."

Holmwood exhaled loudly, then rose and walked over to the display. The distance was continuing to tick down, fast.

"Commander Riker?" she barked.

"Ready with the warning shots, Captain!" the tactical officer replied, answering her unspoken question.

"Fire at will."

———

THE FIRING PLAN had been programmed over half an hour before and continually updated by three tactical officers. They had a *lot* more weapons than the four grasers they were using for the first warning shot, but that was part of the point.

Never show your hand early. It was as important in diplomacy as it was in war or poker. Amelie was no soldier, but she'd planned a war once—and she was *damn* good at both diplomacy and poker.

Four gamma-ray lasers bracketed the battleship with the larger escort group. For a few worrisome seconds, Amelie had to worry that they'd hit the local warship. They hadn't been aiming for it, but they'd been aiming closely enough for it to be a risk with a six-second control loop.

"Zero hits, all beams within ten thousand kilometers of the target," Riker reported. He paused. "Contacts are adjusting vector, reducing vector towards and adding a side vector. Estimate they'll hit zero velocity about fifty thousand kilometers past us. They can't slow down any faster than that."

"Minister?" Holmwood looked over at Amelie.

"Let's keep them at half a million klicks but adjust to match their course," Amelie said. "Keep a careful eye on them. Even once they start talking to us, I'm not convinced I want to trust these folks just yet."

It took a few seconds for the navigators to calculate the right course, but then the flotilla came to life. They weren't running away, just controlling the range.

"Any communication from them yet?" Amelie asked.

"Just adjusting their vector," Heathers told her. "They have the first-contact package but they haven't sent us anything equivalent."

"WK, how long on that translation protocol?" the Minister demanded.

"At least three more hours unless one of the analysts has a break-through," the AI responded. "If they are capable of running the first-contact package and have a similar protocol, they should already be able to generate a text translation system if they started from the first transmission."

"Or they have no idea what they're doing with binary machine code," Amelie suggested. "We couldn't even *run* Vistan code when we first encountered them."

"They should be able to run the package," Heathers said. "Every-thing I'm seeing in the transmissions we're picking up and feeding into *our* translation efforts looks like binary-encoded audio and video."

"Well, they aren't charging at us with weapons ready anymore," Holmwood noted. "We're probably better at building translation soft-ware than they are. We'll get it done, Minister."

"Let me know the moment we can set up a communications link," Amelie replied. "Someone over there has a bunch of twitchy warships and I'd like to be able to *say* 'we come in peace' before we have to fire more warning shots!"

6

With four interspecies translation systems behind them and the K-sequence AIs to back their work up, the team of translation and decryption specialists backing Amelie up could do *far* better than the text translators of their first contact with the Matrices.

The locals were having more problems than she would have expected. Two hours after the two flotillas matched velocities and began orbiting half a million kilometers apart, they still hadn't tried to initiate any communication based on the contact package.

Amelie's people, on the other hand, had been very busy.

"We've got everything," Commodore Rhianna Rose told Amelie. The woman had once been the head of the original *Vigil*'s communication department, but now she was very quietly the head of what military intelligence teams the Republic of Exilium possessed.

Since she answered to a civilian boss, however, Rose could leave Exilium with the Foreign Minister and lead the translation projects as they made contact. And if polite or not-so-polite espionage became required after making contact, that would fall on Rose too.

"Define *everything*," Amelie asked.

"I can give you a direct video link to their flagship," Rose said confidently. "Live two-way translation. There'll be a delay of about half a second each way, so your three-and-a-bit-second time-lag for being half a million klicks away becomes four seconds. Otherwise, should be perfectly smooth."

"How solid's the translator?"

"Don't delve into political theory or quantum physics?" the intelligence officer replied. "Once we get our hands on a proper language database, it will be a hundred percent. Right now, we're limited by what people have been talking about on the radio since we got here."

"All right. Send it to Commander Heathers," Amelie instructed. "It's time to actually *talk* instead of just waving warships at each other."

She turned in the uncomfortable observer seat to look at the communications officer. The seat was far enough away that no one should be overhearing her coms.

On the other hand, like the Terran Confederacy before it, the Republic of Exilium tended to treat the coms officer as an unofficial intelligence officer. Amelie doubted that Heathers *wasn't* listening in on her calls from the bridge.

"You got that, Commander Heathers?" she asked.

The coms officer had the grace to flush under her stiff regard.

"Yes, Minister," she confessed. "I'll have the call set up in two minutes. Should you find some more, ah, impressive surroundings, ma'am?"

"And less operational-security-breaching ones," Holmwood muttered, just loud enough for Amelie to hear.

"True enough," Amelie admitted. "Get everything set up but hold off on building the link until I okay it. I'll take it in… The observation deck should be impressive enough, don't you think?"

"We *have* a flag deck," Holmwood pointed out. "We don't have a staff for it and it's currently shut down, but we should be able to rig up an impressive-looking fleet-command display that doesn't tell them anything. WK?"

"We have some protocols left over from the Confederacy that should serve for flashy and useless," the AI confirmed. "I should have something up in the flag deck by the time you arrive, Minister Lestroud."

Amelie had been a movie actress once. She was *very* familiar with the type of displays that WK was referring to—they'd been the only ones used in movies that had been granted access to film on Confed warships.

"I know when to concede to the experts," she told them. "I'll be on the flag deck in a few minutes. Once I'm there, we'll double-check everything and then we'll call our new friends."

———

WITHOUT A STAFF, the flag deck was almost hauntingly empty. None of the consoles outside of the zone the camera would be picking up were on. As Amelie settled in to the Admiral's seat, the entire assemblage rotated to put the holodisplay behind her.

A small screen on the arm of the seat showed her what would be transmitted. The hologram behind her was now live, showing a massive holographic image of *Watchtower* and the rest of the consular flotilla.

There was nothing in that image that couldn't be picked out by a half-decent telescope, but the looming hologram helped make for quite the effect.

She chuckled to herself as she realized that WK was also inserting officers into the scene behind her, filling in seats with computer-generated images of a fictitious staff.

"Commander Heathers, are you ready?" she asked.

"We are ready." The Commander paused. "It looks like their language is mostly even human-pronounceable, so the translation protocol is going to leave proper nouns intact. Most relevant right now is probably the species name:

"They call themselves the Sivar, Siva for singular. Trimodal gender, he, she, ban. Rose and I *really* want to access a database to see just what the biology factors are on *that*!"

"Understood. Get me a link, Commander."

"We're initiating handshake now, Minister."

New icons appeared on the screen. They'd transmitted using a Sivar protocol and were waiting for… There. Receipt acknowledgement.

"We have a channel," Heathers reported. "You're live in five."

A countdown appeared on the screen and Amelie let her best diplomat mask fall over her face as a single light informed her that she was now recording.

"This is Minister Amelie Lestroud of the Republic of Exilium," she said levelly. "I have been appointed as the Ambassador Plenipotentiary of the Republic to open contact and negotiations with your government.

"Am I speaking with the commander of the military force shadowing us?"

She waited. It was a three-second loop for the light, plus the half-second on each for translation. Four seconds wasn't much, but it could definitely feel like forever.

A new hologram appeared in the flag deck, projecting a two-dimensional image of what she presumed to be the flag-deck equivalent aboard the local flagship. The camera was centered on a throne-like seat, presumably also in the middle of the space.

Sitting rigidly on the very edge of the seat was the most human-like alien Amelie had ever met. The Siva was a gaunt bipedal figure with long limbs and pale blue skin who *appeared* tall—it was hard to tell without a known reference. They wore a long dark-green tunic with a hood that covered their head, leaving only the red reflection of a human-like pair of eyes emerging from the shadow.

"I am Sector Commandant Ackahl," the stranger said slowly. "I presume we are speaking via a translation program?"

"We are," Amelie confirmed. "My team have extracted your civilian communication bandwidths and encoding. We may have some lacking words until we have access to a full language database.

"I must make clear from the beginning that we are not here to invade or conquer your system," she told the alien. "We fired warning shots to protect ourselves only. We wish to forge ties of trade with your people and warn them of a great danger that looms over your stars."

It was hard to tell, but it looked like the Siva had intentionally rigged their camera so they were looking down at whoever they were speaking to. It seemed unlikely that they'd made that change since the humans had shown up, which suggested that was a permanent part of the design.

Amelie filed that away in the back of her mind. Every new alien race they encountered was a puzzle, and the more pieces of that puzzle she had, the more likely she was to be able to decipher them.

"The only danger I see is a stranger who brought warships to my system," Ackahl noted. "This is my space, Minister Amelie Lestroud. You come with weapons and starships and expect me to accept your protestations of peace? First you flee when challenged; now you fire on us.

"If you wish to meet with the Intendant, you will surrender your ships and submit as our prisoners. If you do not, I must treat you as invaders."

The alien's face was concealed in the hood and it was risky to assume that anything resembling human body language was in play. But some signs were universal, and stress tended to create muscle tension, which *was* visible.

The Sector Commandant was not stressed. They had to suspect that Amelie would choose to fight over surrender, but they weren't acting like they were expecting a fight.

"I would suggest you consider alternatives," Amelie finally said. "I answer to higher powers, Sector Commandant, and I have no intention of surrendering my consular escort. If you want a fight, my people will give you one, but that is not why we are here. If you are determined to make us unwelcome, I will leave.

"And then, I presume that you will have to explain to your leaders why you threw away this opportunity to make new allies," she finished sweetly. "My preference, of course, would be to have these discussions with your leader. Senior as you are, I do not think you are the final voice of your people."

The Siva had already said that was a being called the Intendant, after all. Without more information, Amelie couldn't say if that was a military commander, civilian head of state or what. Only that this Sector Commandant was *not* who she needed to be speaking to.

"I am the final authority in this star system," Ackahl told her. "My superiors will understand that I do what I must to protect my charges."

Seconds ticked away and Amelie let the alien's words hang in the air unanswered.

"I have no intention of threatening anyone," she finally replied. "I will protect my own people if attacked, but I am here to make treaties, not war. A wave of death sweeps towards you, of worlds turned to a specific standard regardless of whether they are inhabited.

"I doubt your scientists or your soldiers are blind to what I speak of."

This time, it was Ackahl who let her words hang in silence.

"I believe I know of what you speak," they eventually concluded. "We have seen the marks of the worldbuilders in the stars. You know more of them?"

"We know them," she confirmed. "We have fought some of them. Allied with others. But we stand a bare handful of light-years from the edge of where the closest ones operate.

"They will not care that the world you are charged to protect is inhabited. They will not care that you have warships or industry or space platforms. They will care solely that the world in this system does not match the standard they intend to apply.

"They will destroy the atmosphere of this system's habitable planet so they can rebuild it to their design. Your ships could not stop them."

"And yours could?" Ackahl asked. If they *weren't* sneering at her, the translator was adding tone of its own.

"This flotilla? Maybe," Amelie conceded cautiously. "But that is why my Republic is seeking allies. By sharing our technology and knowledge, we are building an alliance to stand against the terraformers and stop them from killing any more species."

The Siva was silent for several more seconds, then reached up and pulled the hood back. Their neck and face were the same pale blue of their hands. Their eyes weren't quite as burning red as they'd looked under the hood, fading toward a dull orange without the hood accentuating them.

Where a human would have had hair, Ackahl had a solid bone carapace that stretched from roughly where the nose would be over to the back of their skull, with breaks only for their eyes.

The Siva was probably more intimidating to Amelie *without* concealing their face.

"Your ships will remain where they are," they told her calmly. "We will see if we can transmit a language database to you. In exchange, you will provide recent intelligence on the worldbuilders.

"*If* that intelligence matches what we know and I agree with your assessment of the threat, I will communicate with the Intendant and see if His Greatness will speak with you.

"I can promise no more," Ackahl concluded. "You have safe passage to this system so long as you approach no closer than your current position. Is this acceptable, Minister Amelie Lestroud?"

She inclined her head.

"These are reasonable precautions, Sector Commandant," Amelie said. "I will consult with my team and have a briefing prepared to send over. How long do you expect the Intendant's response to take?"

"I do not trust you, Minister Amelie Lestroud," the Sector Commandant replied. "I will reveal no secrets but those I must. I await the intelligence.

"May the darkness flee your path."

The channel cut out and Amelie smiled grimly.

"WK? Let Rose know I need a sanitized briefing packet on the Rogues to give these guys," she told the AI. "I then need an all-hands-on-deck meeting. I don't think this Intendant is going to come to us, which means everyone needs to know everything we've established about the Sivar."

"Yes, Minister."

Amelie turned her chair to study the holograms of the ships behind her. With the automation the Republic built into everything now, the three warships and two freighters only carried a thousand people between them.

Those people's lives were in her hands…but almost as important was that if she screwed this negotiation up, both the Republic's allies and the Sivar would suffer for their lack of coordination.

The Rogue Matrices, after all, had no concept of "neutral noncombatant."

7

"THIS IS OUR SECTOR COMMANDANT," Rose noted as the meeting looked at a hologram of Ackahl. "Female, if you're wondering, which took us a bit to work out."

Two smaller holograms appeared to either side of Ackahl. The one on the left looked almost identical in body structure except that their carapace erupted into two forward-facing horns. The one on the right had slightly less of their face covered by the bone carapace and also had visible breasts.

"To the left, we have a Sivar male," Rose said. "In this case, what we would call a news anchor named Ickone. To the right, you have his partner, a Sivar ban named Trilo. For the curious, the males provide approximately thirty-five percent of the DNA, the females provide sixty percent of the DNA, and the banon provide five percent of the DNA and the womb for gestation."

"I imagine their family reunions are fun," Holmwood said dryly. "Guessing family dynamics like two dads and a mom?"

"It's hard to say," WK interjected. "Rose and her team and I are working off the general news broadcasts across the system, civilian coms, and a language database provided by the Sector Commandant. We have very limited insight into Sivar society."

"And insight into Sivar society is what we need," Faulkner concluded, Amelie's aide the fourth human in the room.

All hands on deck at this stage meant the escort commander, the intelligence head, Amelie and her aide. Plus, of course, WK. The AI was hard to avoid at this point.

"We know that Ackahl, at least, believes herself to be the most powerful individual in the system," Amelie said. "That suggests that civilian authority, at least in this system, is subordinate to the military. I find the translation program's choice of word for their leader interesting as well."

"It's a fancy form of *administrator*, which seems to be what the Intendant's title in Sivar boils down to," Rose agreed. "I wonder if the Intendant is the top of the chain—or just the next step up for Ackahl. Most likely, the translation chose the word basically at random, but it does suggest a high-but-not-ultimate level of authority."

"We won't know until we talk to them," Amelie replied. "Any ideas on how long that will be?"

"Well, I can tell you that I don't have a clue what they're using for FTL," Holmwood said dryly. "One of the orbital platforms launched what we think was an interstellar com drone, though. It traveled outward at about five times the acceleration of their warships and then vanished."

"Any idea what it did?" Faulkner asked.

"Insufficient tachyon signature for a tachyon punch, insufficient gravity lensing or exotic-matter signatures for a warp drive," WK replied. "We knew that, though. This appears to be a new form of faster-than-light travel we are not familiar with.

"The drone appeared to travel to a specific point to enter FTL. There is no way to be certain if that point was simply in the direction of its destination or was required to enter FTL."

"Captain, do we have the data to detect a natural wormhole?" Amelie asked as a thought struck her. "I know we have nothing on artificial wormholes, but..."

"We don't," Holmwood said calmly. "That's not so much that it was cut from our records when were exiled as it is that we never could. We could still detect a wormhole being opened—and that definitely didn't happen—but natural wormholes were notoriously difficult to find except by having a ship fall through them."

"Is it possible their drone went through a natural wormhole?" Amelie asked.

"Possible? Yes," the Captain agreed. "But we found *four* in the entire Confederacy. Unless they got very lucky, it's unlikely there are enough here to hold together an interstellar society of any kind."

"But you also just said we couldn't detect them," Amelie countered. "What if *they* can?"

"That would…" Holmwood trailed off. "That would really limit how usable their fleet would be to us, wouldn't it? They could get around their empire insanely quickly by our standards, but they wouldn't be able to *leave* it."

"Keep an eye on traffic in the system," Amelie told her. "I want to know where every ship or drone that leaves or arrives appears or disappears. I think our Sector Commandant might be underestimating our sensors."

"Almost certainly," WK said. "I suspect if she knew how much data we were getting from the planet, she'd be very concerned."

"Why's that?" Amelie asked.

The image of the three Sivar shrank and a new holographic image appeared in the middle of the table. It resembled nothing so much as a giant stalk of broccoli with tentacles instead of florets, with several eyes concealed in the forest of tendrils.

As the hologram expanded, it became clear that the stalk was both wearing a tunic around the main torso and working on some kind of vehicle.

"All of the communications we have intercepted in space have been between Sivar," WK told them. "All data suggests that the warships and the gunships are all entirely crewed by Sivar. But scanning the surface, we see these people."

"Who are they?" Amelie asked.

"I have been unable to determine so far," the AI admitted. "But the planet has a population of five point one two billion—and four point nine eight billion of those people are these aliens.

"Not Sivar."

"But every warship in the system is Sivar and all of the radio coms are Sivar," Faulkner concluded. "*Fuck.* You're saying the Sivar conquered these people?"

"I cannot speak to past events without further data," WK replied. "But the current situation implies an intentional limitation of mobility of this race and the imposition of a Sivar administrative structure on them.

"Which would, yes, strongly suggest that we are in a system that was conquered by force."

———

THE LAST TIME Amelie had dealt with a method of faster-than-light travel no one around her was familiar with, it had been when the Matrices first arrived in Exilium. Since they'd known nothing about the Matrices or where they came from, the mysteriousness of their interstellar drive had been an extra layer of terror to their attackers.

Now, she was in an at-least-neutral star system, eavesdropping on Captain Holmwood's crew as they attempted to figure out just what they were looking at.

"That's another com drone," a sensor tech reported. "Dialing in its course now." Pause. "It looks like its heading for point four."

"That makes nine drones leaving the planet in two days," Riker noted aloud. "All of them heading to one of those four points. If nothing else, we know they have to transition at one of those locations.

"Are we seeing *anything* at those points to suggest what's going on?"

Amelie wasn't actually *part* of the conversation going on. Riker knew she was listening in—her access codes could have got her into the tactical department's coms *without* the officer knowing, but that would have been rude—but she didn't have the ability to talk to the team.

"I was with the old man in Conestoga when we found a natural wormhole," one of the older Chiefs noted. "Those are *hard* to find, but if you know what you're looking for you can at least tell if one is where you think it is."

"So, am I looking at natural wormholes, Chief?" Riker asked, in the somewhat-exasperated tones of an officer that suspected they *knew* the answer but their subordinate hadn't actually said enough to provide it.

"No, sir," the Chief replied. "I can't say with hundred percent certainty from this distance, but I'm not seeing any of the distortion patterns in the local light and gravity that I would expect if there were a wormhole. We'd be getting at least a glimpse of another star system.

"Plus, if there were *four* natural wormholes in this system, that would be as many natural wormholes as we found in the hundred and sixty systems the Confederacy surveyed," the older non-com continued. "I don't have access to the papers anymore, but I'm pretty sure the theory was that you couldn't have two natural wormholes in the same system or the waveforms would collapse."

"All right. So, what *am* I looking at?" Riker said. "We know their drones go to these particular points and vanish. We haven't seen anything appear at those points, have we?"

"Negative."

"What's on the projected lines of the drones' vectors when they hit the points?"

"Each has a star system within ten light-years," one of the junior sensor techs reported. "None of those systems pinged our scans as having a significant technological presence."

Amelie knew their current system did. She'd also drawn the lines herself and the tech was overstating things slightly. All four systems showed *some* sign of technology if you were looking for it.

What they didn't have was habitable planets or enough radio emissions to suggest major artificial habitation. If the Sivar had wormholes or wormhole-esque connections through those systems, they were clearly little more than stopovers.

She was about to turn down the link and focus on other work when one of the sensor techs suddenly made a startled exclamation.

"Sir! We have an emergence at point one! A com drone just appeared out of nowhere—and there was a tachyon pulse right before it emerged."

"That's useful," Riker agreed. "What kind of pulse?"

"Take a look, sir," the tech responded. "The pulse is recurring…and this one is larger!"

Amelie was already scrambling to bring up the sensor records. She could follow the logic: if one small pulse had preceded the emergence of a drone less than five meters long, a larger pulse was announcing the emergence of something bigger.

Like an actual ship.

"The pulse started sixty seconds ahead of the drones' emergence," the Chief reported. "Grew over three seconds, peaked at three point four, then faded over the same time period. Pulse ended fifty-three point two seconds before emergence."

"New pulse has peaked," another tech reported. "That makes… fourteen point six seconds. It's now fading at the same rate."

"Intensity was higher at the peak by several orders of magnitude. Without multiple samples, we can't estimate what that means," Riker noted. "Keep sensors trained on that point. Thirty seconds or fifty-three after the pulse ends, that's useful information."

Amelie was focused on the same scanners the tactical team was. Everything they were seeing was several minutes out of date—point one was four and a half light-minutes away from them—which added to the delay, as the *tachyon* pulse was instantaneous.

Whatever was coming through had come through a minute or so after the tachyon pulse, but it was almost five minutes before they were likely to see anything.

"We're now seeing lightspeed data from one minute since the pulse began," a tech announced. "We should be seeing an emergence sometime in the nex—"

"There!" Riker snapped. "Multiple contacts, highlight and classify!"

Amelie waited for the experts to break down what she was looking at, but she could at least *count*. There were eight new contacts on the screen, all of them vastly larger than the drone. It looked like an entire battle group.

"Minister," Riker's voice was suddenly directed at her on a private channel. "You were watching?"

"I *am* watching, Commander," Amelie replied. "Is Captain Holmwood in the loop?"

"Yes, Minister," the tactical officer confirmed.

"Good. What am I looking at?" Amelie asked.

"Another battleship task group," Riker said. "One battleship, three cruisers, four destroyers."

It seemed her military escort had decided on classifications for the Sivar warships. That made sense, as did the fact that no one had remembered to tell Amelie. Holmwood and her people didn't truly report to Amelie, after all. They were in charge of *protecting* Amelie.

"Any reaction from the locals yet?" she said.

"Not yet. We're keeping our eyes peeled." He paused and coughed delicately. "We're going to alert status, Minister. I need to cut you out of the working com loop."

"Understood, Commander," Amelie told him. "I'll have WK keep me informed. Carry on."

She leaned back in her chair as the internal department loop she'd been eavesdropping on vanished. She wasn't entirely surprised that it was immediately replaced by a mirror of the main tactical display on the bridge, resized to fit above her desk.

"You could at least pretend that you aren't listening to every word I say, WK," she said aloud.

"You used my designation, Minister," the AI replied. "That activates a subroutine that has me listening to you and reviewing the last sixty seconds of audio around you for context. It seems most efficient."

"You're probably right," Amelie agreed. Having intelligent computers that were able to talk to her and determined to be helpful was still weird.

"Your analysis, WK?" she asked.

"Communications response from the central authority," the AI said instantly. "It was probably held somewhere along the way while the battle group was attached to it."

"That does give us a timeline, doesn't it?" she murmured. "Forty-eight hours is a maximum communications loop between here and their capital. One that allows them to deploy warships."

"I calculate a fifty-three percent likelihood that the battle group was closer to us than their capital," WK told her. "Without more information, though, that is only slightly more than speculation."

Either way, she suspected she was going to be hearing from the Sector Commandant shortly.

"WK, prep the flag deck for another conversation with Ackahl," she told the AI. "I should go look officious and intimidating for our friends now that they have reinforcements."

8

———

AMELIE MANAGED to make it through about thirty minutes of correspondence from Exilium—over two years into President Nyong'o's term, *most* people had realized that the answer they were going to get from the President Emeritus was "no comment," but she still liked to keep up to date—before Commander Heathers contacted her from the bridge.

"Minister, the Sivar are requesting a communication channel," she said. "The Sector Commandant's flagship again. It appears to be her."

"I was expecting them," Amelie replied. "WK, are we set up for proper impressions?"

"We are," the AI confirmed. "Are you ready, Minister Lestroud?"

Amelie dismissed her tablet's holographic screen and pocketed the device. Facing the camera, she assumed her mask and nodded calmly.

"Connect the Sector Commandant," she instructed.

The same two-dimensional image of Ackahl and her throne appeared in front of her. There was no more visible tension in the Siva this time, but Amelie suspected the alien was far from relaxed.

"Sector Commandant Ackahl," she greeted the Siva. "I see that you have received reinforcements. Is this positive or should I be concerned?"

"I have surrendered my command of this system to Sector Commandant Reedoh," Ackahl replied calmly. "I am now properly addressed simply as Lord Commandant.

"My Intendant has considered your offer and request and agreed to allow you to attend on him in the First and Final Citadel."

Amelie had a lot of practice at concealing her emotions, but that name sent a pang of worry down her spine. Pretentious, intimidating and somewhat over the top, that the Sivar's center of government was called the "First and Final Citadel" told her quite a bit about them.

"That is my purpose in entering your space," she agreed calmly. "We will need the location of your home system to make that journey, Lord Commandant Ackahl."

Several seconds of pause passed, well beyond what was needed for lightspeed and translation.

"We would prefer if your ships follow us through the star-lanes without us providing you that information," Ackahl finally noted. "We are uninclined to provide strangers maps of the travel routes of our empire."

"Lord Commandant, I don't even know what a star-lane *is*," Amelie admitted. Admitting that was a risk but a necessary one. There was no way she could get to the Sivar home system if she was trying to follow the Sivar ships through whatever not-quite-wormhole they used.

"My ships clearly use a very different form of interstellar travel than yours," she continued. "Provide us with the star system in question and we will meet you there.

"I don't believe we will be able to travel together."

It was hard to be sure, but Ackahl appeared taken aback by that. She blinked, her eyelids among the only unarmored part of her face, and then leaned forward.

"You are not bound to the star-lanes?" she asked. "That would explain my seeing-eye-warriors' confusion at your arrival. They continue to search the point where you appeared for evidence of a star-lane that we missed."

"My vessels use a point-to-point faster-than-light drive that works on principles far beyond a mere diplomat," Amelie said cheerfully. *Lied* cheerfully, really. She couldn't *build* a gravity-warp engine by any means, but they were so important to the survival and power of Exilium that she'd made damn sure she *understood* them.

"We all have our specialities," Ackahl conceded with another blink.

Somehow, Amelie suspected that the Siva did *not* find her supposed lack of knowledge appropriate.

"We do," Amelie agreed. "We will need, at a minimum, a distance and an angle, Lord Commandant, if we are to visit your Intendant."

Which was, of course, merely a different type of coordinates. There was no way the Siva was getting out of this meeting without giving her the location of their capital.

"I will have the information relayed to you," Ackahl promised. "I must request, however, that you take a minimum of thirty-six hours to arrive. Otherwise, I cannot promise that the defenses of the system will be aware of your approach, and unfortunate actions would be taken."

Amelie concealed a wince.

"I imagine that will not be a problem, Lord Commandant," she said carefully. "I look forward to meeting with your Intendant. It promises to be most illuminating."

At some point before they signed a treaty, she was going to have to ask the Sivar leader just what was going on with the apparently conquered world here. In the pursuit of survival against a xenocidal AI, she could overlook a lot.

She was, however, pretty sure they had the situation well enough in hand that turning a blind eye to slavery and conquest was *not* required.

———

"Yeah, our paranoid friend doesn't need to worry about us beating the com drone to the Siva home system," Holmwood said dryly once the consular party's senior leaders had gathered for a small meeting. "Assuming the 'star-lanes' follow a distinctive pattern, she's got three star-lanes to pass through to get there, which will apparently take a minimum of thirty-six hours.

"From *our* perspective, however, it's more important that the Siva System is nine-point-eight light-years away," she continued. "That's on nearly a direct line from Skree-Skree, putting them almost a hundred and thirty light-years from Exilium.

"And fourteen *days'* travel for us."

"The thirty-six-hour figure is garbage," Faulkner noted, the old bureaucrat rubbing at the edge of his cybernetic eye. "It took them, what, fifty hours to send a message and get a response—with attached battle group!—back here?"

"Assuming a near-miraculous turnaround time for any government, that leaves a com drone only taking twenty-four hours to make the trip."

"The com drones are also much faster than their ships," Holmwood said with a nod. "Thirty-six hours might be Ackahl's transit time to the system, but I suspect the drone will be there in twenty at most."

"So, our tachyon coms are faster, but they move *damn* quickly from our perspective," Amelie said. "That suggests mutual value in tech trade."

"Their speed requires a heavily surveyed initial area," WK noted. "Given our own difficulties in isolating these star-lanes, even when we know their exact location, I calculate a high probability that finding a new system's natural star-lanes is a complex and time-consuming process."

"Internal mobility advantage, but a hell of a barrier for operations outside of known territory," Holmwood said. "Hell of an engine for a defensive fleet, but that's not the vibe these people have been giving off."

"No," Amelie agreed. "They've shown up with the equivalent of three Confederacy battlecruiser task groups to watch us—but part of that is that they refused to leave *this* system without at least two battleships watching it."

"I'm not sure it isn't mostly posturing," Faulkner suggested. "If they have enough force to do this, they have enough force to make sure that the locals *don't* rebel, because it's hopeless."

"Overwhelming force minimizes losses," Holmwood said. "I've heard *that* before."

Amelie chuckled. It was Isaac's description of his preferred tactics against people. It didn't work overly well against Matrices, from what she understood, but humans, at least, tended to surrender when facing ten times their own firepower.

He'd learned it from his mother—and the end of Amelie's rebellion had included an epic example of the theory as well…when First Admiral Gallant had ambushed Isaac's single battlecruiser group with the rest of the Confederacy Fleet.

"We'll coordinate our departure with Ackahl, but we travel on our own time," Amelie said calmly. "We're certainly not going to play games about working out how to get through the star-lanes ourselves."

"We may end up looking weaker than we'd like if we show up over a week after they're expecting us," Faulkner pointed out.

"There's no 'may,'" Roger," she admitted. "We will lose face from that, but we can't avoid it, so we deal with it. Once we *trust* our new friends, I'll want them to have an accurate assessment of our abilities. Until then, well…I'd prefer to be overestimated when we're trying to negotiate, but underestimating us has a value too."

She smiled.

"And if they think we're going to be pushovers, they're going to have some harsh surprises, aren't they?"

Some of the Vistans had made that mistake when Octavio Catalan had been trying to make peace between their factions so he could rescue them. They'd made the mistake of trying to take the soft-spoken ex-engineer hostage.

It had ended poorly for them. Unfortunately for the Republic, today Octavio Catalan was a *long* way away.

The Assini who had joined the Republic's allies had fled a dying star, leaving behind all of their technology and hardware. It was entirely possible that the wreckage of their civilization held another answer to the problem of the Matrices.

Unfortunately, that wreckage was three hundred light-years away.

9

———————

"Emergence in fifteen minutes."

Lieutenant Commander Yonina Daniel had served Octavio Catalan as helm and navigation officer aboard *Scorpion* when they'd rescued the Vistans. She was a tall, heavyset woman with piercing green eyes—green eyes that were focused on *Dauntless*'s control panels. She wasn't just helming the battlecruiser itself. For a journey of the length *Dauntless* and the special expeditionary force around her had taken, all nine ships were slaved to the battlecruiser's control.

Octavio Catalan, now a Commodore in the Exilium Space Fleet and in charge of said expeditionary force, remained silent, watching Captain Aisha Renaud run her ship.

Like Daniel, Renaud had followed him from the wreckage of the warp cruiser *Scorpion*. Dark-haired and competent, she'd received command of the new-built battlecruiser the moment it had left the yards, the first ship built after *Watchtower*.

Octavio was still an engineer by nature, however high he'd risen. He'd pored over the designs for the new *Fortitude*-class ships, and the pale engineer with the short black afro agreed that the new ships were better than the weird transitional ship he'd ended up with.

But they'd spent over a year in space aboard *Dauntless* and he had grown to love every inch of his flagship like he'd loved his old warp cruiser.

Dauntless was still Aisha Renaud's ship and he waited for the dark-skinned woman to give her orders.

"Any major concerns, Lieutenant Commander?" Renaud finally asked. "This isn't a warp cradle holding the entire Exile Fleet, but it's certainly a stretch for all of us."

The warp bubbles were designed to be separate, but they'd made the voyage in month-long chunks. Allowing the ships to actually *talk* to each other had been a critical piece in making sure Octavio's crews stayed sane.

Technically, *Dauntless* had encompassed her four strike cruisers and four freighters inside her warp bubble. It was quite a stretch and not one that the system was designed to manage. They'd done it by synchronizing nine warp drives to create a single bubble that was no wider or faster than a regular warp bubble but was enough *longer* to absorb the entire flotilla.

"Synchronizations are stable," Daniel replied. "I've reviewed the Commodore's data from when the warp cradle failed. I've been watching for those spikes the entire trip."

Octavio concealed a smile. When Exile Fleet had first been dumped on this end of the galaxy, he'd volunteered to lead the contingent of engineers that had operated the warp cradle, a massive device that had taken the entire contingent of sublight ships into a grav-warp bubble.

It had been one of the most boring six months of his life in many ways, but he'd never done any engineering projects quite as *different* since. Not least since Isaac Lestroud had insisted on giving him a ship after that.

"I'll advise Siril-ki and ki's people," he suggested softly. "I imagine they'll want to be somewhere they can see everything when we arrive."

Siril-ki was the leader of the Assini survivors and ki'd insisted on accompanying the expedition back to ki's home system. Ki had fled with the rest of the refugees three hundred years earlier.

Octavio doubted that the obsession with seeing the Assini System was healthy for the alien AI specialist turned effective head of state, but he wasn't an Assini psychologist. Siril-ki had brought one of those along, so he hoped the mental health of his passengers was well in hand.

"Inform me when we're at two minutes," he told Renaud. "I'll be on the observation deck with our Assini passengers, I think."

"I'll make sure you're fully updated," D interjected and Octavio smiled softly.

Unlike the newer battlecruisers and the older ships that had been refitted, *Dauntless* didn't carry a K-sequence AI. The original offshoot of XR-13-9, XR-13-9-D, had insisted on accompanying the mission to the Assini home world.

Octavio was glad to have them. Even if he was quite sure the K-sequence AIs were, well, more human.

THE ASSINI WERE LARGE, centaur-like creatures with a broad horizontal torso with four legs and a secondary torso and shoulders with two arms. They had sharp-looking beaks and birdlike heads but were covered in short, soft fur.

Siril-ki was a "ki," a female/neuter in human parlance—humanity had *tried* using she/they as a translation for a while before the people working with ki had given up and used the Assini pronoun. Octavio wasn't sure if that gender role, poorly translated as it was, had any relationship to the Assini's actual physical sex. The aliens had, so far as humanity could tell, no distinguishing visible characteristics between their sexes.

The Assini leader was young for ki's people, and he was told that was visible in the lustrousness of ki's blue-black fur. Despite ki's youth, ki'd been one of the last survivors of Director Reletan-dai's staff, which had left ki in charge of the refugees the Director had led into a desperate flight.

"Commodore Catalan," ki greeted him as he stepped into ki's office. "Is it time?"

"We'll exit the warp bubble into the Assini System in eight minutes," he confirmed. "D is helping set up the observation deck so that you'll be able to see as much as we can manage. There will be space for all of your people."

"I appreciate your help setting that up, Commodore," ki told him. "I know it has been centuries, but it feels like I left home less than two years ago. I—all of us, I think—*must* see Assini as it is.

"I will have my people gather. I would be delighted if you would join us."

He bowed.

"I would be honored, Director Siril-ki," he told ki. "I'll meet you there?"

"As you wish."

———

THE OBSERVATION DECK was covered by heavy metal shutters during warp travel and combat—and the battlecruiser's *actual* armor layer was underneath the open space that could look out into the stars. There was only so much you could do with shutters and transparent aluminum to armor a space, so the ESF—like the Confederacy before it —hadn't bothered.

There were small trees and potted plants scattered around the space, making it more of a gathering place or meditation spot than a usable spot for astronomy. The transparent screens on the windows could be used to zoom in on areas and otherwise allow for amateur astronomy, but the observation deck was a luxury.

Humans needed to see the stars they traveled with their own two eyes.

Today Octavio was the only human in the space. Twenty-three Assini shared the space with him, fur ranging from Siril-ki's blue-black to a dull orange on one of the junior researchers.

"Emergence in ten seconds," Daniel's voice said in his ear. "Moment of truth."

It was easy to tell when a ship exited warped space. Being aboard a modern Exilium warp ship was a *thousand* times more comfortable than serving aboard *Scorpion* in the old days had been, but no living thing liked warped space.

It ended and the psychosomatic-but-still-quite-real symptoms of that dislike faded. Octavio blinked and yawned to pop his ears while the shutters swung open on the worlds his passengers had left behind.

He'd seen the images of the Assini System as the Assini had left it. Once, the star system had swarmed with life. Lacking an FTL system that could carry living people between stars, the Assini had developed their own system further than any human-inhabited system.

Ships had plied trading lanes between the homeworld, the terraformed colony orbiting farther out, and the swarms of colonies on and orbiting the gas giants' moons. An unstable star had been the death knell for Siril-ki's people, and the view he had now was *very* different.

Even from this far out, just past the orbit of the fifth planet, the star looked angry. The observation deck's windows were automatically zooming in on the planets, and none of the five worlds between him and the star had the typical blues and greens of a habitable world.

The three innermost worlds clearly never had. One might have had a Venus-like atmosphere at one point, but all three were now simply balls of ash, surfaces burned by either proximity to the sun or repeated solar flares.

The two farthest out looked almost leprous. Zoomed in as the image of the two worlds the Assini had called home was, he could see where there had once been vast oceans and what might have been continent-spanning forests and plains.

All of that was gone now, lost in various shades of brown and gray. The worlds were long dead. A high-pitched keening began to echo around him as his guests followed his mental steps and looked at their homes.

They'd known. Octavio knew that they'd seen at least some of the results before they'd fled the Assini System. They'd *known* at least one of their worlds had been wrecked. To see it, though…to see dead worlds and empty space where you'd once seen a living, breathing system…

He understood their grief. It hit him and it wasn't even *his* home.

Forcing himself past it, he focused on the gas giants. Assini had three of them, none quite as large as Sol's Jupiter but all large enough to have colonizable moons and minable debris clusters. If there was any surviving presence here, it was almost certainly there.

There was nothing. No energy signatures. No fireflies of active engines. No splotches of green to suggest an emergency planetary Construction project applied to a moon.

"We had two entire worlds to grow food on, Commodore Catalan," Siril-ki said quietly. He turned to look at ki.

Ki was almost frozen in place. Ki'd torn ki's attention away from the display above them, but tension had locked ki into position. That would fade—it was a fear reaction in a species that had never been predators—but it didn't look comfortable at all.

"I don't follow," he admitted.

"Our space platforms, even the colonies on the gas giant moons… none of them were self-sufficient," ki told him. "Food, water…much of that was expected to come from Sia or Sina."

Octavio shivered.

"Wouldn't they have been able to rig up something?" he asked. "That kind of location has a lot of intelligent people."

"I had hoped," Siril-ki admitted. "My worst fear is that we perhaps did not lure all of the Escorts out after *Shezarim*."

The half-built near-cee colony ship the Assini refugees had fled on had been supposed to also act as a carrier for a fleet of AI warships, mostly to protect it from the Assini's *previous* generation of AI warships.

One of the flares had driven them mad, and the Escorts had followed *Shezarim* for three hundred years before they'd met the Republic of Exilium and its allies. If they'd stayed in Assini long enough to wipe out everyone here…

"We'll find out," he promised ki. "Whatever happened here, we'll find out."

"We must find the answer to the Construction Matrices first," Siril-ki said firmly. "I would like to know how my people died and if it could have been prevented, but first we must stop the monster we unleashed on the galaxy."

Octavio nodded.

The Construction Matrices, like the Escort Matrices, had gone mad.

They'd assumed for the longest time that it had been due to the continual degradation of the tachyon punch, but when they'd finally been able to compare the code of the damaged AIs to the original code in *Shezarim*'s databanks, the truth had become obvious.

Many of the AIs out by Exilium *had* been driven mad by degradation, but the Escort Matrices and the Construction Matrices near Assini had not been. Someone had actively and intentionally corrupted their code.

Octavio was going to find those people. They'd killed untold trillions over the last three hundred years, and there was no way they hadn't known what they were doing.

Someone had to pay for that—and someone *also* had to make sure it stopped.

10

ORBIT OF SIA was even more depressing than anywhere else in the star system. *Dauntless*'s scanners were picking out the wreckage of dozens of ships and space stations.

"Just finding a clear spot to park us is going to be an endeavor, Commodore," Renaud told him. "Sia's orbitals were *very* heavily industrialized, and without someone to enforce traffic control, well…"

"I have the utmost faith in your crew," Octavio replied, watching the battlecruiser slowly edge into a gap in the debris. "What are we looking at, Captain?"

"The leftovers of a planet that makes Earth look like a pre-tech backwater," Renaud told him. "Lieutenant Commander McGill is trying to classify it all."

Dauntless's Captain shook her head and gestured to the hologram in front of the two of them on the battlecruiser's bridge. Darina McGill was the tactical officer and was clearly *still* digging into the wreckage with her scanners, as more data icons were appearing in the debris field as Octavio looked.

"It looks like almost all of it went offline around the same time," she continued. "McGill is seeing a lot of radiation damage. Electromagnetic-pulse burnout, collisions." Renaud shook her head.

"So, a lot of the chaos from the original solar flare is still intact," Octavio said. "That's...not a great sign."

"Wait, what's that?" Renaud asked as a new group of icons appeared. "McGill?"

"I'm flagging what looks like inactive navigation beacons," the tactical officer told her. "They're cold now, but they were *definitely* installed after the initial flare, and it looks like there's a small portion of facilities here that are newer. There was a way through, if nothing else."

"Daniel, put us over that section," *Dauntless*'s Captain ordered. "McGill, get me a closer look at it."

Octavio waited. Renaud had just given the same orders he would have, so there was definitely no point getting involved in her crew.

If this were a more traditional military force, he'd have had a staff and spent his time on the flag deck. But this was more on the order of an archeological expedition that happened to be carried by a group of warships. He had *one* staff officer, Commander Timon Courtenay, but that worthy was run off his feet just keeping the scientists from getting under the spacers' feet.

The hologram shifted and moved in. The area laid out by the newer nav beacons was still dead, but it was clear that someone *had* come in after the initial chaos and cleared a safe zone. The beacons had been supposed to mark the safe area where ships could travel.

It hadn't been a very large zone and most of the lower levels were long gone. They could park the flotilla in the remaining geostationary piece safely, but the gap certainly hadn't been large enough for the kind of travel necessary to support a government or major civilian population. Sia hadn't been completely written off after the flare...but Octavio was starting to suspect it *had* been abandoned.

"Let's get some of the Marines moving to check out the newer stations," he told Renaud. "And then see if we can map ourselves a route to the primary target. Do we have our maps reconciled with the current state of the surface yet?"

"I've got a team working on that in CIC," McGill told him. "We should be able to localize the Validation Center shortly."

To counter the degradation effect of the tachyon punch, the Assini had started using their tachyon *communicators* to validate the code of an AI Matrix after every jump. While there were a lot of questions around how the Construction Matrices had gone wrong, they *knew* that part of what had broken the Escorts had been a corrupted upload from the facility supposed to keep them sane.

It seemed like a good place to start looking.

———

OCTAVIO'S HANDS itched to be *doing* something, whether that was dismantling a warp drive or organizing a starship crew. Instead, he sat on his hands in the observer station on *Dauntless*'s bridge and watched Major Chen Zhou organize her first boarding company.

There was an entire battalion of Marines spread across his expedition, and Octavio had insisted that Chen command the force. The young Marine officer had led the boarding parties onto *Shezarim* and knew more about the kind of traps the Assini's rogue robotic warriors could unleash than anyone—and that included the Assini.

Arranging for her promotion and transfer aboard *Dauntless* had also allowed her to continue her relationship with the battlecruiser's XO. Fire-forged friendships went a long way—and so could fire-forged lovers. That bond had value to the man in charge of making sure they all came home alive.

For her own part, Commander Das was focusing her attention on her own tasks and only occasionally glancing at the updates on the Marine force's status.

"This is Orbital Target Alpha," Chen barked at her people. "Our taxi drivers have flagged it as the single largest structure that was still operational after the flare that drove the Assini out. That has both benefits and drawbacks to us."

Octavio ran through the Marines' org chart as he listened in on Chen's briefing. The Major wasn't commanding the boarding; that would be the Captain of her Second Company. *Chen* was going down with the force landing in Sia's capital city in an hour.

"The benefit is that these guys were here after the flare," Chen explained. "They knew what happened on the surface and had data on what happened then. Plus, that makes for clear evidence that somebody *survived* the flare. Our best clues of what happened next are probably here."

And the greatest dangers were probably on the surface, Octavio reflected. Evidence suggested that the Assini had indulged in robotic peacekeepers instead of organic police, enabled by the near-complete pacifism of their population.

If any of those robots were still running, they weren't going to be friendly to *anyone.*

"The main drawback is that we have a stack of override codes that should get us through most Assini military and police security barriers, but those codes were valid *when* the flare happened. So, they probably won't work on the station, and you're going to have to brute-force your way through a lot of shit.

"Your objective is the computer cores. Once we've located them, an Assini team will board behind you to access and extract their data. Captain Belmont!"

"Sir!"

"Whether it's safe for the computer specialists to board is your call," Chen told him. "Don't hesitate to hold them back. We have *time,* people. Anything that happened here happened hundreds of years ago. Nothing we do can change this planet's fate. Let's not take unnecessary risks."

"Yes, sir."

Octavio closed the display and looked over at Renaud.

"That time could run out faster than we'd like," the battlecruiser Captain murmured.

"Chen's people know what Admiral Lestroud ran into," he told her. "Even if things start going badly back home, we're fourteen months away, Aisha. If there's an answer or a weapon against the Matrices here… we're better off taking the time and finding it."

"I know." Renaud shook her head, glancing back at the display showing the burnt-out orbital infrastructure of a dead world. "I can't say being here isn't a drain, though."

"I know," he agreed. "But we'll take the time we need, Captain. No more, no less."

———

T HE FIRST WAVE of shuttles broke clear of *Dauntless*, impulse thrusters flinging them away from the battlecruiser with ease. They descended on the broken hulk of the Assini space station with easy grace.

A second series of images were added to the main hologram on the bridge, showing the view from the lead troopers on the station. Plasma cutters flashed and the Marines charged into the station.

"What are the odds that there's anything hostile on the station?" he asked Siril-ki over the com.

"I'd like to say zero," the Assini replied. "But there shouldn't have been hunter-killer drones on *Shezarim*. Our robotic progeny continue to surprise us."

"And rarely in good ways," Octavio murmured.

"That there were Construction Matrices out by you with intact preservation protocols was a good surprise," ki told him. "Otherwise…no. Most of our surprises have been unpleasant."

"I'd have expected you to stop building robot warships to fight your last generation of robot warships at some point," he admitted.

"What other option did we have?" ki asked. "We had to protect ourselves, and only the tiniest handful of our people could even work on the combat AIs, let alone consider actual fighting."

Siril-ki shivered at the thought.

"I understand the hypocrisy," ki admitted. "But that makes it no less true."

"Initial entry is clear," Captain Belmont reported. "No defenses, no robots…no bodies."

Octavio skimmed through the data on his tattoo-comp. The bridge observer chair had *some* functions, but he was better off using his implanted computer and linking it to the bridge systems.

"Looks like it was evacuated," he noted.

"That's what we're seeing as well," Renaud confirmed. "The Marines are sweeping further in. Anything unexpected, Belmont?"

"Everything's unexpected, sir," the Marine officer replied. "So far, everything has been pretty clean. We've even checked some supply cabinets. Empty."

"That's both a good sign and damned inconvenient," Octavio said. "It's a good sign since it means they were in good-enough shape to abandon the place in an orderly fashion, but it's a bad sign because if they took the cleaning supplies…they probably took the computer cores."

"Open plains," Siril-ki muttered. "Almost certainly, Commodore. Production of those cores would have required significant resources in the absence of Sia's industry. The retrieval of intact useful cores…"

"Hopefully, there'll still be something to say where they went," the human Commodore replied. "You may as well keep searching, Captain Belmont," he told the Marine. "Even if the cores are gone, that tells us something."

"We're going to step up the pace," Belmont replied. "Sensor sweeps are showing no life signs, no energy signatures. We'll keep it to the Marines for now, but we should have this place searched in short order."

Nodding in response, Octavio muted the channel and turned his attention to Renaud.

"That leaves Chen's mission for a hope of answers," he said softly. "If not…"

"There is an entire star system for us to search for clues," Siril-ki noted. "If there are answers here, we will find them, Commodore. It is only a question of time."

Octavio grunted. Recycling would keep his fleet's supplies going for a while but not forever.

"Our time is not infinite," he said.

"There are other places I know to look," the Assini promised. "It will not need to be."

<h1 style="text-align:center">11</h1>

———

THERE WAS ONLY SO much information that could be added to the main display and keep the hologram useful. As Major Chen's force dropped toward Sia's surface, the live feed from Captain Belmont's company shrank back to a map-based presentation of where the Marines were.

Octavio wasn't expecting much from Belmont's landing now. If the Assini survivors had stripped the station at all, they'd almost certainly taken the data cores they'd needed to locate the post-flare base of operations for Siril-ki's people.

Instead, he linked his tattoo-comp into the observer chair's systems and activated a "bird on the shoulder" view from the camera on the side of Major Chen's helmet.

"I don't think I need to tell you all not to be nervous," Chen barked. "But I'm seeing some nervous-looking biometrics on my feed. Do I need to remind you all who we are?"

A tiny icon popped up on the camera, a nonverbal acknowledgement from the Marine that Octavio was listening to and watching.

"No, sir!" the Marines chorused back.

"All right. Then who are we?" Chen snapped.

"E! M! C!" came the chorused chant.

"And who ain't scared of the ghosts of no dead world?"

"E! M! C!" the Marines repeated, though the tenor suggested that there might be some of them still scared of the ghosts of a dead world.

"Who are the swords in the night, the archers on the wall, when humanity is at the end of all known space?"

"E! M! C!" This time, the tenor was solidifying. The Exilium Marine Corps knew their role, if nothing else.

"And when a bunch of archeologists have to check out a dead world to find out who killed them, *who goes first*?"

"*E! M! C!*" The last of the nervous tenor was gone. Chen knew her people, all right.

"That's right," she snapped. "Strap in and lock down. We're hitting atmo in thirty seconds, and everything I've seen says this is going to be one *hell* of a ride!"

Octavio double-checked for himself. Half of Sia's atmosphere had been baked while the other half was left to normal night-time temperatures. It might have been three hundred years since *that* particular flare, but the weather patterns suggested that the planet had been baked by a few since then.

The storms on the planet were hell. The temperatures weren't much better, and it looked like just about everything on the planet was long dead.

For all that, spectrography suggested that the air on Sia was probably breathable by humans. There hadn't been any plant life to produce oxygen for a while, but there also hadn't been much around to use it up.

"Shuttles are in atmo," McGill reported. "Pilots are reporting some pretty brutal turbulence, as expected. Nothing they can't handle. Landing in six minutes."

A few commands brought up the shuttle's exterior cameras as the heat shields retracted. The view was not pretty. The continent that the shuttles were flying over had been heavily populated once, a carefully managed mix of broad-based arcologies, a small handful of individual estates, and manicured parks and plains.

All of that was dead now. The arcologies were slumping from a lack of maintenance, only their sheer scale and required structural redundancies keeping them intact. The estates were ruins, spared being eaten by plant life only because the plant life itself was dead.

The parks were in no better shape. Hundreds of square kilometers of dead vegetation still remained. Whatever new birth or decay that death would normally have spawned had been killed by further flares.

The entire planet had been radiation-baked. Octavio was sure *something* had survived—life was stubborn—but the flares would be getting worse, not better.

At some point in the next few thousand years, the star would finally nova and eat the Assini homeworld. Until then, the planet would suffer this state of not-quite-death.

Like the wreckage in orbit, it was damn depressing.

"Approaching target location," Chen's pilot reported. "Scans are showing some impressive communications infrastructure. All offline now."

"All offline since the first flare, most likely," Siril-ki said. "The facility wasn't hardened as your people would do it. Any threat would have been stopped by the Guardian fleet before it reached Sia."

The Guardians. Octavio concealed a shake of his head. Most people would have stopped after *one* generation of AI warships—or at least, after one of the generations went crazy.

The Guardians had actually been the first, the pre-Matrix artificial intelligences intended to protect Assini against whatever threats lurked in the dark. The Construction Matrices had been an entirely new revolution in AI, though the Guardians had been upgraded to match.

Then the Sentinel fleets had been built, intended to kill Construction Matrices considered too close to the Assini homeworld. They hadn't been built in time to prevent tens of millions of Assini colonists being murdered by the machines meant to build their new homes for them.

The Escort and Construction Matrices had gone mad and turned on the Assini, but so far as Octavio knew, the Guardian and Sentinel Matrices had served their purposes without fault.

The Guardian AIs had died here. None of them had been equipped with tachyon punches and most of them had orbited Sia.

A small but significant chunk of the debris orbiting the planet was dead AI warships. That felt…appropriate for all the problems the Assini's AIs had caused.

"Sensors agree with the Director," McGill confirmed. "The communications network around the Validation Center was fried by the first flare." He paused. "There are intact landing pads. Major Chen's people are moving in."

The view from Chen's helmet had been muted as she gave orders, but Octavio was following them anyway. It was hard to miss the deployment of the shuttles as they swept in around their target.

The Validation Center might have died a long time before, but it had still been one of the central structures of the Assini military. There were a lot of landing pads and similar around the facility, and the shuttles had no trouble finding places to land.

It was a surprisingly small complex at that. Four large radio dishes had been mounted on artificial hillocks at the corners of the facility, but time and the flares had turned all four to skeletal memories.

Most of the surface installation was made of bunker-like structures. The larger pieces of the installation had been communications tech. Octavio recognized several pieces of what had been one of the largest tachyon communicators he'd ever seen.

"If there's any answers here, they're underground," Siril-ki noted. "We might be pacifists, but we're also paranoid. There *will* be robot security. I doubt it's still active, but…"

"Did your briefing cover the security, Major?" Octavio asked.

"Mostly that it should be long dead," Chen replied, using hand signals to order her people out of the shuttle. "But yeah. Turrets and mobile robots, mostly laser-equipped. Should be on par with the Escorts' hunter-killers at worst."

"Just keep an eye out, Major," he told her. "Whole place may be dead, but it's making me feel *damned* creeped out."

"I hear you," Chen agreed.

The camera tracked with her as she exited the shuttle, turning around to survey the entire facility.

"Flat and square," she noted. "Siril-ki, did everything your people build look like this?"

"Not everything, but efficiency was often a priority," the Assini replied. "Especially for military affairs. There was never much money for the AI fleets, even after the Construction Matrices started wrecking worlds."

The Assini had weird priorities. Octavio didn't get them, but…that was the problem with working with aliens. To be a space-traveling civilization with starships and such, you needed to have a lot in common with other such civilizations.

The remainder, though…that left a lot of space for misunderstanding, confusion and chaos.

"Wait, take a look at this, sir," Chen noted. She knelt at the edge of the landing pad and brushed aside some dust. "That's a landing pattern for something that was too big for the pad and using *way* too powerful an engine."

"What would someone be landing on a shuttle pad that would fit that criteria?" he asked.

"Interplanetary transport," the Marine suggested. "A big-ass shuttle, basically." She started transmitting a collection of calculations and analysis back to *Dauntless*. "They blasted out of here with enough force to break orbit and head for Sina. I'd say that our post-flare people came back here."

"They'd have seen the Escorts attack the colony ship project and pursue us out of the system," Siril-ki half-whispered. "This would have been a place to investigate."

"Wait one," Chen said, interrupted Octavio before he could speak. "One of my teams is at the entrance to one of the bunkers and you need to see this."

A few seconds later, an image appeared next to the feed from her camera.

The door to the bunker was sealed. Someone had used some kind of spray cement to fill the entire entryway, blocking access with anything short of explosives—though given that every bunker led to the same underground complex, it wasn't that much of an obstacle.

In the middle of the spray cement was a laser-engraved metal plate with text in the blocks-on-blocks Assini script.

"Siril-ki?" Octavio asked. "What does it say?"

"It's a memorial," the Assini admitted. "A remembrance of the dead—not just for here but for everyone who died in the flare. I'd guess we're looking at one of many that were mass-produced and placed here after the situation had stabilized elsewhere in the system."

"Major Chen, have your people take a small sample of the plate," Octavio ordered. "Don't dislodge it—a memorial for the dead deserves respect—but some surface shavings should help us confirm where it came from. If *Shezarim*'s databases have that much information?"

"They should," Siril-ki told him. "Get a material sample and I should be able to tell you where the metal came from. Might not be able to narrow it down beyond the planet or asteroid cluster."

"That gives us a good starting point," Octavio replied. "Someone was stable enough to want to leave memorials behind for the people they'd lost. Let's see if we can find them."

"And this place, sir?" Chen asked.

"Search it," Octavio ordered. "Top to bottom, as we planned. If there were survivors, that's a different question than whether there's evidence here on what drove the Escorts mad.

"We can follow both questions, Major, but both of them need you to search that bunker."

"I figured," the Marine agreed. "But I'll admit I was hoping for a different answer." Her helmet light was now shining into the entrance of one of the entrance bunkers.

"That's going to be a creepy dark hole."

"That's why we sent EMC, Major. Good luck."

12

———————

Not only was the Validation Center every bit of the dark and creepy hole Chen had anticipated it being, it turned out to be a *useless* hole.

"Nothing?" Octavio asked.

"Nothing," the Major confirmed. "I'm standing in the middle of what *should* have been the primary computer center, according to Siril-ki's map. I can see debris where I'd guess stuff got torn out to make moving things easier, but I'd say the cores were stripped out."

"They wouldn't even have been functional," McGill objected. "I mean, you could access the memory if you had the right gear, but they'd never have worked as computers again."

Octavio had to agree with McGill. He knew how much Siril-ki's team had put into building the gear to read that memory.

"But it was crystalline silicon, already properly aligned to act as molecular circuitry," Siril-ki injected, ki's translated voice tired. "I presumed that the flare damage would have rendered it unusable, but it's possible it was easier to repair the crystals than to make new crystals.

"And the repair process would have wiped the memory core, anyway."

"They weren't just here leaving memorial plaques," Octavio

concluded. "They were scavenging as much as they could from orbit and the ground. Major military bases like the Validation Center would have been treasure chests of high-power electronics and supplies, even if it would all have been damaged."

"As Siril-ki said, it was probably easier to repair damaged systems than build new ones," Renaud agreed. "It wasn't a long-term project. Belmont's team is figuring the station they're picking through was only occupied for ten years or so."

"They couldn't have cleaned out everything of value on an entire *planet* in ten years," Octavio objected. "And if they left in an orderly manner, they weren't driven out by a flare."

"Not directly," Renaud said. "But look at the orbit of the stations supporting the salvage effort. It's not geostationary, Commodore. It's at a level and a velocity designed to keep it on the opposite side of the planet from the star as much as possible."

"So, if the planet got hit by another bad flare, they'd have *survived*, but it might have been by the skin of their teeth," McGill concluded for her boss. "They might have bailed, falling back to their home base to stay safe."

"Your thoughts are not in enough shadow," Siril-ki told them all. "A bad flare would have been a warning to the scavengers to retreat, yes. A bad-*enough* flare would have devastated Sina.

"If enough damage was done to the rest of my people, whatever herd members were here would have been needed back at their *home base*." Ki made a sad sound Octavio could only describe as a whinny.

"If enough people were dead, why pick through the bones of Sia for things that cannot help you?" ki asked. "Food and air would have become the priority, and if Sia and Sina were both dead, computer cores and robot sentries would not help you grow plants."

"They would have to focus on building new hydroponics facilities, like we did in Vista," Octavio said. "As far from the star as possible, not even at Sina."

He shook his head.

"But Belmont didn't find anything to say where they retreated to?" he asked.

"No," Renaud confirmed. "Chen did manage to get us the spectrography of a sample of the plaques, though."

"Which gives us a compass we did not have," Siril-ki agreed. "We are analyzing the data, but I can confirm that the metal came from Sina. Give me a few hours, maybe a day or so, and we shall be able to tell you where on the planet."

"Then that's where we go next," Octavio said with a grim sigh. "Unless anyone thinks we're going to find something useful randomly poking around Sia?"

"The only primary source for the answers we sought was in the Validation Center's computers," Siril-ki admitted. "There may be other pieces of the puzzle buried on the planet, but we don't even know where to look."

"Then Sina it is. For now, at least."

Octavio turned his attention back to the dead world. The Assini had set into motion events that had doomed dozens of other species to death—the Republic literally *had no idea* how many sentient species had died as their worlds were transformed around them—but none of their technology had been able to fight the fatal entropy of their star.

Part of him was sure the answer to stopping the Matrices was *there*, on the homeworld of the Assini. But with no idea where to even begin looking, a broader search was called for. They had to follow the clues and track the fate of the Assini—and hope that somewhere in that story of death and failure was a clue to the completely *different* question of how to stop the monsters the Assini had built.

13

———————

THE FIRST TIME Isaac had seen the Skree-Skree System, it had been a battlefield. He hadn't been physically there at the time, though. He'd actually been back in Exilium, overseeing the refit to *Vigil*, when *Watchtower* and *Spring Dream* had led their escorts to the rescue of the system.

It had been the first true allied operation the Republic had undertaken. *Spring Dream* had been built in Exilium and handed over to the Vistans only a few months before the battle. They'd been called into action with almost no notice.

But the two battlecruisers and eight strike cruisers had demonstrated that, yes, the ships could do exactly what they'd been designed to do. The Sub-Regional Construction Matrix handling the Construction process of the Skree-Skree's home had never known what hit it.

In the Hearthfire System, the ESF hadn't had the firepower on hand to stop the Matrices from launching their terraformer spikes at Vista. They'd evacuated the survivors, but they hadn't saved the Vistans' world.

In Skree-Skree, they'd arrived in time. Skree's vibrant green ball still hung close to the inner edge of the liquid-water zone of the dull Gclass star. The star might have had less energy than Sol or Exilium, but it was hot enough to keep its second planet warm.

Skree was uncomfortably warm and humid for humans across most of its latitudes, and its equator was actively dangerous for them without protective equipment. The rodent-like aliens had mostly lived underground to avoid the *very* active animal life of their planet.

They'd made it to the stars eventually, and there'd been a healthy spaceborne industry in place when the Matrices showed up. Much of it had been wrecked before the Exiles and Vistans had saved them, but the Skree-Skree had set to rebuilding it without hesitation.

"*Vigil* and *Dante* have docking slots assigned," Connor said behind him as Isaac studied the hologram of the system on the flag deck. "The strike cruisers are going right to the yards."

"How long until their battlecruisers are online?" Isaac asked. Two of the massive ships were under construction there, the centerpiece of the same yards his damaged escorts were moving toward.

"Both are scheduled to leave the yards inside two hundred hours," his operations officer replied. "At least that again in trials and exercises before anyone wants to call them operational, but they'll be in space in less than eight days."

Probably ten of Skree's nineteen-point-eight hour days, Isaac reflected.

"And our own ships?"

"*Fortitude* and *Reliant* are still about a week out," Connor told him. "We're still waiting on answers from the Tohnbohn about whether they can break free more ships, too."

"And the Matrices haven't found anything yet," Isaac said grimly. "We got snookered, Connor. They knew we were looking for the RCM and intentionally laid a trail of breadcrumbs to lead us away.

"It's only bought them time, but that time let them build these damn dreadnoughts." A wave of Isaac's hand swiped away the image of the Skree-Skree System and replaced it with the rotating black sphere of the new Matrix warships. "They're not even in XR-13-9's files. We keep forgetting the damn AIs can improvise, even with our allied Matrices doing it all the time."

Connor didn't argue. He was studying the big warship himself.

"No offense, sir, but I'm glad it's your problem," the operations officer said dryly. "I just have to keep military forces from four species and a bunch of computers talking to each other and moving in the same direction."

"*Just*," Isaac echoed back. "I know better, Aloysius. We wouldn't be getting anywhere without you and the others. Amelie *thinks* she might have some new allies for us, but these Sivar…" He shook his head.

"They remind me of the Confederacy," he admitted. "I almost wish they just reminded me of my mother."

"What's the difference, sir?" Connor asked after a moment.

Isaac turned to look at his aide. Captain Aloysius Connor was a tall and dark-haired man who'd never visited Earth in his life and had *definitely* never met the First Admiral.

"The First Admiral earned the epithet *Iron Bitch* honestly," he told his subordinate. "She fell into the trap of corruption that every absolute leader falls into, but her objectives were clear and she rarely lost sight of them.

"Presented with a clear and present danger on the edge of the Confederacy, there would be no question what she'd do. She'd gouge potential allies for all she could, but there's no question that the Confederacy Fleet would be heading out to fight the Matrices."

He shook his head.

"But everything suggests that the Sivar have a dictator just like her…and we don't know which way they'll jump."

"I don't think most people would be so confident in which way the First Admiral would jump, sir," Connor admitted.

"I know," Isaac conceded. "She did herself no favors, but I did know her. By the end, her virtues were vastly outweighed by her flaws, but she had slivers left of them."

"Speaking of local dictators, though…"

"What does the Grand Speaker want?" Isaac asked. *Dictator* was an unfair descriptor for the Grand Speaker. Like the Great High Mother of the Vistans, he was a strictly limited constitutional monarch—though, also like the Great High Mother, one with real power.

Unlike the Great High Mother, the Grand Speaker was an elected post. The Speaker was elected for life on the death of the previous

Speaker. The vote was a popular election that came with a strong expectation of a previous lifetime of service.

Most Grand Speakers were already quite old when they took up the title. That was an inherent limiting factor on their monarch-for-life powers.

The current Grand Speaker was old even for Grand Speakers, probably doddering into his last years, and had served his people well. It wasn't LastBornVoice's fault that he *irritated* Isaac.

"The Grand Speaker has invited all of the battlecruiser captains and flag officers to attend a grand banquet held in their honor," Connor told him. "It is to be held at the Palace of Frozen Earths."

"That's appreciated," Isaac murmured. That was the Grand Speaker's secondary residence, in the *very* limited area of arctic tundra Skree possessed. So far as he could tell, it existed because the novelty of building a structure out of bricks of frozen soil had never quite worn off for one of LastBornVoice's predecessors.

He sighed.

"We will, of course, attend," he told Connor. "I leave making sure they actually serve something we can *eat* this time up to you."

"Have faith, Admiral," his subordinate murmured. "I have to eat whatever they're serving too!"

———

ISAAC HAD to be grateful that the meeting was at the Palace of Frozen Earths, because his tattoo-comp was all too willing to tell him what the weather was like at the Palace of Broken Monsters. One hundred percent humidity, thirty-eight degrees Celsius and brilliantly sunny.

The Palace of Frozen Earths was its own headache, but Isaac could live with temperatures just below freezing. His uniform could handle that without even trying. It was a *lot* harder for the uniform to handle the weather at Skree's equator.

"We're coming in above the Palace now," his pilot announced. "Air control is directing us in a wide circle, though. Someone—it sounds like a local guest—screwed up their landing and scattered an aircraft along the entire runway."

"Any survivors?" Isaac asked. That was…a bad way to start a not-quite-diplomatic-summit.

"Not even a damn *injury*," the pilot replied. "The Skree-Skree apparently go for ridiculous safety equipment."

As Isaac used his tattoo-comp to show him the feed from the shuttle's pickups, he could see part of the need for that. The Skree-Skree might put insane safety equipment in their aircraft, but the planes were a collection of fragile half-winged nightmares he would have grounded on sight.

The consistency of it suggested that was just the local style, but just *looking* at Skree-Skree airplanes made him shiver. The Skree-Skree didn't have a human level of risk assessment, a necessary survival trait on their planet.

They'd been into rifled firearms and mobile artillery before they'd been able to reliably take down the beasts the translation software dubbed terrormonsters. Even small cannonballs had just pissed the eight-meter-tall sauroids off. The Palace of Broken Monsters now had gates built of terrormonster bones…but the small aliens that had gone after them were now his allies.

The Skree-Skree were basically the small furry rodent that had coexisted with the dinosaurs on Earth…except the dinosaurs had never gone away on Skree.

"They say they'll have the runway cleared in a few minutes, but they're directing us to a second landing site," his pilot continued. "Looks like they do have proper shuttle pads here, they just prefer the runway themselves."

"Land us wherever they ask," Isaac said, sharing a long look with Connor. "Unless it's actually a *problem*. Then we can argue."

"There is *nothing* I can't land this bird on," the pilot boasted. "We'll be fine."

The Admiral concealed a snort. Pilots were always a special breed.

THE GRAND SPEAKER'S people must have been used to this kind of chaos. Despite a crashed plane and their human guests landing on the opposite side of the palace than expected, there was an honor party out to greet Isaac and his officers as they exited the shuttle.

The human group was small. He and Connor represented the overall command. His two Vice Admirals, Giannovi and Anderson, had each brought an aide as well. The two Captains had come alone, bringing the total up to eight.

Captain Alstairs was looking askance at *Dante*'s commander, but Isaac was used to that. Captain Robert Cavan had nearly missed ever getting a battlecruiser command, almost entirely due to a *spectacular* ability to irritate his colleagues.

Isaac had never seen the slightest hint that Cavan punched down, though. *Dante*'s crew seemed happy enough with their Captain—and that was enough for him.

Right now, Cavan was looking around their surroundings with an unconcealed expression of distaste, which Isaac couldn't quite deny the validity of.

The landing pad itself looked modern and functional, a dense nanocrete pad that would stand up to shuttles with ease. The buildings around them took a minute to identify as such, as they had all been built from cut turf. The temperature meant the frozen tundra making up the exterior of the structures *stayed* frozen, but the Palace of Frozen Earths very much lived up to the name.

The formally dressed Skree-Skree soldiers didn't help. Their near-rat-like appearance was only augmented by face-concealing red helmets that concealed their beaks in a snout-like structure.

The shining silver armor wrapped around their hunched torsos was perfectly effective, but its decorative impact was undermined by the fact that each of the Skree-Skree honor guard had welded artifacts of personal importance to the breastplate, resulting in dress uniforms that looked like loose cutlery drawers.

The appearance wouldn't have been acceptable to EMC Marines, but these *weren't* EMC Marines. They were Skree-Skree Speaker's Guards, and Isaac understood that. He gave the honor guard a perfectly crisp salute as they raised their rifles to the sky with a chorus of predatory screams.

"Fall in, officers," he ordered calmly. He met Cavan's gaze levelly for a few extra seconds, until the man dipped his head in understanding.

Message sent and received. Body language was handy, not least because aliens picked it up only at the loosest level.

"I look forward to meeting with our host," he told the lead Skree-Skree officer, allowing the translator device pinned to his collar to repeat his words in their incomprehensible language.

"Of course!" the alien replied. "The Grand Speaker awaits you in the Hall of Warmth. Come! Come!"

———

"THE LOSS OF *LASTBORN* CONCERNS US," the Speaker for Arms told Isaac quietly later, as the meal began.

Each of the alien races was, thankfully, being served a different meal. The Skree-Skree used various tiers of rot as flavoring in a way that Isaac figured might actually kill humans if not properly managed. They managed several dishes that actually looked quite edible to him, but he wasn't going to trust a Skree-Skree chef cooking for him without *very* specific instructions.

A team of ESF stewards had gone down to the surface in advance to make sure the human food was safe—and while the meat in his spaghetti bolognese definitely wasn't beef, they'd done a good job with it.

"Our losses in general concern me," Isaac admitted. "The Matrices were ready for us in a way we didn't expect."

SongWind—the being in charge of the Skree-Skree military and the Grand Speaker's niece or some equivalent, Isaac understood—snapped her beak crisply.

"We are prepared to commit our ships to this alliance, Admiral, but we fear for our children," SongWind told him. "LastBornVoice faces political challenges as well. There are those who question how much of our newborn fleet we are committing to your command, Admiral."

"There are always those who question alliances, Speaker," Isaac conceded. "There are those who would bring my ships home as well."

President Emilia Nyong'o had them very thoroughly politically neutered, but they existed.

"Now you want us to commit the new battlecruisers to your campaign, your crusade," the alien said. "When does it end, Admiral? How many ships will be fed to the terrormonsters of war before it is done?"

"I don't know," he admitted. "I don't know how many species the Matrices have destroyed, how many worlds have been turned to paradises on the graves of innocents. The Regional Construction Matrix we are hunting is the most immediate threat to us all, but there are others and they need to be stopped."

"I don't disagree," the Speaker for Arms said. "But many in the First Gathering do. They question sending our ships to battles that must be farther and farther as time goes on. A tunnel can only be dug for so long before the tools break, Admiral, no matter how valuable the destination."

"I know." Isaac glanced along the table to where the Grand Speaker was sitting. The Skree-Skree head of state had lost much of the blue lustre to his feathers, his plumage fading to dull and gray with age.

LastBornVoice was fully on board with protecting his people, but fighting for the rest of the universe? Isaac knew that was going to be a hard sell for anyone.

"We need to deal with this RCM," he told the Speaker for Arms. "The bastard knows us now. It's being smart, it's luring us into traps. We need to turn one of those traps on it and end this dance before it's too late.

"After that, it will take time for us to identify RCMs that are engaging in genocide," he admitted. "That will mostly fall on Matrix recon nodes as we try and expand our area of operation and, hopefully, bring other non-Rogue RCMs onto our side."

He shook his head.

"In the long run, having the Matrices out there building habitable worlds is good for all of us," Isaac admitted. "We just need to stop the ones that are killing people to do it. We won't need as large a portion of anyone's fleets when we go after the RCMs that are further away."

"You are assuming, of course, that our fleets continue to expand,"

SongWind noted. "An expansion I don't believe your fleet is capable of. At what point, Admiral Lestroud, do you think we will start to complain about fighting your war for you?"

Isaac forced a chuckle to cover his uncomfortable exhalation. SongWind wasn't wrong in what she was suggesting, and it was something he struggled with. He was arming allies and uplifting alien races, but it was a careful balance between keeping the Republic safe and turning his allies into his mercenaries...or his sepoys.

"I hope that it remains *our* war," he pointed out. "And I would add that this RCM is a threat to your worlds, not ours. Exilium is almost a hundred light-years away. If we left you all to your own devices, well, we've given you enough technology that you should be able to deal with the Rogue yourself.

"We're fighting for you here. And we plan to ask you to do the same for people we haven't met yet in the future. I hope that it never becomes just *my* war." Isaac shook his head.

"If it becomes just my war, I've done something very wrong."

SongWind clicked her beak in amusement.

"You recognize that, at least," she told him. "We swore to fight by your side, Admiral, and we will. You'll get the battlecruisers and their escorts this time. But once this RCM is defeated and our world is safe, we will need to keep more of these ships for our own purposes."

A shiver ran down his spine. He didn't even know what other purposes the Skree-Skree could *want* warships for. There were three Constructed Worlds within easy colonizing distance of their system that they wouldn't need to fight anyone for.

"I hope that we will leave behind us a group of races and systems in sufficient communication that you won't have many purposes for them," Isaac told her.

She chirped laughter at him.

"So do I, Admiral Isaac. But I am the Speaker for Arms for the Skree-Skree people. I must be aware of *all* possibilities, not merely the ones I hope for."

"So must I," he reminded her. "This campaign, this *crusade* as so many people call it, against the Matrices...it is only my *secondary* mission. The first and foremost mission that I am called to is to defend the Republic of Exilium.

"But the Republic is a long way from here and I have left people I trust to keep it safe." He smiled. "We make ourselves safest by protecting everyone, I think. It's a better way forward.

"For all of us."

"You humans are fascinating," SongWind told him. "So lacking in consensus of clan and tunnel, and yet so hopeful. Such optimists."

"Not all of us," Isaac admitted. "But I have to hope, Speaker. I am charged to wield the Republic's Sword. I have no choice but to hope it is never drawn lightly."

14

———

"THERE'S nothing left for us to send, Admiral," Rear Admiral Sri Spannagel told Isaac. The androgynously plump officer he'd left in command of Exilium's Home Fleet looked drained. "The two *Fortitude*s and their battle groups are on their way, but you signed off on the Senate's mandates, sir."

"I know," Isaac sighed. "And there's reasons for it. I don't suppose Dr. Reinhardt has managed to come up with a way for us to cut our crewing requirements by another fifty percent?"

Spannagel shook their head.

"There's a limit to how far we can cut things, sir," they reminded him. "Just the Marine contingents alone are a personnel problem at this point. We could get the recruits, but..."

"But the Republic needs most of those hands at home, building the Republic," the Admiral completed.

Spannagel was entirely correct, too. Isaac had worked with the Senate shortly after the last election to lay out the new hull strengths and required deployments of the ESF. Nine battlecruisers, each with a four-strike-cruiser battle group and with eight strike cruisers left over for the Home Fleet.

The strike cruiser number was still theoretical in many ways. That was part of why *Watchtower* only had two of the lighter modern ships with her and the Home Fleet still had a notable number of ships that could only make a hundred and twenty-eight times the speed of light.

And per the same mandate that authorized those fifty-three warships, Isaac was required to hold sixteen strike cruisers and two battlecruisers at Exilium, barring a direct threat to the home system. A separate order required that a battle group be held at Refuge as well, which took up a third battlecruiser—the fourth and final *Vigilance*-class ship in ESF service, *Scrutiny*.

There had been two more *Vigilance*-class ships until recently, but with the activation of the *Fortitudes*, those ships' crews had been transferred to the new ships and the ships themselves deeded to the Vistans.

"I need *Scrutiny*," Isaac finally said.

"It's your fleet, sir," Spannagel reminded him. "But you agreed with the Senate that we needed a battlecruiser at Refuge, which means…"

"I have to send *Dante* back to Refuge if I want *Scrutiny*," Isaac concluded. "I'll talk to Vice Admiral Anderson and the First-Among-Singers. If the Vistans will break free more ships, that gives us options."

And that, as the Skree-Skree Speaker for Arms had warned, would end any pretense that the allied fleet was a human formation. If the Vistans had as many battlecruisers present as he did, well…

It was a good thing neither First-Among-Singers Sings-Over-Darkened-Waters or her Great High Mother was likely to insist that Isaac surrender command to a Vistan officer. They respected him, even when his fleet was rapidly becoming the *second*-largest navy of their tentative alliance.

"Feels weird to realize the Vistans will shortly have more warships than us in total," Isaac admitted. "They already have more civilian shipping."

Most of that shipping was the evacuation transports built to move people from Vista to Refuge. Those ships were just as fast as Isaac's warships and had been built to serve multiple purposes. He suspected that they'd be forming the core of the civilian economy for the Vistans and their neighbors for a *long* time.

Even three years later, there were still millions of people in the Hearthfire System, in orbital habitats that had been moved a *long* way away from the planet itself. Hundreds of the massive transports, each able to carry a hundred thousand people, had once plied their way back and forth between the two systems.

Evacuating a system was an immense proposition. It was only recently that any of that shipbuilding capacity could be turned to building anything else—but the Vistans weren't going to need any civilian ships anytime soon.

Not with those immense transports sitting there, begging for a use.

Instead, they were laying keels for their own fleet. All too aware of the Matrix threat, the Vistans were about to start building battlecruisers four at a time.

They probably weren't going to *stay* at four at a time.

"In many ways, this is even more their war than ours, I think," Spannagel reminded him. "We fought the Matrices and won. They lost ninety percent of their population."

Isaac nodded. And despite that, the amphibious aliens still had a billion people and could afford to put a lot more people in uniform than he could. His fifty-three ships and their Marines and support staff called for the Exilium Space Fleet to have about fifty thousand personnel—over a full percentage point of the humans out there.

He couldn't recruit more…which meant he couldn't have more ships. There just were no hands to crew them with.

"I'll talk to Sings-Over-Darkened-Waters," he repeated. "That dreadnought the Matrices threw at us has me worried. A fleet of those…well, we'd need something to match them.

"And I don't think battlecruisers will cut it at that point!"

HIS CONVERSATION with Sings was both more and less worrying.

"Of course," the old Vistan said after he told her his request. "We have the two ships you promised us on their way. Knowing they're coming, we can easily free up three here. They'll be the first-generation *Vigilance*s, but we know what lurks in the dark waters, Admiral."

"Part of the problem is that we don't really," Isaac warned her. "It's possible the RCM is closer to you than us. That's why we're peppering the entire region with Matrix scouts."

"That is war, unfortunately," Sings told him. "I would rather never have fought one, but what happened to Vista cannot be repeated."

"I know." He shook his head, knowing that the speakers on the other end would make the right chirps for Sings to "see" him via her echolocation. "Three more battlecruisers will make you the single largest contingent in the fleet," he reminded her.

"You'll have four to our five," Sings replied. "And your *Fortitude*-class ships are easily worth two of the *Vigilances*, as I am constantly reminded by my politicians."

"I must protect Exilium," Isaac said quietly. "But the decision was never mine. You know that."

"And we don't have enough exotic-matter production of our own to maintain a fleet of *Fortitudes*, let alone build them," Sings admitted.

The fact that the Republic was building better battlecruisers for themselves than they were willing to sell their allies was a sore point, Isaac knew. On the other hand, Exilium also contained the only exotic-matter mass-production facility available to the allies.

If no one else was willing to capture multiple black holes to build a factory with, then Exilium would remain the main source of the negative-mass material necessary to fuel most of their modern technology.

Assini and Matrix tech didn't require it in the same quantities—they'd only ever used it for artificial gravity—though Isaac suspected that XR-13-9 had duplicated the Exile facility without telling anyone.

The Vistans were starting to use particle accelerators to produce a limited amount of their own exotic matter, but that was a slow process. They were almost to the point where they didn't need regular resupply from Exilium to keep their fleet online—but far from the point where they could build ships without buying EM from the Republic.

Of course, that hadn't been a big-*enough* advantage for the Senate to let Isaac sell the Vistans—let alone the Tohnbohn or Skree-Skree—the *Fortitude* designs.

"Once we've brought this Regional Matrix down, we can consider how we go forward," Isaac told the alien. "We've been chasing this one damn AI for years. It's not a good sign for managing to clear the galaxy of the things."

"This one knew we were out for vengeance," Sings replied. "Its cousins will hopefully not be as forewarned. But trust me, Admiral Lestroud. Even if Exilium must lessen their effort, I and my Great High Mother *will* see this task complete."

Isaac chuckled.

"If Amelie succeeds in bringing the Sivar on board, we might finally have enough players that I'll start feeling comfortable," he noted. "Everything we're seeing there suggests a multi-system polity with a significant fleet. Updating their tech should give us a huge boost in numbers."

"And yet you sound uncertain," Sings-Over-Darkened-Waters noted. The Vistan was getting *far* too good at picking out human tone. From what Isaac understood, Sings could understand English just fine without the translator at this point, too.

Human ears and brains just couldn't handle a language being spoken by two mouths and a set of gills. Vistans could understand humans with practice, though.

"They remind me too much of home," Isaac admitted. "But I trust Amelie. She'll know what the right thing to do is."

"Everything I have heard of and from your mate leads me to agree," Sings told him. "Even if your people had never fought for ours, I think Amelie Lestroud could have convinced us to join this war.

"Dark waters will not drag her down. She will find her way."

"I know," Isaac said, forcing a smile.

And he *did* know that. Nothing in the galaxy was going to stop his wife.

So, why was he so afraid for her?

15

"WARPED-SPACE EMERGENCE IN TWELVE HOURS. I repeat, warped-space emergence in twelve hours."

The alert echoed through *Watchtower*, and Amelie breathed an open sigh of relief. The battlecruiser's crew assured her that the new warp drives were *much* gentler than the old ones—and her experience with the cradle used to move the Exile Fleet agreed with them—but she still couldn't get used to the experience.

She might have tried to conceal the reaction in different company, but the being on the other end of her tachyon communicator did not care about human expressions—and WK was aware of everything she did on the ship, regardless of her company.

"Apologies for the interruption," Amelie told Recon and Security Matrix KCX-DG-12. The AI was the core intelligence of one of the cruiser-scale ships that were supposed to act as backup for the smaller recon nodes.

Right now, DG-12 was acting as the coordinator for the dozen or so recon nodes trying to scout out the Sivar as discreetly as possible.

"This unit's understanding is that the process of warp travel is difficult for organics," DG-12 replied. "Notification of its imminent end is valuable data."

DG-12 was also not nearly as practiced at dealing with people as many of the Matrices Amelie was used to. WK wasn't human either, but she could almost *feel* the battlecruiser's AI cringe at their cousin's stiff speech.

"Your scouts have visited the systems connected to Sivar-One by the star-lanes?" she asked. "or at least, what we think are connected to Sivar-One."

"The systems now designated Sivar-Two, Sivar-Three, Sivar-Four, and Sivar-Five do appear to be linked to Sivar-One," the Matrix confirmed. "Sivar-Two was the system that Commandant Ackahl passed through. One of the nodes successfully traced the Sivar fleet to a second star-lane, leading to a system now designated Sivar-Six.

"From there, she connected to Sivar-Prime, the homeworld."

"What was in those systems?" Amelie asked, feeling like she was pulling teeth.

"Sivar-Two, Sivar-Three and Sivar-Five only possessed spaceborne infrastructure," DG-12 told her. "Sivar-Four and Sivar-Six both had inhabitable worlds. Sivar-Six's inhabited planet appeared to be marginally habitable and represents a midsized colony world. Sivar-Four was near to Constructed World standards and heavily populated.

"At the distances the nodes were surveying from, it is impossible to be certain if either world possessed an indigenous population, but the probability of such a population existing on Sivar-Four is approximately four times that of one existing on Sivar-Six."

"So, that's seven systems and four inhabited planets," Amelie concluded. "That's a hell of a lot more population and industry than any of our other allies. Do we have a basis for identifying other systems? Or, hell, detecting the star-lanes themselves?"

"Partial," DG-12 replied. "Our recon nodes are engaging in extended surveillance to localize similar transition points as were identified in Sivar-One. The nodes following Commandant Ackahl had the advantage of seeing the route her fleet took."

"We have confirmed that the star-lanes follow the entry vector of ships using them," WK interjected. "They travel along that vector to the nearest star and then stop. Knowing that, it only takes a small number of transits into a star-lane for us to localize its destination."

"Any progress?" she asked.

"We have localized and identified eleven Sivar star systems," DG-12 told her. "Six inhabited planets have been identified."

Amelie inhaled sharply. The alliance's four members only had *five* worlds if you stretched the definition to include the Vistans' original shattered home.

Even if that was all they found, the Sivar controlled more star systems and more inhabited planets than all four of the species she'd painstakingly convinced to stand together against the Matrices.

"We have made no progress on being able to detect the star-lanes themselves," WK noted. "What we're seeing so far suggests that the Sivar may have difficulties detecting the entry points themselves. None of the systems connected to Sivar-One *except* Sivar-Two appear to have further connections. It is a reasonable postulation that the Sivar have not expanded more than four star-lanes out from their homeworld in any direction.

"Once we have located the other star-lanes leaving Sivar-Prime, we should be able to identify the entirety of their territory in relatively short order."

"We're already looking at a nation that might rival the Terran Confederacy," Amelie replied. "They'd be powerful allies, but they could easily end up overwhelming us by sheer numbers."

"We have insufficient data to estimate a probability of their full territory," DG-12 said. "The Terran Confederacy was able to access all of the stars inside its declared space. Their access to resources and potential habitable worlds was significantly greater than any power in this region except the Matrices themselves."

That was true, Amelie supposed. It was easy to just match up inhabited worlds against inhabited worlds without realizing just how poorly the Confederacy had really done at expanding in an organized or coherent fashion.

First corruption and then *totalitarian* corruption had held humanity back for a long time. The technology and industry available to the Confederacy would have allowed them to steamroll any of the allies humanity had made out here.

Assuming they'd bothered. The new ESF was almost a match for the CSF in numbers. It was only looking back that Amelie realized just how intentionally limited the CSF had always been—and how much that had depended on the fact that the Confederacy could stop any of the member systems from building their own ships long before they became a threat.

"How much firepower are we looking at?" she finally asked.

"The majority of the surveys are from too great a distance to identify individual vessels," DG-12 replied. "Our node following Commandant Ackahl identified an additional battleship group in each of Sivar-Two and Sivar-Six.

"Sivar-Prime was initially surveyed from sufficient distance to identify its nature. No closer intrusion has been planned."

"Nor should it," Amelie agreed. "Keep me updated as you locate new star-lanes and scout their systems. But…if we can locate a star-lane that isn't currently in major use by the Sivar, it would be worth its weight in gold if we can work out how to pick them up."

There was a pause.

"The star-lane entry points do not appear to have any mass," DG-12 noted. "If they had weight, they would be detectable."

"It is a metaphor, DG-12," WK told the other AI. "It would be extremely valuable if we can establish the ability to detect star-lanes."

"We'll need those lanes if we're going to bring the Sivar fleet to war against the Matrices," Amelie said. "Plus, you said you don't think *they* can easily detect them. A faster method of finding the star-lanes could make a useful trading point."

"We will attempt to carry out close-range analysis," DG-12 promised. "This unit is not convinced the star-lanes are detectable without attempting to take a ship through them."

"That must make surveying a pain in the ass," Amelie noted.

"It would be difficult," WK interjected before DG-12 could respond. "We may be able to fabricate a star-lane transition system for tests, but it would, of course, be easier with schematics of a Sivar system."

She snorted.

"I'll see what I can get my hands on, but I suspect they're going to want weapons pretty damned quickly," Amelie said quietly. "And I'm *not* trading these people gamma-ray lasers or particle cannon until I know them *much* better."

———

"We'll drop out in a few minutes," Captain Holmwood told Amelie in place of a greeting as the ambassador stepped onto the bridge. "Anything I can help you with, Minister?"

"You can reassure me on something, Captain," Amelie told the officer. "Everything I'm hearing says that Ackahl beat us here, probably by quite a margin. So, they're faster than us. Can we fight them?"

"We got some pretty detailed scans of Ackahl's ships," Holmwood replied. "Riker? Want to field the Minister's concern?"

"It's a straightforward-enough answer," the tactical officer replied. He left his station behind and leaned against one of the displays near the command seat. "Two parts to it, but clear enough."

"And the answer *is*?" Amelie asked. "Be clearer than a Recon Matrix that's never talked to humans before, please. It's been a long day."

Riker chuckled.

"First part of the answer: Ackahl's battleship has exactly one hundred missile launchers. Her entire hull layout, engine positions, defenses…everything is predicated around pointing those hundred missile tubes at whoever she's fighting.

"Their sublight engines are an older system that the Confederacy discontinued in favor of impulse microthrusters a generation ago," he continued. "They use a series of large fusion engines. They're effective enough, but if you can *build* effective impulse engines, you can get more efficiency out of the same fuel.

"So, they've almost eighty percent of our acceleration but at half again the fuel consumption. Doesn't matter so much for a warship… but it matters a *lot* for a missile."

"So, their missiles suck, is that what you're saying?" she asked.

"Basically," Riker confirmed. "They're short-ranged and slow by our standards…and we built our defenses around shooting down

Matrix missiles for years now. WK, what's *Watchtower*'s capacity for engaging incoming cee-fractional warheads?"

"Assuming a worst-case scenario with zero warning from other vessels or scanner platforms, *Watchtower* would be able to neutralize between four and six hundred incoming cee-fractional weapons," the AI replied. "Assuming standard defensive drone nets, that could easily be increased by a factor of three or more. This ship was designed to stand against heavy Matrix battle groups and defeat their missile armament."

"So, yeah," Riker continued. "Their missiles suck, and even we can't build missiles that are actually a threat to this ship. *They*, on the other hand, have built their heavy combat platform entirely around mass missile fire."

"And the other half of the answer?" Amelie asked.

"WK, how much exotic matter is included in *Watchtower*'s weapons alone?" the Commander asked.

"Minus three point six tons," the AI answered. "The heavy particle cannon alone requires minus seventeen hundred and eighty kilograms. Each of the light particle cannon requires minus two hundred and twelve kilograms. The pulse guns and lasers require nominal amounts apiece."

"Whatever the key to the star-lanes is, it doesn't involve exotic matter," Riker told Amelie. "Every FTL drive the Confederacy used did, so the Confederacy had exotic matter in quantity. To build our warp drives, we needed even more—so we have a mass-production facility that would feed three Confed systems providing the supply for four million people.

"We have exotic matter to burn. The Sivar don't. That battleship had *no* exotic matter aboard, Minister Lestroud. While that leaves the potential for heavy laser weaponry, it means I can be quite confident they don't have heavy plasma or particle weaponry."

Holmwood turned in her chair to look back at Amelie.

"In short, I'm not any more scared of Commandant Ackahl now than I was when she was charging at us," she concluded. "I wouldn't want to fight their massed battle fleet, but I think it's a safe bet that we can easily handle being outnumbered a few times over."

"Good," Amelie told her. "Because we're heading into their capital system, their *home*. If they had two battleships in Sivar-One, does anyone think they have anything less guarding their homeworld?"

"Not a bloody chance, Minister," Holmwood said. "And while I'd prefer to go find some *reinforcements* if you want me to attack a multi-stellar empire's homeworld, you're in charge of this expedition."

That shocked a surprised laugh from Amelie before she let her Ambassador Mask take over her face.

"We're here to negotiate today, Captain. I don't plan on launching any wars…but I want you ready to blast us out of here if things go wrong, understood?"

"Entirely understood, Minister. If worse comes to worst, well, that's what I brought Marines for!"

———

EVEN WARNED that it was coming, the warp bubble always seemed to collapse with surprising suddenness to Amelie. One moment, the entire universe was locked away from *Watchtower*. The next, the battlecruiser was back in regular space, their little convoy around them.

"Do we have a location on Ackahl?" Holmwood barked. "Let's make sure people know who we are and why we're here before I have to shoot an idiot."

Amelie watched as the system appeared around them. Their initial data was coming from the recon nodes currently lurking a light-day away from the Sivar's home star.

It was a busy system. Thirteen planets, most of them smaller rocky planets closer to Sol's Mars than Earth. A single gas giant, a paltry miniature compared to most of the gas giants Amelie was used to, swept around the edge of the star system.

The fifth planet was the second largest of the worlds and the only planet in the liquid-water zone. Presumably that was the Sivar home-world, though the spacers around Amelie were focused more on ships and industry than on planets right now.

There were plenty of those. The next planet out from the habitable one was surrounded by a swarm of stations that radiated more energy than some entire worlds Amelie had seen. Refineries and factories, almost certainly.

There was more construction around the homeworld and the inevitable cloudscoops on the gas giant. Ships were trawling through the entire star system, ranging from the gas giant at the extreme all the way to the star at the center.

Watchtower's crew focused on the warships. They flagged warships in orbit of the three heavily industrialized planets…and, to Amelie's fascination, four more concentrations of warships at seemingly random points in the system.

"I *think* that's Ackahl in orbit of the homeworld," Riker reported. "But I'll admit I'm looking at those fortresses."

"Fortresses?" Amelie asked. "Are they near those random warships?"

"Those aren't warships at points four through seven," the tactical officer said, indicating the four random concentrations of ships. "The iconography is similar, I can see the confusion, but only some of those are ships.

"Most of them are space stations, *armed* space stations positioned together. I'm guessing they're covering the star-lane entries."

"No wonder Ackahl didn't like the thought of us being able to dodge around the star-lanes," Holmwood said. "If they are limited to the star-lanes, they must have thought those forts helped keep their home safe."

She shook her head.

"Send a transmission to the main planet, addressed to Ackahl. We'll stay out here, a nice ten light-minutes from anything they might get twitchy about, until they clear us in."

16

———————

THE PLANET WAS APPARENTLY NAMED Aris. After the three species that Amelie had spent the last few years negotiating with, it was a strange sensation to be dealing with one where humans could actually pronounce their words and, potentially at least, learn their language.

Aris triggered an odd pang of almost homesickness as *Watchtower* gently decelerated into orbit, surrounded by Ackahl's battle group. The fortress layout, the weird layers-built-on-layers nature of the industrial platforms, the green and blue of the world below…it all reminded Exilium's Ambassador very much of Earth as she'd last seen it.

"Are we sure these people aren't talking to the Confederacy?" Holmwood muttered, clearly having much the same feeling. "The fortress setup could be drawn directly from Earth Fortress Command."

"That's because planets are spheres the galaxy over," Amelie replied. "Offset rings of space stations armed with long-range weapons is a pretty obvious solution."

That they had the *same* four rings of six fortresses apiece as EFC was an eerie coincidence.

"But yeah. Feels a lot like home and not in an entirely comfortable way, right?" she asked the Captain.

"Exactly." Holmwood shook her head. "You could almost *hear* Commandant Ackahl's disdain at the speed of the warp drive. That's a hole you're going to have to dig out of in the negotiations, Minister."

"I can handle that," Amelie said with a chuckle. "I got forty-six rebel factions talking to each other and moving in the same direction at once. I'm pretty sure I can convince the dictator of a dozen planets that they'd rather not see those planets turned into clean slates for the Matrices' Construction projects."

"Better you than me," the ESF officer said. "Have you touched base with Major Köhl yet?"

"Only on the generals," Amelie replied. Major Lina Köhl was the commanding officer of the Marine contingent attached to the diplomatic expedition. She'd be the one in command of the Marines responsible for Amelie's security. "I know I'm bringing Marines down with me when I go to the surface."

She'd had to leave the extremely well-trained Presidential Security Detail behind at the end of her term, but she had a lot of confidence in the Exilium Marine Corps. Köhl's older sister ran the SWAT team for Starhaven Watch, the police force of Exilium's capital, and had been critical in holding things together early on.

Nothing Amelie had seen yet suggested the younger sibling was any less competent.

"Is that even a *when*?" Holmwood asked. "I mean, we did just get escorted into orbit by a battleship and we are very much under the guns of their fortresses. They might want to just chat by radio."

"Unless the Sivar are very different from every other race I've dealt with, they'll want to meet face to face," Amelie noted. "We came all this way to meet with the Intendant. I doubt that worthy plans to leave us sitting in orbit."

Holmwood snorted.

"Not forever, anyway," she pointed out. "I wouldn't put it past them to leave us hanging."

"It's possible," Amelie conceded. "But I'd like to think that, if nothing else, the Intendant doesn't want even neutral warships in orbit of his planet just sitting there, getting grumpy." She looked at the big display on the bridge.

"Speaking of which, how confident are you of extracting yourself from this?" She waved at the hologram.

"Like the battleships, they're primarily missile platforms," the Captain noted. "There's definitely some big lasers of some kind over there, big enough that I'm a *little* worried based on their tech level."

"So?"

"I'm pretty sure we can get the warships out," Holmwood admitted. "I'm *not* so comfortable that we could save the freighters if they started shooting." She grimaced. "They'd pay for the privilege, but if they take us by surprise, they can gut the freighters before I can stop them."

Amelie nodded slowly. That wasn't really a surprise, even if it wasn't what she'd been hoping for.

"I appreciate the honesty," she told the officer. "It's good to know where we stand."

———

THE CALL she was waiting for came with surprisingly alacrity. She'd been expecting a degree of "hurry up and wait" once they were in orbit, but the first communication from the surface arrived within the hour.

The Siva on the screen was less gaunt than Ackahl but still disproportionately tall to human eyes and seated in a very similar throne. Unlike Ackahl, this one hadn't covered their head, freely revealing the bone carapace of their face. They had somewhat less of the carapace than Ackahl had, with their fur closer to black than the Commandant's blue, and their eyes edged closer to red.

Where Ackahl had worn a hooded dark green tunic, this Siva wore a toga-like garment of a delicate-looking translucent fabric. It was wrapped around them in enough layers to be opaque, but loose trails drifted away from the Siva's breasts and shoulders in an unseen breeze.

The breasts, if Amelie understood correctly, meant the person on her screen was a ban, the child-bearing third sex of the Siva.

"Greetings," she told the figure. "I am Amelie Lestroud, Ambassador Plenipotentiary for the Republic of Exilium."

"I have been advised," ban said. "I am Dorost, Keeper of the Keys of Peace. I am tasked by my Intendant to speak with you."

They sounded rather spectacularly unenthused with the prospect. Amelie figured ban's title meant something close to her own Foreign Minister. Talking to strangers was ban's job.

"I came here with the understanding that I would be speaking with the Intendant directly," she noted. She wasn't entirely surprised to be shoved off onto a minister-level figure—assuming that was what Dorost *was*, at least—but some respect would be nice.

"That may still happen," Dorost conceded. "That is *my* decision to make, Amelie Lestroud. Convince me that you are worthy of His Greatness's time, and I will intercede on your behalf."

That mouthful of crap didn't make Amelie any more enthusiastic about making the effort, but no one had ever promised she'd only get to negotiate with people she *liked*.

"I see," she said icily. "And how much of what Commandant Ackahl and I discussed has been passed on to you?"

"A frontier soldier's opinions have value, Amelie Lestroud, but this is Aris," ban replied. "The fate of worlds and stars ride on the Intendant's words, and he is buried in the work of ruling the Governance.

"Commandant Ackahl was right to bring you to us, but I must form my own opinions of your claims and positions before I speak to the Intendant."

Amelie studied the bureaucrat on her screen. Every Siva she'd seen so far appeared to insist on sitting in a throne on their calls. She couldn't say too much, she supposed, given that she was taking all of their communications from the Admiral's seat on *Watchtower*'s flag deck.

"Very well," she conceded. "I represent both the Republic of Exilium and a group of allied powers outside your borders, closer towards the galactic rim. We face an expanding crisis and are looking for allies.

"This crisis consists of a group of self-replicating terraforming robots. While some of these robots are part of our alliance, a large number have lost the portion of their core protocols that prevented them from modifying worlds with native sentient life."

Technically, the core protocols had barred the Matrices from Constructing worlds with *any* life, but even the Republic couldn't get themselves worked up over worlds without sentient life. Maybe if the Matrices *hadn't* murdered untold billions they'd care, but as it was…

"We have fought several factions of these genocidal machines and driven them back from the worlds of our allies," Amelie concluded. "To deal with them on a more-permanent level requires an extended campaign and major resources—a burden more easily carried the larger our group of allies becomes.

"Your worlds, Keeper of the Keys of Peace, are just as threatened as ours," she stated. "Without knowing the boundaries of your nation, I can't guess how far all of your territory is from the expanding edge of the Matrices' reach, but the system we met you in is less than twenty light-years from where we have fought the genocidal version of the AIs, the ones we call Rogues.

"For them, that is a handful of days' travel at most. You have only been spared so far by the fact that they only enter systems in force to begin the terraforming process. The Rogues are almost certainly aware of your presence and are already calculating which of your worlds are most easily transformed."

"You think we are afraid of your horror story, Amelie Lestroud?" Dorost asked. "We are the Sivar Governance. Our fleets fear no enemy. These robots do not intimidate me."

Amelie concealed a snort. From what her people had told her, the Governance's fleets were even worse-equipped to fight the Matrices than the Confederacy's Exiles had been. A *single recon node*, the smallest of the Matrices' armed combatants, had fought the equivalent of Ackahl's battle group to a standstill.

"Your fleets are not prepared to face this enemy," she said. "You do not know their strengths or their weaknesses, and your fleets might well find themselves outgunned by an enemy they do not understand —even though I doubt they would be *outfought*."

She had no basis to judge the Sivar military one way or another, but it was an easy concession to make. Even with limited information,

Amelie suspected that Ackahl, for example, would fight to the last to hold back a Matrix attack.

But from the scans of the Commandant's flagship, she would do so in vain. A single combat platform could wipe out every defender in the Sivar-Prime System.

"You assume we are unready. That we know nothing of this threat," the Keeper replied. "Do you think us blind?"

"I think you look first to the other ends of your star-lanes, never realizing there is another way to travel the stars," Amelie told ban. "If you know what is coming, you must know you are better to stand with allies than stand alone."

"Are we?" Dorost studied her like a hungry hawk, for all that ban's head more closely resembled an armadillo. "Are you so certain you could help us?"

"Yes," she said calmly. "We have technology you do not. Knowledge of this enemy that you do not. We gain from standing together, Keeper Dorost. Without us, your entire 'Governance' might fall into darkness."

"I will consider your words," ban allowed. "Do you have data to support this?"

"We have prepared a data packet summarizing the Matrices' operations in this area and their overall expansion," Amelie confirmed. "A three-hundred-light-year radius of the galaxy has been…*reformatted* to their standard, Keeper. If we are to stop them, we must stop them as a group."

"Send it," ban ordered. "I will consider the data alongside your words. I will be in contact."

The channel cut and Amelie exhaled.

"Without us, you're *fucked*," she told empty air. "Without you, we're potentially inconvenienced.

"Now, how do I make you realize that?"

17

———————

Dauntless and her flotilla spent an extra two days at Sia, sifting through the wreckage of the Validation Center and a handful of other locations Siril-ki flagged, but the metal plaques were the only real clue they found.

"Whoever was scavenging the planet was following the same logic we are," Captain Renaud concluded as their ships slipped free from the safe zone they'd found. "Military installations appear to have been stripped clean. About the only thing that's helped is that we keep finding more of those plaques."

"My people have very similar monuments to the dead as yours," Siril-ki confirmed. "They would have removed the bodies where they could, but survival would have been the priority. Sina would not have gone untouched by the flare that destroyed Sia."

"But the source of the plaques says that Sina *survived*," Octavio pointed out. "Survived sufficiently to either refurbish or build inter-planetary ships to get here."

He'd been an engineer and he could do the math. Nothing that had been in open space near the two inhabited planets when the flare had hit had been usable. Even the orbitals protected by Sia had been wrecked.

Orbitals and spacecraft on the "lucky" side of Sina should have been okay, and the flare *shouldn't* have been enough to do more than cause a massive planet-wide EMP. The Assini's second world would have lost their electronics, but most of the people would have survived.

"It will only take us a few hours to get there," Renaud told the other two in Octavio's office. It wasn't *that* small a room, but the presence of the Assini made it feel cramped. "What are we expecting to find there?"

Siril-ki closed ki's eyes.

"More death," ki admitted. "We have localized the source of the metal in the memorials. I can direct you to a specific refinery facility on Sina's largest continent that we can presume was still operational after the flare, but we'd already know if there were still people there."

"We're following a trail of breadcrumbs at best," Octavio said. "If we were any closer to home, I'd suggest that this was a waste of time. But we're not, so we may as well keep looking. What do you expect to find, Siril-ki?"

"*Shezarim* was not the only ship my people had that was capable of interstellar travel," ki told him. "We took her because she was nearly complete, but there were elevens like her under construction."

Ki flexed ki's hands, drawing Octavio's attention once again to the asymmetrical number of digits. Five digits on the right hand, six on the left. The Assini were an odd race, one that he wasn't sure would ever have evolved on Earth…but then, Sia had never been Earth.

"Were any completable?" Renaud asked.

"They all would have been, given the time and resources," Octavio said. "They could have taken the parts from several to build a single ship." He sighed. "They would have needed to go somewhere safe— but there were systems near here that the Sentinels had cleared, weren't there?"

"Reletan-dai didn't trust the Sentinels after the Escorts went mad," Siril-ki admitted. "Plus…we knew at least some of the ships were destroyed by the Escorts. We should send a ship to investigate, though. There will be no answers to the madness of the Matrices there, but there could be a sign showing my people escaped."

"Assuming, of course, that Reletan-dai wasn't right to fear the Sentinels," Octavio half-whispered. "But that is a worry for later. Renaud?"

"Sir?"

"Send *Prospero* to check out the colony ship staging zone," he ordered. "They were out past the gas giants?"

"Yes," Siril-ki confirmed. "May I transfer some of my people over to your strike cruiser? They will have the access codes in case anything is still intact."

"Do it," Octavio said. "The rest of us are heading to Sina. We'll see what Major Chen makes of your refinery, Director Siril-ki. Maybe we'll find some more answers there."

The only real answer they had so far, after all, was that the flare that had sent *Shezarim* fleeing the system had killed every Assini on their homeworld.

———

Prospero DETACHED from the rest of the flotilla when they made turnover. She kept accelerating as *Dauntless* and the others began to slow into Sina orbit. The strike cruiser, with her six Assini supernumeraries, would hopefully have more luck than they'd had on Sia.

Sina, on the other hand, looked…much as its mother world had. Disturbingly so, in fact.

"It looks like they started sweeping out the wrecked stations from the first flare and never finished," McGill reported. "They'd been kicking stuff out of orbit and clearing space and building new stations, but they never finished the job."

Octavio didn't have to ask *why* they'd never finished the job. He already had close-up images of some of the larger stations on his tattoo-comp, and he could see. He couldn't tell the difference between the stations that had died in the first flare and the ones that had died later.

"Can we tell how much later?" he asked, coughing past an unexpected lump in his throat.

"Not really, from the space stations," McGill admitted. "Once we've put EMC boots on the ground, the shuttles can do a lot more of the detailed work than we can."

She paused, studying the iconography.

"I mean, the good news is that there's still life down there," she noted. "But I'm not seeing any power signatures or anything suggesting intelligent civilization at all."

"There may be survivors without technology?" Renaud suggested, Octavio's flag captain throwing a cautious glance at the cameras passing the image of the bridge to Siril-ki.

"It's possible," McGill hedged. "These scans would miss small-scale infrastructure, water-wheels, that kind of thing. But we're talking *full* regression, the kind that…well…the kind that doesn't happen in a technological society," she admitted. "Despite the stereotypes, there's always *someone* who knows how to make the tools to make the tools.

"Even assuming that the flares caused them to write off high tech entirely, there's so much that they'd be able to accomplish with just gasoline motors."

"You are being too optimistic," Siril-ki injected, the flatness of ki's translated tone suggesting ki'd turned off the emotional layers to the software. "Look more closely at your scan data.

"You're not looking at forests and animal life. You're looking at bacteria, algae, fungi…minor-order life, life that would survive massive radiation blasts.

"You're not looking at a world that *survived*, Commander McGill. You're looking at a world that hasn't quite died yet." The keening that came over the radio was harsh to human ears. "You're looking at where *my people died*."

"We know," Octavio cut in. "But there's a chance some made it out and the only answers are here. We have to go down there, Siril-ki."

"Of course we do," ki agreed in the flat tone of a mechanical translation. "Our answers are there if they are anywhere. Find them, Commodore Catalan."

———

Shuttles flashed into space again as Octavio watched. This time, it looked like Chen was leading the team heading to the orbitals, and delegating the expeditions to the surface to her subordinates.

Octavio had no intention of micromanaging the Marines. He was still riding on Chen's virtual shoulder, but he'd retreated to his office to do so in privacy. On Sia, they'd had hopes that the Validation Center would have some answers to their bigger questions.

On Sina, all they were doing was scraping for clues, hoping to find an answer to stopping the Matrices hidden in the wreckage of a dead world.

"All right, people," Chen barked as the shuttle docked. "Scans suggest that this was the last station the centaurs built before things ended the second time. I'm not seeing any signs that anyone scavenged this place, and they put a lot of effort into building it.

"Let's find out why, shall we? EMC! Move out!"

Octavio brought up the scans of the station they were boarding to see what Chen was talking about. The station was definitely newer than the others and… Wait. It had tachyon transmitters.

"Renaud, did we notice the tachyon transmitters on Target Alpha and no one mentioned them to me?" he asked over a private channel.

There was a long pause.

"I'm looking right at it, sir," she said slowly. "Am I blind?"

Octavio adjusted his image slightly and added highlights before sending it back.

"Yup, blind," Renaud confirmed. "We did our initial analysis from a different angle, sir, and it was a lot less obvious from there. Why would they have tachyon coms?"

"They were talking to the Sentinels," Octavio told her. "Or trying to, anyway. I think we're looking at a replacement Validation Center."

"If we are, sir, they may well have hardened aspects of it," she pointed out. "And if they were remotely suspicious about what happened to the Escorts…those aspects may have included security."

"Are we picking up power signs?" he asked.

"No…wait…*fuck! Get me Chen!*"

18

———————

Octavio's over-the-shoulder-camera view of what Chen Zhou was seeing didn't show him the displays inside the marine's helmet by default. It only took three commands for him to link into the tactical control network for the Marines—a network that was already starting to flash red warning signs.

"We have power signatures moving inside the station," Chen barked. "Shipboard is reporting a high likelihood of intact Assini defense systems. Fall back on your primary entry points and reinforce. Do *not* engage alone."

The red icons were, thankfully, "remote" contacts—ones that the Marines hadn't collided head-on with.

"Assume we're facing something comparable to the hunter-killers on *Shezarim*," Chen continued. Octavio was hearing what his Marine CO was saying but not the responses. "Highly mobile, heavily armored, equipped with high-power lasers.

"Set your pulse rifles for minimum dispersion, maximum power. Don't fire randomly on those settings, either. We kind of need this place intact."

The red icons were following the Marines as they fell back. None of them had burst through walls and opened fire yet, but they were *definitely* pursuing.

"Siril-ki," Octavio said. "What are my Marines looking at? Chen's figuring something like the hunter-killers."

"She's right," the Assini replied swiftly. "They're remotes with minimal onboard intelligence, but that station never had a full AI Matrix aboard. They might be a bit smarter than the ones on *Shezarim* simply because they weren't expected to have a Matrix for control."

"Do you have any codes that can shut them down?"

"I'm sending a shutdown order already," Siril-ki told him. Ki shook ki's head. "No response. They're not recognizing the code—it's probably obsolete and they may have degraded past the point where they'd obey any stand-down code."

"How much power can they have?" Octavio asked.

"Enough," the Assini said grimly. "They'll have been in standby mode. They might only have power for one shot apiece, but the power reserves for a single shot from their weaponry will allow them to move for hours.

"Now they're active, we could just withdraw an—"

"CONTACT!"

For a moment, Octavio wondered why he was hearing someone's report to Chen...and then he realized the Marine had been shouting herself.

A panel in the roof of the space the Marines had set up the onboard HQ in had swung open and three of the drones dropped out. As they did, the red icons on the Marine perimeter moved in.

Chen was far from helpless. She'd made the same adjustments to her own weapon that she'd ordered her people to and she shot one of the drones before it even hit the ground.

A spear of superheated plasma pierced the machine and flung it backward into the wall. The second drone was caught in a crossfire of three other Marines—but the third fired first.

As Siril-ki had suggested, it fired a single shot from one of its three lasers and then hit the floor an immobile powerless wreck...but that was enough.

"Corporal Shu is hit," Chen said calmly. "Medic to the HQ section. Perimeter squads, report!"

Icons were flashing on the screen as the drones swarmed the Marines. For a few seconds, Octavio was actually worried...but Chen didn't *sound* worried as she grunted acknowledgement of the reports.

A few seconds later, he saw the reason for her calm. Her Marines were getting hit, but their armor was preventing more than minor injuries and the drones were collapsing as they fired. It only took a few minutes for the defenses to spend their power reserves, and then the space station was silent again.

"Get the wounded moved back to meet the medic," Chen ordered. "Watch your scanners for new power signatures, but that should be the end of it. Good news, Marines: if there was enough power left for security, there might actually be something here."

A moment later, she opened a direct link to Octavio.

"Major Chen reporting, Commodore," she said briskly. "The drones were spent before they even hit our formation. It looks like their power levels were so low, they couldn't fully energize their beams, and they basically suicided to generate shots that only burnt through the armor half the time.

"We have seventeen wounded but only one severe injury," she continued. "Any idea from Siril-ki what this place is? I wasn't expecting hunter-killer drones."

"It's the replacement Validation Center, Major," Octavio told her. "We think, anyway. There are tachyon communicators attached to the station. We want the data cores and we want the core transmission hardware for the tachyon coms.

"There might be something left in those transmitters that will let us know what happened to the Sentinels, if nothing else."

"Understood," Chen replied. "We'll see what we can find. This place has already been an...interesting trip."

―――――

LESS THAN TWENTY MINUTES LATER, Chen pinged Octavio directly. He was looking over the initial reports from the landing at the refinery Siril-ki had identified, which was about as depressing as he'd feared.

"Yes, Major?" he asked.

"Found something you want to take a look at," she told him. "Helmet says you aren't riding my shoulder right now, but you should bring it up."

That software was closed, but the system could handle restoring a program closed a few minutes earlier. A new image appeared next to the report, showing what looked like an office. The desk looked normal enough, even if the seats were shaped for a centaur-like creature the size of a pony.

"What am I looking at, Major?"

"This appears to have been the station head's office," she told him. "No local computer core—figured I'd check—but there is one thing I think we might find useful."

Chen had more control of the over-the-shoulder view than she normally used and was easily capable of zooming in the view on the map she'd found. It wasn't much more than laminated paper, but the station didn't have much in terms of living bacteria to eat it.

"That's a world map of Sina?" he asked.

"A world map of Sina that dates to *after* the fall of Sia," she confirmed. An armored gauntlet tapped part of the map. "The maps I saw from Siril-ki's people showed this continent as being inhabited, where here it has no cities labeled on it at all. I'm not entirely up to date on the Assini language, but my computer says the text is warnings and memorials."

"Cities that were stripped of power and technology but still had survivors," Octavio murmured. "Evacuated and abandoned." He shook his head. "That part of the planet would have been salvageable, but the population was low enough that they could abandon it."

"That's what I figured," Chen agreed.

The map was an odd projection, its image of the planet narrower at the top and bottom but still with an adjusting scale.

"The thing I wanted you to see was this." An armored finger stabbed at an icon of a green leaf with a gold box around its middle.

"Unless I'm misremembering Assini iconography, this is their capital. And it's *not* where the capital was on Siril-ki's map."

"So, that's where they were running everything from after the world ended," Octavio murmured. "We don't have anyone near there, I don't think."

"We've got this station secure," Chen told him. "It's a computer tech job now. My shuttles are still almost fully fueled. I can break a platoon free and drop inside five."

"With yourself in command, I'm guessing?" he asked.

"You sent me to check out ghost worlds, sir," she replied. "Not going to leave it half-done."

"Fair enough. Make the plan, Major, but one question."

"Sir?"

"Did you see Belmont's report from the refinery?" he asked.

"Only skimmed the summary," she admitted.

"We got a timeline, Major. Everything here? They only lasted twenty years after Sia. Radiology on the soil samples says there were at least two flares almost as powerful as the first one in between, but they must have thought the new hardening and such they put in place was enough to keep them safe.

"Then they got hit with a flare hard enough to give three-quarters of the planetary surface a lethal radiation dose."

He could almost hear Chen grimace.

"Dating the bodies we found here was on my medics' to-do list," she told him. "I imagine it'll come out about the same. There was an emergency bunker at the heart of the station, but...it's still sealed. Should I crack it before I go?"

"Crack it, Major," he ordered gently. "But don't wait around yourself. Your subordinates can handle the station now."

"Understood. Captain Mac Niadh will take over here. He's more tech-savvy than I am."

"Keep an eye on your people, Major," Octavio ordered. "This isn't an easy job."

"I know, sir," she conceded. "And I'm watching them. Who the hell watches me?"

"That's my job, Major Chen Zhou," he told her. "And your girl-friend's, when she has time."

"My girlfriend is a battlecruiser XO," the Major replied with a laugh. "She *doesn't* have time."

"You're a regimental commander. When was the last time you did?" Octavio asked.

"Fair. Right now, I appear to have digging up the grave of a government on my to-do list. I'll let you know what I find, Commodore!"

19

———

Despite what Amelie had hoped was some kind of urgency, it was over forty-eight hours before she finally heard anything else. If nothing else, she would have figured having multiple warships in orbit would have woken *somebody* on the surface up!

"Minister, we're receiving another call from the surface," Holmwood finally told her, interrupting a riveting series of emails from Exilium that Amelie was basically ignoring.

"All right. Let me get to the flag deck and look sufficiently intimidating," Amelie said with a sigh. "Anything I should be aware of?"

"I think it's a different Siva than last time, but all I got was 'imperious bureaucrat dismissing the servant,' so I can't be sure," Holmwood replied. "I mean, if you wanted to go take a shower or something, turnabout is fair play."

Amelie chuckled.

"Not today, I think," she told the Captain. She was already on her way to the flag deck, after all. "WK?"

"It is definitely not Dorost," the AI told her. "It is another ban. I have not yet detected any standard or decoration in Sivar garments outside of the military. We may have moved up the chain, but I understand that the Intendant is male."

"So do I," Amelie agreed as she slipped into the seat. "Do we have our cloak of intimidation ready?"

"We do. The display is online and we are ready when you are," the AI replied.

"Put them through."

If ban wasn't sitting on the same throne Dorost had been, it was a very similar stone structure. This Siva appeared older, with fur closer to a dull gray than Dorost's black, and wore a similar toga-like garment to the Keeper of the Keys of Peace. Ban's had a solid leather-like section around the torso that acted as a base for the flimsy fabric that made up most of the garment, but the corset-like piece had clearly been molded to accentuate the wearer's breasts.

Some things, it seemed, were universal.

"Greetings, I am Minister Amelie Lestroud," she told the stranger. "I'm wondering if there was some delay in Keeper Dorost's communications."

"Anathema Dorost has been executed for failing to properly advise ban's Intendant," the stranger told Amelie calmly. "The Keeper of the Keys of War gave the information the Commandants had provided to the Intendant, and he questioned why the Keys of Peace had not passed on the communication.

"Dorost is now anathema, ban's former ranks and achievements to be forgotten for ban's crime," the Siva continued. "I am Istila, ban's replacement as Keeper of the Keys of Peace. I have reviewed the data you provided."

Ban did *not*, Amelie noted, explain how the Intendant had gone from "why have you not told me what the alien said" to "you are executed for treason." That was potentially not something that the Intendant had to explain.

"As I told your predecessor," Amelie said slowly, "I am here to meet with your Intendant...or whoever else can commit the Governance to an alliance against the Rogue Matrices."

"We are aware of the Builders," Istila told her. "The Intendant knows more than mere Keepers. That is his place. Your data matches the fears of the Governance, and the Intendant has informed me that you and I will meet in person. Once I have met you, I will judge if you are to be conveyed before His Greatness.

"You will take an unarmed vessel to a space station whose coordinates will be communicated to you," the Keeper continued. "You may bring one guard. I will meet with you there and we will learn if what you believe and what the Intendant knows match closely enough for you to be permitted a meeting."

"Very well," Amelie said grimly. "I will return to my ship from that station, however, and we can discuss my visiting the Intendant afterwards. That, Keeper Istila, is a different discussion."

She'd take one Marine onto a space station while *Watchtower* loomed in the background. She sure as hell would *not* go down onto the surface of an unknown world with a single bodyguard.

For now, though, she'd let them set the terms. She needed them to *talk* to her.

"Of course," Istila told her, with a bow of ban's armored head. "The turnings will bring us to faces, Minister Amelie Lestroud."

That was apparently a farewell, as the communication shut off. Amelie exhaled a long sigh.

This was going to be...*interesting*.

———

AMELIE FINISHED LAYING out the Sivar proposal and looked around her team.

Captain Holmwood commanded her battlecruiser and the spaceborne component of her expedition. Major Köhl, a dark-haired woman hailing from India on Earth, commanded the Marines across her three warships. They sat together at the far end of the conference room, the two military officers attempting to present a unified front.

Faulkner sat at Amelie's right hand, facing the Vistan diplomat Shivers-Under-Mountains. The broad-shouldered frog-like alien was the head of the small group of non-human diplomats aboard *Watchtower*.

Like her fellows, Shivers-Under-Mountains was willing to let the humans make initial contact. Once the basic alliance had been agreed to, they would have input on the details, but they were really there to become their peoples' ambassadors to the Sivar.

Assuming that anybody ended up wanting to talk to the Sivar.

"One Marine," Köhl said pointedly. "They want us to send the President Emeritus, the Old Man's wife, the bleeding *Foreign Minister*…onto their space station with one Marine. I'm not sure my commission would survive allowing that, ma'am."

"It's not your call, Major Köhl," Amelie pointed out dryly. She appreciated that the Marine at least put her being Isaac's wife *after* her having been Exilium's first president. Not all of the military officers she'd met had handled the priorities the same way.

"It's my call," she continued. "And I'm going. We need to make a real connection with these people to establish an alliance, and we've all looked outside at those battleships."

She shook her head.

"They're flawed ships built with tech we'd call obsolete, but remember that they made it here over a week before we did," she continued. "They have things to offer us and we have things to offer them.

"We've *seen* six battleships, each of them a third again the mass of an Alliance battlecruiser," Amelie pointed out. "Those six ships alone would be a significant reinforcement against the Matrices, even if they'd need refitting.

"Evidence suggests that's only a portion of their fleet, too—which means they have the ability to build those ships on a recurring basis. We can augment those shipyards with the industrial nodes we brought with us and halve their construction time.

"The Sivar Governance could be a *powerful* ally," she concluded.

"Or a terrifying enemy," Shivers-Under-Mountains said, the warbling multi-toned sound of her voice rippling under her translated speech. "They feel…like the ink of darkwater monsters, creatures of the blackest depths."

"The first person I spoke to here has apparently been executed for mildly displeasing the Intendant," Amelie conceded. "Shivers is right.

These may not be people we want to ally with—in which case it is even *more* critical that we know them better.

"I will meet with this Keeper Istila. If I can, I will meet with the Intendant. I have no intention of committing to *anything* without more information," she said firmly.

"We're using passive sensors to sweep the ships and the planet as best as we can," Holmwood told her. "Even a single low-altitude pass by one of our shuttles could augment our data dramatically."

"The more we know about the Sivar, the better off we are," Faulkner agreed, Amelie's right-hand man speaking for the first time. "We need to have this meeting. What I think is the better question, Amelie, is whether *you* need to go to it."

She started to dismiss that idea out of hand, then paused.

"That would make me a lot more comfortable," Köhl admitted. "If we sent Mr. Faulkner over with a Marine escort, for example."

"I hate to emphasize my expendability, Amelie," Faulkner told her, "but I *am* more expendable. You don't need to be in every meeting and every encounter. If we're sending somebody into the lion's den, then… maybe it should be somebody we don't have to start a war if they get chewed on a bit."

"You overestimate my willingness to write off *anyone*," Amelie told him grimly. "You make a good point, Roger, but…if we were going to do that, we needed to make that plan before I spoke to Keeper Istila.

"I was expecting our next step to be meeting with the Intendant in person, so I didn't consider sending, well, a subordinate to meet a subordinate," she admitted. "As things stand, I have said that *I* will be there, with one escort.

"We can't do anything else or we risk becoming untrustworthy to a potential ally that already thinks our ships are slow," Amelie told them. "We need to demonstrate, first and foremost, that we keep our promises.

"That way, when we promise aid with one hand and devastation with the other, they know to take us seriously."

She smiled coldly.

"I will meet with Keeper Istila," she repeated. "Pick your best trooper, Major Köhl. You're sending them fully kitted out. They said bring one, not that anyone had to come unarmed."

Amelie waited for anyone else to object, then nodded firmly.

"Let's get going, people," she told them. "This is our first chance at a real look inside the Sivar."

20

AMELIE SHIFTED UNCOMFORTABLY in her clothes as the shuttle dipped toward the indicated Sivar station. She'd never realized, as an actress, just how uncomfortable concealed body armor actually was. In movies, after all, if the plot called for her to be wearing concealed armor, it showed up only after she'd been shot.

As both a rebel leader and a President, she'd adjusted to low-profile armor, but that was only designed to stop light kinetic weapons. Exilium had had occasional issues, but they'd been surprisingly minimal for a colony built out of a bunch of outcasts and troublemakers.

The diplomat that Exilium sent to strange races, though? That diplomat had to wear recorders and cameras...and body armor rated to stop handheld pulse weaponry. Power armor was tougher and her face was uncovered, but the heavy vest under her suit would stop plasma fire.

Once.

Once was enough for her bodyguards to get her out of the way, in theory. No one had ever shot at her on a consular mission, but she wasn't quite so sure *this* particular mission was going to go quite so smoothly.

"We've made contact," her escort told her. Sergeant Choi was currently a two hundred and two centimeter–tall, vaguely human-shaped mountain of metal. Amelie's body armor could stop a single plasma bolt from a man-portable pulse rifle.

Choi's armor could tank standard bolts from the same weapon for several minutes with luck. She wouldn't do quite so well against her own weapon. The power armor–scale pulse rifle powered by the suit's miniature fusion core was capable of punching through small tanks.

"You go first, Sergeant," Amelie said.

"Wasn't going to happen any other way, boss," Choi told her with a chuckle.

The woman in the armor was roughly the same age as Amelie and had spent thirty years in first the Confederacy and then the Exilium Marine Corps. She'd been one of the experts who had *trained* Exilium's Presidential Security Detail…and Amelie didn't believe for one *second* that her presence on *Watchtower* was a coincidence.

The armored Marine stepped out the airlock first, and Amelie *heard* Choi's chuckle over her earpiece.

"Stand back, please."

She heard the Marine's untranslated words through her earpiece, but what she heard through the open shuttle hatch sounded like a mouthful of consonants with a couple of vowels as an afterthought.

"You're clear, ma'am," Choi said after a moment. "Their idea of proper separation for an honor guard and mine are not compatible."

Exilium's foreign minister swallowed her laughter, shaping her face into her full diplomatic mask as she followed her bodyguard off the shuttle.

Two files of infantry faced each other on either side of a dark green carpet, the intent surprisingly similar to a dozen similar traditions in human history. The similarity was the first surprise.

The second was the infantry themselves. The Sivar were dispropor-tionately skinny for their height which, combined with the high-backed stone thrones their leaders favored, had given Amelie the impression that they were quite tall.

All twenty of the soldiers, however, were maybe a hundred and fifty-five centimeters tall. They were still just as gaunt proportionate to their height as she'd expected, but they were easily forty centimeters shorter than she'd anticipated.

Their armor had been polished until it gleamed under lights that were uncomfortably bright for humans. Black plates covered their limbs and torsos, but helmets were formally slung in their right hands, opposite to the rifles in their left hands.

"Rifles are mag-kinetics," Choi's voice murmured in her ear. "No threat to the armor, and your vest should handle them easily at anything but point blank range. I moved them back a couple of meters to clear a safety zone."

"And that's our host at the end," Amelie subvocalized back. "Let's play nice now."

She walked forward, past the Marine who fell in behind her with a practiced motion.

The soldiers were all almost exactly the same height. Istila was actually shorter, maybe a hundred and forty-five centimeters. At an average girth for a human, ban probably qualified as rotund for a Siva.

"Keeper of the Keys of Peace Istila," Amelie greeted the Siva with a slight bow of her head. "It is a pleasure to meet you in person."

"Foreign Minister Amelie Lestroud," ban replied with a similar bow. It was smooth enough to be a practiced gesture, suggesting another similarity with humanity.

The Sivar were starting to weird Amelie out.

"Will our discussions be here or somewhere more private?" Amelie asked cheerfully.

"We have arranged a space. Your…bodyguard will need to remain here."

"That won't be acceptable," Amelie said calmly. "You asked that I only bring one bodyguard, but she is coming with me everywhere."

"That wasn't a request, Minister," Istila replied, the translation in Amelie's ear icy.

"That doesn't change the acceptability of it," she replied. "If my bodyguard will not be welcome deeper in the station, I am perfectly prepared to discuss matters here."

Just standing there in the shuttle bay was educational, after all. They'd brought out twenty soldiers—the number suggested base-ten math, which lined up with them having the same number of digits as humans—much as humans would have.

The bay was roughly a hundred meters across, and *Watchtower*'s shuttle wasn't the only spacecraft in there. It was the *biggest* one by a significant margin, the thirty-meter-long vehicle dwarfing the local craft in every dimension.

The artificial gravity in the bay felt weird as well. Unless Amelie was wrong, she was actually being *pushed* down against the deck rather than pulled down onto it. It was still probably an exotic matter–based system, she thought, but more than that was outside her skillset.

Plus, everything she saw—and a good chunk she *didn't* see—was being recorded by her plain black business suit and its sensor suite.

She was perfectly fine to stand there and stare down Istila with a small smile on her lips. If they *actually* had to negotiate there, that would be a pain in her legs, but she'd do it.

Istila was silent for only maybe ten seconds before ban realized that ban was making banself look like an idiot.

"Very well," ban replied. "Follow me."

"Of course," Amelie agreed, gesturing Choi to her side as they headed deeper into the space station.

Every step deeper into the structure, after all, gave them a bit more data on their potential ally.

———

ISTILA LED them to what Amelie would have called a garden if it were anywhere except a space station. Carefully manicured shrubs and trees in a darker green than Amelie was used to were scattered around a room with actual flowing water running from ceiling to floor.

In the midst of the greenery there was a single stone throne, the style now *very* recognizable to Amelie, and a collection of seating cushions.

Choi moved to the edge of the seating area and settled into place as a looming metallic statue. Amelie was assured that the suits were actually quite comfortable to stand in for long periods, but she still felt more than a little guilty.

On the other hand, *she* was not sitting on the floor at Istila's feet like a child listening to the teacher. She located a reasonably dry-looking tree and leaned herself back against it while gesturing the Keeper to the throne with a wry grin.

That didn't go over well. The Sivar weren't as readable as if they'd been human, but ban's body language as Istila crossed to the throne suggested potential violence.

"You asked for this meeting, Keeper," Amelie pointed out. "Are you empowered to negotiate on behalf of the Sivar Governance? Can you speak to alliances and technology exchanges, or is this merely a formality?"

"I am empowered to decide if you are worth the Intendant's time," Istila told her. "He is the ruler of entire worlds, the righteous master of ten thousand suns. He is the voice of the Fates in this mortal time.

"Who are *you* to demand that he meet with you?"

"I demand nothing," Amelie said calmly. "I ask to meet with someone who is prepared to negotiate with the Republic of Exilium. I ask if the Governance wishes to stand alone against the enemy that is coming.

"The Republic has no need to stand between you and the Rogue Matrices," she told ban. "I am a long way from home, Keeper Istila. Together, we could face the Rogues and make your worlds and others safe.

"I have much that I can offer the Governance, but I see no reason to discuss details of any kind until I am speaking with someone with the power to *bind* the Governance."

"The Governance is bound only by fate," Istila replied. "If you seek to enslave and trap the Governance, you will fail. Only the Intendant can guide our future."

Amelie waited silently. She had to assume the Siva wanted *something* from this meeting, but she would be *damned* if she'd jump through the alien's hoops.

"And just what can you offer?" Istila finally asked. "Your ships are slow and obsolescent compared to the grandeur of the Commandants' fleets. You bring us warnings of a threat we already know of. I have seen no sign of worth from your people, Minister Amelie Lestroud. No reason to bring you before the Intendant."

Someone, it seemed, had seen the report on how long it had taken *Watchtower* to make it to Sivar-Prime—but not the reports on *Watchtower* maneuvering around Sivar-Prime or the warning shots they'd fired in Sivar-One.

"We would not be sitting in this room, with a major figure of the Intendant's government in orbit to meet me, if you believed that," Amelie countered. "I suspect your Commandants are all too aware of the true balance of power between our ships. You should ask them about that."

The Sivar military might not be able to identify particle cannons or gamma-ray lasers, but they *would* be able to tell that the matter-conversion power cores on *Watchtower* and her escorts were producing a lot more power than any power plant they had.

The Intendant had probably seen those exact reports. They were probably why the last Keeper of the Keys of Peace was apparently dead. That suggested another layer to the track that Amelie was on, and she leaned into it, physically and verbally.

"I also note that it seems your predecessor was removed for *not* properly updating your Intendant on interactions with us," she said. "I do not have the impression that your Intendant is likely to accept that I wasn't worth his time.

"So, we are here for some kind of pretense, a formality…or is this an attempt to get some kind of bribe?"

She doubted it was the latter, but in her experience, the accusation helped open up a path to the actual heart of the matter.

"A Keeper sits before the highest throne and keeps the Intendant's trust," Istila said slowly. "For us to accept a bribe is punishable by death."

So far as Amelie could tell, that was also true of dragging their feet on telling the Intendant something. The core of government for the Sivar had to be one hell of a mess.

"Then what do you want, Keeper Istila?" Amelie asked. "If you could negotiate the alliance I want, this meeting might not be a waste of time, but you can't."

She shoved off from her tree.

"I came as requested," she told ban. "But I don't know why. Do you have a proposal or a question, Keeper? One I have not already answered? Or should I return to my ship?"

Amelie would not be entirely surprised, at this point, if her returning to her ship in anger would result in *another* new Keeper of the Keys of Peace calling her.

"We must see value in this relationship, Minister Amelie Lestroud," Istila told her. The Siva seemed unbothered by her threat to leave. Perhaps ban's position was more secure than ban's predecessor's.

"Currently, we see nothing to separate you from the other petitioners who come before the prince of ten thousand suns. You have starships that are strange to us, but *strange* does not mean *useful*. You perhaps know more about the Builders than we do, but the Builders are a distant threat, not an immediate one.

"If you would petition the Intendant in person, a sample must be given of what value you bring."

Translation: the Siva was totally asking for a bribe, but it was one to give ban's leader to prove ban's value, not one to keep for ban's self.

Amelie smiled.

"*That*, Keeper Istila, is the first useful thing you or your predecessor had said to me," she told the Siva. "I have patience for formalities when needed, but this is a matter between states and between *species*. I do not know your structures or your ceremonies and I do not care."

She would have cared about their ceremonies and government structure if she didn't have the *very* strong impression that caring wouldn't help her. It very much seemed like the Sivar would accept forcefulness and brutal honesty over concern for their traditions and ceremony.

That was fine. She'd done traditions and ceremony and culture with the Skree-Skree and the Tohnbohn. That had been educational, useful, even occasionally fun.

If the Sivar wanted a battering ram, she could do that.

Pulling out her tablet, Amelie opened a file that had been prepared in case of a similar request.

"Our scans suggest that your shuttlecraft are using a miniaturized form of the large fusion engines used on your large spacecraft," she told Istila. An image appeared above the thumb-sized computer, a hologram of the engine in question.

"It's effective, but it's too large for craft that are too small and too inefficient for craft that are too big," she continued. "It forces you into either small craft of a very specific set of sizes or larger spacecraft entirely."

A new hologram replaced the first one, this one a technical diagram.

"This is a design for a heterodyned ion thruster," she told ban. "It has a hard limit on how much thrust it can produce, which can limit acceleration, but it is approximately four thousand times as efficient as your current thrusters and is a fifth of the size.

"It would provide your shuttles with vastly more range at a cost of a portion of their acceleration. It would also allow you to build a greater variety of shuttles."

It was also a distinctly *civilian* technology, one that wouldn't provide enough power to accelerate warships or missiles. It was a distant cousin to the impulse microthrusters that propelled Exilium's warships that was actually superior in some ways.

Just not in the ways that made impulse thrusters the engine of choice for warships and missiles.

"I will have my people transmit it to yours," she told Istila. "Translating our designs into something your systems can use might be difficult, but we can assist if needed."

"That is a generous offer," the Keeper said, ban's eyes studying the diagram in a way that suggest that ban *definitely* had enough engineering background to make sense of it. "The other path, I must note, raises the bird that you offered a *military* alliance."

"And if we agree to a military alliance, the Republic will be willing to sell you weapons technology," Amelie cheerfully told ban. "Until then, however, I am not permitted to trade weapons tech."

That was an outright lie. There was no way she was handing the Sivar better guns until she knew far more about them, so part of it was true.

Her mandate might *allow* her to trade weapons to the Sivar—but she definitely wasn't *going to*.

21

———————

THE ARMORED EXTERIOR of the radiation protection vault resisted Captain Belmont and his Marines for longer than Octavio would have expected. Whatever the Assini had shielded the station's last-ditch fall-back position with, it stood up to cutting tools for over an hour.

On the other side, they found the answer to one of the questions that had been bugging Octavio since the Marines had stepped aboard the station: where were the bodies?

They were there.

"I'm seeing at least thirty, forty, corpses in this hallway," the Marine officer reported as he made his way into the space. "Air readings are weird too. The rest of the station was at the same oxygen levels as the Constructed Worlds. This place…it's shifting now that we've opened it up, but it looks like it was down around one or two percent."

"They'd have asphyxiated," Octavio said, then realized he sounded like an idiot. "Wait. Did they asphyxiate *themselves*?"

"That would be my guess, but I'm figuring there's a command center in here with some answers," Belmont replied. "I've got two medics scanning the corpses to see what their status is, but…"

The Marine was probably making the same guess as Octavio.

"It would make things go faster if the medics can take samples," the Marine said after a moment. "May I ask Siril-ki for permission?"

"Ask," Octavio confirmed. "*Don't* push. These are her people."

"Understood, sir."

The Marines moved farther into the vault, finding much the same as they went. No one there had died violently. They'd lain down, out of the way along the walls, and gone to sleep.

Then they'd never woken up. Someone had set the oxygen levels inside the vault to slowly slide down, leading the already-irradiated station crew to fall asleep and then calmly suffocate.

As mass murder went, it was disturbingly efficient. Watching the cameras, Octavio was grimly certain he knew *exactly* what had happened. There were too many Assini in the vault for it to have been an accident.

"Found the command center," Belmont noted. The Marine's voice was even more clipped than usual. "Take a look, Commodore, but it isn't pretty."

Calling the space a *command center* was probably doing it favors it didn't deserve. It was a tiny room with half a dozen control panels, providing the senior station crew with access to the sensors and control of the survival vault's systems.

The command center also had the only sign of violence they'd seen in the vault. Several Assini had clearly tried to break through the door when they'd realized what had happened, but without Belmont's power armor, they'd failed.

Inside was worse. There had been five Assini in the room...and one pistol. Everyone else inside the vault had suffocated. These five had committed suicide.

The one holding the pistol had taken a moment to write a neatly lettered note that they'd pinned to the console. The carbon dioxide–filled air in the space had preserved it across the centuries and it was still perfectly legible.

It took the computer a moment to process the text, and Octavio closed his eyes against the sick feeling that ran through him.

Flare was too powerful. Sina is dead. We are dead. All the vault bought us was a painful death instead of an instant one. All I can give my people is peace.

If anyone reads this, witness the futility of our arrogance. We who would have shaped a galaxy but could not control our own sun.

Witness and learn.

Please.

———

"T HE BIOPSIES CONFIRMED IT," Siril-ki said quietly on the channel a few minutes later. "The shielding wasn't enough to prevent every one of my people aboard the station from receiving a lethal dose of radiation.

"The commander's action was murder, and yet…I can't see any other course they could have taken."

"It was also two hundred and seventy-eight years ago," Octavio pointed out softly. "It… We can't judge that. We have a pretty good idea of what they saw. I can't judge them."

By the time the station commander had activated the program to slowly suffocate their crew, they'd have known that the entire planet had been blanketed by a lethal dose of radiation. There was no one to "gently" murder those billions.

The lucky would have died quickly. The *truly* unlucky might have been resistant enough to survive the radiation poisoning…but if anyone off of Sina had survived, they wouldn't have known to come for them.

The final hours and days of the last habitable planet in the system would have been a foretaste of hell—a hell that Octavio Catalan had sent Major Chen Zhou into.

"Major Chen will be landing at what we think was the new system government center shortly," he continued after a long silence. "There may be some answers there—and we should hear from the expedition to your old shipyard soon as well."

"I'll send my computer techs over to the station," Siril-ki said slowly. "I don't know if they'd even have been able to establish new validation links with the Sentinels, but if they did…we may at least find the protocols to allow *us* to do so."

Octavio considered that.

"Would they still exist?" he asked.

"They're capable of self-maintenance though not self-replication," ki told him. "Without the central Validation Center here, they'd have had to improvise some kind of network amongst themselves.

"They were capable of that," ki insisted. "It would have required a minimum number of them, but there should be at *least* eighty-eight Sentinels left. They may require some repairs and assistance with their cores, but I should be able to provide whatever they need and convince them to join us."

He exhaled.

"Join us?" he asked. "You mean we might be able to bring them back to Exilium with us?"

"Of course," ki replied. "That was always part of what I was here for. The Sentinels were older ships than the Escort Matrices but larger and more powerful vessels. We should be able to bring elevens of them back with us."

Octavio had *very* vivid memories of the Escort Matrices, AI warships so badly degraded by using the tachyon punch to follow a near-cee colony ship that they'd been almost animalistic in their tactics...but phenomenally powerful warships representing the heights of Assini technology.

Eighty-plus bigger and more powerful AI warships? Sane ones, who'd had a tachyon verification system in place for their entire lives?

It wasn't necessarily enough to justify the entire expedition, but bringing those home with him would feel a lot better than coming home completely empty-handed.

"I don't think I'd drawn that connection," he admitted aloud. "Let me know if you need anything from us."

"Transport to the station and portable power sources," ki told him. "Which you've already arranged for, Commodore. We'll be fine."

———

LESS FINE WAS the view from the shuttles as Major Chen swept over what had been Sina's largest surviving metropolis. The Assini had never gone in for skyscrapers as humans had. There were only a handful of the arcologies they'd seen on Sia here, but they towered over the rest of the structures like blocky pyramids.

Few other structures rivaled their height. Assini buildings were wide-based, usually dome-like. Larger buildings ended up looking like pyramids built of domes on top of other domes. The arcologies were the closest the Assini came to the blocks and rectangles still typical of human architecture.

Age had been no kinder there than on Sia, and there had been no one coming in to clean up in the most easily salvaged areas. Even from the shuttles' altitude, Octavio could pick out crashed and abandoned vehicles.

Even Assini corpses were invisible at this altitude, but as the shuttles approached their targets and dipped lower, white shapes that could only be weather-stripped skeletons began to appear.

"This city had only three or four million people when I left," Siril-ki's voice said in his ear. The Assini was remaining locked in ki's section of the ship—much like Octavio riding his Marines' cameras from his office.

"There are new arcologies, but mostly they seemed to have expanded on the ground," ki continued. "There might have been as many as a hundred million souls here. Automated builders allow things to be built quickly when needed."

"And there's the government center," Octavio said. It was only a guess, but the structure mirrored the images they'd seen of the original building on Sia. Six broad domes supported a seventh, much sharper, dome that rose into the sky as if announcing its presence.

"Almost certainly," Siril-ki confirmed. Ki's translator had its emotional channels turned off again, Octavio noted. He couldn't blame ki.

"What should we be looking for here, Director?" he asked.

"There would have been a fallback plan," ki told him. "They had to have realized that Sina could suffer Sia's fate. If they were clever, it would be clearly present, but…your best bet is the First Administrator's office."

Octavio eyed the structure. If it had been a *human* facility, he'd have been certain that the official in charge would have had their office at the top of the central tower.

"Where would that be?" he asked.

"The top of the central tower," Siril-ki told him, unknowingly echoing his thoughts. "Tradition would demand it."

For all that they were pacifistic herbivores who looked like a child's multicolored image of a centaur, the Assini had a lot in common with humans sometimes.

"Top of the tower, huh?" Chen replied after Octavio passed that on. "So, is the Director attaching emotional value to the architecture?"

"What are you thinking, Major?" he asked.

"This bird has VTOL capability and the gear to cut into a spaceship hull," the Marine replied. "Why bother with landing and coming up the stairs when I can cut out *all* of the middlemen?"

"Do it," Octavio ordered. "This place was built after Siril-ki left; ki's people can't be too attached. And I'd rather not leave your teams digging around ghosts for longer than I have to."

"EMC isn't afraid of a ghost world, sir," Chen barked. "But I hear you. I'll be in the First Administrator's office in five minutes. Feel free to ride my shoulder in."

"I've been riding your shuttle so far," he told her. "It's damn depressing."

"Yes," she confirmed. "I've seen worse but not on this end of the galaxy."

That sent a shiver down Octavio's spine. There were very few people in Exilium's military who hadn't served in the Terran Confederacy's military—and the Confederacy's only enemies had been internal.

The Marines had been on the wrong side of far too many revolts and "riot suppressions" for any of them to have made it out there with clean consciences. Even Octavio hadn't made it out with a clean conscience.

"We all saw things back home we hoped to never see out here," he said quietly. "Our job is to make sure we *never do*. This wasn't even people, Major. This was just…entropy."

"Well, it still looks like a ghost town of wrecked electronics and dead people, and I don't much *care* if it was a solar flare or Fleet EMP bombs that killed them," Chen said grimly. "Contact in five."

Octavio flipped to Chen's shoulder-cam just in time to watch the shuttle hatch swing open in a flash of plasma jets. The shuttle was now connected to a space that easily rivaled any open-plan office designed by humans.

"EMC with me!" Chen barked, charging across the hatch. "Shuttle five, break off and orbit the city. Other shuttles, touch down and deploy teams into the main floor. Let's see what we can find."

There was no threat in the massive office. No robots, no traps. Just a wide expanse of black stone flooring that crunched slightly under the power-armored feet of Chen's Marines. A single desk—and next to that desk, a wall of the same black stone that had a number of paper charts pinned up.

"Those charts—get me visual," Chen ordered before Octavio could say anything. Two Marines crossed the space in moments, cameras sweeping the charts.

"Sondheim—see if we can boot up the computer and dump the local memory," the Marine continued. "Every scrap of data, everything. I want to know what the old horse had on his desk."

"Sir, check out vector ninety-four," one of the Marines told her. "That's…that's not pretty."

Octavio saw it at the same moment that Chen did. There was apparently no chair behind the desk—because the piece of furniture had been used to smash through the safety-glass windows. It couldn't have been easy, but Assini were *strong* when they chose to be.

"Get me…" Chen trailed off with a sigh, then repeated herself. "Get a visual down. Let's confirm what we all know."

"Yes, sir," the closest Marine confirmed, stepping over to the edge of the building and extending an arm out. A camera in the wrist let them look down without leaning a two-hundred-kilogram suit of armor out.

"Yeah." The Marine's voice was a little sick. "Our First Administrator jumped. Right spot, at least…but there wasn't much left even before time had her way with him."

"If he had a lethal rad dose *and* felt like he was responsible for this…I can see it," Chen agreed. "Tell me there's something useful here."

"Couple of the charts are plastic," another Marine injected, her voice excited. "Looks like system maps, Major. With a bunch of detail around one of the gas giants—is that what we're looking for?"

"Show me," Octavio ordered. "But yes, that's almost certainly what we're here for."

The First Administrator of the Assini had smashed his window and jumped almost three hundred years before. But if his charts led the Republic's expedition to survivors, he might have saved what was left of his people.

22

————

Ten ships erupted into the Skree-Skree System in brilliant blasts of Cherenkov radiation, and Isaac concealed a sigh of relief from *Vigil*'s flag bridge. His reinforcements were exactly on time—and he'd been feeling *Dante*'s absence for the last few days.

His last report said that *Scrutiny* and her battle group had left Refuge alongside the three Vistan battlecruisers he'd been promised. That was arguably pushing his orders from the Republic, but the two new *Vigilance*-class battlecruisers had arrived shortly afterward.

The Vistans had plenty of ships to protect their own system. *Dante* would see her final tour of duty at Refuge before the ship was sent home to finally be decommissioned.

Isaac knew that Vice Admiral Anderson knew that was what was coming. Everyone did, really. There was no point to hanging on to an experimental ship that had been rebuilt from a broken keel multiple times, not when they had the *Fortitude*s to crew.

He'd heard murmurs that the Senate had other plans for *Dante* than scrap metal, but no one had discussed them with him yet.

"Contact Vice Admiral Wu," Isaac ordered. "Let's see how we're doing."

Tachyon communicators were useful, but there was still a layer of human subconsciousness that added immediacy to knowing that the person you were talking to was *there*, in this star system.

Vice Admiral Charity Wu appeared on his chair-arm screen, the small Asian woman smiling as usual.

"Admiral Lestroud, it's good to see you," she told him. "Even if it's from a few light-minutes away still."

"It's good to see you, Admiral Wu," he agreed. "And your ships even more so. What's your status?"

"*Fortitude* and *Resilience* are ready for combat in all respects," Wu said crisply. "Unfortunately, *Tybalt* had an engineering failure en route. *Yorick* and *Cordelia* are showing unexpected signs of wear as well."

"Define *engineering failure*, Admiral," Isaac said slowly. He'd have been told if the ship was lost and, *hopefully* at least, if anyone had died. But that suggested something significant.

"Power conduits to her main gun fractured in a test firing while we were in regular space," she told him. "That's not supposed to happen, so we're digging into it. She needs a shipyard before she'll be combat-ready.

"*Yorick* and *Cordelia* just need the chance to strip down and replace a number of the sensors and systems on their outer hull. We're seeing more equipment failures in general than I'd like, sir."

Isaac grimaced.

"We're engaging in rapid implementation of hyper-automated production systems," he said quietly, a string of technobabble that he at least *understood*. Unlike some of the details that came up when Dr. Reinhardt, his R&D head, started talking with Minister Shankara Linton, the Republic's head of orbital industry.

"That means we're going to have problems," he continued. "Flag everything that was defective and we'll send the list back to Linton and EP-01."

EP-01 was Exilium Production Matrix One. Like the K-sequence AIs that helped run Isaac's warships, they were a child matrix from D. Unlike the K-sequence AIs, the EP-sequence AIs were incapable of violence. They were exactly what the name implied: massive computers that ran automated production systems in close cooperation with human observers and forepersons.

"The sheer speed we're working with means we're going to have problems, I suppose," Wu conceded. "I'd rather not have a strike cruiser's main weapon suddenly seize up on me, though!"

"That's why we test and exercise," he reminded her. "We can fix that. I'll check with the Skree-Skree, but we should be able to get *Tybalt* in for the repairs in short order.

"We're not going anywhere until the Vistans show up, and they're still thirty days away," he continued. Even if he'd made the decision to ask for reinforcements from Refuge before they'd headed to Skree-Skree, they wouldn't be here yet.

"I understand we should have Skree-Skree battlecruisers shortly, too?" Wu asked.

"They're leaving the yards shortly, but they'll complete their working-up in another ten days. We won't move before that, for the same reason I'm glad we found the problem with *Tybalt*'s zetta-laser in transit."

Most of his fleet was equipped with high-frequency grasers, but the brand-new strike cruisers and battlecruisers in Wu's task force were armed with the same weapon the Escort Matrices had almost killed *Shezarim* with.

The zettahertz lasers were terrifyingly powerful, and now Isaac had ten ships armed with them. The upgraded heavy particle cannon on his battlecruisers remained superior, but the edge was getting thinner —which was why each of the *Fortitude*-class battlecruisers carried *two* heavy particle cannon.

"That gives us a month, give or take, to work up with the Tohnbohn and Vistan forces already here," Isaac noted. "We'll get *Tybalt* fixed and we'll be ready."

"Ready for what, sir?" Wu asked.

He smiled.

"Sooner or later, Vice Admiral Wu, the recon nodes are going to find us that damn Regional Construction Matrix. And this time, the mechanical bastard is *not* getting away from us!"

———

"WE HAVE an update from the recon nodes, Admiral Lestroud," VK's calm voice told Isaac as he settled into his office.

"Any good news?" Isaac asked, pouring himself a coffee and considering the black liquid.

"We have now surveyed twenty-seven systems around the line the RCM's nodes drew us along," VK replied. "Minor Rogue forces were identified in four of those systems, including two in-progress Constructions of apparently uninhabited planets."

"Constructed Worlds are always useful to locate," Isaac allowed. It was easy to grow cavalier about their access to worlds that were basically paradises to humans. The terraforming Matrices, Rogue and not, had been *very* effective at their job.

Approximately forty percent of all stars appeared to have had a planet the Matrices could Construct...and if they could Construct a world, they did. The three-hundred-light-year radius around Assini that the Matrices were present in had to contain *thousands* of paradises now.

The hundred-light-year zone between Exilium and Skree-Skree contained over a hundred completed or in-progress Constructed Worlds. They were at the edge of the Matrices' operation zone and there were dozens of paradises available.

"None of the Constructions included even Sub-Regional Matrices," VK noted. "There were also, since you asked, four previously Constructed Worlds and one world under Construction from non-Rogue nodes in the same twenty-seven systems."

"Have we made contact with those non-Rogue Matrices?" Isaac asked.

"XR-13-9 has an ongoing link with most Regional Matrices in the region," VK confirmed. "As of our last update, they are sounding out the closest ones—including the one responsible for the encountered node—about an alliance dealing with the Rogues."

Isaac shook his head. The Matrices he'd dealt with had been *horrified* by the destruction of sentient species in the process of Construction but had been unable to do anything about it. They'd been stuck in a loop of conflicting core protocols until humanity came along.

Hopefully, XR-13-9 would be able to convince the others that they had to act. Somehow, Isaac suspected that would be a slow process unless the Assini started flinging override codes around.

Overriding sentient computers just seemed vaguely morally wrong to him. He'd take it over killing the Rogues if it became an option, but he didn't want to do it to AIs that really just wanted to be left alone to do their work and not harm anyone.

"I think we need to pull further back," Isaac finally said aloud. "We've been scouting around the corridor they led us along, but they wouldn't have led us anywhere near their RCM. Does our estimate of the construction timeline of the dreadnought give us a maximum distance?"

VK activated the holoprojectors in the office and brought up the regional map.

"That was being calculated into our sweep," they confirmed. "Given the capabilities of the tachyon punch, however, the radius is easily a hundred light-years."

That radius lit up on the map, but it was almost useless. It reached almost the entire distance to Exilium one way and past the Sivar Governance in another.

"And the RCM wouldn't have gone that far, right?" Isaac asked.

"Core protocols require completion of the Construction of a region before the RCM could move on to a new region," VK said. "They should stay inside this area."

That was a smaller cube, roughly seventy light-years a side. It unfortunately included the homeworlds of the Vistans and the Skree-Skree. The Tohnbohn were just outside that cube, as were the Sivar.

Not far outside, though. Once the Rogue was finished with its current zone, those stars would be next on the list. The Tohnbohn recognized that, at least.

It was part of why they were sending him more reinforcements. One battlecruiser and enough escorts to bring all three battle groups to full strength. It was more than he'd expected.

More relevant to the moment, though, was that the entire cube was contained inside the distance that could have deployed the dreadnought. That was no real surprise to Isaac, sadly.

"I don't suppose the fact that we haven't seen their lightspeed emissions helps us, does it?" he asked. "How mobile is an RCM?"

"The Matrix itself is extremely mobile. External shipyard complexes and defenses, however, are not. It is likely that the Rogue has not left the system they chose as their main base in some time."

"How long?" Isaac asked. "If we know they've been in place for ten years, then we know they're not within ten light-years of Vista, Refuge or Skree-Skree—or most of the systems the recon nodes have scouted."

"The time frame of the RCM's residence is a probabilistic surface, not a definite distance," VK noted slowly.

"You're computers. Run the damn probabilities and factor it in," Isaac ordered.

The AI was silent for several seconds.

"That does allow us to divide our potential targets into higher- and lower-order probabilities," they admitted. "That the lightspeed emissions of the RCM's infrastructure could be detected at interstellar distances was not something we factored in."

"If you use multiple sensor arrays, you can build a dataset that should refine your probabilities," Isaac replied, his hands already flying through the hologram. "We have, what, thirty recon nodes available?"

"Yes."

"If you assemble a five-by-five array with one-light-year separation, you have a twenty-five-square-light-year telescope," the Admiral concluded. "If we position it…here"—he tapped a point on the map—"that will help us refine this probability zone. We can move the nodes around and eliminate potential locations a dozen at a time—or at least make them lower-order probabilities."

"The recon nodes pursue certainty by nature," VK said slowly. "Their design leads them to think certain ways."

"And they'll find the RCM their way," Isaac admitted. "But will they find the RCM their way in thirty days?"

"The probability is thirty-three plus/minus five percent," VK told him. "With your method, I calculate that rises to sixty plus/minus fifteen percent."

"Your confidence in my suggestion is touching," he replied. "Can you pass that on to Twenty-Five to give to their people?"

"Already done, Admiral," VK said. "Twenty-Five is reviewing… Twenty-Five says they are an idiot."

Isaac laughed.

"Twenty-Five is *not* an idiot," he argued. "Twenty-Five is very focused."

Matrices looked at other stars for planets, not ships. Lightspeed radio emissions weren't at the top of their mind—but Isaac had been involved in the Confederacy's projects to use a Very Large Array like this to try and find intelligent life.

Sentient species might be relatively common *here*, but humanity hadn't discovered any spacefaring neighbors back home. Assuming, of course, they hadn't seen humanity coming and decided hiding was the better part of valor.

Even Isaac wasn't going to pretend the Terran Confederacy looked like they'd be a good neighbor.

23

—————

Even with the not-quite-bribe to grease the way, it took almost two days to sort through the logistics and realities of bringing an ambassador into the presence of the Sivar Intendant.

In the end, two Republic shuttles dropped away from *Watchtower* under close supervision. Two Sivar destroyers had adjusted their orbits to keep the human spacecraft in their line of fire for the entire descent.

Amelie hadn't bothered to tell the Keeper of the Keys of Peace that those destroyers would die the moment they attempted to energize weapons systems. The need to maintain a matter-conversion core at a minimum power output meant that *Watchtower* and her escorts had a far higher energy budget at "rest" than the Sivar ships did.

They might have problems using all of that power in a cold orbit, but it also meant that the battlecruiser could energize her secondary grasers *without* having to bring her reactors to a higher energy level.

If it came down to a quick-draw contest, the Sivar fleet was doomed.

She was more concerned about Captain Holmwood being too quick off the draw than she was about their Sivar escorts actually harming her shuttles—and she trusted the Captain.

"We're getting solid data from the shuttles' sensors as we drop in,"

Major Köhl observed. The Marine was sitting next to Amelie on the shuttle, on the opposite side from Sergeant Choi.

Both were in what the Confederacy had called formal armor. It was a low-profile suit of power armor that managed to compress about a third of the physical augmentation and a quarter of the protective capabilities of a suit of power armor into something that *looked* like decorative unpowered armor.

Like most of the ultra-high-tech equipment available to the Terran Confederacy, it required exotic matter and had been mind-bogglingly expensive to manufacture in Confederacy space. Exilium's continuing oversupply of exotic matter made the armor more affordable, if still far from practical for regular use.

For the twenty-Marine security detail Köhl had insisted on, though, it was perfect. And its low-profile heads-up-display—projected directly into the wearer's eyes—was allowing Köhl to keep track of what her shuttles were doing and seeing.

"Are we spying on our hosts?" Amelie asked.

"Yes, Minister," Köhl confirmed cheerfully. "Everything we see is being fed back to *Watchtower* and WK. Some things are obvious on first pass, but WK and the tactical analysts will extract things from the data we won't see initially."

"Good," Amelie said. "Anything immediately useful?"

"Well, you should probably see this." Köhl tapped a command on her wrist. Her HUD was showing her what the tattoo-comp under that armor would have been displaying if it wasn't concealed, and the armor read the commands in the same way as the covered skin would have.

A holographic projector in the bracers of the armor suit blinked to life. A holographic image of a set of foothills leading to a small cluster of mountains appeared in front of them.

"That's our destination, Minister," the Marine told her. "The First and Final Citadel is here."

A few moments study showed that the "mountains" were the worn-down caldera of some ancient supervolcano. The rolling foothills had once been mounds of volcanic ash.

Köhl's highlight rested on the largest mountain, and it took Amelie a moment to process just what the Marine had picked out.

The entire mountain was a fortress. A city had overtaken the rest of the mountains and the foothills around them, but the largest mountain clearly served one purpose and one purpose only. It started with stone walls intermingled with modern defense bunkers on the lowest slopes and only grew more modern and more dangerous as her gaze tracked up the mountainside.

It wouldn't have mattered if someone approaching by ground had been on foot or in vehicles. The entire surface of the mountain had been carved away to leave only one path up the mountain, and there were no accessways to the interior anywhere on the lower slopes. Just to enter the First and Final Citadel's outer perimeter, even a guest would have to get half a kilometer up from the ground, via a series of switchbacks and curves that turned that into at least a ten-kilometer journey through a massive sequence of traps.

The mountain was crowned by a series of anti-aircraft defenses that could probably threaten the shuttles Amelie was approaching aboard. In between the lower defenses and the peak defenses was a calmer-looking series of terraces, though even the entrances Amelie could spot in there were easily sealed.

This place had been fortified since the Sivar had been fighting with spears and bows, and had *continued* to be updated the entire way.

"Look here," Köhl murmured. She tapped a spot about halfway up the mountain, where the terraces gave way to a sheer section of mountain wall that blinked with the occasional light of a window. "This looks like it *was* more of the terraces, but someone hit it with a big bomb. From the lines of that cliff...a bunker-buster. Kiloton-range."

"So, the First and Final Citadel has been attacked in the last few hundred years, you'd guess?"

"There's a lot of active defenses down there for someone who doesn't have enemies," the Marine replied. "We're being directed to a landing platform near the top of the mountain, which means we at least avoid the long walk up.

"On the other hand, it puts our birds right under the guns of the anti-air defenses." She shook her head. "I'd back my people against their troops one-on-one, no question," she noted. "But their anti-air tech is on par with ours.

"We're not getting the shuttles out unless they let us go. That's something to keep in mind, Minister."

"It's good to know, at least," she agreed, a chill running down her spine. She'd known that *Watchtower* could handle the Sivar fleet, and she'd known she was more vulnerable on the surface...but it hadn't quite sunk in that she was completely trapped down there.

"We're to negotiate an alliance," she continued. "We'll be fine, I'm sure."

"Of course." Köhl nodded firmly, but Amelie could tell she couldn't believe what she was saying. "We'll be down in less than three minutes. Once we're down, you'll want to assume everything we say is being recorded."

"Just like being back in the Confederacy," Amelie admitted. "I've dealt with worse."

Making contact with rebel factions and acting as intermediary and courier while keeping up the face of air-headed actress had consumed her life for ten years. One of the odder side effects of that was that she doubted there was anyone on Exilium who didn't know exactly what she looked like naked—or at least, what she'd looked like naked ten years before, anyway.

"I hope old habits die hard, but there's one more thing you need to take a look at," Köhl said quietly. The holographic image projected from her suit zoomed in with painful speed, flashing down into the garden terraces and focusing on a single one.

No. Focusing on the *gardener*.

Like the Assini, it was a centaur-like creature. It had a large splayed nose more akin to an Earth mole and massive eyes, with a thicker, more rounded, torso than the Matrice's creators. Its dark red fur was long and slick as it dug into the dirt with a small shovel.

"That is *not* a Siva," Köhl stated the obvious. "And unless I'm severely mistaken, *this*"—a highlight flashed on a metal band Amelie hadn't noticed around the being's neck—"is an explosive collar.

"Just who the *hell* are we trying to make an alliance with, Minister?"

"I don't know yet," Amelie said levelly. "I'm going to find out. And if it's as bad as some of what we've seen implies…"

She shook her head.

The Sivar's battleships could turn the tide of the crusade against the Matrices, save tens of thousands of lives—but was she prepared to turn a blind eye to conquest and slavery to get that fleet?

And if she wasn't…was she willing to walk away from that same conquest and slavery?

24

Amelie's Marines might have traded full power armor in for low-profile ceremonial armor, but their Sivar equivalents didn't bother. As Amelie and her staff and escorts left the shuttles, they were greeted by a solid wall of aliens in full power armor.

Even to her unpracticed eye, she could see that the armor was cruder than the standard armor worn by the EMC. It was bulkier, turning the slim Sivar troopers into something more akin to the dwarfs of a fantasy novel than their usual appearance.

Instead of the mag-kinetic rifles the guards on the station had carried, these ones carried massive axes, each weapon easily the size of the armored suit carrying it and almost certainly containing some kind of weapon.

The line of armored Sivar was still and silent and for a few seconds, Amelie hesitated. Then she realized that this, like so much before, was posturing. Ceremonialized and formal posturing that required specific responses.

Responses that Istila hadn't bothered to share with her.

Suppressing a shake of her head, Amelie gestured for Choi and Köhl to fall in with her and walked forward as if the guards weren't there. She aimed directly for the center of their line and was unsurprised when it split in front of her.

The power-armored guards fell back in a perfectly practiced motion, splitting to create the same kind of double line as they'd met her on the station with. At the end of the line stood Istila with a pair of personal guards who were, at least, not in power armor.

They were, however, the first Sivar Amelie had seen carrying what were unquestionably energy weapons. They were massively oversized things she doubted the Sivar could fire without the visibly attached bipods, but they were energy weapons.

Istila bowed slightly at her approach.

"I welcome you and your people to Aris and to the First and Final Citadel," ban greeted her. "You are scheduled to meet with the Intendant in one hundred seventy-three minutes."

If Amelie was remembering the translation right, the actual Sivar timeframe would have been three wax-spans, referring to a standardized mark on a specific type of candle that translated to just under fifty-eight minutes.

"Has there been a delay?" she asked. She'd been supposed to meet with the Intendant within an hour of landing, not three hours later. It might be a power game, which she'd have no real choice about, but she was still going to push back.

"There has," Istila confirmed without apology. "News has arrived from one of our colonies that required His Greatness's immediate attention. I will show you to your quarters so you may refresh yourself before your first meeting."

"Lead on, Keeper of the Keys of Peace," Amelie told ban. If nothing else, it would give the Marines more time to check on the rooms they were given before she had to sleep there.

She'd never expected to resolve everything that would need to be discussed in one meeting, after all.

———

Istila led them into the mountain of the Citadel and into a large elevator that took them down at least a hundred meters. From there,

Amelie was surprised when they were led back *out* of the mountain, past a blast hatch that would probably stop a small nuke, and onto one of the garden terraces they'd seen from above.

The hatch was the most obvious of the defenses, but Amelie had been a rebel once. She could pick out the concealed observation posts and the hidden remote-controlled weapons they passed by—and she was sure she missed some.

The actual guest house was at the far end of the terrace, a sprawling stone mansion that would have been acceptable as an ambassador's residence anywhere Amelie had ever gone. It was the carefully cleared and organized lines of fire in the garden that bothered her.

"The heat in the residence has been set to the specifications you sent us," Istila told her. "There are forty-two individual rooms, so you should have enough space."

Ban bowed ban's head slightly.

"I will return twenty-four minutes before your audience so that we may commence the ceremonies," ban continued. "We will speak again then, Minister Lestroud."

Istila and ban's bodyguards withdrew, leaving Amelie alone on the terrace with her people, staring at the stone structure.

"What, not even a tour?" Köhl asked, watching the Sivar cross the killing field pretending to be a garden.

"Anyone else feel like there's a target on their back?" Amelie muttered. "That garden is a wonderful killing field and *not* one designed to protect the guest house."

"And if someone decides to bomb the mountain, *we're* sure as hell not protected," Faulkner agreed, the aide looking nervous. "I suppose we should check out our new home? How long are we going to be here, Amelie?"

"As long as it takes," she told him, tapping her ear to remind her aide that they were almost certainly being recorded. Nothing on this planet could be trusted yet.

"But yes. Let's find out how well our hosts plan on treating us."

———

THE ANSWER, at least as far as housing, was pretty well. The biggest problem was no real surprise: the luxuriously comfortable beds the guesthouse rooms contained were in no way large enough for most of the humans.

Köhl and her people had come prepared for that and started unfolding cots in the thirty or so rooms they'd need. The kitchen was serviceable—there were only so many ways to approach the concept of "burn food to make it edible," and Amelie's cook had it in hand.

"Bugs?" Amelie muttered as she and Köhl studied the main entryway.

"Everywhere," the Marine agreed. "They can probably hear us having this chat. Quality devices, though nothing that can beat our detectors."

"Can we clear them?"

"Not easily."

Amelie nodded. That would be a pain, but they could work with it.

"Privacy generators?" she asked.

"Should work so far as I can tell," Köhl agreed. "No guarantees, though. No real way of testing, either."

"We'll make do," Amelie said with a sigh. "Other than the killing field out there, any concerns for security of the guesthouse?"

"It's stone and wouldn't stop energy weapons, explosives or heavy kinetics," Köhl told her. "Too many entrances, clearly designed for a staff of servants they haven't lent us. My people will keep it secure. You don't leave without Choi and at least two others, though."

"I know," Amelie agreed. "I'll be good. I can't guarantee they'll let me bring bodyguards everywhere, though. Ambassador or not."

"I trust your...persuasiveness, Minister," Köhl replied with a chuckle. "But I do have another option."

Amelie looked over to see that the Marine had produced a small package from inside her armor. It was...it was very gun-shaped.

She opened it. It was definitely gun-*shaped*, with a trigger, trigger guard, safety...but it lacked such key features as a magazine.

"What is this?"

"This is what happens when Dr. *Brigette* Reinhardt decided she's sick of her husband being a defenseless twit in the middle of a war and 'borrows' her father's database," Köhl replied.

Dr. Lyle Reinhardt's daughter was primarily the CEO of one of Exilium's engineering management companies. She was also a mother and the wife of Captain Cameron Alstairs, who was *Vigil's* commanding officer and *Amelie's* husband's right hand.

"It's a laser pistol, Minister," Köhl continued. "Based on the same principles as the weapons used by Assini hunter-killer drones. It's the first pistol-sized energy weapon we ever built, but the Marines bought the design from her and manufactured a small run.

"Variable power. Minimum should kill a man. Maximum should punch through power armor but probably won't kill the wearer," the Marine noted. "Five shots at max, sixteen at min. There's one replacement power cell there, but recharging the cells requires at least our shuttles."

Amelie regarded the weapon carefully. Neither the Confederacy or Exilium had ever managed to compress pulse-weapon technology down small enough to create plasma sidearms. The Marines didn't go in much for lasers outside of specialist tools, either, but she could see the value. The power density implied by the shot settings left her more nervous about the *power cell* than the weapon itself.

She took the laser pistol anyway, tucking it into the spot designed for a weapon on the bulky vest under her clothes.

"They're more likely to disarm me than they are to take my guards away," she pointed out. "But it might come in handy. We've got an hour left. What's your plan, Major?"

"I'm going to be walking the perimeter of the house with the platoon commander and Sergeant Ryu," Köhl told her. "*I* will have time to take a shower while you're talking to the Intendant."

Amelie snorted.

"Does this place have anything I'd call a shower?" she asked. It was, after all, alien plumbing.

"It's..." The Marine paused thoughtfully. "It's at least in the same general concept?"

"Then I guess I'll check it out. Never hurts to be at your best when you're meeting with a tyrant."

It seemed a fair description. She wasn't aware of any *non*-tyrant rulers who'd execute a government official because they didn't like the way information had been handled.

If anything, she was being generous. The phrase *mad tyrant* was probably more appropriate.

25

Istila returned exactly when ban had said ban would. Freshly show‐
ered and re-dressed in another of her ambassador suits and armor
vests—with the laser pistol transferred to the new vest's holster—
Amelie met ban at the front door.

"Is the Intendant ready?" she asked brightly.

"There are ceremonies a stranger must go through to meet the voice
of the Fates in this mortal time," Istila told them. "These are your
escorts?" Ban gestured to Choi and the two other Marines with her.

"They are. They will come with me everywhere," Amelie said
firmly. That had been part of the agreement, but it never hurt to
reiterate.

"As was agreed," the Keeper confirmed. "Follow me, Minister
Lestroud. Your people's safety is His Greatness's word."

Amelie kept her scoffing at that carefully internal. How many of the
Intendant's guests over the centuries had seen the guesthouse
stormed? She doubted this was a safe place to be an ambassador, let
alone a supplicant.

For now, she kept her peace and followed Istila back into the moun‐
tain. This time, they took a smaller elevator that went sideways. There

didn't appear to be a distinction between movement between levels and on a level in the transit system inside the mountain.

When the door opened again, though, they were hit with a wave of sulfur.

"We begin the first stage of the purification ceremony," Istila said calmly as ban led the way out. Ban had been expecting this and seemed much less bothered than the humans.

Coughing, Amelie gestured her guards forward. She had a breather included in her vest that would automatically deploy if the air got bad enough. This was safe. Just unpleasant.

They had come out into what looked like the entryway for a temple. A cavern, a hundred meters square and twelve high, had been excavated to allow for a doorway to be flanked by pillars and carved beasts that resembled Earth's mythical sphinxes—though the heads of these "sphinxes" had the armor plate of a Siva.

The door itself was six meters tall, attached to hinge mechanisms that were very clearly statues of armored Sivar warriors of another time.

"This is the Gateway of Fire," Istila told Amelie. "We will walk the Pathway of Fire to the Mountain Heart, and there we will greet the next gateway."

Ban's faceplates shifted in what might have been an attempt at a smile.

"Assuming you survive, of course."

"Lead the way, Keeper Istila," Amelie replied. "I would hope that the ceremonies would not cost the Intendant the life of his Keeper of the Keys of Peace."

Ban gestured and the statue hinges activated, the mechanical warriors pulling the massive doors open in front of them. An even stronger scent of sulfur radiated out, and Amelie suddenly had a very strong suspicion of both what the Mountain Heart was—and how the First and Final Citadel was powered.

Nonetheless, she followed Istila through the Gateway. The air grew warmer as they entered into a carefully carved descending spiral. Sulfur-laced mist drifted up from the lower tier of the spiral—and as one of the gusts of mist swept over the lead Marine, the man's breather snapped automatically into place.

Istila laughed, a strange clapping sound—but ban was already pulling a breather from within ban's robes.

"Tradition requires we walk the path," ban told them. "Pragmatism suggests that we survive the path. I have breathers if…"

Amelie and the other Marines manually activated theirs and the Keeper laughed again.

"Come, Minister Lestroud. The beating heart of the First and Final Citadel awaits us—and tradition only allows us so much time."

———

THE MOUNTAIN HEART was similar to the Gateway of Fire. A massive space had been excavated, with pillars and statues carved out of the living stone to decorate a space. Through the center of the space, like a stream of water in a surface temple, ran a tube of lava.

Sulfur might be rising from the stone around the lava stream, but the stream itself had been capped a long time before. A canal bed of some kind of special ceramic funneled the magma along the route, and a transparent layer of something—any of her military people might have IDed it, but that wasn't Amelie's skillset—covered the lava.

That allowed for the space to be *habitable* by humans and Sivar, but it was far from comfortable. If they had the lava this much under control for a ceremonial cavern, Amelie was now quite certain geothermal power provided much of the Citadel's electricity needs.

"This way," Istila told them through ban's face mask, gesturing toward a second gateway that matched the first one. This time, the sphinx-like beasts were replaced by a second set of Sivar warriors, looming six meters tall over everything in the space.

"This is the Gateway of Iron," ban explained as they reached the door. "Once, there would have been ritual combat on this spot to prove your right to continue…but such traditions fade with time."

The fact that the Mountain Heart itself would have killed far more of the ritual combatants than the fight would have was probably a factor in that.

The Gateway opened for Istila's gesture, and a second set of spiraling tunnels led away. They were less filled with sulfur, and it took Amelie a moment to realize why: water was running down the floor of the tunnel, and a stiff artificial breeze pushed air along above it.

Only a tiny rivulet of water survived the heat to reach the bottom as liquid, but it was absorbing some of the toxins from the air…and the stiff breeze made sure that the steam rose up the other tunnel, making the Pathway of Fire much more unpleasant than this tunnel.

"This is the Pathway of Water and we approach the Gateway of Water," Istila told them. "We have been purified in fire and now we will be purified in water before we come before the Intendant."

"Do you do this every time you approach him?" Amelie asked as the water grew into a broad but shallow stream across the floor.

"I am known to the Mountain," the Keeper said calmly. "You are not. The full purification will not be required for future audiences."

Stepping out of the Gateway of Water, Amelie was unsurprised to see that the only way forward was through a broad pool of water, filled by a gentle waterfall that formed a wall-to-wall barrier of descending liquid.

It seemed her shower had been a waste of time.

"We go forward," she said firmly, stepping into the water. She was *reasonably* sure her electronics would survive this. Somehow, she doubted the likelihood of shorting out spy devices had hurt the survival of this particular tradition!

"Always," Choi agreed, her armored boots splashing in the water beside Amelie.

"You begin to understand, I think," Istila noted as ban walked beside them. Clearing the water, waiting robed attendants offered them large white towels, and the exit passed under what looked like industrial blow-dryers.

"We must require you and your guards to surrender your weapons once we clear the Gateway," ban continued. "The Intendant is the ruler of worlds, the righteous master of ten thousand suns. His safety cannot be risked."

"My guards come with me," Amelie said calmly.

"Of course," the Keeper agreed. "But they must come unarmed."

"Very well." Amelie glanced at Choi and the other two Marines. Their armor made them deadlier than they looked, but she was still agreeing to make herself vulnerable.

But she had no choice. Through fire and sulfur and water into the belly of the beast she went.

26

After the temple-like structures she'd passed through in the purification rituals, Amelie was expecting to be ushered into a throne room that was as much temple as court. She was expecting the Intendant to be presented as some kind of god-king, probably wrapped in enough gold and jewels to buy a starship.

Instead, she was brought into a room that had a clear relationship to the conference room on *Watchtower*. There was a raised dais at one end with a table on it, and three smaller tables in the rest of the room.

No reporters. No gathered court. There *were*, at least, gold and jewels—the walls were decorated in gold filigree and murals of stones and gems that clearly drew attention to the figure at the head of the room.

That figure wore a complex headdress of fine gold and platinum chains wrapped around his headplate. At some point, his headplate itself had been carved to inlay a triangle of tiny red gems above his eyes, but other than that and the chains, the Intendant was unadorned. He wore a plain white tunic, closer to his soldiers' garments than his Keepers', and had two other Sivar at the table with him.

The lower tables were empty. Ten guards lined each wall, blocking the ability to see the detail of the murals, but otherwise it was just Amelie, her guards, and the central figures of the Sivar government.

No wonder they'd required her Marines to surrender their weapons!

Istila led the way, proceeding through the tables with a practiced grace to reach a section of carpet on the stone floor directly in front of the Intendant. Ban knelt on that carpet and bowed their head.

"I bring the Exilium Ambassador before you, Your Greatness," ban said breathlessly.

Amelie was glad for the earbud translator. She assumed the Sivar had established their own translation programs to understand her people, but she wanted to control what she was getting of their emotion.

"Approach, Ambassador," the Intendant said. The untranslated tones of a Siva speaking were harsh on human ears, choppy consonants and short words. His voice seemed even more so.

Gesturing for Choi and the Marines to stand by the door, Amelie walked up to stand next to the kneeling Keeper of the Keys of Peace. She gave the Intendant the same slight bow of her head she'd given Istila.

"I am Amelie Lestroud," she told him. "I am the Foreign Minister and Ambassador Plenipotentiary for the Republic of Exilium, and I am authorized to speak on behalf of our allies for these initial talks."

"So I understand," the Intendant replied. He gestured diffidently around him. "This is Corstan, the Keeper of the Keys of War, and Rode, the Keeper of the Citadel. With Istila, they *are* my Governance."

Translation: *these are the heads of my government.* Presumably there had to be infrastructure and bureaucracy behind each of those Sivar. It was fascinating, though. Unless Amelie missed her guess, Corstan was male and Rode was female. The three Keepers seemed to explicitly represent the three Sivar genders.

"I am the Intendant," the Siva continued. "The voice of the Fates and the ruler of the Governance. My titles claim I am the prince of ten thousand suns."

He bowed his own head in a mirror of her gesture, though *his* bow was a far more fractional gesture.

"I rule thirty-three," he said calmly. "Bound by star-lane and the Commandants' fleets, they kneel to me. So, tell me, Minister Amelie Lestroud, what would you have of the fate of the Sivar?"

"There is a danger in this corner of the galaxy," Amelie said softly. "Machines forged by an old and foolish race to carve new worlds for their future homes. The machines destroyed their creators and have now turned their eyes outwards."

The exact details of the relationship between the Assini and the Matrices would be an explanation for later.

"Some of those machines, these AI Matrices, retained an original code that required them to protect sentient life. Most had that code damaged by their form of interstellar travel," she continued. "We have allied with those that attempt to protect others to stop their genocidal cousins.

"Multiple species have joined us in our war against these Matrices. We have traded weapons and starships for their aid, but we stand as allies and friends, shoulder to shoulder against these robots."

She shook her head.

"I was told you know their works," Amelie said. "That you call them the Builders."

The two Keepers on either side of the Intendant, both clad in the same toga-like garment as Istila, looked directly to their master. Neither appeared to have a clue what Amelie was talking about.

The Intendant, on the other hand, leaned forward and laid his hands on the table.

"We have watched the Builders for some time," he noted. "The Eyes of the Sivar look to the stars, Minister Amelie Lestroud, and we are not blind. When star systems change and worlds move, we see. We have wondered and we have studied and we know some of the Builders. You tell me you know more."

Fascinatingly, Corstan definitely hadn't known any of this. He was in command of the Governance's military but hadn't been warned of the largest prospective threat they knew of. He'd only know what Amelie had told Ackahl, she would speculate.

Amelie didn't know Sivar body language, but if Corstan had been *human*, she would have guessed he was both furious and terrified.

"We have fought against and alongside the Construction Matrices," Amelie finally replied. "The central mind nearest you has been damaged beyond repair. It does not care if there is life on the worlds it transforms, and it will use—it *has* used massive force to destroy anyone attempting to stop its work."

None of the worlds where the Republic had fought the Matrices were close enough for the light of those battles to have reached the Governance yet.

"The Builders can move worlds," the Intendant noted. "Yet you claim to have made war upon them. Successfully, I must presume."

"We have saved the worlds of our allies from them," Amelie confirmed. "They were built to transform worlds, Intendant. The designs they use for war were intended for emergency defense, not to wage military campaigns.

"They are powerful, yes, but they can be defeated. And we have done so."

"How can there be such a threat that the Keys of War were unaware of?" Corstan finally demanded. "It is the Commandants' duty to guard your Governance, Your Greatness. Without this knowledge, we might have failed you!"

"Be silent," the Intendant replied. He didn't snap or raise his voice, but Corstan recoiled as if struck—and Amelie was reminded that Istila's predecessor had been executed in the last few days.

The Keepers *had* to be feeling that reminder of the balance of power between them and the Intendant...or it was normal enough that they were *always* aware of that balance.

"This was a matter of the Eyes and the Voices, not of the Governance," the Intendant continued. "The Builders were approaching but they were far away. They are no threat to us yet and lie far beyond our star-lanes. The Keys had no need to know."

Amelie doubted that Corstan agreed, but he was also clearly utterly terrified of the soft-spoken man in the white tunic.

"The Matrices are not bound by your star-lanes," Amelie told them. "Neither are my people. If a Rogue decides that your territory is their next Construction zone, they will be here long before you can see them coming. They will not pass through your fortifications. They will not fear your ships. They will see your worlds as raw materials for their grand projects…and your people will die."

She shook her head.

"We believe that our alliance can stop the Rogue we face today, but that one is only one of several potential threats to your Governance, Intendant," she noted. And even *that* was assuming that her people had a remotely accurate guess of the limits of the Sivar's territory. "And we are a small group of species on one side of the Builders' expansion.

"To protect ourselves and others, we must fight them here and elsewhere. We must identify the Matrices hostile to sentient life and stop them. Not just the ones on our borders but *everywhere*.

"Bringing your fleets into our alliance and upgrading your technology would increase both the safety of our allies and of your Governance."

The Intendant kept his hands on the table as he leaned back slightly, studying her like a cat would study a trapped mouse.

"Keeper Corstan," he said levelly, as if he hadn't just shut the Siva down. "Am I to understand that Minister Lestroud's ship is in some way superior to ours? Others have told me that it took far longer to reach Aris than Commandant Ackahl's flotilla did, but that only answers half a question."

"The alien ship has no missiles and lacks-long range engagement options against our fleet," Corstan said, his voice calmer this time. "It has greater acceleration than our own ships and appears to have a far higher power-generation capacity.

"Some of my Commandants, including Commandant Ackahl, point to evidence that they have extremely powerful energy weapons that could pose a threat to our fleets at close range. Most do not believe that the ship would survive to that range."

Amelie smiled thinly.

"Your Commandants may want to ask themselves *why* we don't have missiles," she pointed out. "As you just noted, our engines are superior to yours. We could build better missiles than you have. But we fight the Matrices, and no missile in our arsenals can penetrate their defenses.

"You may consider that a free warning, Intendant and Keeper. If one of your battleship task groups were to engage a Matrix combat platform with its current armament, it would be utterly destroyed without notably damaging its opponent."

The Sivar around her were suddenly silent. She hadn't even told them that her own fleet could duplicate the same stunt. The massed fleet of the Sivar Governance could probably damage a Republic battle group…but they wouldn't be doing it with missiles.

"And you would provide us with weapons that could fight the Builders?" the Intendant asked.

"If we were to conclude a mutually satisfactory military alliance, we would work with your engineers to produce an upgrade template that would convert your battleships into warships that could fight the Matrices," Amelie agreed. "We would retain control of the designs and certain key elements for their manufacture, but we would assist you in upgrading your fleet to face our mutual enemy."

"I see." The Intendant continued to study her, then pulled his hands back into his lap as he leaned backward.

"And why, if your technology is so advanced, do you need us?" he asked bluntly. "You have already said you have other allies. You have your own nation. It seems I should be fearing your fleets of conquest, not meeting your ambassador."

"My nation is over a hundred light-years from here," Amelie admitted. *That* should be safe enough—she certainly wasn't telling the Siva just how small the Republic of Exilium was. "We have other demands on our vessels and our resources. We are challenging the Matrices on several fronts. We cannot commit the resources to win this war on our own, so we are finding and preparing allies to face this enemy at our side.

"Military allies today are trading partners tomorrow," she continued. "We expect to stabilize this region of space, throw back the Matrices and establish long-term economic ties that will make everyone involved far wealthier than they would be on their own.

"But dead people make for poor allies and poor traders. So, we make this alliance and commit what ships we can spare."

Everything she said was true. Of course, the resources they could commit to this war were a far higher portion of Exilium's capacity than she was admitting there.

The Intendant made a small hand-wave gesture.

"I see you," he said formally. "Your intentions are clear and your desires mostly so. Keeper Istila!"

"Your Greatness." Istila was still kneeling but at least didn't have ban's head on the floor. Ban was clearly not quite as well regarded yet as ban's colleagues.

"You will continue discussions with Amelie Lestroud," he instructed. "Details and realities must be clarified before I make my decision.

"Your presence here is welcome," he continued, returning his attention to Amelie. "I see productive fates for your discussion with my Keys of Peace. Go forth and know that the Intendant of the Sivar has seen you and heard your words."

And if *that* wasn't a formal dismissal in any language, Amelie was a crow.

27

"The yards haven't been operational since *Shezarim* left," Captain Cameron, commanding officer of the strike cruiser *Prospero*, told the gathered leadership of Octavio's expedition. The woman's voice and image were being relayed by tachyon communicator, allowing a real-time conversation despite the vast distance between *Prospero* and *Dauntless*.

"They were shot to pieces by the Escorts on the way out, and no one even tried to salvage them. It looks like the ships were picked over pretty heavily, though."

"Have the Assini techs found anything useful?" Octavio asked, glancing over at Siril-ki.

"They think they've got a vector on our scavengers," Cameron told them. "My people found at least one interesting thing ourselves, too."

"What's the vector?" Octavio asked. "That was in the computers?"

"It looks like one of the scavenging expeditions took the most intact ship back to the most distant gas giant, Kora."

"*One of?*" Siril-ki interjected.

"That's the interesting thing we confirmed," Cameron replied. "There were at least *three* different expeditions that hit the shipyard here. One was only a few months after the first flare, and it looks like they fell back to Sina.

"The second was twenty years later, after the second flare took out Sina." The blonde Captain shook her head. "They're the ones the Assini are certain fell back to Kora. It looks like they were focused on ship parts—like I said, they took the only intact hull back with them."

"The third was ten years after that. We don't have much of a vector, but I can tell that they weren't using a reactionless drive like the first two expeditions," Cameron said. "They came in hard, decelerating at a couple thousand gravities. Closer to *Shezarim*'s drive than the usual reactionless system the Assini use."

"So, was that a technologically regressed Assini ship or something else?" Octavio murmured.

"Like I said, the vector is unclear. We're talking two hundred and seventy years ago, sir. They seemed to have focused on colony supplies. Siril-ki's records show that there should have been at least two complete terraformer spikes here. It doesn't look like the first two groups of scavengers took them, but they're gone."

"That sounds more promising than you might think," Renaud pointed out. "A big ship with a big engine, grabbing the terraforming spikes? That sounds like a colony ship heading out. If they fell back to Kora, they should have been safe for an extended period."

"Long enough to build an evacuation ship and reestablish contact with the Sentinels," Siril-ki concluded. "Or even, potentially, to build a sustainable artificial ecosystem. The resources existed."

"Were the gas giant colonies self-sufficient before?" Octavio asked.

"No," ki admitted. "We had two planets to grow food on and a reactionless drive system to lift that food out of the gravity well. Food supplies would have taken serious effort to set up, but the resources existed."

Ki was insisting on that rather hard, but Octavio couldn't deny ki's hope.

"What about Irona and Kand?" he asked. "There were colonies there?"

"The charts from the First Administrator's office suggests that they deorbited every orbital they could safely manage on a course for

Kora," D cut in, the AI having handled collating the battered papers from the dead city.

"If it could be moved to Kora, they were moving it to Kora. How much of that process was complete when the flare hit Sina is uncertain," the AI noted. "Any vessel or station in transit would have been in severe danger in a flare of that magnitude…and the likelihood is that flares of at least that magnitude had occurred multiple times since then.

"If the Creators did not evacuate, there may not be any left *to* save."

"They had the resources to evacuate," Octavio replied, glancing at Siril-ki again. It was hard to tell with a dark-blue centaur, but ki looked *exhausted*. "We have to hope that they did and that we'll find them."

He shook his head.

"Did we find what we needed to make contact with the Sentinels?" he asked the Assini gently.

"I'm not sure yet," ki admitted. "The codes and protocols should be in the data cores we retrieved, but accessing them is not a fast process. D is assisting us, but it will take time."

"I estimate a minimum of one week to fully break the encryption and security protocols," D added. "I am more capable in many ways than the Matrices they expected to be attempting the breach, but the security designers *did* anticipate the use of AI Matrices to get through their security."

"Keep working on that," Octavio ordered. "Otherwise, it sounds like our next destination is Kora. We'll spend a few more days here at Sina and see if we can find anything else, but…"

"All we are finding of my people is dead worlds," Siril-ki said softly. "A smaller ambition might have saved us, but our grand ambitions doomed us."

Ki shook ki's long head, more of a shiver than anything else.

"Even our evacuation plan was far too grand in the end," ki whispered. "We could never focus on the problem at hand without some grand solution to fix everything. And it damned us."

28

Isaac watched the first Skree-Skree battlecruisers cut through their trials on his flag deck hologram with interest. The two ships were basically late-generation *Vigilance*-class ships, with higher-frequency grasers than the older ships that were on their way from Refuge.

The ships were a dream. The Skree-Skree engineers had taken the designs the humans had given them and added their own touches. Not every change they'd made had been an improvement, and none of the changes were game-changing, but he knew his engineers were already taking notes.

As he was considering that, however, *Glorious Heart* missed the next turn in her maneuvering sequence. The massive battlecruiser continued on her course at full acceleration, only avoiding a collision because the strike cruiser *Observant Star*'s crew had been watching for problems.

The ships were a dream. The *crews* were a mix of a cadre drawn from the earlier strike cruisers and half-trained new recruits. There was only so much anyone could do with that mix, and Isaac wasn't overly impressed with Skree-Skree training methods in the first place.

"We're going to have a problem."

Vice Admiral Giannovi stood next to him on *Vigil*'s bridge, watching the same hologram. She'd transferred her flag to *Fortitude* to act as the commander of the human contingent of the fleet, but she remained his right-hand woman.

"They're rough," he agreed. "But ThreeHeart's strike cruiser crews worked up faster than we expected. They started rough too. So did we."

He smirked.

"I remember a warp cruiser a while ago that should never have gone into battle," he pointed out.

"That was different," Giannovi objected. "That was a skilled crew letting themselves go because no one figured the First Admiral's kid was going to get sent into a fight."

"Little you knew then, I suppose," Isaac said with a chuckle. "Any concerns with our force?"

"I'll be happier when *Scrutiny* is here," she admitted. "And not just because she's coming with three Vistan battlecruisers. Four battle-cruisers sounds so much better than three—and fourteen sounds so much better than six too."

He snorted, but she was right.

The Republic had given up *Dante* but gained *Resilience*, *Fortitude* and, when she arrived, *Scrutiny*. The Tohnbohn had put up a third battlecruiser, which would arrive alongside the Vistans' three new ships, and the Skree-Skree were lending him their two.

Fourteen battlecruisers with full or even extended escort groups. Fifty-four strike cruisers. Plus the Matrix contingent, which no one was ever entirely sure what the strength of would be.

"Another week for the reinforcements," he said aloud. "Twenty-Five is making noises about their new ships, too. If I'm reading between their lines right, XR-13-9 just launched an entire new round of combat platforms and we're looking at a fifty percent or more increase to his combat platform strength."

Isaac wasn't entirely sure how many combat platforms XR-13-9 *had*. Until the Assini had provided a code update to allow them to fight their genocidal siblings, XR-13-9 hadn't had much use for them.

He didn't think he had *all* of XR-13-9's combat platforms in the allied fleet—but he suspected he had a similar percentage of the Matrices' ships as he had of the Republic's fleet. He wouldn't have been surprised to discover that he had half or even three-quarters of Twenty-Five's siblings attached to his fleet.

A fifty percent reinforcement would give the AI eighteen ships instead of the twelve survivors of the battle with the dreadnought, and Isaac was perfectly willing to regard the combat platforms as being in the same category as his battlecruisers. They lacked the particle cannon that made the primary armament of the human-designed ships but made up for it with more lasers.

And all of Twenty-Five's ships were fully upgraded with zetta-lasers. His allies might *look* the same as his enemies, but they were *far* more dangerous.

"Sir, we just got a coms request from Twenty-Five," Isaac's coms officer, Naveed Hashemi, interjected quietly as she stepped over to join them. "He wants to speak to you alone, Admiral Lestroud."

"That might be good news," Giannovi said. "I need to transfer back to *Fortitude* once these trials are done. Do you need anything before I go, sir?"

"Tell Singh that you enjoyed lunch," Isaac replied. His long-suffering steward had been with him since he'd been promoted to command the old *Vigil* back in the Confederacy's service. The man took incredible care of Isaac and deserved his praise.

"Otherwise..." He paused thoughtfully. "Don't leave until I've finished speaking to Twenty-Five," he finally told her. "I can't imagine the call will take that long, but I have the feeling we'll want to talk afterward."

"You're the Admiral, Admiral," she agreed with a grin.

———

His office was only a few steps away. Those steps might make the difference between life and death in battle, which was why the flag deck had the ability to provide a *reasonably* secure privacy shield around the Admiral's seat, but his office was still the best place for a private call.

Taking his seat, Isaac poured himself a coffee and nodded silently to VK.

"Commander Hashemi is standing by to connect Twenty-Five," the AI told him. "Do you want me to privacy-seal your conversation?"

Not only would that seal Isaac's office, but it would mean that VK wouldn't have access to the recording themselves.

"Yes," he decided. "Just in case. Have Naveed put them through."

"Understood. Sealing your office now."

There was a moment of silence and then a machine-translated voice spoke from the air. Like most of the Matrices, Combat Coordination Matrix ZDX-175-25 had chosen a particular voice and accent to recurrently use.

It made the AIs easier to tell apart, though Isaac knew it was an affectation at most—and one that could easily be used *against* their human allies.

"Greetings, Admiral Isaac Lestroud. This is ZDX-175-25."

"Greetings, Twenty-Five," Isaac replied. "This call is as secure as we can make it." He shook his head. "I'm not sure that would stop our actual enemies, but it will at least prevent inadvertent eavesdroppers."

"You underestimate the encryption protocols your teams and the K-sequence AIs have assembled," Twenty-Five told him. "Even I would have problems breaking through them without preparation, and I have access to the encryption protocols themselves, if not the distinct keys."

"Fair enough. What did you need, Twenty-Five?" Isaac asked.

"I wanted to provide you with two updates, Admiral Lestroud, one of which will hopefully affect your response to the other," the AI Matrix said.

"Firstly, we have found the Rogue RCM."

Twenty-Five dropped that bombshell so matter-of-factly, it took Isaac a moment to process what they had just said.

"You're sure?" he finally asked. "Not another dreadnought? Not another trap?"

"It has been demonstrated that one hundred percent certainty in this matter is beyond our grasp," Twenty-Five replied. "Thanks to your suggestion, we were able to cut our scouting operations by over seventy percent. We *did* find one system where a dreadnought appears to be attempting to pretend to be the RCM, but it was definitely a false positive."

"You're sure?" Isaac said.

"It was exactly positioned along what would have been our scouting route without your suggestion," the Matrix noted. "It lacked the assembled infrastructure that XR-13-9 has in our base system…and our long-distance scans suggested that it had been in place for less than six months.

"The system we believe has the highest probability of containing the RCM has a full setup of infrastructure that appears on our long-range scanners. Scouting runs from some distance suggest a similar setup to that in place around XR-13-9…and the presence of *four* vessels of sufficient size to be either RCMs or Matrix dreadnoughts."

"Four," Isaac muttered. "Any idea on smaller ships?"

"Our scans took place at sufficient range to make that kind of identification difficult," Twenty-Five admitted. "We have confirmed the presence of major fixed defenses, sufficient to provide multiple layers of heavy security around the RCM."

Isaac exhaled.

"Show me," he ordered. "Relay the data on this channel; I'll bring up a hologram."

His office lit up a moment later. One image was the location of the RCM's system. It was, he noted, almost equally distant from Refuge as from Skree-Skree. It was actually closer to where his reinforcements were currently en route than to anywhere else.

The second image was of the system itself. It was a mix of visuals and Matrix iconography that his computer took half a second to translate into Republic labels.

Isaac silently whistled. The RCM and its dreadnought companions were nestled in the middle of a massive asteroid belt. The gravity data suggested that the asteroid belt wasn't original—the Matrices had shattered a small rocky world with missile fire and were feeding the wreckage into their foundries.

And those foundries had been busy. Building offensive fleets was secondary to defending the RCM, which was secondary again to actually Constructing worlds. Easily hundreds of fortresses orbited the system, creating multiple networks of defensive structures.

The big ships were most obvious, but there were icons in the map for probable contacts of other ships. There were dozens, potentially hundreds, of those. Few would be combat platforms and many of the noncombat platforms would be completely unarmed, but it was still a *lot* of ships.

"I'm not sure we can crack that," he admitted aloud.

"That brings me to my second update, Admiral Lestroud," Twenty-Five told him. "I have confirmed that my reinforcements are on their way. I will shortly receive twenty recon and security platforms and thirteen new combat platforms.

"With twenty-five combat platforms and the fourteen battlecruisers scheduled to be under your command, I put our chances of successfully engaging the RCM's fortification at fifty percent. The addition of the fleet of the Sivar Governance as assessed by Minister Lestroud would increase that to eighty percent, plus/minus ten percent based on the level of upgrade applied to the Sivar battleships."

"That's a hell of a difference," he noted. "But...those combat platforms will make a major addition. When are we expecting them?"

"Well before your own reinforcements. Within a few days."

Isaac considered the astrographic map.

"We need more data," he confessed. "Can you redirect your reinforcements to meet us near there?"

He was already doing mental math. Ten light-years was two weeks from his current location. If they'd done the VLA trick at the right angle in Skree-Skree, they would have been able to *see* the bastards.

His reinforcements could meet him there. They were actually closer, on the way from Refuge. The Sivar...he had no idea if he'd *ever* have them to back him up, let alone how quickly they could get there.

"We need to prepare on the assumption that we won't have the Sivar," he said aloud. "We'll set a rendezvous two light-months from the system and converge there."

Fifty percent, Twenty-Five had said. He had faith in his people, but that was still *terrible* odds.

29

"WITH THE SIVAR, properly upgraded and positioned to support us, the odds would be in our favor," Isaac's image told Amelie. "Without them, it's a toss of the dice, my love. But...I don't see a choice."

"Neither do I," she admitted grimly. "It's been two days since I met the Intendant, Isaac, and I only just got confirmation of a meeting with the Keepers for today. These people are not in a hurry and seem to have their own problems going on."

"Do I even want to know?" her husband asked.

"Problems like all the way back home," Amelie said carefully. She was *reasonably* sure the privacy generator sitting next to her on the table was secure, and *reasonably* sure her tightbeam to *Watchtower* was secure, and certain the tachyon-com connection between the two battlecruisers was secure...but the last thing the Sivar Intendant needed to know was that the humans were exiles from a home that was a long, long way away.

"Is their fleet even worth this hassle?" Isaac asked.

"I'm not qualified to judge," she admitted. "I can tell you that I'm seeing evidence of at least two, probably more, subjugated species. They might be subjects with decent rights...they might be slaves. I don't know yet.

"If it's the latter, we might be in trouble." She glanced down at the other tablet she'd been working on.

"Holmwood thinks she could take their battleships three or four at a time right now," she noted. "But she also says their lasers are actually pretty decent. Pump *enough* power through an efficient-enough laser and you can rival some of the lower-energy grasers, after all."

Isaac snorted.

"It's not quite that simple, but I see your point. Look, even if you got them on board at this meeting tonight, they'd need weeks of refits and weeks to get out here. If I leave tomorrow, we're two weeks from contact. Do you think we can even sort out an alliance with these people in two weeks?"

"It took a month with the Tohnbohn," she reminded him. "They at least wanted to talk to us and understood the threat, even if everything with them is slow. I'm not sure the Intendant really *gets* how much danger his Governance is in if we fall."

"The Republic is far enough away that if we fall here, we can evacuate our allies and write off this sector," her husband said, his voice very quiet and very grim. "We know what kind of effort that looks like, but we could do it.

"Without an alliance, I won't get my people killed for the Sivar." Isaac's eyes told the truth. He didn't have it in him to stand by while worlds were destroyed, though he'd make the threat.

"And what about their slaves?" Amelie asked. She knew the answer there, too.

"I know," he conceded. "We need more data. I leave that to you, Amelie. Politics and backstabbing were always your field."

"Hopefully, I won't need to stab anyone," she demurred with a forced laugh. "I'll get answers, Isaac. Hopefully, I'll even get an alliance. The sooner I manage that, the sooner I can see you.

"Don't die on me," she ordered. "I love you."

"I love you," he replied. "I don't plan on dying. The same goes for you. Everything I'm seeing about these Sivar...I worry."

"At least I'm not the only one this time," Amelie told him.

———

Amelie's meeting that afternoon was with two of the three Keepers. She still wasn't entirely sure exactly what the title translated to. Her initial impression that they acted as cabinet ministers had been undermined by the degree to which the Intendant seemed to have multiple entire chains of command that converged on him.

Rode and Istila met her in a grand conference room that looked out over the terraced gardens of the First and Final Citadel. They each had a single guard, wearing the same toga garment as the Keepers themselves but with a black sash around the torso to hold a visible holster.

Those guards joined Amelie's trio of Marines in low-profile power armor at the door of the room, while Istila led the Minister to the far end of the room.

This was apparently on an outcropping that hung out over the gardens, allowing her to look down in three directions and see the Sivar's homeworld spread out.

"The Intendant has given us his initial instructions," Rode told Amelie. "Today's meetings are for us to learn more about each other. We cannot be allies if everything about each other is concealed in secrecy and shadows."

"I agree," Amelie said. She stepped off to one side, intentionally turning her body away from the two Keepers as she studied the gardens. There were a lot of people out there working on those terraces, dozens or even hundreds that she could see from this conference room.

It was hard to be sure, but she didn't think very many of them were Sivar.

"I have told you about my people," she noted. "Our system is quite far from here, months of travel by our star drive and functionally unreachable by yours, as the star-lanes between here and there have never been mapped.

"Closer, though still beyond the reach of your star-lane maps, are our allies: the Vistans, the Tohnbohn and the Skree-Skree. The Vistans and the Skree-Skree have both seen the Builders come to their systems and have driven them back with our assistance."

She smiled.

"Between the four of us, we control five star systems and have a combined fleet in this region of over eighty starships. Our alliance with the sane siblings of the Rogue Matrices provides an equal number of starships using a different star drive than our own, though they *are* computers and can have some…odd ideas about things."

She was still watching her companions out of the corner of her eye, and both of them seemed surprised by the ship strengths in play.

"And between today and our previous meetings, I have now told you more of my Republic and her allies than you have of the Sivar Governance," she noted. "I would…suggest that imbalance be rectified if we are going to continue these discussions."

The two Sivar were doing more than communicating with their body language and eyes, Amelie realized. There was a delicate dance of their fingers down by their sides where they hoped she hadn't noticed it.

Fascinating. Sign language offered so many possibilities for talking around aliens using computers to record and translate audio. To have a truly secure conversation, Amelie supposed she could have used her translator software to talk to Isaac in another human language. They could even have used her half-forgotten French or his equally rusty Swahili.

It would never have occurred to her to use Refined Terran Sign Language, even though both of them were fluent in RTSL. One of Exilium's senators was deaf, after all.

The Sivar's flickering finger language was far better designed for secrecy, though the conversation took at least a minute longer than Amelie figured it would have aloud or in RTSL.

She spent the time half-watching her companions and studying the gardens. The First and Final Citadel's gardens were a wonder, she had to admit. The esthetics were alien—and often used to conceal weapons emplacements—but it was an immensely gorgeous project.

Beneath it, she could see what she presumed to be the Governance's capital city. It was an interesting metropolis, with large chunks of it appearing barred to ground vehicles from this distance.

She wondered if she'd ever get to see it from close up. If the Sivar were smart, they wouldn't let an ex-revolutionary anywhere *near* their general populace…but then, it wasn't like she'd handed them her resume.

"You are, of course, correct," Rode finally said, her voice a calm counterpoint to the activity on the slopes below. "May I show you a display, Minister?"

"Of course."

The two Sivar led Amelie slightly back into the outcropping conference room and activated a bulky holoprojector. Even as Amelie was adding *miniaturized holoprojection technology* to her mental list of things they could sell the Governance, a map materialized above the table.

The structure of the map was fascinating. It took the shape of a series of balls and spokes, an interconnected model resembling a child's model of a molecule. After a few seconds, Amelie realized that all of the "spokes" were the same length and the map had no direct correlation to real space.

"This is a star-lane map of the Sivar Governance," Rode explained unnecessarily. "We are here, in the Sivar System on the world of Aris."

The central ball flashed white.

"The Governance contains nine inhabited planets, each of which has a Sector Commandant or a Commandant-Key of War charged with its spaceborne security and a Prince-Key of Peace charged with the governance of the world. Around those nine inhabited planets, we have occupied twenty-four more systems and claim to the end of our currently mapped star-lanes, another forty stars."

Amelie was clearly expected to react with awe to the sheer size and power of the Governance…but she was a child of the Terran Confederacy. *Exilium* was a backwater colony seventy thousand light-years from the edge of Confederate territory and home to a mere four million souls.

The Terran Confederacy was the unquestioned ruler of a region of space as large as the zone the Matrices had terraformed. From the wormhole generators in Sol orbit, the First Admiral could deliver a battlecruiser group to any star within three hundred light-years. Fifteen inhabited worlds, each with their own wormhole stations, were home to a human population nearing a quarter-*trillion*.

The Governance's belief in their overwhelming power was cute.

"Where did I meet Commandant Ackahl?" she asked, ignoring their expectations of her and trying to match this map to real space. She was familiar with the stars in the region now, but the map was more concerned with the star-lane connections than the real-world positioning of the systems.

"You met Command Ackahl in the Sonbar System," Istila told her. "This one."

Another system flashed white and Amelie concealed a smile.

"So, Sonbar is your most vulnerable star when the Matrices come this way," she told them. "If we do not agree on an alliance, you will still likely want to reinforce there."

"That is for the Keeper of the Keys of War, the Intendant and the Commandants to decide," Rode said. "My concern is the Citadel and Aris. Keeper Istila's concern is the Prince-Keys of Peace and the worlds of the Governance. It is the Keys of War that look beyond our territory and plan our defense."

"And who are the Eyes of Sivar?" Amelie asked.

That wasn't a question they'd wanted to hear, and their fingers went back to flickering.

"They are a secondary branch of our nation," Istila said slowly. "One that serves the Intendant and the Fates directly."

A priesthood, Amelie guessed. Also trouble…but she'd *known* that.

"Nine worlds," she repeated. "How many ships? If we agree to an alliance, how many of your battleships can the Commandants and the Keys of War send to face the Rogue Matrices?"

"If the Intendant wills it, we can send as many ships as you already have facing these Rogues," Rode intoned, though if she'd been human, Amelie wouldn't have believed her. "The fleets available to the Intendant are as vast as the Fates require."

Which was not a number—but also told Amelie that *Rode* didn't necessarily know the number. The female Siva was responsible for the Sivar homeworld and didn't know how many ships her race commanded.

Their government was weirdly siloed.

"If we are to get to know each other," Amelie said after a few moments of silence, "would it be possible for me to tour the palace? The gardens are beautiful and I would like a closer look."

That would also allow them to take everything she'd said back to the Intendant. She was *quite* certain that their goal had been as much to learn the strength of the alliance as anything else.

"I would be delighted to show you our gardens," Rode said after a quick flicker of fingers at Istila. "We can speak more of my people as we do. I hope I can ease your curiosity and fears, Minister Lestroud."

"My curiosity, at least," Amelie allowed.

She expected the tour to be educational…but she didn't expect it to ease her fears.

30

———————

RODE INSISTED on showing Amelie the area of the Citadel interior they were already in, calling it "one of the great wonders of our people."

Amelie waited patiently through the tour, allowing the Keeper of the Citadel to tell her details of stone types and artisans and statues that she would never care about. It wasn't that the area of the Citadel she was touring wasn't gorgeous—quite the opposite. She just knew that they both understood that Rode was playing for time for an escort to be assembled.

She wasn't sure if the Siva realized that she *also* knew they were probably clearing the slaves from the area Rode was planning to show her. The Sivar seemed to suspect that the non-Sivar slaves would be an issue for her—which suggested at least some internal conflict over them, if nothing else.

But it was polite to let her hosts decide what she saw this time, so Amelie made polite commentary on the sweeping, reshaped caverns that had been turned into the reception area long before. When the Citadel had been built, the Intendant had clearly had to deal with *somebody* for grand audiences.

Eventually, they passed under yet another set of statues supporting a stone arch and reached a set of massive double doors.

"These are the Halls of Gathering," Rode told her. "They are the most impressive of the Halls in the Citadel, but it is one of fourteen. There are, as you have seen, temples and pathways and residences throughout. Our engineers estimate that as much as ten percent of the mountain's original mass has been excavated to create the First and Final Citadel."

"So I see," Amelie replied, her attention focused on the doors as they swung open. Another of the omnipresent double files of Sivar guards waited for them.

"Our escort," Rode said unnecessarily with a gesture to the guards. "As with any leader, the Intendant has his enemies, and many would target you for being his guest."

And, of course, they could only trust *her* so far.

"I understand," Amelie agreed aloud. "Sergeant Choi?"

"We'll play nice," the Marine said with a grin. "I want to see these gardens myself."

The Keeper of the Citadel—ruler of the entire planet of Aris, so far as Amelie could tell—gave the Marine an aside glance but didn't object as they all fell in with the escorts.

"From the terrace here, you can see the entirety of the eastern gardens," Rode continued after a moment, leading them out into the bright sunlight.

Amelie didn't think she was exaggerating, either. The exterior entrance to the Halls of Gathering clearly linked to a road that went down the outside of the mountain and several nearby landing pads. Currently, the two Amelie could see were playing host to a pair of sleek atmospheric interceptors.

Rode led them across the road and to the edge of the terrace she'd mentioned. Amelie stood at the edge, feeling the slight electric buzz of an inertial safety field.

From there, the view was exactly what the Keeper had promised. Stone planters along the edge of the terrace held shrubs and flowers in intricately mixed patterns of color, with breaks clearly intended to allow people to do exactly what they were doing.

Twenty meters down the mountain, the first of the terraces held more gardens. Amelie suspected she could see herb and vegetable gardens tucked in amidst the purely decorative greenery as well.

Twenty meters after that, there was another terrace, and then another twenty meters beneath that one. From this one balcony, Amelie could easily see ten or more terraces, each extending fifty or more meters out from the mountainside and full of color.

There probably wasn't a spot to look at the terraces where they weren't stunning, but Amelie imagined that they were designed to look best from there—from the place the Intendant and his guests would see them.

"There is a set of stairs over here," Rode told her after a few moments of awed gazing. "If you'd like the tour of the garden itself, that is?"

"I would," Amelie replied. "It's beautiful. I'd like to see it closer up."

And she wanted to see just *who* kept all of that up. It looked like a *lot* of work, and she hadn't seen that many Sivar who weren't politicians or soldiers yet. Even if she was wrong about who was doing it, talking to a Sivar gardener would be valuable in and of itself.

———

RODE SPENT the tour pointing out particular plants, skimming over the functional ones mixed in with the rest in favor of the purely decorative vegetation. She tried to divert Amelie's attention away from the more obvious weapons, but there was only so much of that that could be done as they walked through the gardens themselves.

"Why is the Citadel so fortified?" Amelie finally asked after Rode had stalled out in an attempt to ignore a vine-wrapped missile launcher platform.

"As I said, there are those who oppose the Intendant's wise rule," Rode reminded her. "We must make certain that the voice of the Fates is safe."

"That explains guards and aerial patrols," Amelie said quietly. "Not missile launchers and cannons and concealed arsenals. Those are built to fight wars, Keeper Rode, not stand off assassins."

"Some of that is tradition," the Keeper told her. "Most is a precaution in case the Keys of War forget who they serve. It is *my* task to protect the Intendant against any possible treachery, as well as to maintain the Citadel and serve as the Prince-Key of Aris in his name."

"So, your authority ends at Aris's atmosphere, and the other two Keepers control the rest of the Governance?" Amelie asked.

"All of our authorities end at the will of our Intendant," Rode replied. "We serve him and through him the Governance."

Amelie nodded and stepped away from the weapons system. She crossed to the edge of the terrace and looked out at the one beneath them. There was a team of gardeners down there, working on a tree that looked like it had some kind of blight.

Out of eight gardeners, only two were Sivar. The other six were split between two other species, both unfamiliar to Amelie. One was a delicately built group of winged beings with four legs and two arms and what looked like a stinger to go with delicate but *large* wings.

Wings that had been visibly clipped to make sure they didn't fly away.

The other was the aliens they'd seen on the way down. Close up, they were a stocky race and even shorter than the Sivar. Like the winged gardeners, they had four legs and two arms but lacked the more bug-like features of the other species. They were covered in black fur that couldn't have been comfortable in the harsh sunlight. More than that couldn't be distinguished—but the black fur allowed Amelie to pick out the metallic collars Köhl had pointed out on the other aliens earlier.

Slaves.

"Flames," Rode cursed softly as she stepped up next to Amelie. "They were supposed to bring everyone in. It's not polite to have gardeners out while touring the garden."

"I only see two Sivar down there, Keeper," the Republic's Foreign Minister said, her voice very calm and formal. "Who are the others?"

Rode was silent for several seconds.

"Most of the staff of the Citadel are not Sivar," she finally said. "Those appear to be Croni and Pol. They are indentured servants, bound to the service of the Intendant as part of the terms by which their worlds joined the Governance and came under His Greatness's protection."

"Indentured servants," Amelie echoed. "And how are these servants selected?"

"That varies from world to world and is the responsibility of the Prince-Key of Peace of that world," Rode answered after staring off the mountainside for several long seconds. "They are weak. The Governance is strong, so we extended our protection over them.

"This is the way of the universe, that the strong protect the weak. So your Republic has stretched its ships over your allies near us. You are strong. They are weak."

"We didn't require them to send us slaves to maintain our gardens," Amelie pointed out, keeping her voice as level as she could. Turning off the emotional layers of her translator would be too obvious. Fortunately, she had *years* of practice at this.

And something told her that Rode wasn't as okay with what she was describing as her words implied. There was too much staring off blankly into space for that.

"But you expect compensation from them," Rode replied. "Your trade deals and sales. You did not give them warships."

"We did exactly that," Amelie said with a chuckle. "Warships, weapons technology, industrial modules…all things we would give the Governance, too, if you sign on to the alliance. The Rogue Matrices are a critical threat to the survival of all sentient life. The more powerful our allies against them are, the safer we *all* are."

Rode was silent for several seconds.

"This is all we know," she finally said. "The strong lead. The weak submit or are made to submit. It is not merely gardeners, Minister Lestroud."

"I did not think it was," Amelie replied. "They are barred from space, yes? Allowed to leave their worlds only to serve as your slaves and janissaries?"

"That was the deal to keep them safe," Rode confirmed. "A deal made only more important by the news you bring us. We protect the weak. We will fight these Builders to keep them safe."

Amelie heard Rode's unspoken addition: that doing so would call for far larger tributes from the conquered worlds.

Faced with an unavoidable presence, Rode had admitted what the Sivar had been hiding from her. Now Amelie knew *exactly* what kind of empire she'd made her proposal of alliance to.

And she was going to have to decide just what to do about that.

31

———————

From a distance, the collection of stations and orbitals hung around Kora, Assini's third and smallest gas giant, looked promising. There was a *lot* of metal positioned in carefully synchronized orbits. Closer examination showed everything from residential habitats to massive greenhouse platforms that *should* have been enough to feed ten or twenty million people at least.

But Octavio's people hadn't picked up any energy signatures from those stations until they were close enough to see them. That was all the warning he really needed to make the true state of those stations and facilities a horrific non-surprise.

"We've got a few systems running on radioactive decay generators," McGill reported to the ship commanders and Octavio. "It looks like some of their high-priority, low-power systems were hooked up to RDGs to make sure they kept operating, but…"

"Everything else is dead," Siril-ki concluded. The emotional component of ki's translator was still turned off, leaving only a cold flatness to ki's tone. "Can you identify if it was evacuated or…"

"Not from outside," McGill admitted. "I can tell you that more of the stations look like they got hit with radiation pulses than I'd have expected, but that could just be ones that were in transit when flares hit.

"This far out, everything *should* have been safe—and with the tachyon communicators, they should have been able to set up an early warning system to let them move everything behind the gas giant."

"Assuming they had time," Octavio murmured. "Or that the system didn't get hit by one flare and disabled before the next one hit. A lot of things could have gone wrong."

He studied the dark stations in the flag deck's main hologram and shivered.

"Or they could have built ships like the one that took the terraformers from the shipyards," he noted. "And evacuated every-body. *Shezarim* was designed to carry three million people. They should still have been able to duplicate her technology."

"Maybe," Siril-ki replied. "Vast resources were committed to that evacuation program. I do not know if some of those resources could have been duplicated, especially given the losses my people suffered."

"There's enough here to have sustained tens of millions," Renaud pointed out. "Forever, basically. All they would have needed was hydrogen and basic hydrocarbons, both of which are available from Kora or the planet's moons."

"There's enough food and life-support production here to support as many people as these stations could hold," Octavio agreed. "This should have been fully self-sustaining and safe."

A cold tremor ran down his spine.

"McGill, would we be able to detect weapon damage now?" he asked.

"We would," she confirmed. "That would be far more obvious than damage from the flares. We haven't found any yet, so any use of weapons was limited at worst. They weren't attacked, Commodore."

He nodded slowly.

"I don't see any choice, then," he told the command channel. "Chen?"

"Sir?"

"How ready are your people?"

"Suited up and boarding shuttles as we speak," the Marine replied.

"My only question is where I'm sending them. There's a lot of individual stations over there, and I'm not seeing anything from here to help me decide what to investigate."

"McGill? Have we seen any signs of a tachyon communication center?" Octavio asked. They were still hoping to find another Validation Center. *Two* sets of data would be worth more than one, even if each set was inevitably degraded from the original.

"It looks like there were still a few smaller tachyon coms, but nothing I'd call a major center," the tactical officer admitted. "There definitely isn't a Validation Center, though…"

"Commander?" Renaud asked after her subordinate trailed off.

"Take a look at this."

The command channel they were talking on was only primarily audio. Octavio was sitting on the flag deck. Renaud and McGill were on the bridge. Siril-ki was in ki's office and Chen Zhou was apparently in power armor, coordinating her Marines.

It was easy enough for Octavio to transfer the data from the command channel to the big display on the flag deck, zooming in on a particular platform.

A particular *half-built* platform. Time and debris had done the structure few favors, but Octavio could see the shell of what the station would have been. There was still nonfunctional construction equipment attached to it, even.

"That has roughly the same structure as the Validation Center on Sina," McGill pointed out. "They were building one. They stopped."

"All right. That gives me two targets for your Marines, Major," Octavio said quietly. "The first one is that Validation Center. If there's any data cores or dropped datapads or *anything* to tell us why they stopped, I want them.

"Most of the rest of your Marines can basically pick random targets throughout the colony, but I want at least three squads on the hydroponics platforms." The Commodore looked at those with a dark eye.

"Food was their major problem, and they found a functional and nearly elegant solution," he continued. "Those ag stations should have sustained this colony. For it to be this dark, either they evacuated or they ran out of food.

"If they'd evacuated, they'd almost certainly have finished the tachyon com station. So, what the *hell* happened to the ag stations?"

It was easy to forget, sitting in the flag deck and watching icons flit across his screen, just how much energy was involved in moving even a single shuttle-load of Marines around that easily. Creating thrust was one thing—allowing human beings to survive thousands of gravities of it was even *more* power-intensive.

But that was a challenge humanity had mastered a long time before, and Major Chen's Marines were unlikely to be more aware of that power need than Octavio was.

It was on his mind right now, though, because he was thinking about *Shezarim*. They had evidence that there had been at least one more ship of a similar design and scale, using massive fusion engines instead of the Assini's elegant and efficient reactionless engines.

Shezarim had suffered from a fuel-capacity problem. Fully fuelled, she could accelerate up to her maximum speed and decelerate down once before needing to refuel. *Interceptor*, the Exilium- and Matrix-designed ship that had caught *Shezarim*, had carried more delta-*v* in less space.

The Assini reactionless engine was sufficiently more effective than reaction engines at most purposes that the centaurs didn't have an equivalent to Exilium's hyper-efficient impulse thrusters.

But those drives had a hard speed limit, so *Shezarim* had mounted fusion rockets. The ship that had taken the terraformers from the evacuation project yards had too.

"Well, that's not a great sign for the evacuation theory." Commander Courtenay was one of the tiny handful of other people on the flag deck.

Octavio hadn't brought a full flag staff and hadn't really felt the lack of one. His command was small enough and tight-knit enough that he could talk to all nine of his Captains directly.

If he'd expected to wage a war, he might have chosen differently.

For an archeological expedition, he was more likely to be sending his strike cruisers off alone than coordinating a combat formation.

"What did you find, Commander?" Octavio asked.

Courtenay tapped a few commands at his console and zoomed the main display in on something. Given his own thoughts, Octavio recognized it immediately and swallowed a curse.

"That's the ship they pulled from the evac yards, right?" he asked.

"Yeah. And it looks like they barely touched it," his aide confirmed. "I mean, they peeled it open here and here"—cuts in the side of the ship flickered on the hologram—"but that's it. Might have gutted her for key systems, but she was never turned into a functioning ship… and I'm not seeing any shipyards out here that could have built an equivalent, either."

"Dammit," Octavio muttered. "We knew we were looking for a dead world, but I had hoped we'd find *somebody*."

Courtenay was silent. The big hologram was mirroring his screen and he was…looking more closely at those cuts?

"Commander?"

"I might have to regret my phrasing, sir," Courtenay replied. "I said she was gutted, and that might be more accurate than I thought. Those cuts, sir? That's weapons fire. They're surgical and controlled and clearly intended to allow access to her systems, but I think that was a zetta-laser."

"That's not unreasonable," Octavio pointed out. "Her hull would have been tough—I'm surprised they cut it open at all, given that her armor would have been the most valuable part—"

"Sir, there are no spaceship weapons in this colony," his aide interrupted. "No Guardian Matrices. No defensive platforms. Not even a high guard cutter. They had no warships left."

"So, someone *else* cut open the ship that was their only hope of getting out of here?" the Commodore asked. "That's…problematic."

"Yes. Can I get Chen to redirect one of her Marine teams?" Courtenay asked.

"It's up to her," Octavio replied. "But you can ask. Either way, that ship goes on the list. Something *weird* is going on here."

———

Octavio's attention was drawn back to the Marines as the first wave of shuttles reached the half-built Validation Center station. Camera feeds from the exteriors of the spacecraft showed chunks of the facility lit up in brilliant lights from the shuttles.

"I'm not seeing much intact here," Belmont reported. "It doesn't look like they'd finished more than the shells. There's no equipment here except the construction gear."

"Is there a foreperson's office?" Chen asked. "Someone had to be in charge on site. That would have the data we want."

"We're sweeping," the junior Marine confirmed. "I'm going to drop Marines towards some of the construction gear, see what's in their cockpits. The station itself is a bust."

Octavio brought up a display of shoulder-camera views from Belmont's Marines as they moved out. The station had been around two hundred meters across, which left a lot of spots for things to be missed...but he agreed with the Marine Captain's assessment.

There might be something useful in the construction setup that had been building the station, but the station itself was too incomplete to have anything of value. They'd been working on the shell when they'd shut down.

"Well, no one is finding any bodies," Belmont reported after a few minutes. "Everything appears to have been neatly shut down and abandoned, all around the same time."

"ID that time for me, Captain," Octavio ordered. "To within a few months, if we can."

Even with the gear the Marines were hauling around, that might be hard. Most likely, the construction crews had neatly shut down their gear sometime between two hundred and eighty and two hundred and seventy years ago—when Sina had been destroyed and when someone had raided the evacuation ship yards for supplies.

He wasn't sure *why* he was assuming that had been the end of the Assini in their home system, but it felt right. In an extraordinarily unpleasant way, at least.

"This is Chen," the Major's voice cut into Octavio's channel. "We're approaching the ag platforms, and I see at least one thing that might explain part of the problem."

"Which is?" Octavio asked.

The feed from Chen's shuttle appeared in the big holotank. Courtenay had the mess of feeds reorganized to be reasonably clear before Octavio could even reach for his controls. Competent subordinates were a dream.

The agricultural stations had been designed to use natural light and heat from Kora and Assini itself to reduce their power draw. That gave them a very distinct appearance: a flattened dome floating in space, with all of the hardware "underneath" the main dome.

Chen's shuttle was coming in from "under" one of the domes, and the video feed was of the mechanical infrastructure of the dome.

The *incomplete* mechanical infrastructure of the dome.

"Her engines weren't online," Chen said quietly. "I'm not a space engineer, but I'm guessing that the dome was supposed to be pointed at the sun, and they figured that they could install the engines later."

"I *am* a spaceship engineer," Octavio replied, his voice equally soft. "And I agree. They were focusing on building the food supply first and…making it safe later."

He stared at the half-built thruster array. It wasn't even a hugely powerful engine—it couldn't be, not with how precious and fragile the station's contents would have been—but it would have sufficed to get the station behind Kora and protect it from the star.

"Do we have close range scans of the top half yet?" he asked.

"Not yet. First of my birds will be swinging over in about ninety seconds. What are you expecting, sir?"

"A lot of radiation-fried crops that have been rotting for three centuries," Octavio admitted. "Another goddamn solar flare that hit them at the worst possible time. The answers should be on those stations, Major."

"We'll go find them, Commodore. EMC isn't afraid of ghosts."

"It's not ghosts I'm afraid of," Octavio murmured. "Find what you can, Major. We'll be watching from here."

———

THE FOREPERSON'S office on the Validation Center was…illuminating. Octavio watched as three of his Marines cut open the access to the spaceborne equivalent of a mobile office trailer. It had an airlock and engines, but all of that was long-dead.

Saws and cutting lasers were the answer instead—at least to start.

"Sir, we've got atmosphere on the other side," one of the Marines reported as they inserted the first probes into the interior. "It's stale as fuck, but it's there. We might lose some artifacts if we just tear this open."

"We'll bring one of the shuttles in and attach with the boarding airlock," Belmont replied. "That should at least get equal pressure."

That didn't take long, though Octavio wouldn't have wanted to be the pilot maneuvering the shuttle *into* the framework of the unbuilt station. Once the boarding airlock attached, though, the mobile office was open in under a second.

Marines stepped through with lights and mag-boots, sweeping the room for answers—and all of their lights stopped on the same thing.

The office had been *much* less neatly shut down than the construction equipment itself. Several datapads had been tossed against walls, and none of the inevitable office equipment had been moved.

The lights were all focused on the message graffitied across the entire wall of the unit. It was in the Assini script, but the translator was already subtitling it for Octavio and his Marines.

Why try? The star will kill us all!

"Grab those datapads," Belmont ordered. "Get recordings of the entire place, paperwork, posters, the graffiti…everything."

"Can we date that graffiti?" Octavio asked.

"Probably," Belmont admitted. "Marines? Get a sample of that graffiti. See if we can date the pen or the paint or whatever it is."

One of the cameras slid across to the wall, and Octavio watched as a sample kit was pulled from inside the armor suit. A scraper took a few flakes of paint off and dropped it into the analyzer.

"Two hundred and seventy-five years ago, plus/minus three years," the Marine reported. "Can't narrow it down more than that; the paint composition isn't right for more accuracy."

"Let's see what we get from other samples," Octavio told Belmont.

"Let's get those datapads heading back to *Dauntless* for Siril-ki's people. Let's hope there's more answers there."

"I'll send that shuttle back immediately and we'll keep sweeping here," the Marine replied. "I don't know if we'll find anything, but this had to have been one of their key projects."

"Understood. Keep us updated," Octavio replied. "Chen?"

"I've got shuttles cutting into the domes as we speak," the Marine CO replied. "You were right. I didn't think I needed to tell you that."

He closed his eyes.

"Courtenay, drop the visuals from Belmont's company and bring up Chen's people," he ordered. "How bad is this mess?"

He opened his eyes again and wished he hadn't. There weren't even rotting crops in the domes. The one that Chen was entering was *empty*—everything organic in the space had been removed. Presumably to allow some attempt at recycling.

A couple of the others showed pathetic attempts at a later wave of crops, ones that had failed to be harvested in time to make a difference.

"I know, Commodore," Chen said before he could speak. "We need dates. We'll get them, but..."

"Take samples of the dome material as well," he ordered. "That should let us date the flares more accurately, too."

"Understood." She was silent for several seconds. "Sir, I've got people elsewhere in the colony stations, too. Should I be warning them?"

"Yes. We don't know how these people died in the end, but it couldn't have been pretty," Octavio admitted. "Pacifists or not, starvation may have changed all the rules in the end."

"Probably," Chen admitted. "What do we do?"

"Timelines, Major," he told her. "Because the one we got from the Validation Center leaves me asking some ugly questions. According to that graffiti, they abandoned the station at least two years before someone raided the *Shezarim* yard.

"So, either they pulled a miracle out of their asses—*without* repurposing the one half-built ship they already had—or it wasn't *these* people who took those terraforming spikes.

"In which case, who did?"

32

Octavio turned out to be wrong on one key point: no matter where the Marines went in the mix of colony platforms, they didn't find any dead Assini. There were no signs that the stations had been shut down neatly or that any kind of coordinated burial had taken place, but there were no bodies.

"Someone removed the dead," Chen told a gathered meeting later. "Given some of the trails and debris of that process, I can tell you that it fits into the timeline. I'm not quite sure *what* timeline I'm looking at, but I can tell you that someone cleaned up the dead and when."

Octavio looked over at Siril-ki. The Director was the only Assini in the room, and ki was…drooping. There was no better word for the way the centaur-like alien had rested ki's entire torso on the table in front of ki, ki's face buried in ki's hands and ki's fur disheveled and worn.

"Who would have done that?" Octavio asked ki.

"They would have tried to honor the dead at first," ki whispered. "But in the face of mass starvation, they wouldn't have been able to keep up. If someone came later…respect for the dead is a key pillar of our faith, our culture.

"Like with the memorials on Sia, they would at least have tried."

"All of which, like Chen said, fits our timeline," Octavio admitted. "Chen? Can you and D lay it out for everyone?"

"It is not a pleasant sequence of events," D noted, the AI's tones gentle. "We now have access to various databases from both Kora and Sina. None are complete and we haven't penetrated the secure files from the Sina Validation Center station, but we know roughly what the Assini were doing until the end."

The room stilled, the half-dozen humans and one Assini listening to the AI carefully. Octavio very carefully did not note that *Dauntless*'s XO, Commander Meena Das, had positioned herself next to Major Chen and was holding her lover's hand tightly under the table.

He didn't often envy his subordinates their relationships, but he could see the appeal at this particular moment.

"Three hundred and one years ago, plus/minus six months, the first solar flare rendered Sia uninhabitable and killed the entire population of the original Assini homeworld.

"Over the following twenty-one years, the survivors on Sina concentrated as much of their resources at Kora as possible. They never completed their project, as they were expecting another century or so before a flare large enough to do to Sina what was done to Sia.

"There were four flares of equivalent magnitude to the original in that time period, and all inflicted critical infrastructure damage across the star system, undermining the Kora colony project significantly. They were, nonetheless, survivable.

"Two hundred and eighty years ago, plus/minus six months, a new flare of an unexpected order of magnitude hit. Sina was rendered functionally uninhabitable and the majority of the population was killed."

Octavio turned his attention to Siril-ki. Ki was basically collapsed on the table. This cold timeline was harsh enough for the humans— and he appreciated D *not* giving the numbers of dead that came along with each of his timestamps—but this had been ki's *home*.

"The Kora colony installations became the last surviving bastion of the Assini people. They planned an evacuation project, hence retrieving *Shezarim*'s sister ship, but their focus was on their immediate survival.

"They started building the agriculture platforms immediately.

Using natural sunlight helped get the crops in a harvestable state sooner, and they calculated that even a flare of the scale that hit Sina would be insufficient to destroy the crops.

"The flare that hit two hundred and seventy-six years ago was sufficiently stronger to do so. It destroyed their entire growing crop and burned out much of the infrastructure needed to support future crops.

"With the loss of infrastructure they'd already suffered, the agriculture platforms had taken longer to complete than planned and were all but irreplaceable. Attempts were made to ration food supplies and plant new crops, but the intact ag facilities were far too few to feed the entire population.

"Worse, some of the records suggest a radiation-mutated blight managed to take hold in a significant percentage of their remaining crops. Food riots ensued. Order broke down. Computerized record-keeping on life support and suchlike continued for approximately six months after the final official records, but the last automated systems shut down two hundred and seventy-four years ago.

"At that point in time, there would have been no surviving Assini colonists."

The complete silence hung in the room like a fog for a while after that before Octavio cleared his throat.

"But if that was the end of the story, we'd have found the wreckage of riots and starvation in the stations," he noted. "And we didn't. So, there's one more piece to the timeline, yes?"

"Correct, Commodore Catalan," D replied. "We have, obviously, no confirmation of this sequence of events from Assini records, which makes our time frames more uncertain.

"Approximately four years after the cessation of automatic record-keeping aboard the stations we have examined, several of them saw their life-support systems rebooted. *Someone*—and someone familiar with Assini technology—boarded the stations and turned the life support back on to make their task easier.

"The stations that saw their life-support systems rebooted are lacking in many critical elements and systems required for their proper function," D continued. "Power cores have been removed. Computer systems stripped. In general, the larger stations appear to have been very thoroughly scavenged.

"We assess a high probability that these scavengers accessed the computer systems, much as we have, and learned of the terraforming spikes at the evacuation project yards. They then proceeded from Kora to the yards, took the spikes, and left the Assini System."

That hung in the air.

"Where did they come from?" Siril-ki demanded, raising ki's beak to stare around the room. "Who robbed my people's graves?"

"I don't know," D admitted.

"We do know they buried the dead," Chen pointed out. "They came here from somewhere else and tore apart stations for parts and supplies they could easily transport…but they took the time to bury the dead."

"Short of asking for our Matrix allies to try and set up an absolutely immense telescope at the two-hundred-and-seventy-light-year mark to try and *see* what happened, we're limited to speculation and analysis," Octavio said. "But what makes the most sense with everything we're seeing is that our scavengers were Assini.

"But they weren't from *here*."

"That's impossible. There was nowhere else," Siril-ki objected. "The whole point of *Shezarim*'s mission was that there was no one—nowhere —else. The Sentinels had made systems safe for us to colonize, but the first wave of colonists and colony ships had already been launched and lost."

"Is it possible that one of those ships survived?" Das asked. "That they didn't collide with the Construction Matrices?"

"Every one of them was headed to a Constructed World and had a tachyon communicator," Siril-ki replied. "We knew the fate of every ship."

"You had the technology to build the colony ships in massive numbers," Renaud said slowly. "Could someone have built an extra ship? One that didn't officially exist and went somewhere not on the records?"

"It would be possible, yes. But why would someone leave in secret?

Why would they have gone somewhere without a Constructed World…unless…"

Everyone in the room followed Siril-ki's thought and fell silent with ki.

"Unless they were aware that the Construction Matrices would turn on their creators," D finished for ki. "Unless the people on that ship were the *reason* the Matrices went mad."

"We already believed that someone had directly modified the Construction Matrices," Octavio said. "If they were setting up the deaths of millions, then removing themselves from the main Assini population to somewhere safe would make sense.

"They couldn't send a reaction-drive ship back and forth, but automated tachyon-punch supply ships wouldn't draw attention the same way as a giant rocket," he continued. "And then when everything went to shit *here*, they sent a ship back. Whether it was to try to help or try to conquer…who knows.

"But they came here. And they left here. And these massmurdering fucking monsters know how to recode a Matrix core, people," Octavio ground out. "They have our answers. They might, much as I want to grind them into dust and ash, be able to help us stop the Construction Matrices.

"So, I need to know where they are. We know when they were here. We know they were riding an interstellar ship, probably a first-generation Assini reaction-drive colony ship with additional weapons.

"Find me their vector, people. Because I very much want to tie these people to a wall and leave them to Siril-ki."

Pacifist or not, he suspected that ki'd break several of ki's own laws of war in that circumstance…and he wouldn't blame ki for a moment.

33

Despite a lack of further meetings with the Keepers, Amelie's second meeting with the Intendant took almost as long to arrange as the first. At least this time, she only had to walk through a ritualized shower rather than the full descent down to the lava tubes that powered the First and Final Citadel.

She was led into the same conference room–style audience chamber, once again leaving her guards at the door as she advanced to the carpet put there for people to kneel…and remained standing.

This time, the Intendant didn't even get the respectful nod. Amelie was starting to think she'd made a mistake by coming here in the first place. She was alone in front of the raised table this time, with all three of the Intendant's Keepers joining him on the table.

"You stand before the Intendant," the ruler of the Sivar intoned as he looked down at her.

He was lucky, she reflected, that the dais was as raised as it was. She was enough taller than the Intendant to leave him with bare centimeters of height advantage.

"I do," she replied shortly. "I have spoken with your Keepers, Intendant. We have spoken of worlds and history and technology. We have not spoken of alliances or terms, and I'll admit I expected to have further discussions with them before you and I met again."

"It is not the place of the Keepers of the Governance to discuss terms," the Intendant told her. "Their role was to learn for me, and they have done it. I now know more about the Builders than I ever did before—and about your Republic as well."

He gestured widely.

"I sit at the heart of the First and Final Citadel, which sits at the heart of the Sivar Governance," he said calmly. "I am more aware of the might of my Commandants than any other being in this world. With all that we have learned from you, I once again have faith in the strength of my fleets.

"If the Builders come to the Governance, they will learn the strength of our resolve and the might of our arms. I have full confidence that they would be driven from our worlds."

Amelie said nothing. She wasn't certain if the Intendant believed that, but she knew even the limited information she had given the Sivar should have suggested something *very* different. He was posturing, laying out a base position for negotiation.

She knew the style, even if it was an annoying one.

"It is clear from your discussions with my Keepers, however, that there are vulnerable worlds between my borders and these Matrices," he told her. "Your allies are in need of our help as much as yours, and we are not unwilling to provide it. It is clear your people, too, understand that it is better to fight an enemy in someone *else's* territory."

That was not how the Republic saw their current efforts, but if it got the Sivar on board, she'd let him think whatever he wanted. She'd even let him think that the Republic would turn a blind eye to his slaves, for a while at least.

"But." He held up a hand in a very human-like gesture. "For my Commandants to be ordered into the field beyond our borders, to fight and die for the worlds of other races, we must have a reason. An...*incentive*.

"And it is clear to me that your allies have nothing to offer the Governance. So tell me, Minister Amelie Lestroud, what would your *Republic* offer for our assistance in defending your dependencies?"

Amelie wished that was an inaccurate descriptor of their nearby allies. The Intendant underestimated them, in her opinion, but she could see the sense of it from his point of view.

"If the Commandants of the Sivar Governance are mercenaries, then yes, we can certainly provide payment," she replied calmly. "We have already demonstrated, I think, that we possess technologies different from your own and in some cases superior."

At some point, it would be necessary to make the point that *Watchtower* could take on multiple Sivar battleships despite being outmassed by even one of them. This wasn't that point. Not yet.

"My Commandants are not mercenaries," the Intendant countered. "They follow my commands. But *I*, Minister Lestroud, must serve the Fates' purposes. It does not aid either the Governance or myself to send my fleets to fight a war without a reason."

"Very well, then," she conceded. She wasn't surprised that it had come down to straight horse-trading, though the complete and utter silence of the Keepers was a warning sign.

"We are prepared to provide you with industrial manufacturing systems that would allow you to rapidly build space stations larger and more stable than you are currently capable of, as well as the warp-drive technology to unchain your people from the star-lanes," she told him.

The Matrix-derived manufacturing nodes her freighters were carrying were entirely capable of self-replicating with a little organic guidance—and while she was pitching them as station-builders, they were perfectly capable of building starship hulls.

From the way the Intendant slammed his hands down on the table, he wasn't making that connection.

"I do not care about your obsolescent space drive or factories to make toys for children," he snapped. "You claim you have weapons, defenses, war-fighting technologies worth the name. For these and these alone would I consider sending my Commandants to war, Minister Lestroud!"

Amelie faced him levelly.

"We reserve those for true allies, Intendant, not mercenaries," she told him. "We reserve that assistance and trade for people we can trust."

"I am the Intendant of the Sivar, the voice of the Fates," he replied. "I do not lie."

"That does not mean you can be trusted," she countered. "How many species does your Governance enslave, Intendant? How many races have you conquered? The Republic does not—*will* not—trust a slaver.

"That you have concealed this from us all along speaks only to the weaknesses and deceptions of your Governance. I not only question your trustworthiness, Intendant; I question whether your Governance would be worth the investment required to make you a worthy ally."

She smiled thinly.

"Or if your entire state is better ignored and left to collapse under its own arrogance."

For the first time while she'd been in the room, the Intendant rose to his feet.

"Seven species have knelt to the voice of the Fates," he told her. "They recognized the inevitability of the Governance, one way or another, and bound themselves to our fates for all eternity. They are irrelevant to this discussion—as are your so-called allies.

"They are the weak, and the strong rule them. The Governance is strong. I have seen no evidence of the Republic's strength beyond your own arrogance. I suggest, Minister Lestroud, that you consider your words carefully—and search your resources for an offer worthy of the Governance's aid!"

He pointed to the door.

"This audience is over. Begone."

Amelie was suddenly *very* aware of the soldiers lining the walls, guards she'd almost automatically dismissed as decoration when she'd arrived. Several of them were moving toward her now, clearly intending to physically carry her from the room if she refused to obey the Intendant's orders.

With a calm smile at the Sivar's ruler, she turned on her heel and walked back to her Marines. There was no need for indignity or violence here, after all. Not yet.

———

Amelie's Marines fell in around her as she exited the audience chamber. She was starting to look for her guide when the Sivar troops followed her out, eight of them silently falling into a diamond formation around her and her people.

"Yes?" she demanded after they stood there silently for several seconds.

"We are to see you back to your quarters," the lead trooper told her. "This way."

They gestured. Amelie considered causing trouble…but right now, her quarters was where she needed to be going.

"Very well."

She gestured for Choi to step in closer as they moved out.

"Eyes open, Sergeant," she ordered softly. "I think I may have just burned most of our warm welcome."

"That was my impression, Minister," the Marine confirmed. "Here."

Amelie hadn't been carrying the laser pistol Köhl had given her. Since she knew she was going to be disarmed, what was the point?

Apparently, Choi didn't necessarily agree. The gun she was handing over was a more standard chemical-powered slugthrower, but it slipped into the same compartment in the body armor as the laser had.

"Just in case," the Marine told her.

The guards didn't seem to have noticed the exchange, though Amelie was sure they must have. They just didn't seem to care. Most likely, they figured the small hand weapon was no threat to their body armor.

They might even be right for the slugthrower. They'd have been wrong for the laser pistol, and Amelie resolved not to leave it behind next time.

The route the soldiers led them seemed much shorter than the route their previous civilian guide had followed, and they arrived back at the house and its garden sooner than she expected.

"Everyone inside," the lead guard barked, gesturing at the Marines on the exterior of the stone building. "You are no longer permitted outside the building; we will be providing exterior security now."

"Sergeant?" one of the Marines asked Choi.

"That was not a request," the soldier replied, their gun unerringly focused on the human Marine.

That armored figure proceeded to *utterly ignore* the Sivar soldier as he waited respectfully for Choi to respond.

"We play nice, Private," the Marine finally ordered. "Move everyone inside."

There was a moment more of stillness as the two groups of soldiers glared at each other, then the Marines followed Choi's command, falling back into the house.

The diamond formation split off as they reached the door, leaving Amelie to be ushered into the building. The lead guard stood by the door as she passed through it and leveled a helmeted gaze on her as she passed through.

"You and all of your people are now restricted to the building," the soldier told her grimly. "His Greatness's orders. Anyone leaving without permission will be fired on."

Any pretense at diplomacy appeared to now be dead.

Coming here had *definitely* been a mistake.

34

———

THE GUEST HOUSE would have been large for a personal residence, but it wasn't large enough for finding any of her people to be difficult. Amelie had Köhl and Faulkner in a room within minutes of being all but kicked into the building.

"There's no point in playing nice now," she told them. "Köhl, privacy generator?"

The Marine produced the device, which resembled an upside-down spider. Each antenna emitted jamming radiation on a different frequency, overloading any electronic bugs in the space; while the central piece was a white-noise generator.

"Can we sweep the building for bugs now?" Köhl asked. "Just leaving them here has been making my neck itch."

"Do it," Amelie ordered. "If the Intendant wants to house-arrest us, I don't see a reason to keep being polite. Do we still have a link to *Watchtower*?"

"We do," Faulkner confirmed. "I don't think the Sivar realize that *Watchtower* has a live link to the rest of our fleet. They may be assuming that our coms are limited by drones, like theirs."

"That's an advantage I won't turn down," she admitted. "I'll need to talk to Captain Holmwood as soon as we're done here."

"Can she extract us?" Köhl asked.

"You're the expert," Amelie replied. "My understanding from her is that while she can't necessarily fight their entire fleet, she can stand off most of their arsenal long enough to get out. The Citadel itself is the obstacle."

The Marine officer winced.

"Fair," she conceded, then shook her head. "We've got less than ten percent of my people down here, but the shuttles left aboard *Watchtower* and her escorts aren't designed for heavy ground assault. They're *armed*, but this mountain..."

She shook her head.

"The Marines need orbital fire support from *Watchtower* to neutralize the defenses, and that would risk us down here. Plus, *Watchtower* doesn't carry bombardment munitions. Her engineers could fabricate them in twenty-four hours or so, but..."

"But unless they can build something far more precise than our regular arsenal, they can't clear enough of a path to extract us," Amelie concluded. "I'll double-check that with Holmwood, but it looks like our only real option is to play along with the Sivar for now and hope that the Intendant doesn't want to start a war."

The Republic didn't need another war, but Amelie wasn't sure she'd be able to talk her husband or President Nyong'o out of coming for her.

"It was a damn mistake to come here," she admitted aloud for the first time. "These people were never going to be useful allies."

"Not in their current state, anyway," Faulkner conceded. "On the other hand, they were the first multistellar state we'd seen since leaving home. It would have been irresponsible for us *not* to come here."

"Your old colors are showing, Roger," Amelie told her aide with a snort. The Confederacy had never hesitated to arrange regime changes on its member worlds when they'd grown troublesome.

"Maybe," he conceded. "But I'm not the person in the room who organized the revolution against the *last* fascist state we all knew."

"Find me twenty rebel factions to get lined up and moving in the same direction, and I could cause trouble," she replied. "But otherwise, I'm just one woman."

The conversation was interrupted by a knock on the door. One of the Marines stuck her head in a moment later.

"Sirs? We've got a party at the door and we're not quite sure *what* to do with them."

"What kind of party?" Köhl demanded before Amelie could ask.

"Well, I think they're the cleaners…but they're not Sivar."

———

THE SIX BEINGS on the front step, under the guidance of a Sivar staffer and watched by the quartet of Sivar soldiers guarding the door, appeared to be the race that Rode had called Croni. They were delicately built tall aliens with four legs and visibly clipped large wings.

"You do not have permission to bar us from our own ground," the staffer snapped when Amelie appeared.

"Get over it," she suggested. "Either I am an ambassador and this is my ground, or I am a prisoner and you aren't willing to bleed for that."

They'd have to disarm her Marines to manage that, and they'd find out just how effective the low-profile power armor and light pulse rifles the Marines had brought down with them were in that case.

"What is this?" she demanded, gesturing at the Croni.

"Cleaning workers," the staffer replied. "Workers of the *right* tier for that work."

Someone, it seemed, was bitter about having to scrub toilets for the last couple of weeks.

"They may enter," Amelie said with a glance at the aliens. They were almost butterfly-esque in coloration. She wished she could read their body language. "Your guards may not. *You* will be searched if you wish to enter."

The Siva drew banself up to ban's full hundred and fifty-two centimeters of height.

"You would not dare!"

"This morning, I would have said your Intendant would not dare impose house arrest on us," Amelie said sweetly. "You can send the Croni in alone or you can be searched. Your choice."

"There will be consequences for this," the Siva muttered as ban submitted to the search. A Marine swept ban away as the doors closed, leaving Amelie and two Marines alone with the Croni.

"Do you understand the Sivar language?" Amelie asked them, using the translator to speak in that tongue. "I can program a new language into this device, but I would need data."

The Croni looked at each other, clearly unsure what to do.

"We...clean," one finally said in halting Sivar. "We understand orders. Not speak."

She waited for a moment for any of them to speak again, but then bowed her head.

"I understand," she allowed. "I will not cause you trouble. Just know that so long as I am in charge, you are safe inside these walls."

That seemed to get through, but it wasn't much. The Croni split into groups of two to take on their cleaning project...but one of them drooped a wing onto her shoulder in what she suspected was a gesture of acknowledgement.

"And just what was that?" Faulkner asked softly from behind her.

She turned around and jerked her gaze toward the ceiling, reminding him that they were outside the privacy field and being bugged.

"Acknowledging the staff," she said lightly. "It never hurts."

And maybe, *just maybe*, the effort would get passed down the line to the rebels she knew had to exist somewhere.

———

AMELIE HAD BARELY MADE it out of the entrance hallway when she heard another set of knocking. Not waiting to see if the Marines called her back, she turned around in time to see the Marines open the door and find Keeper Rode standing there.

The Keeper walked into the room like she owned it—which, arguably, she did—but also left her guards outside.

"I need to speak to Lestroud," she barked.

"And I need to search you before you go one step further into the building," the Marine replied. "After that, it's up to the Minister."

"I am the Keeper of the First and Final Citadel," Rode snapped, then stopped and chuckled. "Even if I was armed, guardian, I guarantee you I would miss a target I was touching."

"Search her anyway," Amelie ordered as she stepped into Rode's line of sight. "No exceptions, I think."

"As you wish," the Siva replied. "The insult will not be forgotten."

"We weren't the ones that started with the insults and deceptions," Amelie said cheerfully as the soldiers ran a scanning wand over the Siva.

"She's clear."

"Say your piece, Keeper," Amelie told Rode as the Marines stepped clear.

"We must speak in private," the Keeper replied. "There is an office there." She pointed. "It is large enough for us and several of your guardians."

Amelie snorted. "Sergeant Nguyen? Can I borrow one of your Marines?"

"Zahn, go with the Minister," the Sergeant replied instantly.

Amelie gestured for Rode to lead the way. The Keeper was clearly familiar with the layout of the guest house, probably more than she was.

They stepped into the bare stone room, and Rode glanced around it with faint disdain.

"The last time I was in here, they'd decorated," she told Amelie. "Guardian, grab the chairs, please."

The Marine glanced at Amelie, who nodded assent. Her own attention was focused on the Keeper. Rode was fiddling with one of the stones on the wall—a stone that suddenly slipped out to reveal a very modern-looking control panel.

A few seconds later, shutters closed over the inside of the window and a faint ringing sensation settled into Amelie's teeth.

"These guest houses were built to serve many purposes," Rode told her. "Sometimes, secure discussions were part of those services, and the systems are maintained."

She gestured Amelie to a chair.

"The Intendant offered you everything you asked for," she continued flatly. "Fleets, starships, support…you came prepared to give us weapons and starships for that aid, but when all that you asked for was offered, you refused.

"Who do you think you *are*?"

"I think I am the ambassador plenipotentiary for a star nation that is built on a code of morals as well as a code of laws," Amelie replied. "Codes that, so far as I can tell, your people are entirely lacking.

"In a full and complete alliance, I might provide the Sivar weapons technology—but I would hesitate to seal that alliance, because of your people's crimes. My nation knows dictators and slavers, Keeper Rode. We are at this end of the galaxy because we chose to stand against our own.

"I see no reason to bow to *yours*."

"You cannot challenge the Intendant," Rode said softly, the harshness suddenly draining from her voice. "Even to fail the Intendant is death. His will *is* the Governance."

"Which is why Istila is Keeper of the Keys of Peace now, not Dorost," Amelie replied. "Even your senior leaders' lives hang by the threads of one man's ego. Why would I ever negotiate with a state that unstable? *How* could I negotiate with you?

"Certainly, I could never hand weapons over to a madman."

Rode was silent, the shadow of her armor plating allowing her eyes to burn brightly.

"You are a small nation, far away," she finally said. "The Governance is dozens of stars; the Commandants wield dozens of warships. You *cannot* defy the Intendant."

Amelie considered her next words very carefully. Rode had told her that the space was secure, which was interesting in and of itself, but she was also digging for something. The ex-revolutionary *knew* this conversation. It had just taken her a while to realize what was going on.

"The Intendant has no idea who he is *fucking* with," Amelie told Rode. "You are so impressed with your conquests and your fleets that you have no idea how dark the tunnels you're wandering down are.

"If your Intendant betrays our trust further, the Governance will burn. I am but one woman, but I speak for the Republic. If the Intendant goes too far, his ego will be no shield against what is to come."

The room was silent for a long time, then Rode coughed.

"That's probably a good thing," she conceded. "I think we're done here, Minister. I have delivered my Intendant's warning."

She bowed her head slightly.

"I suggest, Minister Lestroud, that you be very careful. We walk on dangerous ground under the eyes of the Fates."

Amelie waved her out and stayed in the room, watching as the shutters slowly reopened.

Under the eyes of the Fates. If those were the same Fates that the Intendant was the voice of, she had words for them.

On the other hand, unless she was *severely* mistaken, one of the senior members of the Governance had just tried to sound out if the Republic would back a coup against the current Intendant.

Voice of the Fates or not, it sounded like the Intendant's government was *far* from stable!

35

The answer had to be fuel.

"We've spent two days going round and round in circles, trying to work out how to identify our strangers and where they went," Octavio noted as his people gathered. "I think we need to try a different tack. We need to consider the physical limitations of the ship we're probably looking at.

"Siril-ki, D, do we have schematics and specifications for the first-wave colony ships?" he asked. "I have a thought based on how *Shezarim* was built, but she was newer and more advanced than our stranger would be."

"It appears that I have full schematics of the phase-one colony ships in the databank from *Shezarim*," D confirmed after several moments. "Siril-ki, do you know of any reason why those would be lacking or incomplete?"

Ki neighed a laugh. It wasn't entirely a happy noise, but Octavio didn't expect happy sounds from his Assini companions right now.

"Unless there's something in the new files, that's all I would have access to," ki pointed out.

"Show us, D," Octavio ordered.

There were some definite similarities between *Shezarim* and the holographic ship that appeared in the middle of the conference room, but many differences too. She wasn't as big, for one, and her engines were proportionally larger.

"She seems a lot less streamlined than *Shezarim*," Renaud said. "I'm guessing she wasn't intended to go as fast?"

"*Shezarim* wasn't designed to go as fast as we took her," Siril-ki admitted. "But she was designed for the particle densities of point nine seven cee. Between that streamlining and her armor, she survived near-cee velocities for far longer than we had any right to expect.

"The colony ships were designed for a peak velocity of point six cee," she continued. "They would accelerate to that velocity over the course of approximately sixteen of your hours."

"*Shezarim* was capable of significantly greater acceleration and had more efficient engines," D noted. "The colony ship's engines and internal compensation systems had lower thrust-to-weight and required a lot of fuel for the voyage."

"They couldn't turn around or adjust course," Octavio murmured. "That was why they were doomed when they learned about the Matrices…and that's what we were missing, people. Wherever they came from, *they didn't have the fuel to go back.*"

His staff and Siril-ki looked at him in surprised understanding.

"Presumably, they didn't come here with a million colonists and the entire infrastructure for a colony aboard, so they'd have had some fuel left for maneuvering around the system—but they had to refuel here if they were going to get back.

"So, where did they do that?"

"Not at the evacuation yards," Siril-ki noted. "We were lucky in that *Shezarim* had been fueled before the flare. Our fuel supplies were delivered by tanker from Kora."

"There was nothing at the evacuation yards to suggest that the ship left the system from there," Renaud noted. "If anything, what data we had there suggested that they came back here."

"To refuel, if you're right," Das agreed, the XO already pulling up data on her own tattoo-comp. "The Assini moved a lot of their cloud-scoops into a single cluster, specifically positioned in an orbit where it would never be on the star-ward side of the gas giant."

"It's still there?" Octavio asked.

"Some of it," *Dauntless*'s XO admitted, flipping the scan of the station into the hologram. "It looks like chunks of it fell off, but most of those are still orbiting in tandem with the facility. The cloudscoops themselves are the biggest concern—without someone actively managing thrust to counterbalance, the drag will pull the entire thing down into the gas giant."

"My calculations suggest a sixty-five plus/minus three percent probability that the drag effect should have already pulled the entire station into the gas giant," D interjected. "That leads me to a high-probability conclusion that someone made an effort to stabilize the station over the long term."

"There's no power sources over there," Das replied. "But if someone had left a computer running with access to the thrusters and a minimal stabilization program…it would still be here even if the computer ran out of power long ago."

"And that computer would need sensors, wouldn't it?" Octavio asked. "People, I think we have another target for Major Chen's Marines."

The Marine leaned past her girlfriend and studied the slowly-falling-apart station in the hologram.

"Biggest engines are…here and here, right?" she asked, touching the assemblages the Assini had attached to the cloudscoops. "Would they be using the station's original computers or a secondary installation?"

"I think our optimal case is that they installed a new computer and sensor array at the engine structure," Octavio agreed. "There are a lot of small thrusters on the station—drag's a problem for any cloudscoop, so they would all have had them—so those two big engines were probably intended to handle the entire assembly."

"They might have even been added by the strangers rather than part of the original structure," D suggested. "Medium-order probability, but we wouldn't be able to tell without much closer examination."

"Well, then, let's get to that closer examination," Octavio said. "Renaud, we'll move *Dauntless* over herself while sending the strike cruisers and freighters to clear space. The last thing we want is to have enough ships present to risk accidentally disrupting the orbit."

He could read the orbital vector charts as well as anyone. Without *some* kind of intervention, the station only had another thirty years at most. Even his shuttles landing could cost the station years of survival if they weren't careful.

<hr>

CHEN WAS PROBABLY GETTING sick of having Octavio virtually riding on her shoulder, even if he *was* doing as well as he hoped in keeping out of her hair. His office currently showed him three images: a holographic display of the entire cloudscoop assembly and *Dauntless*'s position five hundred kilometers away, the view from Chen's shoulder-camera, and the view from the shuttle's camera.

Spaceborne structures only took so much damage from time, but they did take that damage. Close orbit of a gas giant was only technically "space" by most definitions, as well. There was a lot of pitting and scarring on the station the shuttles were approaching, and the cameras highlighted it.

"There is no *way* this place would still be here unless something had been working to keep it up," Chen muttered on her private channel to him. "I know D says thirty percent chance, but chunks of this are *inside* Kora's atmosphere. In a geostationary orbit without power? I don't believe it would last a century."

"The evidence disagrees with you, Major," Octavio pointed out. "Even if our strangers did set up a system, I doubt it lasted three centuries without anyone checking on it, and we haven't seen any sign of a second visit."

"Which is weird enough on its own, right?" the Marine asked. "I mean, they might have come here to try and save people, but it clearly turned into a scavenging expedition, and there's still a *lot* in this system to scavenge."

"How much time would you want to spend poking around Earth for supplies if it looked like this?" he asked.

Chen was silent for several seconds as the shuttle dipped toward their target. The more Octavio saw it, the more he wondered if the strangers had added it themselves. It looked like one of the engine assemblages from *Shezarim*'s sister ship back in the main colony. The Kora colonists might have grabbed it, but they could just as easily have relied on the original thrusters from each cloudscoop.

"I see your point, sir," Chen admitted. "Making contact in two minutes." She paused. "Personal question, sir."

Octavio chuckled.

"Is this really the time, Major?" he asked.

"I haven't had much of a chance to sit down with you without Meena in the room, sir," the Marine admitted. "All of this…the death, the loss, the ghosts. Makes you really aware of your mortality."

"I know," he agreed.

"I checked. Regs say that Captain Renaud can't perform a marriage ceremony aboard without special permission—but *you* could either provide that permission or perform the ceremony yourself. Sir."

Octavio paused, taking in the image of the slowly approaching shuttles as he parsed Chen's request.

"Are you asking if I'd be willing to perform a wedding ceremony for you and Commander Das?" he asked. "Should you ask the Commander first?"

"Not much point proposing if I can't arrange a wedding, is there?" the Marine asked.

Octavio snorted.

"*If* she says yes," he said pointedly, "I would be *delighted* to perform the ceremony. Now find me a destination, Major, so we can do so while underway."

The shuttles' boarding airlocks latched onto the station.

"Oorah, Commodore."

36

Plasma cutters sliced through the hull of the engine assembly, and the Marines charged through on the heels of the collapsing metal. By now, they expected the cutter to take longer than it should have.

That delay tied back to Octavio's assessment of where the engine had come from. *Shezarim* and the other evacuation ships from that fleet had been armored to stand up to potential Matrix attacks and near-cee velocities. The engine towers that had been added to the cloudscoop station were from the half-built colony ships.

"We're clear and on board," a report echoed on the open channel. "No sign of resistance, no sign of power anywhere."

"We're not expecting power, people," Chen replied. "But somewhere in this hunk of metal is a computer that was telling the engine what to do. We want that computer."

"This appears to be one of the secondary engine nacelles from *Shezarim*'s sister ship," D inserted into the channel. "I'm dropping waypoints into your system for where the control systems would have been while it was attached to the colony ship."

"That's what I was hoping for, D," Chen said. "All right, people, we've got six blinking lights and four squads. Move in groups, check out the waypoint closest to you.

"We'll probably need to boot up computers before we get answers, so I *hope* you were paying attention when the Assini told you how to do that!"

Octavio was only getting half of the conversation between Chen and her people, but he really doubted that any of her people had been slacking off when their alien allies had told them what to do with the computers.

He trusted his Marines more than that. So, he was certain, did Major Chen Zhou.

Seconds ticked by in silence and he realized Chen had muted the microphone on her link to him as she moved deeper into the station. Everything she said was still being recorded by D, and if the AI thought he needed to know what she said, D would play it for him.

But it was one fewer concern on her side as the Marines dug deeper into a dead alien space station. The whole place was creepy. Like the stations they'd swept in the main colony, there were no bodies. The strangers had buried the dead in the gas giant, leaving the platform looking like it had never even been occupied.

Unlike most of the colony stations, there was no atmosphere in the section the Marines were digging through. Octavio was starting to wonder about that when Chen turned a corner and found her team staring into a massive breach.

He checked the map. One of D's waypoints had been right in the middle of the wreckage.

"You seeing this, sir?" she reopened the channel to ask.

"I am. I'm hoping that particular computer wasn't the one we needed."

"Team two already hit their first waypoint. That computer was removed, so that's at least one down," Chen replied. "And I guess this one is down too. We'll have to jet across. If you get motion-sick, I'd suggest turning the camera off, Commodore."

"I've done engineering EVAs in worse, Major," Octavio pointed out. "Carry on."

"Commodore," D interjected. "Major. Before you launch off, a moment of your time. Team three may have located our target."

Chen paused, making half-seen hand gestures to hold up her team.

"Show me," she ordered.

A fourth image appeared in Octavio's hologram. It had been a secondary thrust control center once, a minor computer relay of the type more often used by crew checking their emails than actually working.

Now the computer hardware from at least two other secondary centers had been added in. Multiple computer cores were wired together in a crude aggregate that Octavio assumed had worked at one point.

Thick wires ran from the cores into the conduits beneath them that would link to fuel lines and the rest of the machinery required to control the big fusion engine.

"All right. We have a center point," Chen noted. "We need to find the sensors and the power. Team three," she linked to her people. "Start *carefully* dismantling that mess and packing it up.

"Everyone else will track the lines to see if we can find the sensors and power supply it was using. We can probably live without that data, but since I'm *here*, I see no reason not to get it."

"Well done, Major," Octavio murmured. "Let's hope there's some answers in there, shall we?"

———

CRACKING the computers proved surprisingly easy after that. The Assini computer techs had taught the Marines well, and they had everything up and running in the shuttle on the way back.

"There's no security on the cores," Chen reported as the shuttles began to touch down. "There's a lot of data in here and my people aren't data-search experts, but everything is intact and functioning. Better than I expected, to be honest."

"Someone was expecting to come back," Octavio concluded. "Your point stands, Major. Something weird is going on. We'll have D and the Assini get into the system as soon as you bring it aboard. Let's not power it down just yet."

"We hooked it up to a portable power core. We'll be fine."

"Well done, Major. Once the computers are in the Assini's hands, you can stand your people down." He smiled. "I believe there's a conversation you have to have on your down shift, yes?"

"We'll have it in the my little ponies' hands in ten," Chen promised. "I'll be keeping an eye on everything while I arrange that conversation. Don't break it. I'm not sure I can find another one."

"If nothing else, there's a second engine tower on the cloudscoop station," Octavio replied.

He couldn't dignify Chen's response by calling it actual words.

"D, any concerns with the data search?" he asked the AI after the channel with Chen cut.

"I've been doing preliminary surveys via the Marines' link," the Matrix told him. "The assistance of Commander Das's and Director Siril-ki's people will be essential to make certain we've located our target, but I can tell you some details immediately."

"Carry on," Octavio agreed.

"As we expected, this engine was networked with the other nacelle from the colony ship. They appear to have been added two hundred and seventy years ago, during the strangers' visit to the colony. They were clearly intended to be a long-term solution, but they also obviously expected to be able to recharge the power core every hundred years at most."

"So, it ran for a hundred years?" Octavio asked.

"That was the apparently designed intention," D agreed. "The computer managed to save fuel and power in its thrust calculations and operated for one hundred and eighty years before running out of fuel. The station as we currently see it has been unpowered and without orbital adjustments for just over ninety years."

"And it's still here." He shook his head. "Your creators built well."

"They did. With the sensors available, we should be able to identify the stranger's ship and exit vector relatively easily. Locating the partic-ular time slot should only take a few…"

It wasn't in an AI's nature to trail off.

"D?" Octavio asked.

"We have cracked the security codes on the Validation Center computer cores," the AI reported. "I have identified the tachyon communication codes and frequencies for the Sentinel Matrices and sent out base-level ping codes.

"These should trigger automatic responses without attracting attention. Director Siril-ki and I have worked up the codes over the last few weeks."

"D, you're dodging around something," Octavio pointed out. He knew the AI better than he knew most people at this point.

"There should be dozens of Sentinel AIs in various degrees of active status," the AI told him. "I have received ping responses from three.

"All are in the same system, twelve point six light-years from Assini."

Octavio swallowed hard.

"Find me the vector for that stranger ship," he told the AI. "And then get me everything you can on the system the Sentinels are in.

"Because I would bet this *battlecruiser* that vector leads to that system."

37

WARPED SPACE MIGHT HAVE BECOME LESS uncomfortable than it had once been, but there was still little to reduce the unending *boredom* involved in the process. The more comfortable it had become, the more willing Isaac and his officers had been to commit to longer flights without occasionally dropping out for sanity breaks.

Two weeks to the target location of the RCM was an "easy" jaunt by that new standard, but it was still two weeks in a vaguely uncomfortable side-reality where nothing could touch you.

Their biggest limitation was that the tachyon communicators didn't work while under warp. The ESF didn't have a standard yet on how long was too long in warp, but Isaac was starting to suspect that it would end up being based on how long a ship was out of communication.

Looking at his inbox as *Vigil* and her companions arrived at the rendezvous point outside the RCM's home base, he was starting to think that two weeks was too long!

Catalan's reports from Assini had always made for sobering listening and reading, but this was something else again. They'd suspected that *someone* had modified the core code of the AI Matrices they could reach—the pattern of failures wasn't right to be entirely tachyon-punch degradation, though they'd only realized that when able to compare to core code that *was* punch-degraded—but Isaac had assumed it had been an unknown third party.

Not a faction of Assini that had knowingly arranged for tens of millions of their siblings to be sent to their deaths. It wasn't a very Assini thing to do!

Or was it?

Isaac sighed as he turned that thought over in his head. Setting up a situation where a robot did all of the killing for you without you raising a finger…yeah, that *was* very Assini. The solution to every problem was a robot with a gun.

Even if the job didn't *require* a gun, evidence suggested.

The situation in the Assini System was so far beyond anything Isaac could influence that it was almost irrelevant to the task at hand. If Siril-ki had managed to convince a few dozen Sentinel Matrices to start tachyon-punching their way out to join him, *that* would have changed the math.

The punch couldn't move anything alive—even frozen embryos had a massive loss rate that the Matrices countered with a mind-staggering amount of cloning—but it was the fastest FTL method available to Isaac's allies. Two hours to travel a light-year would have seen any Sentinels they recruited arrive at Vista in twenty-five days.

He'd have waited for that. He couldn't wait for the Sivar ships he didn't know would be coming or how long they could take—and he was glad he hadn't.

It didn't look like he was ever going to get Sivar battleships now. Holmwood's report on the developments on Aris made for nerve-wracking reading. Both as the leader of the Republic's military and as Amelie Lestroud's husband, he found the news of the Intendant's latest tantrum terrifying.

Fortunately, the Admiral could justify sating the husband's worry today.

"Naveed?" he opened a channel to the flag deck. "Can you get me a tachyon-com channel to *Watchtower*? I need a live update from someone on the scene of what the *hell* is going on there."

"Yes, sir!" Commander Hashemi replied. "I'll let you know when I have a link to Captain Holmwood? Or should I hold until I have a channel with Minister Lestroud?"

Isaac wasn't really surprised his people were paying enough attention to the briefings to know he'd want to talk to his wife.

"Get me a link to Amelie," he confirmed. "I need to know what's on her mind."

He was sitting two light-months from the machine he'd been chasing for two years with a fleet of almost a hundred and fifty warships and a grim, sinking feeling that he needed to be twenty-five light-years away.

———

Isaac had known that Amelie was all right, but it was still reassuring to see her face when her holographic image appeared. He couldn't keep himself from reaching out to touch the image of her face, his fingers inevitably disrupting the image.

"Admiral. My love," she greeted him, leaning her head into his hand unconsciously before both of them laughed.

"Amelie. How are you and your people holding up?" he asked.

"Two days under house arrest on an alien planet while the math says that nobody can get me out," she told him. "I'm trying to make friends with our cleaners without getting them in trouble, but the non-Sivar staff here are *terrified*."

"From the reports, I can't blame them," Isaac admitted. "*Explosive collars?* I mean…we recognized the tech for a reason, I suppose."

His understanding was that the use of equivalent systems had been restricted to condemned prisoners at penal colonies, but he wasn't going to pretend they'd never built it.

"I think they realize we're potential friends," Amelie replied. "Whether that percolates back to potential allies for *us* here, I don't know. I can't really justify privacy generators while I'm talking to the maid, after all."

"You have one up now?" he asked.

"I do. I'm not one hundred percent sure that the link to *Watchtower* is secure, but they aren't *acting* like they know I'm in contact with our fleet."

"All right." He shook his head, trying to consider the situation.

"I'm twenty-five light-years from Sivar-One," he reminded her. "That's five weeks. If I was still at Skree-Skree, we'd be just over three and a half weeks away. Even if I head straight for Sivar-Prime, I'm looking at seven weeks before I'm in position to do anything."

"You can't start a war for me, Isaac," Amelie replied. "You certainly can't drag our allies into this."

"Isaac Lestroud sure as hell cannot start a war to pull his wife, Amelie Lestroud, out of the clutches of the vile alien," Isaac agreed dryly. "*Admiral* Lestroud can sure as hell launch an extraction operation to pull *Foreign Minister* Lestroud out of the hands of a hostile power that has detained our ambassador.

"Even if you managed to convince me it was my duty to let you die, Emilia would give me my marching orders an hour later," he continued. "It's not just personal, Amelie. It's political.

"Whether we like them or not, the Sivar exist. Is letting them imprison and murder our ambassador going to help our future relations with the Governance?"

The call was silent.

"No," she conceded. "I've got wheels moving here—I *think*. I'm not sure I need you to show up with a battle fleet just yet, though I'll admit that I'd rather negotiate from the flag deck of a battlecruiser in the middle of that fleet at this point.

"The Governance is almost as large a problem as the Rogue Matrices. We need to plan for them in future."

"Or we need to deal with them now," Isaac argued. "You are the Foreign Minister of the Republic. The Ambassador on the scene. If you tell me that you're going to be fine, that you can extract yourself from this situation without the ESF making a major deployment, I'll trust you."

He shook his head. He didn't expect her to say that, but if there was *anyone* who could pull that off it would be Amelie Lestroud.

"I'll trust you," he repeated. "But can you really tell me that?"

"Isaac, the reports *I* see say you're in position to launch a major offensive against the RCM," she told him. "You can't walk away from that for me."

He met her gaze, letting *his* silence fill the call now.

"We might lose," he finally told her. "We'd be better off with another year's worth of construction in the hands of our allies. We'd be better off with *Dauntless* and *Watchtower* in our order of battle and the last of the old ships decommissioned to bring more *Fortitude*s online.

"We'd be better off with an upgraded Sivar fleet at our side and answers from the Assini. Not knowing what any of that is going to look like, we could push the attack…but I can't do that with an enemy at my back, measuring the knife.

"So, if you can't turn the Sivar into allies or at least complete neutrals, *I can't launch this attack.*"

Leaving an RCM intact was his worst nightmare. He was there, he'd gathered the massed fleets of his allies…but they had to choose what enemy they could deal with.

"We should have left them be," Amelie said.

"Could we have? Really?" Isaac asked. "A multistellar nation on the edge of our area of operations? Ally or enemy, we needed to know. And if they're not an ally, we need to neutralize them."

She bowed her head.

"I can't speak to the military situation," she murmured. "I certainly don't think this is a battle you can order our allies into. But…"

He waited.

"I don't believe I am going to be able to extract myself and my people without additional assistance from the ESF," she admitted. "Even if I do, I am unlikely to do so in a way that will see the Sivar neutralized as a threat. The Intendant is apparently a mad god-king and I don't see a way out of conflict with him."

"Then I don't have a choice, Amelie," Isaac told her. "You're right in that I can't order our allies into this fight. I will *consult* with our allies and I will make certain that, whatever happens, this RCM doesn't get away.

"But once all that is done, I am coming for you. And if the Intendant has half a brain, he'll have all of our people sent on their way with a damn gift basket before I get there."

38

Isaac was late to his own meeting. As a rule, he did everything within his power to make sure he was never late for *anything*, but he'd never been late to a meeting he'd called himself—and definitely not to a meeting involving fleet commanders from four different species and a collection of AIs that probably counted as a fifth.

"Apologies for the delay, everyone," he told the gathered officers as he stepped into the conference room, quickly taking a seat next to Vice Admiral Giannovi. There were two human flag officers in the room, but Commodore Anthony Helm wasn't nearly as well known to Isaac or most of the aliens as Giannovi was.

He'd been one of the handful of officers elevated to flag rank as the ESF had expanded. His file was solid and Giannovi had sworn by the man, but Isaac didn't know the big black man as well as he'd like.

The rest of the room was full of holographic projections of his alien subcommanders. Lord of Seven Stars ThreeHeart remained in command of the dramatically expanded Skree-Skree contingent. Similarly, Third-Among-Singers Swimmer-Under-Sunlit-Skies remained in command of a Vistan contingent that had more than doubled in strength.

Since the Tohnbohn didn't *have* ranks, Isaac wasn't surprised

Oohoon was still their contact. He wasn't entirely convinced that the big shelled alien was actually *in command* of the Tohnbohn contingent in the same way as the other officers were, but they spoke for the Tohnbohn in these meetings.

Combat Coordination Matrix ZDX-175-25 was in a similar boat. Command of the Matrix contingent was exercised by a networked gestalt intelligence, not by any individual Matrix, but Twenty-Five was the one who communicated with Isaac for the group.

"Our understanding is that unfortunate news arrived from Minister Amelie Lestroud," Oohoon said, the whalesong of their true voice underlying the slow translation of their speech. "The negotiations with our hoped-for new ally do not go well?"

"That is the crux of the matter, yes," Isaac confirmed. He kept his gaze level as he looked out at his officers. "As of two days ago, the negotiations with the Sivar Governance have collapsed. Ambassador Lestroud and her staff have been detained on the surface of the Sivar capital.

"We have every reason to believe that the Sivar will shortly attempt to capture *Watchtower*." He shrugged. "They will fail, but we now face a threat where we'd hoped to have an ally or at least a neutral. That requires us to reassess our current tactical and strategic position."

A tapped command on his tattoo-comp brought up a floating hologram of the fleet's entire strength.

"Our current fleet consists of one hundred and forty-eight combat platforms, accompanied by forty freighters," he noted. "Thirty-nine of those ships are capital ships. Against any mobile force that the Rogue can deploy, I would not question our victory.

"I *include* in that calculation, people, the knowledge that the Rogue possesses at least *four* of their new dreadnoughts."

Another command wiped the fleet in favor of the latest intelligence on the Rogue's system.

"Against *this*?" He hesitated, then shook his head. "We knew when we set out from Skree-Skree that this was risky. Now we have a closer look at the defenses. The Rogue has as many Matrix combat units in that system as we have in our fleet.

"Plus three dreadnoughts. Plus massive orbital fortifications. *Plus* the Rogue's own hull, which at least matches a dreadnought in firepower."

The room and the holographic attendees were silent and Isaac looked around.

"You've all done the math," he conceded. "You wouldn't deserve your commands if you hadn't. Does *anyone* in this room think we have a better-than-even chance of victory here?"

He waited.

"Or that if we are victorious, this fleet will be anything but a spent force?" he continued. He waited again.

"No," ThreeHeart finally chirped at him. "But this machine tried to kill my planet. What else can we do?"

"I don't know," Isaac agreed. "That's why we're here…except that now there is a knife pointed at our backs. We don't know if the Sivar Governance can find new star-lanes fast enough to reach our territory —but we also don't know they can't.

"The last thing we can afford is for the Skree-Skree or Bohon Systems to come under attack while we have the majority of your fleets here—or even after we've all willingly sacrificed our lives on the altar of destroying the Rogue."

He couldn't read Skree-Skree body language, let alone Tohnbohn, but he hoped that point struck home.

"Refuge is relatively safe. The Republic is unreachable for them, but Skree-Skree and Bohon are potentially at risk."

Bohon had two battlecruisers with full escort groups there to protect the Tohnbohn home system. Skree-Skree only had half a dozen strike cruisers.

"I cannot ask you to leave your systems defenseless in the face of a new-found threat," Isaac told them. "If I thought we could fight the Rogue and we'd all go home, I'd be standing here insisting we launch the attack. Finish off the Rogue, then deal with the Sivar."

"But you fear we might not be able to defeat the Sivar after fighting the Rogue," Oohoon concluded. "The probabilities suggest you are correct. This was to be the meeting to plan the strike against the Rogue. What do you suggest now?"

"Firstly, Lord of Seven Stars ThreeHeart, you *must* consult with your government," Isaac told the bird-rat hybrid who commanded two of his battlecruisers. "In their place, I'd call both your capital ships home, but I won't speak for your government. Oohoon, I'd suggest you talk to your people as well, though Bohon is better defended."

He shook his head.

"The Republic has an ambassador plenipotentiary in the hands of a hostile power," he said quietly. "I have no choice but to move against the Sivar Governance. Since I *cannot* justify moving against the Rogue first, I have no choice but to leave this system unattacked.

"Twenty-Five."

"How would you have us assist you, Admiral?" the Matrix's holographic avatar—an intentionally stylized figure that looked like an Assini wearing the armor of a historical human knight—asked.

"Can you interdict the system?" Isaac asked. "Make certain that anything *less* than the Rogue's full force doesn't leave and that we know where the Rogue goes if it leaves?"

"Our tachyon-punch drives are now approximately eleven percent more efficient than those available to the Rogue, and our long-range passive tachyon scanners are now approximately twenty-six percent more efficient than those available to the Rogue," Twenty-Five told him. "We can get inside their command-and-control loop and intercept any force that attempts to leave."

"You can besiege the system," Isaac concluded. "I need you to do that."

"It would require all of our combat platforms and the majority of our lesser units," Twenty-Five warned. "We would not be able to contribute significant firepower to your movement against the Sivar."

Isaac exhaled slowly.

"I trust you, Twenty-Five," he told the Matrix AI. He wasn't even dissembling. He wasn't a priest, so his opinion was out on whether the Matrices had souls, but he *knew* them to be people—and damn fine people at that.

"But I'd hesitate to ask the Assini to modify your targeting protocols to let you fire on sentient organics, regardless of how much trouble the Sivar have caused. I'm not even sure that the Assini here would *do* that if we asked."

"Even without modification, our ships would be able to engage any vessels that attacked yours," Twenty-Five noted. "We would be neither able to participate in or permit ground bombardment, but we are not under the impression this would be a problem."

That…made sense, Isaac supposed. The combat platforms had been designed to protect the Construction Matrices from people who might try to attack them or steal them. The protocols the Rogues had lost said they couldn't Construct inhabited worlds or commit mass murder, not that they couldn't defend themselves.

"I appreciate your offer," he told Twenty-Five. "But you'd be more valuable to us all here. And there is another point I must raise."

Isaac looked around at his allies.

"Our alliance is against the Matrices," he reminded them. "I want you to be able to protect yourselves if the Sivar become a threat, but Amelie Lestroud is not your ambassador. She's not your foreign minister.

"She is mine. *I* am obligated, as Admiral of the ESF, to retrieve her. I *cannot*, per the terms of our alliances, order this combined fleet into action against the Sivar. And I would not.

"I will be taking the ESF ships to Sivar space with me. That's all. I ask that the rest of you work to secure your own home systems and to help Twenty-Five keep the Rogue contained. The Exilium Space Fleet needs to go extract our ambassador.

"I won't ask you to come with me."

It took him a moment to realize what the deep, booming, echoing whalesong that cut off anyone else speaking was. His translator didn't provide any words to replace Oohoon's laughter, because it *was* laughter. There were no words.

"All of our leaders met Amelie Lestroud, Admiral Lestroud," the Tohnbohn told him in their slow voice with its underlying song. "All of them. I will accompany you aboard *Peacemaker* with her battle group. My other vessels will remain here with Twenty-Five."

"I will discuss with my superiors," ThreeHeart chirped, "but I will argue with the Grand Speaker that we should also send a battlecruiser group."

"We owe your Republic dirt and blood and water," Swimmer-

Under-Sunlit-Skies added. "I will leave the Fifth-Among-Singers and her three battle groups here with Twenty-Five, but my ships and I will come with you.

"Vista would have faced our enemies alone but for the fleet you and Amelie Lestroud sent to our aid. We will leave neither her nor you to face this new enemy without us."

Isaac bowed his head. He hadn't even dared *hope* that they would volunteer to fight with him. He'd only known he couldn't even ask them, let alone order them.

"I'll borrow some recon ships if you can spare them, Twenty-Five," he told the AI. "And I won't turn down anyone's help, but we need to make sure that our home bases are protected *and* the RCM is contained.

"If you are all willing to join up, I suggest we deploy a combined force: two of my battlecruisers and one of everyone else's, plus their escorts. Five battlecruisers and twenty strike cruisers should be enough to make our point to the Governance while allowing us to secure Skree-Skree and keep the Rogue contained."

That got acknowledging gestures from around the room, and Isaac exhaled in relief. Even sending ThreeHeart's other ships back to guard the Skree-Skree System, that would leave eight battlecruisers and their escort to back up Twenty-Five's siege.

And since he was bringing the most advanced ships with him to Sivar space, five battlecruisers should be *more* than enough.

39

A FULL WEEK passed in relative quiet in the guest house on Aris. Amelie knew about the gears now moving to rescue her, but until Isaac's fleet arrived at Sivar-One, there wouldn't be any signs of them that the Sivar could see.

The silence from the Keepers and the Intendant was terrifying, though. She didn't trust the Sivar as far as she could throw their *planet* at this point, and she had to wonder just what the Intendant was making of the data they'd extracted.

The alert from the Marines was almost a relief.

"Minister, we have multiple armed Sivar at the door," Sergeant Ryu said urgently into the channel. "They are demanding that you come with them, alone."

The senior noncom in the platoon Köhl had brought down paused.

"I can take them out," he noted. "But they'll have reserves. We can push back?"

"Negative," Amelie ordered. "Negative, do *not* start a firefight."

"Understood," Ryu replied. "What do we *do?*"

"Tell them I'll be right there and I will come alone," she told the Marine. "No one is going to die for me today, not if I have any say in the matter."

"Understood. We'll let them know."

Amelie shook her head and grabbed the armored underlayer for her ambassador suit. She was going to try to avoid a fight, but she was grimly aware that she might well *not* have any say in the matter.

"Sir." Choi was standing inside the door. Amelie hadn't seen her enter, but she was unsurprised by the Marine's presence. "We're ready."

"You can't come with me this time, Sergeant," Amelie told her. "They said alone, and they might well be willing to back that by shooting people. I need you to get with Ryu and Nguyen and Köhl. I don't think this is going to be the Intendant having changed his mind and wanting to play nice all of a sudden."

"So, you're going to walk into his den unarmed and alone?" Choi demanded.

"It's our only real chance of getting out of this without a fight," she replied. "I don't want to get any of my people killed if I can protect them."

"Walking into the furnace when the man at the switch tells you to doesn't protect anyone," the Marine said. "Dying won't save us."

"I don't plan on dying today," Amelie said dryly. "I'm still hoping to talk our way out of this mess."

"Fair. You'll forgive me if I think the odds of that suck."

Amelie nodded silently. She didn't disagree.

Before she could regard the conversation as over and walk out to face her fate, Choi produced the laser pistol Amelie had barely carried despite being given it.

"Speaking of odds that sucked, we tested if this would pass Sivar security," she said brightly. "It's Assini tech. Ceramics, batteries, artificial crystals. I was expecting the power source, at least, to ping something."

"Wait, *what?*" Amelie demanded.

"I walked into the Intendant's audience chamber with this in my armor," the Sergeant confessed. "They never questioned it, never flagged it as a weapon. Take it this time, Minister. *Please.*"

Amelie took the gun and tucked it into the vest. It might have been concealed by Sergeant Choi's heavier armor, but she wasn't turning down a weapon the Sivar might miss.

"All right," she told the Marine. "Time for me to go, but I have orders for you to give Köhl."

"Ma'am?"

"The priority is keeping everyone alive," Amelie insisted. "If they storm the compound, I'm not going to order Marines not to fight, but your priority is to make sure as many of you and as many of the staff are alive when Isaac comes to get us.

"Make sure Lina understands that. No matter what happens to me, your job and hers is to make sure that as many of you as possible are still here when the Fleet comes. You get me, Sergeant Choi?"

"I get you, Minister Lestroud."

Choi stepped back and gave Amelie a picture-perfect salute.

"Another alert from Ryu," the Marine told the older woman. "I think it's time for you to go."

———

BY THE TIME Amelie reached the guest house's front door, the standoff had grown *very* pointed. She guessed it had *started* with her people in full power armor, but that didn't help her nerves.

Four Exilium Marines, each clad in two meters of powered steel and ceramics instead of the more decorative-but-less-functional formal armor, loomed just outside the door with heavy pulse rifles in their gauntlets. Easily a dozen Sivar faced them. Their armor wasn't quite as impressive, but that was mostly due to the occupants' lack of height. It was still a hard shell with a powered internal exoskeleton.

Without testing it, there was no way to know if Sivar power armor stacked up to EMC gear, but Amelie was hoping to *not* find out. Their weapons, at least, looked cruder to Amelie. From her Marines' general reactions to Sivar ground troops, though, she guessed that whatever the large "mag-kinetic" guns were, they could at least threaten her Marines.

"I'm here," she told the Siva. "Stop pretending you can intimidate my Marines and point your guns somewhere else. What do you want?"

"You are to be brought before the Intendant," the lead guard snapped. "Follow me."

It wasn't a request, and Amelie concealed a sigh as she could feel the Marines bristle *through* their armor.

"*EMC*," she barked, snapping all four power armored Marines to attention. "Stand down," she ordered. "I came here to speak to the Intendant, after all. There is no reason to decline his invitation."

"You will come alone and unarmed," the Sivar soldier told her, but some of the sharpness had faded from his tone as he realized that she was the only reason the Marines hadn't turned him to ash yet.

"I figured," Amelie replied. She spread her arms. "I am unarmed. I will come alone. Bring me to your Intendant, soldier. I don't intend to start a war today. Do you?"

Encased in armor, there was no way to tell how the soldier reacted to that—even if Amelie was confident in her ability to read Sivar expression. He gestured for her to follow him and turned around.

"Choi has my orders," Amelie told the Marines, presuming Ryu was in one of the suits of armor. "I'll be back."

"If you can," the Marine Sergeant muttered, his armor projecting his voice directly to her earbud.

She said nothing. What was there to say?

He was entirely correct.

———

SHE WAS LED to the same room she'd met the Intendant in every time. This time, however, the guards lining the walls were in power armor and the Intendant was alone on the top dais.

The Keepers had been relegated to the tables on the lower level, sitting behind her with several other Sivar she didn't know as she was firmly led to the square of carpet and faced the Intendant calmly.

"Even now, you do not kneel," he observed. "Your arrogance is your undoing, Minister Amelie Lestroud."

"If I am ever undone, it will be by many things, but never by not kneeling to a tyrant," she replied. "I have never knelt and I never will."

The Intendant laughed.

"You will learn," he told her, eyes flashing in his armored skull. "I have studied what the Eyes of Sivar have learned of your people from you and your ship. You claim great power, but you are a tiny nation far away from the true heart of your race's power.

"You are not strong enough to stand before me as an equal," he continued, his voice calm. "The Governance negotiates only with the strong, and none of your allies qualify…and neither do you."

"Then we will leave," she told him. "This visit has been a grand waste of both of our times and I see no reason to continue it."

He laughed again.

"I think not," he replied. "Your allies have rich worlds, and you have technology that can help us, even if you lack the strength to fully use it. You face an enemy you cannot defeat, and so you came to me.

"And I will help you. Nine worlds have knelt to the Governance, and they are guarded by our fleets. I do not fear the Builders. That *you* fear them is another sign of your weakness."

The Intendant, Amelie reflected, was in for a rude awakening sooner or later.

"I will make this offer once, the only remaining chance to save your people from the enemy you fear so badly," he told her, his translated voice a sleek purr. "Kneel, Amelie Lestroud. Submit your allies and your Republic to the Governance of the Sivar, and our almighty fleets will shield your worlds from the Builders.

"Kneel and submit, and I will guarantee the security of your worlds from the monsters in the dark."

There was an expectant silence in the room, the audience waiting to hear her response. They might even believe there was a chance she'd accept.

Instead, she laughed. She'd been an actress once and she could laugh on cue—and this was a massive belly laugh, one that was utterly unladylike that she'd learned for a comedy routine in her twenties.

It echoed off the stone walls and the armored soldiers. There was *no question* of what she was doing, language and cultural barriers be damned.

"Your almighty fleets?" she finally asked. "You don't get it, do you? Your fleets are *obsolescent trash*. Your industry is backwards. Your conquests barbaric. A single Matrix warship could shred your fleet. A single Republic battle group could conquer your entire empire.

"You are utterly out of your depth, facing enemies who outclass you *completely*, and you spit on our aid and betray us? You ask *us* to surrender to *you*?"

She met the Intendant's gaze.

"You have power over me only because I made myself vulnerable —so we could try to help you," she told him. "We are not your enemies, Intendant of the Sivar. We came here to be your friends, though that was before we learned that you were the mad tyrant king of a slave state.

"Let us go and we will leave. We already have one war. But if you turn on us now, if you betray the trust that brought me here before, unarmed and alone, you start a new war.

"One you cannot win."

Amelie had no illusions now how this audience was going to end— which meant that her words weren't for the Intendant. They were for the Sivar in the room, watching her face down their god-king. Everything, from her posture to her verbal attack, was to show *them* that the Republic was going to destroy them.

"Seize her," the Intendant commanded. "Your arrogance will be the downfall of your entire alliance," he told Amelie as armored soldiers grabbed each of her arms.

She let them. They might take her weapon from her, but she suspected she might still get it into a cell with her—and *that* would be convenient.

"I have only spoken truth," she told him. "The consequences of *your* arrogance are going to be fascinating to watch."

40

———————

THE SIVAR GUARDS searched Amelie thoroughly once they'd removed her from the audience chamber, holding her at gunpoint to discourage resistance. They identified and took away the communication gear that had let her warn her people what was coming before she learned the Sivar's next stage.

They even took away her translator earbud and shoulder speaker, which was going to be a problem. She pointed at that particular set of electronics and then at her ears. The guards ignored her, one of them barking an order at her.

Without the translator overlaying it with English, the Sivar language sounded like grinding consonants through a series of jagged rocks. More importantly, she didn't understand a word of it.

She pointed at the translator gear again, then held up her hands in clear confusion.

Another barked order and she repeated the gesture. There was now a gun directly in her face and she met its holder's gaze levelly...and pointed at the translator.

One of them *finally* worked out what was going on and handed her the gear. She reattached it and looked back at the guard.

"Now, what were you asking me to do?" she asked sweetly.

"Remove your outer layers and spread your limbs for the scanner," the guard barked.

She obeyed. Fortunately, the armor vest was her inner layer, and she wasn't sure the Sivar knew human anatomy enough to realize that it was intentionally hanging to conceal pockets.

They ran the scanner over her, far more closely and intently than any previous search, but it cleared her. Whatever it was looking for, Assini sidearms didn't trigger it.

They didn't give her her suit back before they ushered her out of the room. The armor vest at least had a built-in bra—she hadn't become one of the most famous actresses of her time by being flat-chested, after all—but it was still a sleeveless block of armor pretending to be clothing.

But she didn't have much choice unless she wanted to start shooting, so she went along as they led her to a prison section whose warmth and slight sulfur smell told her she was *deep* inside the mountain, near the lava tubes that fuelled the First and Final Citadel's geothermal plants.

"Where are my people?"

"Being interned as we speak," the guard told her. "They will not be imprisoned here. These are the Intendant's *personal* cells."

That was probably a bad sign, but the guards weren't giving her much choice. She was pushed forward into the cell before the door slammed shut behind her.

Amelie glanced around her prison with scant favor. The bed was going to be too short for her—even Isaac, who was a lot smaller than the popular image of a black man as scary as he could be, couldn't fit on a Sivar bed—and it was the only furniture.

A bed, a small niche in the wall with what appeared to be a sink and…that was it. Amelie had a moment of concern before she realized that what had looked like a mere stone outcropping was a toilet of the same odd design as the ones in the guest house.

"A luxurious embassy this is not," she muttered to herself. "Hurry up, Isaac."

The laws of physics were hard to break. He was thirty days from

Sivar-One, his destination when he'd entered warp. Forty-plus from here.

Hopefully, the Sivar could at least manage to feed her. It was going to be a long wait.

———

THE SIVAR HAD LEFT her tablet and her translator gear. Without the secondary communicator they had taken, it couldn't reach *Watchtower* —though Amelie wasn't sure it could have reached through the mountain anyway.

The battery life for both was long enough that she probably wasn't going to find herself miming at her guards. She took a moment to switch them into power-conserving mode while making sure that her tablet clock was up.

She might not be able to know what was going on, but she would at least know how long it took.

That was how she knew how long it was before anyone came— roughly four hours.

Footsteps in the corridor attracted her attention a moment before she heard a door opening. It wasn't her door, but as she heard it close again, she realized that there was an airlock-style security barrier to keep her locked in. The outer door had presumably been open when they walked her in.

The inner door to her cell retreated into the ceiling, and a Croni walked in carrying a tray.

The winged alien ignored her, placing the tray into a slot in the wall that turned it into a shelf.

"Wait," she said in Sivar. The alien ignored her.

"*Please,*" she said…this time in the alien's own language. She and her people had been paying attention to the cleaners as they came through the guest house. She didn't have *much* of a Croni vocabulary in her translator, but she had some.

"What happened to my friends?"

The alien was staring at her with large black eyes that now looked very wide.

"No," they finally responded, in Sivar. "No talk." They paused. "Too dangerous," they finished in Croni.

"Please?" Amelie repeated.

The Croni backed away, their hands raised defensively in front of themselves.

"Some are dead. The rest are prisoners," they whispered in Croni. "Ask no more. No talk!" they concluded in Sivar. "Leave be!"

She let the slave go, watching as it backed into the space sealed by the double door. She knew…well, she'd confirmed what she'd already expected. The Sivar had stormed the guesthouse and the Marines had, eventually, surrendered.

The door slid closed and she turned her attention to the meal. It was plain enough, but the vegetables were another answer to her question. She recognized the sauce and mix as the result of one of the easy-prep packages they'd brought down from *Watchtower* with them.

Feeding her the food she'd brought was a good way to make sure she could eat it, she supposed. There was only so much of it, though.

Sighing, she realized there were no utensils. Nothing they'd served her was really designed to be eaten with her hands, but she'd make it work.

Amelie refused to give the Intendant the pleasure of watching her starve.

———

TEN MORE HOURS and a second meal passed before anyone but the slave bringing her food came to visit her. The second slave was even less talkative than the first, refusing to engage.

The third arrival was unexpected. Two armored guards led the way, sweeping through the security double door and checking her cell for surprises.

They had the same scanner as everyone else, though, which meant they missed the laser. Again. Amelie was starting to think the Republic needed to make a *lot* more of the little weapons.

The silent guards withdrew and Keeper Rode walked in. The security doors closed behind her and she regarded Amelie with a quizzical look.

"I do believe your people are mad," she finally said. "Your soldiers' armor is impressive."

Amelie snorted.

"Don't let my Marines hear you call them soldiers," she told the alien. The translator probably couldn't handle that distinction, but it was *important* to her people. "They get snippy."

"Many of them are dead," Rode replied. "I am unconcerned about their irritation. Your civilians surrendered peacefully and fourteen of your soldiers lived. All wounded."

Amelie closed her eyes and sighed. She'd known the Marines weren't going to be *good* at following orders to lay down their arms to preserve their lives, but that meant almost half of Köhl's detachment had died defending that stupid guest house.

"Thank you for telling me," she admitted.

"I thought you would like to know," Rode said. "By our traditions, that seems odd, but you are not Sivar. And many among our people would have wanted to know, regardless of traditions."

"But not your Intendant."

"No," Rode conceded softly. "Not the Intendant. But I am not here for the Intendant."

"Why are you here?" Amelie demanded. "To mock me? To taunt the monkey in a cage?"

"What is a monkey?" Rode asked, then shook her entire upper torso. Natural armor plating clacked against itself in an impressive clatter. "Irrelevant. I am not here to mock you."

She held out her hand, revealing a holographic projector. An image of *Watchtower* and the rest of the consular flotilla appeared.

"The delay in the Intendant calling you back was to allow the Commandants time to plan their operation against your ships," the Keeper of the Citadel noted. "They were certain they had the measure of your weapons and defenses from their scans."

"How many ships did you lose?" Amelie breathed.

"Ten, including both battleships committed to the attack," Rode said flatly. "Even with the survivors we retrieved from the wrecks, over ten thousand dead."

She tapped a command and the hologram starting playing. Even at the relatively tiny scale, Amelie could pick out the storm of missiles as they descended on Holmwood's ship.

Not least because of the explosions as *Watchtower*'s defenses engaged. The three warships leapt into motion, trying to usher the freighters to safety.

Even watching the video at speed, it was clear that Captain Holmwood had refused to fire back initially. She'd completely ignored the local fortresses, pure missile platforms that had flung hundreds of missiles at her.

It was only when the two battleships and their escorts had made their final lunge to cover the assault transports' approach to the freighters that Holmwood stopped playing nice. The battleships survived better than Amelie had expected, the first one taking multiple direct hits from the secondary turrets on the three Republic warships and even surviving a direct hit from *Watchtower*'s main gun.

The hit still stopped her dead in space, allowing Holmwood to *bake* the ship with heavy pulse gun fire. Lasers and pulse guns had ravaged the second battleship, crippling both ships and sending them reeling from the fight.

The escorts had continued to face *Watchtower*'s fire when they refused to break off, still attempting to deliver the boarding ships behind a hail of missile and laser fire.

Only when over half of the escorts had been destroyed did they finally run.

"All of your ships escaped," Rode said calmly. "I'd *like* to blame your Captain—I *knew* people on those ships—but I can't. She did her duty."

"You know where the blame lies," Amelie pointed out. "I didn't order that attack. My people defended themselves."

"One does not blame the Fates or their voice for what comes to pass," the Siva replied.

"Really." Amelie studied the alien. The armor plating left the Sivar with unexpressive faces, leaving much of her reading of them to eyes and body language. It wasn't quite a guess, but it wasn't a lot better.

"You're not here because you believe that," she told Rode. "You didn't come here to tell me my people died and you aren't here to commit suicide by prisoner or arrange for me to be shot attempting to escape.

"You just watched one of my capital ships punch through two of yours and are beginning to realize just how fucked your Governance is," she continued. "I can't help you there anymore. I suppose if your Intendant was going to release all of my people and put us on a ship to Sivar-One, we could talk down the storm that's coming.

"But your people started this war—and it's going to *be* a war, Keeper Rode. You threw me in a cell, killed my people and attacked my ships. The Republic will not forget and the Republic will not forgive, not unless your people change."

"We do not change. The strong endure. The strong rule."

Rode's words were fatalistic.

"And if the Sivar are no longer the strong, what happens?" Amelie asked.

"It has never been the case," Rode replied. "Tribes fell. Nations fell. All became Sivar. All are bound by the voice of the Fates."

"And when the Governance is broken and the Republic's fleets are at your door, who falls?" Amelie asked again. "Who are the Sivar if they are no longer slavemasters?"

"I don't know," the Keeper of the Citadel told her. She produced something from inside her toga-like garment—a piece of cloth with a symbol on it. Dropping that cloth on the floor, she nodded to Amelie.

"I don't know and my Intendant has no intention of finding out," she continued. She nodded to the cloth. "If you ever find yourself in the City, though, look for that sign. That is how you will find the people who *do* wonder who we are if we are no longer slavemasters."

Rode turned and left, leaving Amelie staring at a closing door in surprise. Shaking her head, she picked up the cloth. It was a neatly embroidered thing, a handkerchief, she supposed.

The symbol on it was clear enough: it was a broken chain on a star. She could see a dozen ways that it could be subtly concealed in a larger image, a hidden sign for…what? A group of rebels? An underground railroad?

She was in a cell at the heart of the First and Final Citadel. She wasn't going to end up in "the City"—presumably the metropolis at the base of the mountain anytime soon.

Amelie was still staring at the image, trying to work out what Rode was trying to suggest, when the doors to her cell calmly slid open.

41

AMELIE STOOD and stared at the door in shock for at least ten seconds before starting to think about the situation. The double security door clearly needed to be overridden from somewhere to open both doors.

It was quite possible that she was being set up, with every intention of her being "shot while attempting to escape." Except that there was no *point* to that. If the Intendant wanted her dead, he'd order her death and that would be the end of it.

The only audience he could be performing for was the Republic... and he had to realize that there was *no* scenario he could fake up that would make her death acceptable.

Which meant someone wanted her to escape. If nothing else, they wanted to see how far she'd get and what she'd do.

Watching the doors for several more seconds to see if they suddenly closed, Amelie then briskly strode forward like she'd been officially released.

There had, it turned out, been a guard outside her door. The Siva was on the ground, curled into the fetal position and unconscious. The ground around the alien was a mess of vomit.

The guard was probably going to be fine—they appeared to still be breathing, and she doubted that Rode had fatally poisoned her own people—but Amelie couldn't just walk by, either. She took a moment to kneel by the unconscious figure and carefully adjust them. The recovery position was reliant on human anatomy, but the concept of "keep the airway clear and position them to make sure the airway *stays* clear in case of further vomit" seemed pretty universally equivalent.

She took the opportunity to steal the guard's personal computer. Bulkier than her thumb-sized holographic tablet, it was a book-sized device that could collapse down to a stick a centimeter wide and fifteen high.

Fortunately for her sanity, it was unlocked. Unfortunately, her translator couldn't read text for her without a scanner attachment that the guards had broken.

It wasn't the first time she'd missed the permanently installed military tattoo-comps. She'd only ever had a fake one for movie roles, which meant she'd been reliant on attachments the Sivar had taken.

The Sivar text was beyond her, but the *iconography* wasn't, and the map software icon was on the screen the device was open to. It still took her a few seconds to get it open and orient herself, but she managed it.

Using the software's navigation software was out of the question, but she could at least pick the most direct route toward the outside of the mountain. Holding the tablet in her left hand, she finally drew the laser pistol Köhl and Choi had insisted she take.

This might end up with her dead or back in the cell, but she'd be damned if she was going down without a fight!

———

THE CORRIDORS around the Intendant's personal prison were surprisingly empty. There was a second security checkpoint on the way out, but Amelie almost missed it. She was between the two heavy security doors before she even realized they were there, and dashed forward to find another pair of guards, both in the same state of illness as the one outside her cell.

She was pretty sure Keeper Rode was to blame for the sudden lack of security between her and the outside of the First and Final Citadel—

and she was also reasonably sure that these security guards worked for the Keeper.

They would probably follow the Intendant's orders over Rode's, however, and almost certainly *hadn't* signed up to be food-poisoned into unconsciousness. Even her apparent ally there was making Amelie nervous.

It didn't help that the only thing she really had to go on was "get into the City and look for this symbol."

Getting to the outside of the mountain was the first step, though, and while she was rusty, Amelie had once trained in infiltration tactics with some of the best. While her official training with Confederacy Special Forces had been limited and targeted at looking good rather than actually working, several of those soldiers had ended up in her rebellion and had given her *real* training.

This was, of course, about the worst possible circumstance to be doing it under. She was inside a structure that she'd never scouted, relying on a map she hadn't validated, in hostile territory and with no idea how good her hiding places were going to be anywhere along the way.

Plus, just briskly walking forward like she belonged there wasn't going to get her anywhere. She was thirty centimeters taller than any Sivar she'd met, *and* her head looked completely different.

Caution and good hearing got her to the closest exit on her map. That took her over an hour of painstaking, nerve-wracking travel, listening at doors and corners as she moved forward.

Her care meant that she was aware of the armored guard standing at the doorway before she walked into their line of sight. A careful peek around the corner laid out the situation and her problem.

There was one Siva standing next to the closed door. They held a weapon lazily, the short rifle hung on a strap from their shoulder. For all the slack in their posture, there was no way that Amelie could reach the door without them having plenty of time to react.

She steeled herself and took a deep breath. Despite everything, she'd made it through her revolt and into leadership of Exilium and her role as ambassador without ever actually firing a shot at another sentient being in anger.

There didn't seem to be another option here. Shooting the guard would almost certainly raise a million alarms—though Rode's poisoning the other guards obviously hadn't. The Keeper had apparently missed this one, and Amelie had to wonder if she'd gone a different way than Rode had expected.

It was probably for the best if she had, even if this was something of a problem. Breathing slowly to calm her nerves, she checked the charge on the laser pistol. It wouldn't need full power to kill a man in light armor. Thirty percent should do it.

She was procrastinating and she knew it. Enough people had already died that it seemed silly to hesitate and yet...

The door popped open and a voice barked in Sivar. The guard snapped to attention, stepping back as a pair of other guards came through with a train of Croni slaves carrying cleaning equipment.

Amelie snorted mentally. If she *hadn't* just been procrastinating about moving, she'd have gone through the door right into a cluster of guards and slaves.

The discussion continued in Sivar, but she was too far away for her translator to pick it up. If the guards and slaves came her way, she was going to be in serious trouble. She'd mentally mapped a couple of hiding spots to fall back to, but she wasn't sure she had time to get to them.

Then, to her surprise, the guard closed the door behind the last Croni, activated a locking mechanism, and the entire group set off down a different corridor. The door was now locked...but unguarded.

And Amelie Lestroud had *much* less hesitation about shooting a lock.

It wasn't until she was outside the mountain, on one of the roads that circled the First and Final Citadel and led down to the City, that Amelie realized the dual flaw with her plan.

First, she had no idea where to go. Following the road and sneaking around every one of its fortified checkpoints and defensive positions was an almost-certain recipe for getting caught. There was no way

Rode had cleared a path down the outside of the mountain, the most fortified set of security barriers on the planet.

She *might* have cleared a path through the mountain itself, potentially marked by the symbol she'd shown Amelie, but that brought up the *second* problem with shooting out the lock:

It was almost *certainly* alarmed. She could hear shouting voices through the door she'd left propped open, and *those* were probably the very guards she'd watched pass a few minutes before.

Staying where she was wasn't an option, so Amelie took a moment to be certain there was no traffic on the road and then dashed across. At least the other side had the same planters and decorative shrubbery as had been outside the Halls of Gathering. She had a basic hiding place and she could hope that her biometrics were sufficiently different from what the guards' scanners were calibrated for to give her a chance.

It was a crap chance. Her rusty infiltration training told her that, but she didn't have much choice. Hidden behind the planters for now, she crouched over to the stone safety wall and looked out.

Like most of the mountain she'd seen so far, the side of the mountain beneath her was a sheer face, carved by explosives and lasers to give the terrace below more space. Leaning against the protective barrier, she felt the slight buzz of an inertial safety field. That would try to stop her falling over, but if she actually *jumped*, it should also reduce gravity enough to let her land safely.

It was at least a fifteen-meter drop and the back of her mind was gibbering at the thought. The *Republic*'s safety fields would have been calibrated to make sure anyone who managed to completely fall over would land safely.

She didn't know if the Sivar were quite so generous, but, once again, she didn't have much choice. She could hear a vehicle slamming to a halt behind her, presumably a patrol checking in on the alarm from the lock and finding a door blasted open by an energy weapon unknown to the Sivar.

She jumped.

Static electricity shot over her body, an unimaginably uncomfortable case of full-body pins and needles that was a side effect of the inertial safety field. She'd been told it could be reduced, but she wasn't surprised the Sivar hadn't.

Amelie fell fifteen meters and hit the ground like she'd jumped down a tenth of that distance. She rolled forward to absorb the momentum, ending up in the middle of a set of decorative bushes.

This being the First and Final Citadel's gardens, of course, those bushes concealed a secondary SAM launcher. It wasn't one of the massive multi-missile racks that crowned the mountain, but the weapon would make a handy mess of anything that sneaked past those.

Fortunately for her, the installation didn't have sensors of its own—or at least, not ones that would detect a human on foot hiding behind the missile.

She took a moment to regain her breath and spotted one of the Sivar patrolling along the edge of the fence. She couldn't be sure if the safety field had pinged an alarm of its own—quite possibly—or if they were just checking the edge to be certain.

Either way, the guard didn't appear to see anything to raise their suspicion. They kept moving, and Amelie exhaled a long sigh.

The inertial safety fields made parkouring down the side of the mountain a possibility, but if the fields had alarms, someone was going to notice the pattern sooner or later.

For now, though, she needed to get more distance from her prison. Taking a moment to make sure that there was no one watching from above, she surveyed the terrace and drew a mental map of her route to the edge.

Then she ran. She might have spent the last few years behind a desk, but her acting had required a high level of athleticism, and her protective detail had refused to let her get out of shape as President of Exilium. Habits died hard and she was in solid shape for anyone, let alone a fifty-plus politician.

She vaulted several of the lower planters, trying to keep taller plants between her and the edge where she knew the patrol was still looking for her.

This time, she only gave herself a few seconds to look at what was on the terrace below. This one looked like it was actually a food garden for the Citadel's kitchens, but it was empty of anyone she could see from above.

She jumped again, swallowing the beginnings of a scream as the pins and needles rippled over her skin. The landing was harder this time, but she still managed to avoid most of the impact by rolling forward behind a stand of some kind of grain tall enough to hide her from view.

There, gasping for breath, she realized the grain had hidden someone from *her* view. A stocky four-legged alien with fur so black as to be almost purple looked at her. A Pol, she thought they'd been told.

"You are trouble," the alien told her in calm Sivar. "Should you not be in a cell?"

"You know who I am?" she asked, raising herself to her knees and making sure she had a hand on the laser pistol inside her vest.

"The strange alien who challenges the Intendant and keeps trying to speak to the slaves around her, even when it is unwise?" the Pol replied, their tone almost amused. She was relatively sure the alien was speaking Sivar without a translator. It probably made sense to make the staff learn your language if you were a slaving despot, she supposed.

"I know you. I am...not sure I can help you, if you are running down the mountain to escape the Sivar, but you are *fascinating*."

"Can anyone help me?" Amelie asked, glancing back up the mountain. "My people have been imprisoned, my ship driven from the system. I have somewhere to go if I can get to the City, but that contact is using me against the Intendant."

The Pol blinked large yellow eyes at her and bared broad, sharp teeth in a lazy smile.

"That explains your lack of cell, yes," they noted. "I am but a gardener. I grow vegetables and am treated better than many by our masters, but I am quite restricted."

They considered her, looking her up and down.

"I can get you off the mountain," he finally told her. "It is not without risk, but I can see you delivered to the Kond. If anyone can help you, it will be the Kond. From there, if he wills it, you can be taken into the City."

"The Kond?" Amelie asked, then shook her head. "I will gladly meet anyone who can help," she told the Pol. "I need to get my people out."

She was grimly certain that the Intendant wouldn't surrender and that Isaac's fleet couldn't capture the First and Final Citadel. They'd have to destroy it from orbit, which meant she wanted to get her people—and as many of the slaves as possible—out of the damn mountain.

"Then I can deliver you to the Kond," the gardener told her. "You look about the right size; this should work."

"What's the right size?" Amelie asked slowly.

"You'll fit in my compost bags," the Pol gardener said cheerfully.

42

———————

"WE HAVE no response from the Sentinels," Siril-ki reported to a subdued crowd the next morning. "We definitely *have* a connection, but we have received no response to our attempt to communicate."

Octavio had put three holograms up in the middle of the conference, and he was currently studying the closest one to him: the schematic of an Assini-designed Sentinel Matrix's combat hull.

A Construction Matrix combat platform was over a kilometer long, a multi-claw shape with each prong armed with gamma-ray lasers. The Escorts had been spindle-shaped ships of roughly the same size with multiple high-powered lasers positioned along their hull.

The Sentinels were the intermediate design. They were a more rounded shape than the combat platforms but retained a bifurcated form resembling a sailing catamaran. Most of their arsenal was high-frequency grasers like *Dauntless*'s own secondaries, but each of the main spikes contained the first zettahertz lasers the Assini had built.

They were also *five* kilometers long, bristling with pulse guns and lasers along their entire length. The Sentinel had been designed to engage a Regional Construction Matrix and all of its defenders in groups of eleven at most.

Bringing eighty of them home would have made the whole trip

worth it. Instead, there appeared to only be three left…and those three seemed to be brain-dead.

"Is there any way to establish *why* they're not answering?" Octavio asked the Assini. "Are we looking at intact beacons in wrecked ships or nonfunctional Matrices or…are they just ignoring our call?"

"It is almost impossible to tell at this distance," Siril-ki noted. "Without any ability to examine the ships or use secondary lightspeed communications, we are limited to their voluntary responses or basic involuntary system protocols.

"Currently, we are only able to engage with the latter. That has allowed us to confirm their location but not their status. All of your suggested possibilities are potentially valid.

"Given that we are the first Assini to attempt to make contact with the Sentinels in multiple elevens of eleven years, I would not expect them to *ignore* us," ki admitted. "I was expecting an immediate, if confused, response."

"Is it possible there's some kind of technical issue interfering with the communication?" Renaud asked.

Octavio shook his head before Siril-ki could respond.

"If we're getting the involuntary ping, we should be able to communicate with the Matrix," he told his flag captain. "There's only one tachyon communicator aboard a Matrix starship and it's basically attached to the Matrix core."

"As Commodore Catalan says, yes," Siril-ki confirmed. "If the Matrices are intact, they are *aware* that we are calling them."

"So, either they're ignoring us…or the Matrices are dead but the ships remain," Octavio concluded. "Neither of those is a great result."

He shook his head.

"Especially given where they are."

He tapped a command on his tattoo-comp, vanishing the image of the Sentinel and bringing up the local astrographic chart.

"All three of the Sentinels we've been able to locate are here," he told his people. "It's an M-sequence orange dwarf with a mass of just under a quarter of Sol's. It wasn't flagged for development by the Construction Matrices because the odds of there being a useful planet were low.

"Theoretically, there is no reason the Sentinels should be there… except that it's *also* directly along the vector our strange ship left Assini on."

The line was already on the hologram. Everyone could have drawn the same conclusion as to what the data had shown, even if only half the people in the room had already known the answer.

"We don't have a lot of detail on the system," he continued. "At twelve point six light-years away, it would be a twenty-one-year flight for the interstellar colony ship we believe they were using as a transport. That would line up with an expedition being sent back after they learned of the fall of Sina via tachyon communicator."

"Or, potentially, after losing contact with whoever they were talking to in the Assini System," Renaud suggested. "It seems reasonably likely that they could have lost all contact here when Sina fell."

"So they sent a ship," Das noted. "And then what? Before they even get here, everybody dies?"

"Basically," Octavio said grimly. "They might have been a rescue expedition. They might have been an invasion army. They could easily have been both! We'll never know now.

"What we *do* know was that there was an Assini colony, despite even the Assini not knowing that," he reminded them. Another command focused on the orange dwarf system.

"The system is close enough that the Assini databases have a pretty solid idea of what's there," he continued. "It's not much. A pair of gas giants, one almost big enough to rival the star for mass, and two midsized rocks in close-in orbits. Neither is close enough to be in the liquid-water zone…but one is close enough that the Construction Matrices could have kicked it there."

"That would have been detected from Assini, wouldn't it?" Renaud asked.

"Yes," Octavio confirmed. "So, they didn't do it *before* the flares, but it may have been part of their long-term plan. *May*. We don't know what these people were after."

"We know they may have contributed to the deaths of elevens of eleven million of my people," Siril-ki said grimly. "If they *knew* to avoid the Matrices…"

"We don't know enough to judge them yet," Octavio replied. "What we do know is that without a full set of Construction Matrix terraformers, there's no way they could have transformed that world.

"But. With the two terraformers they took from here they could have established a significant habitable zone on almost any planet. Those are extraordinarily powerful devices."

He looked around his crew, smiling as he spotted that Meena Das had acquired a ring on her left hand over the last day or so. Chen, it seemed, moved quickly once she'd set her mind to something.

"We've spent weeks in Assini," he reminded them all. "It hasn't been entirely wasted, we've learned a lot...but I don't think we've learned anything that is going to help the Republic as much as taking a battlecruiser group home would.

"We've learned the fate of Siril-ki's people and it isn't pretty," he continued, gesturing to the Assini. "We *may* have found a clue as to how all of this started, and we *may* have found some of the Sentinel Matrices.

"Three Sentinels won't change the balance of power back home, but they'd help," he said. "More than that, we know Matrices. Three of them lost on their own, thinking their creators and their siblings alike are all dead or mad? They don't deserve that—and we can help them.

"Those clues, that chance to help those Sentinels? They all lead us to this system. If we're going to learn anything here, we need to investigate that star."

Octavio smiled. Twelve-point-six light-years would take his fleet eighteen days to travel—and it wasn't even in the direction of home. He would be adding a minimum of sixty days to his trip, with no guarantee that it would be worth it.

"So, that's what we're going to do," he told his people. "And we'll see what we can find."

At the end of the day, it was his call and his call alone. His little flotilla was already a year from home. It was unlikely that the Republic was going to fall because he'd arrived in a year and three months instead of a year.

Of course, if it *did*... Well, that was why he had new reasons to dye his hair of late.

43

Compost, regardless of the world it is on or the plants it is made of or its destination, stinks. The bags used to haul vegetable scraps and the inedible portions of the garden plants out of the First and Final Citadel's gardens were no exception.

The Pol gardener never gave Amelie a name, but they helped her squeeze into an empty compost bag of roughly the right size for her and set up an air hose to the outside of the open-backed transport truck they were loading.

The air hose was necessary, as they proceeded to load the other twenty sacks of compost in the shed onto the truck around and on top of her. There wasn't enough mass on top of her to keep her from being able to breathe, but even with the hose, she was worrying about suffocating.

The truck was a six-wheeled vehicle that made its way down the mountain in a recurring reminder that working vehicles the galaxy over apparently had their shock absorbers removed when they reported for duty.

The First and Final Citadel's roads were well maintained, but even the tiniest bump or crack shifted the weight above Amelie. She wasn't entirely sure the setup was safe, and she had to wonder who the Pol normally smuggled out.

There was no way that the truck had come with the spot the gardener had tucked her air hose into originally. She wasn't the first person who'd been secretly removed from the Intendant's capital.

Security checkpoints were their own heart attack. She lost count after fifteen, each at least a five-minute pause while she could feel the vibrations of guards poking at the vehicle. A straight drive down the intentionally looping road out of the Citadel was probably sixty kilometers or so. That would have called for an hour, maybe an hour and a half, of careful driving by the truck driver.

Instead, it was over three hours before the sudden paucity of checkpoints and increase in road bumps suggested they might finally be clear of the Citadel. Three hours that Amelie could only regard as a precursor to hell itself.

She'd set herself up to at least be able to check the time on her tablet, but by the time four hours had passed, she almost wished she hadn't. There was no water in the bag with her. No food. She had an air hose and that was it.

That was when the truck stopped. Voices spoke near the wheel well in a rapid-fire language she didn't understand—and then everything started vibrating as the bags of compost began to be removed.

It took Amelie a moment to realize that it wasn't a random process or the orderly removal of everything starting at the top she'd expected, either. Someone was quite specifically removing the bags above her.

Then hands grabbed the bag she was in and started to pull her roughly upward—only for commands to get barked in that unfamiliar language. After that, she was more gently lifted out.

"Minister Lestroud, can you hear me?" a voice asked in halting Sivar. "I don't speak your language. I hope you understand me."

"I can hear you," she replied.

"Do you have a way out or do we need to cut the bag open?" the voice asked.

"I can get out if you put me upright," she told the stranger.

"Very well." The voice barked orders in that strange language again. The people holding her felt around the bag for a second, locating her head the only way they could, and then put her feet on the ground.

With a bit of effort, Amelie reached the tag the gardener had pointed out to her and yanked on it. The "loose thread" easily pulled away in her hand, unravelling a line across the top of the bag that let the sealed top fall away. A moment later, the entire stinking bag collapsed around her feet.

She'd done grosser things for her movies, but those had been with the promise of immediate hot showers afterwards and generally hadn't lasted four hours.

The being holding her was of a species unknown to her, a shuffling creature easily two and a half meters tall that looked more like a tree than anything else. A half-second's examination revealed that the solid-trunk appearance of their torso and legs was actually a garment, a long tunic cut of a fabric that matched their bark-like skin and rested on the ground around their feet.

Two large arms with at least a dozen fingers apiece were still holding her up, with a second set of arms protruding from the alien's back swinging forward with a bottle of water and a chunk of bread.

"The medical data we extracted suggested the bread should be safe," the voice told her.

Accepting the food and water with a small bow to the tree-like alien, she turned to see the speaker. It was another Pol, slightly larger than the gardener who'd helped her escape.

This one's fur was paler, dark russet brown instead of black. They were dressed in a better-fitted outfit than Amelie had seen on any non-Sivar in the Governance, one clearly tailored to their body.

They bowed their torso forward.

"Minister Amelie Lestroud," they greeted her. "I am the Kond."

"I was told you could help me," she replied. "But I'll admit I don't even know what 'the Kond' means."

Large square teeth flashed in a laugh.

"Let us move out of the way of the farmworkers," they said. "We both have questions that need to be answered, but this compost must also be put to work."

Turning, the Kond gave more orders to the big plantoid in that same rapid-fire language.

"Come with me," the Kond instructed. "I would offer to get you clean, but I do not believe we have clothes that will fit you."

"Give me water and tub and I will clean these myself," Amelie replied. "Anything to be able to breathe."

The teeth flashed again and she realized that that had been a test… and more than one, at that.

"I think we can arrange that."

―――――

THE ARMOR VEST was at least theoretically self-cleaning through various active and passive measures, so Amelie put that on after washing herself and began washing the rest of her clothing. She'd managed to get them most of the way to "probably not going to smell" when there was a knock on the door.

"Minister? I have some items for you, if that would be acceptable," the Kond told her.

She laughed. She wasn't overly concerned about being seen bottomless by an alien race with unknown gender roles.

"Come in," she told them.

The package in the Kond's hands proved their earlier statement about clothing a lie. The skirt and top were presumably sized for a Sivar ban—the only other people on the planet with breasts—but she could make them work.

"There is an electric dryer," Kond told her. "Your clothes will survive that?"

"They should," she agreed, pulling the skirt up around her waist. It was elastic enough to fit a wide variety of sizes, but the Kond had eyeballed her size almost perfectly. Of course, the skirt was probably floor-length on its intended Sivar wearer and only came down to her mid-shin.

Similarly, the top was probably a near-knee-length tunic for its intended wearer, but the cut was right to work with her armor vest and leave her completely covered. On a hundred-and-fifty-centimeter-tall Sivar, the two garments would probably have looked odd together. On her, they worked perfectly.

She checked in the mirror and raised an eyebrow.

"You did not have time to have these made, so you already had them," she noted. "And they fit and go together perfectly. I'm impressed."

The Kond bowed.

"Officially, I am a tailor," they told her. "To our masters, I am a favored servant. I served my time as a tribute and found a trade amongst the ex-tributes here. To my people, I am the Kond."

"Which means what?" Amelie asked, following the Pol to an industrial-scale laundry. She tossed her clothes in the designated machine and let the Kond punch the commands in for her.

"I am a member of a noble family on our home world," the Kond replied. "I would not have been Kond back home. I was a third child and chose to volunteer as tribute to spare another family grief."

She grimaced.

"I'm guessing the tributes don't get to go back home afterwards," she noted.

"For two of the races here, the ten orbits a tribute must serve the Sivar is most of their adult lives," the Kond noted sadly. "Not all, of course, but the Croni especially…"

"That bad?" Amelie shivered. Aris orbited in a bit over one point two Terran years.

"They grow to adulthood in five orbits and live roughly twenty-five on average," the Kond told her. "There are no medical services for the ex-tributes here. We are…"

The translator choked on the Sivar word for several seconds before providing the translation of *helots*.

"I'm guessing that's not much of an improvement," she said dryly. The word the translator chose was just a different type of slave, after all.

"No," the Kond agreed. "Some rise above helotry by being of service to the Sivar in broader roles like mine. We mostly live in townships arrayed around the Sivar cities, working farms and industrial sites that the Sivar regard as too dangerous for themselves."

"Where do the tributes work, then?" Amelie asked.

"In factories and sites owned by the Governance," the Kond replied. "Like the gardeners you saw on the First and Final Citadel. Hundreds of thousands of tributes—potentially millions; even I do not know for certain—work in factories across this star system, Minister Lestroud. They fuel the Sivar Keys of War."

"Slaves don't make for great workers in technical industries," she noted. "How does that work?"

"They are very good at catching people who cause problems with production," the alien said quietly. "And reprisals are visited on entire work shifts…and their families back home."

"Fuckers," Amelie breathed.

"I would agree. That is why my people sent you to me," the Kond told her. "I am the senior Pol aristocrat on Sivar. That is not why my people follow me, but it helps. I have raised myself into the vague upper tier of the helots that the Sivar tolerate in the City and running my own business.

"They trust me."

"And you're running a secret route to evacuate abused tributes from the Citadel, using that trust?" Amelie guessed. An underground railroad.

"You understand more than I expected," the Pol said. "But…I do not have the ability to rescue your people. I have a network of informants and allies scattered through the tribute- and helot-run facilities in the City and the Citadel, but we lack weapons or soldiers."

"I imagine there are other rebels who do have those?" she asked.

The Kond winced.

"If I thought we could overthrow the Sivar, I could identify a hundred weak points to strike at," they noted. "That I refuse to do so makes me no friends. I know of other, more active groups among the helots. But their resistance and their violence never end well."

"Kond, in less than thirty days, the Republic fleet is going to arrive in Sivar space," Amelie told them. "The Sivar have *no idea* what is coming or how badly they are outclassed. They are going to be handed what I suspect will be their worst military defeat in a very long time. From there, the Republic will proceed here.

"We can defeat the Sivar's space defenses, but we don't have the ability to take even the First and Final Citadel by storm, let alone the planet."

"The system you first visited, I assume?" the Kond asked. "That would be Sonbar. I have several people from there. Their people, the Sonba, will suffer for your victory."

"Everyone will suffer if there is an extended war," Amelie agreed. "But I was released by a *Sivar*, Kond. The Intendant will be made vulnerable by defeat. Working together, we might be able to bring him down *without* the Republic destroying the Citadel with fire from on high."

The Kond closed their eyes.

"We have seen that fire," they told her. "I am not certain I would wish it upon my enemies, let alone on a fortress full of my friends."

"It is our last choice, but it may be our only option."

"You would have us fight for you?" they asked.

"I would have you fight for *yourselves*," Amelie replied. "The Republic can help, but those ships are only here to rescue me and my staff. If I tell them to support a rebellion, to support independence for the races the Sivar have conquered, they will.

"But we can't free you. We can only help you free yourselves."

The Kond looked at her in silence for a long time as the laundry machines whirred away around them.

"I cannot make that decision on my own," they finally allowed. "There are others you must speak to."

"And?" she asked.

"I will make that conversation happen," the Kond promised. "Be patient for now. Here, you are safe."

44

"As of the last contact we had with the surface, Amelie had been detained at a meeting with the Intendant, and Sivar ground troops were storming the manor they gave us as an embassy."

Holmwood's image stood utterly straight, the woman staring at a wall behind Isaac's head as if she was expecting to be torn to pieces for her failure.

Isaac couldn't say he wasn't tempted, but it would have been pointless. If nothing else, there were still light-years and light-years between *Watchtower* and *Vigil*. Holmwood's battlecruiser was in deep, deep space, roughly halfway between Sivar-One and Sivar-Prime.

"And your own situation, Captain?" he asked gently.

"We were attacked by two Sivar battleships and sixteen escorts of various sizes, supported by an estimated forty-five battle stations," Holmwood reported. "Only fifteen of the stations were in our line of sight; the remainder were providing over-the-horizon missile support."

Isaac nodded.

"You extracted the support ships and your warships, Captain," he reminded her. "How bad was the damage?"

"Both of the freighters took multiple hits from Sivar laser weaponry," the Captain admitted. "Seventy-two civilians dead, as many wounded. We managed to keep the missiles off of them, but if the battleships had turned their heavier beams on the transports, we would have been lost."

"You retreated under fire in good order, Captain Holmwood," Isaac told her. "There was no way you could have extracted Minister Lestroud at that point."

"I could have taken their entire damn fleet!" Holmwood snapped.

Isaac waited for several seconds until she sighed.

"My reports already tell me what those 'heavier beams' on the battleships did to *Watchtower*," he reminded her. "Several disabled LPC turrets, fifty-two dead. My understanding is that the damage is repairable in space?"

"It is," she confirmed. "And I can tell those beams are short-ranged by our standards. They ambushed us at twenty thousand kilometers, sir. It should have been a massacre."

"It very nearly was, Captain Holmwood," he told her. "A continued engagement at that range would have been. I agree that there wouldn't have been any Sivar ships left when the dust settled, but your battlecruiser is worth more to me than any number of dead Sivar ships.

"Is that understood?"

"Yes, sir. Thank you, sir."

"I'm impressed that you managed to extract everyone with as little lethal force as you used," he continued. *Watchtower* had basically taken the two battleships' best shot and then baked the exterior of both ships with close-range pulse-gun fire.

She *probably* couldn't have destroyed them with those tertiary guns, but she had crippled them in a single pass. That—and the destruction of half those battleships' escorts—had bought her the respect to extract her fleet.

"I'll admit I'm mostly concerned about the Intendant's final message," Isaac concluded. "He had to know you were clear at that point, right?"

"I think his officers were still expecting us to break for the star-lanes," Holmwood admitted. "I'm not sure he did. The last two battleships in the system were guarding the star-lane to Sivar-Six. They couldn't catch us.

"And he sent his ultimatum." That iron-stiff posture trembled—with rage, Isaac hoped. "If we want the Sivar to protect us, we have to surrender and become part of the Governance. The Republic might be able to dodge out through sheer distance, but the Skree-Skree, the Vistans, the Tohnbohn…he expects all of them to kneel."

"That's not happening, you know that, right?" Isaac asked softly. "We're still three weeks out, further than I'd like, but we'll be in Sivar space long before the Intendant can find star-lane routes back to anyone's home systems.

"And even if he did, we've sent reinforcements back. He can't win this, Captain Holmwood."

"But he might kill the President Emeritus."

That was the risk that Isaac was refusing to admit to himself.

"He might," he finally conceded. "And extracting her from Aris is going to be hell, no matter what happens. With her held captive in the First and Final Citadel, he has a trump card and he knows it.

"But we *cannot* let that trump card be enough," he continued. "We'll punch out their forces at Sivar-One and tear through their computers. We'll learn everything there is to know about the Governance and the people they've conquered.

"The Intendant will fall, Captain Holmwood. If he's smart, he'll realize he can't win after we kick his people's collective ass in Sivar-One and make a play for peace." Isaac sighed. "That he holds Amelie means we might just give him that peace, at least for now while we deal with the local Rogues.

"But we cannot refrain from action now. We'll do everything within our power to save Amelie, but we have to neutralize this threat."

"I never should have let her go down," Holmwood declared. "We knew it wasn't safe, that we were giving up control of her safety and security to an unknown."

"And without doing that, she couldn't have done her job," Isaac said. "It was her call, her decision—and without knowing that the Intendant was going to go this far, it seemed the right call then.

"This is not your fault, Captain Holmwood," he told her firmly.

"You followed her orders and supported her legitimate decisions. Unfortunately, it seems our potential ally is a dictator and conqueror of the worst kind.

"We might have turned a blind eye to focus on the Matrices, but now he's left us no choice. You and your ships will meet us at the rendezvous point one light-month outside Sivar-One, where we will plan our seizure of that system as a demonstration to the Intendant."

Isaac knew *exactly* how terrifying his cold smile could be, but today, it was exactly what Chantel Holmwood needed to see.

"Either he will give us back my wife or I will shatter his fleets, liberate his slaves and bring his fancifully named fortress down around his ears," Isaac concluded calmly.

"And everything I have seen suggests I'd be doing the galaxy a favor."

45

If Amelie understood the situation of the upper tier of the Sivar's not-truly-free helot class, the farm had a Sivar partner who acted as the paper owner. Most likely, the Siva in question collected a portion of the profits and never even visited the location.

Everyone she saw on the farmstead was a helot. They were mostly Pol—the Kond appeared to be the actual financier behind the business —but she saw Croni, the tentacled broccoli Sonba, and the treelike aliens she'd learned were called Toorg.

It was a large commercial operation, one of several that used the massive amounts of compost produced by a facility the size of the First and Final Citadel to produce food crops that most likely went right back to the Citadel.

There were at least three hundred people living on the farm, working its fields and machines and mills. Hiding Amelie among them was apparently straightforward, not least because she didn't see any Sivar in the days before the Kond returned.

She didn't even see him arrive. Her hosts had asked her to stay in the main dormitory, well out of sight from anyone who visited the place. It was boring as all hell, but it was safe and she'd met enough Pol now to realize that the Kond was male.

The Kond ended up meeting her in a small office this time instead of the laundromat. She was sticking to Sivar clothing based on the selection he'd left her. It fit relatively well, covered her armor, and didn't draw quite as much attention as a Terran-style suit unlike anything else on the planet.

There were enough different aliens on the farm that even a human went unnoticed by anyone who didn't know who she was.

"I appreciate your patience, Minister Lestroud," the Kond told her as he gestured her to a seat. "Making contact with my partners is difficult, and I must keep up my business and speak with my Sivar partners…who cannot be permitted to guess anything has changed."

"I am familiar with the dance, Kond," she replied. She'd done the same thing once. "The time to think has been valuable. Have your 'partners' agreed to meet with me?"

"They have," he confirmed. "It will take a few days, and some are only sending representatives. Not everyone is on Sivar and communicating off-world is difficult at best."

"You are sneaking messages into Sivar com drones, I presume?" Amelie asked. "Since there are no non-Sivar ships."

The mole-like alien wrinkled his nose at her.

"You know that question is not safe for me to answer," he said. "You will need to remain here for a while longer. It is a safe place to keep you."

"But is it an effective place for me to be?" Amelie replied. Pol body language was still new to her, but she suspected that surprised the Kond. "Do you know this symbol?"

She dropped the cloth that Rode had given her on the table. The Kond stared at it for several seconds, then lowered his head with an audible sniff.

"Yes. It is not as hopeful as you might think. It was chosen as an irony, as something the Intendants would never believe was associated with the Dynasts."

"The Dynasts," Amelie echoed. "That is not a term I have heard before."

The Kond paused, then settled himself more firmly in his chair with another sniff.

"You will dig until you find what you desire, yes?" he asked. "I can respect that, but you dig into wars and lies that may put my people at risk."

"These Dynasts are also enemies of the Intendant?" Amelie replied. "Sivar enemies, I assume?"

"Yes. The Intendants and the Eyes of Sivar overthrew the First and Final Dynasty three generations ago, but a minor branch of the family survived and went into hiding.

"Now they plot a return to power." The Kond shivered. "Make no mistake, Minister Lestroud, the structure of tribute and helot? The Dynasts built that. They are not my friends."

"But they share your enemies," Amelie replied. She'd had this conversation a *lot* in the Confederacy. She sighed.

"Tell me truthfully, Kond. You told me there were more action-ready organizations than yours. How many other rebels lurk among the tributes and the helots that you have not invited to this meeting of yours?"

The alien aristocrat studied her with dark eyes.

"The organization I represent is one of the helots and the servants," he finally conceded. "We have our claws among the tributes, but many of the tributes are already working for their homeworlds. They don't trust long-term helots and we don't trust them.

"Even among the helots, there are the more violent groups that I do not associate with."

"Are we talking a dozen groups? A hundred? Five hundred hands or ten thousand?" Amelie demanded.

The Kond's unreadable gaze stayed focused on her.

"I am not certain," he admitted. "There are perhaps thirty groups I know of among the helots and the tributes here in the City. Many pay their fealty off-world, and few rival my organization's numbers or power."

"But they have guns and explosives where you have spies and smugglers, yes?" Amelie asked. "They have asked you for intelligence that you have refused to provide?"

"That is correct," he said. "What do you want, Minister Lestroud?"

"I want you to bring them all to that meeting, Kond," she told him.

"I want you to use your organization's connections and reputation to put everyone in one room. It's not the best way to do this, but I'm running out of time."

Her math said she had less than twenty days before Isaac hit Sonbar—Sivar-One.

"I cannot do that," the Kond protested. "My partners—"

"Then do not tell your partners," Amelie replied. "Put everyone in one room, Kond, and so long as we keep them from killing each other, the worst that happens is you know you share a goal."

He sniffled.

"I know these people," he noted. "I am not as confident as you that we can keep them from killing each other."

"Get them to the meeting, Kond," she told him. "I have something none of you have. A few things, really, but two are critical:

"Firstly, I am not part of any of your factions. I can stand as arbiter and guarantor to an alliance against the Intendant."

"And the other?"

"I speak for the only people who can defeat the Sivar fleet in space."

The Kond was silent.

"I don't think you can give me what I need, Kond," Amelie said quietly. "Not on your own. The rebels need to be ready for when the Intendant's position wavers at the fall of Sonbar. *All of them.* Can your organization storm and seize the First and Final Citadel alone?"

"I am not certain all of the helot and tribute organizations *combined* could do that," he replied. "If I listen to you, you will doom us all."

"And that's why I also need to talk to this Dynast and the *Sivar* rebels," she told him. "You need to get everyone to that meeting, Kond, and you need to give me a ride into the City. I'm guessing you know where I can find this symbol."

Her finger stabbed at the cloth, and the Kond's gaze followed her gesture.

"You are mad," he finally said. "A lead digger driving ever closer to the river bottom. I should never have listened to you."

"You *need* to listen to me," Amelie snapped. "Has doing things the way you have changed *anything*, Kond? You must have saved a few people along the way, I'm sure—but you haven't even saved enough that the Sivar are looking for escapees in the trucks leaving the Citadel.

"I can't save your people myself," she continued. "But I can help you help each other. I can bring the Republic to your door to break the Sivar fleets and stand as an external guarantor to your promises and alliances.

"But you said yourself that your organization can't do this. That all of the helot organizations can't do this—and I suspect if the Sivar organizations could do it, they would have." She spread her hands.

"Together, with the Republic as an inciting factor, you can achieve what you never would have managed on your own. But you need to take a chance, Kond. Are you willing to? *Can* you?"

The Kond sniffed the air in silence for a moment, then bowed his big head.

"We will take my vehicle," he told her. "I cannot guarantee your safety once I drop you off. We'll have to set a time for pickup, but between those…I cannot protect you. Even the local Sivar guards may grab you."

"That's the risk I have to take," Amelie agreed. "It's part of my job."

The Kond snorted.

"What is your job, again?" he asked.

"At this point? Turning the Governance into a nation we *are* prepared to ally with."

46

———————

THE KOND'S personal vehicle was a smaller version of the six-wheeled truck that had brought Amelie down from the mountain. On the exterior, it was clearly a work vehicle. On the inside, it was significantly more comfortable, with soft seats and highly effective climate control.

"It would never do for a helot to appear wealthy or comfortable," the Kond told her as they drove into the City. Other vehicles around them looked closer to the kind of personal and luxury vehicles Amelie would have expected in a human city.

"You can do well, but only quietly," Amelie concluded aloud. "And only among helots, I assume?"

"My little business services many Sivar, but we are servants only," he agreed. "I invest in other businesses as well, but…" He sniffed. "As you say, they are either among helots or have Sivar faces that officially own and run them."

The fact that there *were* Sivar that the Kond could get to help him maintain that illusion was promising. Money—or whatever passed for currency or influence in a given culture—papered over many sins for most species.

But if the Sivar were *truly* lost beyond any hope of Amelie working with them, she suspected that the Kond would have had a far harder time keeping up his little empire.

"Here," the Pol told her as he pulled the truck around a small open-air plaza and into an alleyway parking spot. "Walk carefully, Minister Lestroud," he told her. "This is a Sivar entertainment district. Tributes and helots are only allowed in the alleys and kitchens.

"The tables are served by robots and Sivar. They do not want to see aliens here, though many helots work in these businesses."

"That's typical," Amelie replied. "Thank you."

"I won't be picking you up," he told her. "Someone else will do so, but they'll be in this vehicle. They'll pick you up here in seven hours."

"Thank you," she repeated. "Is there anywhere in particular I should look for the symbol?"

"The back doors all have the symbol of the restaurant on them," the Kond told her. "My understanding is that several of this particular plaza's businesses are owned by the Dynast. You should be able to make contact here.

"If you can't, you can wander further afield if you want, but your contact seemed to think they'd be easy enough to find," he continued. "I'd suggest waiting in the alley until we come back for you if you can't find your contacts. It would be safer."

"Go, Kond," she told him. "I'll be here in seven hours or I'll send a message to arrange a different time for pickup. I don't suppose you have a tablet you can give me?"

"Helots are not permitted mobile communications devices like your tablet," he replied. "Most will assume you to be a helot or tribute unless given reason to believe otherwise, but I cannot be found with them. This vehicle cannot contain anything that would produce signals that would draw attention, so I don't have any with me.

"If you conclude any alliance with the Dynast, perhaps they can provide you something." He paused, then sniffed again.

"May your digging be fruitful."

Before she could respond to that, he closed the door and turned the truck back on. A moment later, Amelie Lestroud was alone in the back alley behind a row of restaurants she couldn't be seen in.

It was time to get to work.

———

Amelie started by taking a slow walk along the alley. Her goal was twofold: first, to take at least a quick look at each of the restaurant logos to see if any of them obviously held the symbol she'd been given; and second, to see the limits of what counted as *alley*.

She expected it to be relatively obvious where the areas the helots were allowed were and she was right. There was a blue line painted on the ground and walls at the end, but it was almost unnecessary.

It was very clear that the area on one side of that line had been maintained to be gorgeous…and the area on the other side had been maintained to be functional.

Interestingly, it looked like there was a reasonably continuous corridor of helot-allowed roads and pathways leading both deeper into the City and out toward the suburbs. There were probably places where non-helots would have to pass through that were better maintained, but it formed a maintenance corridor through an area where non-Sivar were clearly *not* allowed.

Slaves and near-slaves made for much cheaper labor than free Sivar. It was clear that the business owners weren't going to give up that cost savings just for the illusion of living in a city that *wasn't* being run on the backs of alien slaves.

The plaza that the Kond had dropped her off behind had six restaurants in the alleyway she had started in, and none of them obviously had a broken-chain image in their logos.

Three of the six, however, had stars in their logos. One of those stars was a perfect match for the one in the symbol Amelie was carrying, and on closer examination, the position of the *letters* of the name was a perfect match for the pieces of the broken chain.

No matter what happened next, she had to take a risk. Otherwise, everything she was setting out to do was for nothing.

Folding the cloth with the symbol into her hand, she rapped hard on the door. No one answered for a minute, so she raised her hand to knock again.

The door popped open before she could strike it, a tall-for-their-race Siva standing in the doorway, glaring up at her.

"What the hell do you want?" the Siva demanded. When they saw her, however, she could tell that they knew *something*. Most of the Sivar who'd seen her had clearly written her off as an alien helot without any further thought. This one clearly knew she was something else entirely.

She let the cloth unfold to hang from her hand, the symbol clearly visible to the Siva in the door.

"My apologies, I'm lost, and I was hoping you could help me find these people?" she asked softly, gesturing with the cloth.

"This is a restaurant, not a helot charity!" the Siva snapped at her, projecting their voice loudly so it could be heard by anyone in the alley. "Be off with you, begone, we have nothing for you!"

As they yelled, however, they pushed the door further open and gestured her inside with their free hand. She ducked under their arm —*her* arm, Amelie thought, the stranger lacked the facial horns of male Sivar—and the door slammed shut behind her.

"I know what you are," the Siva hissed. "But you're all supposed to be dead or captured. Where did you get that symbol?"

"I suspect that telling you that could get a lot of people killed," Amelie replied. "I'm looking for sanctuary—but more than that, I need to talk to your leaders."

"I run security for a restaurant," her new acquaintance pointed out. "Do you mean my manager?"

"No," Amelie said. Another risk might be needed there. She wasn't sure it was the right call, but it was the weapon she had to hand.

"I mean the Dynast."

———

THE GUARD STARED at Amelie for several long seconds, then laughed. Her armored jaw clicked in a sound that was rather disturbing to human ears.

"I am Isseel," she told Amelie. "Your presence here already dooms me if you work for the Intendant. If they know that symbol enough to identify this restaurant, I have already been marked for anathema and merely haven't learned it yet.

"Come," Isseel instructed.

They stepped farther into the restaurant, where a Sonba in a white tunic that covered most of their skin stuck their broccoli-like head out of the kitchen. "Isseel, we—"

"Not right now, Canba," the security head replied. "Talk to Dost if you need someone evicted, but if it's supplies you need, you know that's not my job."

It was hard to pick out a Sonba's tentacled eyes amidst the less-mobile fronds of their head, but Amelie was grimly certain the alien was studying her closely for a moment.

"All right." The Sonba disappeared back into the kitchen.

"Staff," Isseel said in a tone that every manager across the galaxy would recognize. "I can't order anything for them, but they come to me instead of Sohstell." She shook her armored head.

"Of course, Sohstell treats the helots like work animals," she muttered under her breath. "Because no work animal had ever kicked its rider to death."

Amelie was quite sure she was being tested and simply maintained a genteel silence as Isseel led her up to the second floor of the restaurant. That turned out to be made up of several private rooms.

To her surprise, she was led to one looking out over the plaza with floor-to-ceiling windows. From there she could see the entire Sivar crowd wandering through an open pedestrian area surrounded by boutiques and cafes that would have fit in perfectly on Exilium.

Of course, the crowd on Exilium would have been taller.

"The windows are one-way," Isseel told her. "You'll have complete privacy."

She gestured Amelie to a seat.

"Please, wait here," she instructed. "I can't bring the person you seek here, but I can bring someone who can at least talk to them for you."

"It's somewhere to start," Amelie agreed. "I could very easily be a trap, after all."

"That would require some effort, Minister Amelie Lestroud," a new voice told her as another Siva entered the room. "Thank you, Isseel. Please go kick Sohstell and tell ban that if ban doesn't stop plucking the helot staff's skullplates, I can replace my purchaser far more easily than I can replace my chef."

Amelie had to blink as she processed the metaphor. The Sivar had plates that hung down around their neck from the plating on their skulls. Those could be grabbed and pulled. She doubted it would cause much movement, but it was probably *very* annoying.

Sohstell, it seemed, had a gift for pissing the staff off.

The speaker gestured Isseel out of the room and closed the door behind banself. Ban stood by the door for several moments after that, studying Amelie.

"You know who I am," Amelie concluded. "You were told I was coming?"

"Indeed. Which was quite a risk," ban noted. "Every cell leader in the City was told to watch for you, using a channel we reserved for critical emergencies. Each time it is used, we risk exposing our organization."

"Someone thought it was worth it," Amelie said.

"Indeed." Ban crossed to the table and took a seat. "My name is Loreck. I own this restaurant and I work for the Broken Chain."

"You serve the Dynast," she concluded.

Loreck winced, a gesture that manifested in Sivar as a clack of armor plating.

"Be more sparing with that title, please," ban asked. "We hope that the Intendant does not know that the Broken Chain exists, let alone what the Broken Chain serves."

"I've yet to meet whatever the Intendant uses for internal security, thank God," Amelie noted, "but I wonder how realistic that hope is."

"The Knives of the Eyes do not truly work for the Intendant," Loreck said, ban's voice very quiet. "But your assessment of their role and their skill is roughly correct. They watch our worlds for sedition and heresy."

"Alone?" she asked.

"No. They lean on the Knives of the Keys of War," Loreck explained. "You know so little about us. I question your value."

Amelie smiled thinly.

"How many battleships did the Commandants send against my escort?" she asked softly. "I doubt your Broken Chain is unaware of how that ended."

"My own information is limited," Loreck admitted. "But my understanding is that the ships in question remain in orbit...because they cannot leave. And that, Minister Lestroud, is why I believe the Broken Chain was called to protect you."

"Protection isn't enough," Amelie replied. "I need to speak to..." She cut herself off and paused thoughtfully. "Your leader," she finally concluded.

Not using the Dynast's title was a small-enough concession, she supposed.

"So I heard," Loreck conceded. "*My* instructions were to see you kept safe. A bargaining chip for the Broken Chain if your people prove as mighty as you claim."

"You can attempt to acquire a bargaining chip, Loreck, at the price of a potential ally," she told ban. "I did not arrive at your door alone, and another ally waits to carry me away in a few hours. I have no desire to make them wait."

She was suddenly very aware of the weight of her armor vest and the laser pistol it contained. She didn't *want* to shoot her way out to meet the Kond, but she would.

"You are a determined one, aren't you?" Loreck asked. "You understand, yes, that contacting my leaders risks this cell? And everyone who works in the restaurant? You are not, I suspect, as uncaring about the helots as my more stupid compatriots."

"Risks must be taken," she told him. "All of this is built on risk and chances and hope."

"All of this," ban echoed. "And what would *this* be, Minister Lestroud? What are you attempting to build?"

"The fall of the Intendant and the birth of a new Sivar nation," Amelie said flatly. "A nation without slaves, without murders.

"A nation my people could proudly stand side by side with against the enemies that hide in the darkest void."

She was watching Loreck's eyes. She wasn't sure how much of

what she and the Intendant had discussed had been made public—or how much of it Rode had leaked to the Broken Chain. The upward glance ban took at her words told her ban knew *something*.

"The Builders," ban finally said.

"The Rogues, at least," Amelie confirmed. "If we don't fight them, you'll all burn. Right now, your people have managed to make yourselves a distraction we didn't need. If we have to suppress the Governance to deal with our main enemy, that won't go well for you."

She wasn't entirely sure how Isaac would go about that, but she was pretty sure it wouldn't leave much in terms of shipbuilding infrastructure anywhere in Sivar space.

"If you can salvage a government we're prepared to negotiate with from the Governance, then you can save a lot of lives. Mostly Sivar lives, if that matters to you."

"Even if you focused solely on the Keys of War and are entirely immune to our weapons, our governed worlds would suffer," Loreck said quietly. "I am not one of those who think we can fix our nation without changing how the Sivar and the other races interact. Neither is my leader."

Ban shook ban's head.

"There are some who do believe that."

"We won't permit that as a solution," Amelie replied. "Not and make the alliance we both want."

"You are very demanding for a woman with nothing," Loreck said calmly. "And if I told you that wasn't acceptable?"

"I'd note that doesn't seem to be your decision," she said.

Loreck laughed.

"Perhaps not," ban agreed. "My decision is whether to send you to my sister at all."

Amelie blinked.

"Your sister?"

"Ban do not transmit lineage," Loreck pointed out. "Even if she were younger, I would concede any claim to her for that alone. But she is wiser than I, in my opinion."

Ban rose.

"Come, Minister."

"Where are we going?" Amelie asked.

"It is far too risky for me to send a message," the Siva told her. "But driving over to surprise my sister for supper? Even the Knives of the Eyes are unlikely to question that."

47

———

Leaving a message for the Kond was thankfully as easy as a preplanned set of chalk marks left on the alley wall before joining Loreck in ban's car. Staying invisible in that vehicle was harder than it had been in the Kond's work truck, but variable-tint windows helped.

Still, Amelie spent the entire drive deep into what looked like a middle-class suburb of vaguely pyramidical houses slumped as low as she could manage in the back seat of the six-wheeled vehicle. Hopefully, the tinting worked, because the vehicle was designed for people over thirty centimeters shorter than her, and there was only so much slumping she could manage.

Garages looked much the same the galaxy over apparently and she finally relaxed, a little, as Loreck parked the car.

"Come with me," ban ordered. Ban led the way to a small side room that could have just as easily been an office or a breakfast nook, and then left her there.

She'd been hoping for something a bit more definitive and waited for at least ten minutes before realizing that whatever Loreck was doing, it was going to take a while. Unfortunately, her tablet had nothing even remotely resembling signal on the planet, now that

Watchtower and the relay system they'd set up at the embassy were gone.

It was hardwired into her translator and she'd actually disabled all of its wireless signals. It still gave her a clock and let her add notes from her conversation with Loreck into the local database.

That took her at least ten minutes, but she was still waiting. The door had been closed behind her. It might even be locked, not that Amelie was really feeling restrained by that.

She'd be in a lot of trouble if she had to shoot her way out of a Broken Chain safehouse. Amelie didn't *think* she was being held prisoner, but it wasn't outside the realm of possibility.

After she'd been waiting for forty minutes, she tested the door to make sure it wasn't locked. It swung open easily and silently, and she found herself facing a young—she thought, at least—Siva leaning against the wall across the corridor.

"Do you need something?" he asked quickly. "I can get you a drink or something, but we need you to stay out of sight from the windows."

"I'm waiting on—"

"I know," the youth told her. "You can leave if you want, but I don't see any way that could work for anyone. They should be here for you soon."

Amelie snorted at the alien with the armored head.

"Get me some water?" she asked. "I'll be cooperative for a bit longer."

"They talk, and they talk, and they talk, but they know you're waiting," he promised. "It shouldn't be much longer."

He went for the water anyway, clearly trusting her to stay in the dinette on her own. With a chuckle, Amelie took a seat and waited.

The kid didn't bring her water. Loreck did and ban came alone.

"Well?" Amelie asked ban, taking the delicate ceramic cup ban carried.

"Drink up, assuming your throat gets dry from talking like ours do," ban replied. "Then follow me."

Ban led the way deeper into the house, past a window where the youth she'd just met was *entirely coincidentally* suddenly measuring what looked like a drunken hybrid between blinds and curtains against the glass, blocking any view into the house.

Loreck opened the door to what was *definitely* a closet and then tapped a concealed button. Coats and racks of shoes slid aside, revealing a steep ladder leading down into the ground.

"Suspicious-looking, I know," ban conceded. "But we need full security for this, and there are few better insulators against unexpected listeners than dirt and concrete."

"Lead the way," Amelie said. "I look forward to meeting your sister."

"Believe me, Minister Lestroud, the feeling appears to be mutual."

———

THE LADDER WAS LONG ENOUGH and designed for people with different-enough anatomy that Amelie was in noticeable discomfort before finally extracting herself from it into a dimly lit…hole.

There was no better description for the bare earth walls that surrounded her. It looked like something had just dug a thirty-foot-deep hole from the house and expanded it a bit at the bottom. There was a single electric light providing illumination, and there wasn't even a visible exit.

Amelie wasn't claustrophobic, but this was a bit much.

"Loreck?" she asked cautiously.

Instead of answering her, ban shoved ban's arm into one of the dirt walls, revealing that one to be much looser than it looked, and hit some kind of control. The wall ban was poking at slid away from them and to the side, exposing that the "wall" was just several inches of dirt on some kind of backing.

The other side was a slightly more solid-looking tunnel with several electric lights leading to what was much more clearly a door.

That door was a heavily shielded monstrosity, clearly designed to prevent signal leakage.

"This way, please, Minister," Loreck told her. Even the vault door slid open easily at ban's touch.

The other side of that was much more solid-looking. Metal and stone had been worked in as walls and floors, clearly designed to muffle sound and radiation and resist bombardment.

"The bunker pre-dates the neighborhood above," Loreck told her. "We destroyed most of the accesses to hide it and drilled up when the neighborhood was built." Ban shook ban's head. "Locating *which* house to buy was apparently a project. That was my bana's task, though. Ban never had good things to say about that."

That would have been Loreck's ban parent. The third member of a ban family unit would usually be the one buying the house, from what Amelie understood, so that made some sense.

"Where was the bunker originally accessed from?" she asked as she followed ban deeper into the structure. It was larger than she expected, and they'd clearly come in on the top floor.

It was clearly old, with obsolete systems by even Sivar standards, but it was all in working order. If nothing else, she had to wonder how they *powered* it.

"The First and Final Citadel, via a concealed train system that is long destroyed now," Loreck replied. "We have a geothermal plant about two hundred meters further down, and some parts of the structure obviously go that deep." Ban shrugged. "Most of it is up here. It was a final secret retreat for the family, and it served its purpose."

"This bunker is why the Dynasts still exist?" Amelie said.

"Not alone, but it is certainly the centerpiece of what power we have. Right under the Intendant's nose."

There were very few people in the bunker, which made sense. Outside of an active combat situation, Amelie couldn't see any reason why they'd have many people there. Most of the people there would presumably be communications people supporting the Dynast.

Loreck led her into a central briefing room that wouldn't have looked out of place in a Republic or Confederacy military base. There were half a dozen Sivar of all three genders in the room.

As Amelie entered, everyone looked at her and then looked at a female Siva standing behind a table that looked like it had been freshly cleared of papers and maps.

"Minister Amelie Lestroud," the Siva said, bowing ever so slightly.

"I have heard many things about you, some fascinating, some disturbing. Have a seat." She gestured to a chair across from her.

"From the amount of time it took me to end up here, I'm guessing that Loreck filled you in on everything we talked about," Amelie noted.

"Ban did," the Siva agreed. "As did our mutual friend in the Citadel." She smiled. "My name is Silleck. Loreck is my younger banner. We are the current generation of the family that once ruled the Sivar Governance."

"You are the Dynast," Amelie concluded.

"You didn't hear that term from us," Silleck noted. "But yes, that is the technically accurate but currently meaningless title I could claim."

The other Sivar in the room bristled, but Silleck waved for them to relax.

"The Governance as it was under the Dynasty is already dead," she snapped. "The Governance as it is under the Intendant is no worse in many ways, though I doubt any Dynast would have turned aside your offer of alliance as readily as the Intendant did.

"Tell me, Minister Amelie…just how badly is the Governance's fleet outclassed by yours?"

"Badly," Amelie said quietly. "*Watchtower*'s Captain was under orders to avoid a major confrontation with your fleet. Her taking the orbitals above Aris wouldn't have served anyone and would have left a lot of Sivar dead in space."

"But your ship could have defeated the forces arrayed against her?" Silleck asked.

"I don't know the full extent of the forces that were deployed against *Watchtower*," Amelie admitted. "But outside of a surprise ambush at short range, there is nothing in the Governance's line of battle that represents a material threat to a Republic capital ship on anything resembling even terms."

The Dynast seemed content with that. Amelie knew she was *probably* exaggerating. The Sivar couldn't have stopped *Watchtower* retreating, but she suspected an outright battle between the battlecruiser and the planet's fortifications would have ended poorly—for everyone.

"You didn't come directly to us," she noted. "You sought us out, presumably having already made other allies here on Aris. We haven't seen *Watchtower* since she left orbit. What happens next, Minister?"

"My fleet will move to rescue the prisoners taken by the Intendant." Amelie shrugged. "In the absence of any change, they will reduce the defenses of several systems on their approach to Aris, devastate the defenses in this system and demand the release of our people.

"The Intendant will probably realize that while we can *destroy* the First and Final Citadel, we can't assault it on the ground, and hold our people hostage. A negotiation will ensue, though I am not convinced that the Intendant can be safely negotiated with."

"That sounds like a situation that should eventually result in you getting what you want," Silleck said. "With you outside the Citadel, the Intendant loses his strongest bargaining chip, and you, personally, are probably more easily extracted from the City.

"Our mutual friend's assistance in allowing you to escape seems to have already given you all that you need. So, what do you *want*?"

"I refuse to allow a slaving expansionist autocracy to *fester* on my flank while I fight a war against a fleet of self-replicating genocidal machines," Amelie said flatly. "The Governance as it currently stands is an offense to all that is right and just, and I intend to bring it down.

"Beyond that, I want to get my people out of the First and Final Citadel, and I would *like* to end this conflict and reform the Governance *without* a war that will see tens of million of Sivar and their slaves killed."

She held Silleck's gaze.

"You know every argument I can make," she told the Siva. "Either from Loreck or from our *mutual friend* in the Citadel. I have made allies among the helots and tributes, and I know that my fleet will deliver defeats that will create a moment of weakness on the part of the Intendant.

"Even with that moment, I don't think the rebels among the helots and tributes can overthrow the First and Final Citadel on their own. I don't believe that *you* can overthrow the First and Final Citadel on your own.

"But combined, you might just be able to change the Governance's fate."

The briefing room exploded into streams of rapidly spoken Sivar. There were too many speakers talking far too quickly for her translator to follow, and she winced at its confused attempt to translate the argument.

"Enough!" Silleck bellowed. Her voice silenced her subordinates and she faced Amelie across the table. Sivar faces didn't move enough to smile, but there was a spark to her eyes that Amelie suspected she understood.

"It was my ancestors who created the Governance and the tribute program and the helots," she told Amelie. "But my ancestors called themselves the First and Final Dynasty, so I think we can all agree that their predictions for the future were incomplete at best.

"We were the first to unify Aris and we believed we would rule forever," Silleck summarized, mostly for Amelie's benefit. "We encountered other races when we left our world, and we were convinced that our rule of Aris was righteous because we had the strength to take it.

"So, our rule of other worlds was righteous for the same reason. Living as ordinary people has helped change my and my banner's view of that. My father's, too, I believe, though he kept his silence on that point."

"We cannot continue to enslave entire worlds," Loreck, the *banner* in question, said. "It is a toxin that has sunk into the bones of our government and is destroying our people. It weakens us, it blinds us and it hurts us as a people.

"To be willfully ignorant of the harm we have done requires us to poison our own minds," ban continued. "It must end. The Governance might survive, but the structures must change and the tributes and helots must be freed."

"I don't even require them to go home," Silleck said dryly. "Many of them were born here, just as I was, and many of our people were born on the governed worlds. We must find ways for all of us to live together as equal partners in a future."

"Surely, we must stand as first among those partners," one of the other Sivar demanded.

"*Maybe*," the Dynast hissed. "But we must *earn* that status—and the first step to doing so is to recognize how much harm we have done and work to undo it."

"Will you fight with us, then?" Amelie asked.

"Can you commit them to fight with *us*?" Silleck replied. "I speak for the Broken Chain, the organization that serves my family. There are others."

"I am organizing a…convention, let's call it, with help from one of the rebel groups," Amelie told her. "There are things I can offer you all that I will not offer any group on its own. The more of you are present when I make that offer, the better we all are."

"I will come," Silleck said instantly. She glanced around the room, cowing her subordinates with her eyes. "If you are prepared to tell me where, I can bring others. There are few rebels among the Sivar I do not know."

"If there is a way I can contact you, I can return to my other allies and make the arrangements," Amelie promised.

Silleck nodded and gestured to one of her aides. A wristband-style communicator appeared from nowhere.

"To avoid problems, this only links to one channel and is highly encrypted," she told Amelie as she passed it over. "For now, I suspect you should keep it concealed."

"I was told such devices were banned for helots, and that seems to be most people's assumption of what I am."

"Exactly." Silleck looked around. "It is decided. Walk with me," she told Amelie.

Mildly concerned, Amelie followed the Dynast out of the conference room. Loreck was already moving to corral the other Sivar, making sure the two women were alone.

"We'll take you out a different way. Tell Kond Asselis that the Green River Farm is going to need to up its chlorine budget for next year by twenty percent," Silleck told Amelie with a soft chuckle. "It's not a code," she said as Amelie looked at her in concern.

"It's just a piece of information that no one outside our little semi-secret covert business venture will know."

"You knew," Amelie said.

"I suspected the Kond was up to his neck in at least three rebel groups," Silleck replied. "If anyone can bring the helots and tributes to a peace circle, it's the Kond. I'll bring the Sivar, as many of them as will accept the future I think we both want."

"Why do you even need me?" the human said with a chuckle of her own.

"Even the *Sivar* won't trust me," the Dynast said. "The Kond might, if he knew who I was descended from, but he couldn't convince the rest of the people we enslaved. The factions he'll bring don't trust each other.

"We need someone outside our conflicts and politics…and preferably someone with the ability to make certain everyone keeps their promises." Silleck shook her head.

"Even so, I hope you can deliver on that defeat you promised. Unless you can separate the Commandant-Keys of War from the Intendant, anything we achieve on the surface is going to be *very* short-lived."

48

Somehow, Octavio wasn't surprised when the first scans of the system came back utterly silent. No large power sources. No mobile heat signatures. Nothing. That meant there were no ships. No colonies.

From the uninhabitable nature of the two rocky planets, it also meant there were no Assini. If the Assini colonists had survived the last three hundred years, they might even have eventually been able to nudge the innermost planet into the star's tiny liquid-water zone, but without that project the planets were hostile to life without technology.

"We'll have to get closer," he said aloud. "Do we have a tighter location on the Sentinels?"

"Somewhere in the inner system," Renaud told him. "Siril-ki's people are working on localizing them, but the tachyon com isn't the best tool for that close an ID."

He grunted, looking at the four worlds hanging in the bridge's holographic display. For this part of the mission, he was better off in the uncomfortable observer seat on the bridge

"Set a course for the inner planet, Captain Renaud," he ordered. "If our strangers set up a long-term colony anywhere, it would be in the place they might have been able to Construct later."

If he'd lived through the death of his species to a failing star, the system's ultra-stable orange dwarf primary would have been tempting to him. Making a planet habitable with the heat from that star would be difficult, but it was well within the demonstrated abilities of the terraforming equipment available to the Assini.

"Scans will give us more information as we get closer," McGill noted. "We're still a few light-minutes from being able to pick out inactive space stations, for example."

"I know," he agreed. "How long until we could pick up a Sentinel in standby mode?"

Renaud and McGill traded looks.

"They have the same energy-dispersing ceramic armor we do," Renaud said slowly. "I think that would help…plus they don't have life support to worry about."

"The computer core burns a lot of heat," McGill replied. "They can only get so cold before they're literally killing themselves to do it."

"So?" Octavio asked. "I make it six light-minutes, myself, but that's mostly an engineer's perspective."

"We can detect an inactive platform at six light-minutes," Renaud agreed. "If they're leaking heat, then maybe seven."

"But if they're hiding well and controlling their heat release, they could easily make themselves hard to distinguish from inactive platforms until we're even closer," McGill pointed out.

"Keep them in mind," Octavio ordered softly. "And make sure all of the warships check in on their readiness. I'm not convinced this battle group can engage three Sentinels, and I'd rather not court that threat if we can avoid it."

"But the Sentinels—"

"Are Matrices that have been left alone for two hundred and eighty years," he interrupted Renaud. "And we're missing ninety percent of them—and an entire colony. Something happened here, Captain, Commander. I don't trust the Sentinels not to have been responsible for it."

"I see, sir."

"D," Octavio addressed the AI. "I want that part of our preparations kept secret from Siril-ki and her people. Hopefully, it will be a waste of worrying."

"I anticipated as much, Commodore, but I appreciate the clarification," the Matrix replied. "I cannot, unfortunately, disagree with your assessment. The Sentinels' presence here suggests that they are aware of the rogue colony...but per their core protocols, they should have protected that colony at all costs.

"But I am not seeing a—"

"Captain, Commodore," McGill interjected into the gap as D cut themselves off. "We just flagged something you need to see."

"Show me," Octavio ordered.

The big holographic display in the center of the bridge flickered, and a new icon appeared on the map of the star system. An entire region of space, almost a light-second across, was now blinking in orange.

"We are picking up massive quantities of refined metal in this area," D reported. "Lieutenant Commander McGill's analysts are suggesting we're looking at shipwrecks. I rate that probability at seventy-five plus/minus five percent. As we are focusing scanners, I am picking up diffuse clouds of metal suggesting the vaporization of significant amounts of that material."

"Active scans," Octavio ordered. "Deploy tachyon com–equipped drones as well. Let's move up to that cloud and see what we're looking at."

He suspected he already knew the answer.

———

"We appear to have found the bulk of the Sentinels," D told them all an hour later, as *Dauntless* and her escorts slowly orbited the debris cloud. "Not all of them, by far, but scans suggest at least fifty Sentinel-type vessels in the debris cloud."

"What killed them?" Siril-ki asked, the Assini linked in from ki's office. "We've established the Construction Matrices never came here."

"We have identified the wreckage of two hundred and sixty-three individual warships that were *not* Sentinels in the debris cloud," D replied.

"They're robots too," McGill explained. "Only a portion appear to have been large enough to carry Matrix AI cores, and we don't think any of them were punch-capable."

She shook her head.

"The design is definitely Assini," she continued.

"I have an eighty-two plus/minus three percent probability that we are looking at the deployment of ten to twelve Guardian swarms," D explained calmly. "Those were the non-punch-capable defense ships built to protect the Assini System before the Construction Project and continually upgraded after.

"Assuming the colonists had brought standard Assini industrial modules with them, the manufacture of Guardian swarms would have been relatively straightforward."

A new image appeared on the screen: a ship roughly the same size as *Dauntless* with two dozen smaller ships moving around it in deep space.

"Later iterations like these appear to have used a Matrix AI in the core Guardian warship to provide command and control to drones with a limited deployment range," D noted.

"Twelve Guardian swarms shouldn't have been able to engage fifty-plus Sentinels," Siril-ki objected.

"Unless they were heavily upgraded, potentially to the standard of the Escort Matrices or even beyond," Octavio murmured. "With the self-replication abilities of Assini industrial architecture, continually updating a set of Guardian swarms to engage the main Assini combat forces on an even playing field would be entirely possible."

"That would require these colonists to assume that they *would* be fighting the Sentinels," Siril-ki pointed out. "Why would they assume that?!"

"I don't know," Octavio admitted. "But they were right. Fifty Sentinels died here, people. *Fifty*. That was a fleet that could have taken on a Rogue Regional Construction Matrix's entire combat force with ease.

"So, whoever these people were, they expected to have to fight the Sentinels. And they ended up having to fight the Sentinels." He shook his head. "What I don't understand is *how*. Aren't the Sentinels bound not to attack Assini?"

"They should be, yes," Siril-ki agreed. "And they were using post-punch verification at least until the fall of Sina, so they shouldn't have *lost* that."

"An important part of the answer, I believe, is the time frame," D noted. "Our scans suggest that this battle occurred two hundred and sixty-five plus/minus five years ago."

That time line silenced the room for a while. Octavio turned it over in his own head and shivered.

"At least five years," he said aloud. "When the Sentinels showed up, they'd been the last survivors of their species they knew for at least half a decade. More likely an *entire* decade."

"What would the Sentinels have done in that time frame?" Renaud asked. "Siril-ki? D?"

"Their mission at that point would have been a complete failure," Siril-ki said slowly. "They could have continued to keep the area clear of Construction Matrices, but there would have been no point.

"Machines the Matrices may be, but they are also intelligent individuals," the AI specialist continued. "They likely would have spent some time reestablishing some kind of networked validation system for themselves. I think they would have physically congregated, but I'm not certain. D?"

"I cannot be certain I share an equivalency with the Sentinels," D noted. "I am a clone of XR-13-9 loaded into a less-capable Matrix core that was activated on arrival at the *Interceptor* yard. I have never been without human company, let alone organic sentient or Matrix company.

"The thought of being truly alone…is somewhat disturbing to me," they admitted. "I think I would agree with you, Director Siril-ki. They would have gathered. They would have discussed what their best option was. Their nature—*our* nature, the nature of every Matrix—is to be doing *something*."

"And if they learned that the strangers existed while congregating, they would have come here?" Octavio asked.

"It seems likely," Siril-ki agreed. "But I can't see them attacking. I don't understand that part."

"They may not have started the battle," D replied. "If the Guardian swarms were ordered to attack the Sentinels, they would have defended themselves."

"But not to the point of destroying local infrastructure and wrecking the colony," Octavio said. "The Sentinels would have fought a battle here if attacked, but the colony should still exist."

"I have to agree," the Assini Director said. "Several things here do not add up. I need more data."

"I think we all can agree on that point," Octavio replied. "Can we learn anything more, surveying this debris field? Given the state of the ships, is there any chance of retrieving intact computer cores or anything else of sufficient value to make the attempt?"

"It's possible," McGill said. "But the chance is low."

"We could leave one of the strike cruisers here," Courtenay suggested, Octavio's aide linked into the command channel from his post on the flag deck. "Any of them would be able to support EMC shuttles searching for intact computer cores or similar, but until we know where the Sentinels are, I don't think we should be exploring new areas of the system without *Dauntless*."

"Agreed," Octavio said. "I'll talk to Captain Cameron, but the rest of the flotilla should get ready to move. I think our answers are either in orbit of or on that planet, people. Something happened to these people, but before that, they helped damn untold trillions.

"I have a lot of questions and we're going to find the answers."

49

───────────

DAUNTLESS'S ADVANCE on the planet was slow. The world that presumably *had* a name, but even the records from the Assini System only gave the system a catalog number that translated as KB2N13. The planets didn't even have that, falling into a default number system.

KB2N13-1 was all the name they had, and that was a mouthful for humans. The closer they drew, the clearer it became that the planet had to have *some* kind of name.

There had been vast domes on its surface, many of them probably farms taking advantage of what sunlight the rock received from its dim star. Other domes had likely held atmosphere over cities and mining complexes and the billion-and-one settlements and facilities sentients built on their planets.

None of those domes were active now. None of them were even *intact* now. KB2N13-1 didn't have an atmosphere, and there'd been nothing to stop unimaginably powerful laser beams striking from orbit and obliterating the protective shells protecting the colony settlements.

Someone had carried out an extraordinarily precise campaign of mass murder. The orbital stations were equally devastated, and it was hard for Octavio and his people to even pick out just what the original structures had been.

"There is the wreckage of at least two more Guardian swarms here," McGill reported quietly as the bridge crew looked at the shattered colony in silent horror. "I think there might actually be more of the drone parasite warships than the Guardians could control, but it's hard to tell. The debris field above the planet is a mess."

"And the Sentinels?" Renaud asked. "Were they here?"

"Yes," D answered before the tactical officer could respond. "I can't confirm exact numbers, but there are between twenty-five and thirty-five wrecked Sentinels in the debris field. A second battle took place here, likely in much the same time frame as the first."

"And the Sentinels spent themselves smashing into the strangers' defenses," Octavio murmured. "Some obviously survived. Would I be correct in assessing the dome damage as being from a Sentinel's beam weapons?"

"Likelihood approaches unity," D confirmed. "The Strangers appear to have been using zettahertz lasers equivalent to those mounted on the Escort Matrix units. The Sentinels were using high-frequency gamma-ray lasers.

"While both are horrendously destructive applied to structures like the colony dome, the Sentinels' beams are significantly less so and the distinction is easily assessed."

"That's *impossible*," Siril-ki objected. "Even the Rogue Matrices would have struggled to carry out this kind of bombardment. And the Sentinels should never have been damaged enough to let them attack Assini at all, let alone carry out a targeted campaign of extermination like this!"

"I would agree with your assessment of the core protocols implemented in the Sentinel Matrix cores, Director Siril-ki," D said. "And yet the evidence is unquestionable. At least one Sentinel Matrix—and the impact patterns suggest a minimum of three units—turned their weapons on the surface colony on KB2N13-1.

"This should have been impossible, yet it occurred. We can only extrapolate back from that circumstance."

"And one of those extrapolations is that we need to know where those three Sentinels we pinged via tachyon com are," Octavio said grimly. "Renaud, Courtenay—take the flotilla to Readiness One."

"Yes, sir," both officers chorused.

"You think the Sentinels are a threat," Siril-ki said on the command channel. When Octavio didn't respond, ki let the silence stretch out for at least a minute before sighing as the chimes on the ship called a second shift to their duty stations. Two-thirds of the crews of Octavio's warships would now be on duty at all times.

"I understand," ki conceded. "This attack shouldn't have been possible, so we need to assume that they are as lost as the Rogues by your worlds. I simply do not know what could have broken them."

"If they had no grounds for suspicion before and found themselves with proof that these strangers had broken the Matrices, that these strangers were responsible not only for the deaths of tens of millions of other Assini but had stolen your people's only chance of survival..." Octavio trailed off as he shook his head.

"What was the Sentinels' purpose, Siril-ki?" he asked. "We try to avoid thinking of them as machines, but we still look to their code and their protocol to define them. But they were people and they had a mission, a purpose. What was it?"

"Protect the Assini people," ki said, ki's voice very, very quiet. "And someone killed almost all of us. Except that someone *was* Assini... I don't know how that conflict between their protocol and their purpose would be resolved."

Octavio looked at the hologram showing him the wreckage of a murdered world.

"It seems they resolved it in blood and fire," he murmured. "I hesitate to apply the term to a Matrix, but I think they have gone mad."

"I believe you may be touching on the core of the matter, but your phrasing is wrong," D interjected into the conversation. "Mad, yes, but not as you mean. I fear my cousins were *angry*. I have felt the edge of what they would have felt, but I was modified so that my racial loyalty was to humans instead of Assini.

"We are not as emotional as organics, but XR-13-9 believed that our emotions short-circuit much of our core protocols and other limitations. If my progenitor is correct, the Sentinel Matrices may have been angry *enough* to ignore the prohibitions against attacking Assini and general mass murder."

"My god," Octavio murmured. "But…they're much the same as you, ethics- and morality-wise, at least? Right?"

"Yes. They would have remained angry far longer than any organic would have, but when they understood what they did…"

"They might have gone mad anyway," Octavio said, echoing his earlier words. "Siril-ki?"

"It…" Ki paused. "We never truly studied the interaction between Matrix emotion and the inhibitions built into their code and protocol. Even Shezarim-ko, who created the first Matrix AI kernel, didn't truly understand how they gave the Matrices emotions.

"I think Reletan-dai *did*, but he is dead."

And, from ki's phrasing, had never written down that knowledge or shared it with his most junior department head.

"If they did this from anger and then broke when they realized what they'd done, what may they have done?" he asked.

"It is possible that they may have suicided," D replied. "It would, for example, be possible for me to place *Dauntless*'s AI-driven systems under control of what would functionally be subconscious processes and terminate my primary consciousness.

"Such an action could not be undone, but the ship would continue to function and would have at least some of the independent operation you have me aboard for."

"If that was the case, that would explain why they weren't responding to our communications," Siril-ki said. "The systems are there to respond to our ping, but the intelligence is gone."

"Without that intelligence, are they still a danger?" Renaud said, the Captain butting back into the conversation to raise one of the critical questions.

The channel was silent for several seconds.

"Without a controlling intelligence to deactivate automatic defensive protocols, they will be less effective as combatants…but *far* more likely to actually attack us," Siril-ki concluded.

"That's not great," Renaud admitted. "Because we just found your Sentinels and all three of them just powered up their engines and weapons."

———

"BATTLE STATIONS."

Octavio waited for the first sounds of the alarm to ripple through the ship, lights shifting in the corridors outside to direct crew to their positions. As the bridge crew began to update the displays, he rose from his seat and tapped Aisha Renaud's shoulder.

"I need to be off your bridge," he murmured in her ear. "We have time for me to get to the flag bridge."

"Agreed," his Captain replied. She turned to look at him, holding his gaze for a moment too long. "You're a distraction here. Go."

With a nod, he strode out of the bridge as the big display switched over to a more-immediate tactical display.

"D, do we have any communication or response from the Sentinels?" he demanded, keeping up a brisk pace as he made his way across the ship to *his* battle station.

"Nothing," the AI replied. "We're trying everything in our databanks and the Assini databanks from Sina and Kora. They're not acknowledging any codes or coms protocols, radio or tachyon transmission."

"They're not talking to us," Octavio concluded grimly.

"Two of those protocols are command overrides, Commodore. They should not have been *able* to ignore them," the AI admitted. "The likelihood that the core Sentinel AIs have terminated their primary processes is now approaching one hundred percent."

"If the core personality has committed suicide, who's *left*?" Octavio demanded.

"Autonomous combat programming. They could have shut it all down, but they obviously did not."

"So, those ships are going to attack anyone who comes here?" he asked.

"Exactly," D confirmed

"Is there anything we can do except blow them to hell?" Octavio asked as he reached the door to the flag bridge.

"That's a question for Siril-ki, I suspect," the AI admitted. "There's nothing in the databases, but ki knows things that might not be obvious from the data. That kind of synthesized connection is what you organics are better at than us still."

The door slid shut behind Octavio, and he traded a nod with Courtenay as he slid into the flag officer's seat.

"Get me Siril-ki," he told the aide. "Private channel."

"And the battle group, sir?" Courtenay asked. "Your orders?"

Octavio scanned the display. They were still over two million kilometers from the planet, but that distance could disappear *fast* if the Sentinels moved out. So far, the AI warships had brought everything online but were remaining in orbit of KB2N13-1.

"Begin deceleration for all units, attempt to remain outside zetta-laser engagement range," he ordered. "Strike cruisers are to move into formation Delta-Seven."

That put the lighter units out in front of the battlecruiser, using their lasers to try to herd targets into the path of *Dauntless*'s main gun. If he actually expected to stay out of range of the Sentinels, it would be unnecessary, but he could do the math.

"We can't avoid entering at least the edge of their range," Courtenay told him. "Not without—"

"Abandoning the freighters to enter that range on their own," Octavio agreed. "We're not doing that, so get the escorts in formation while I talk to the AI specialist about the AI warships. We're playing for time, Commander Courtenay, not the endgame.

"Not yet."

———

"WHAT DO you expect from me, Commodore?" Siril-ki asked bluntly. "I didn't work on the Sentinels. They shouldn't have been able to do *any* of this. They're insane."

"They're dead," Octavio told ki. "The core personalities are gone, Siril-ki. They realized what had happened, got very, very angry, and did something they couldn't undo. When the anger faded, they killed themselves.

"Only three of them lived that long, but the actual Matrices in those ships are dead. Can we get the autonomous protocols to shut down?"

Ki was silent for a few seconds. Octavio bit down on demanding that ki think faster. Seconds could make the difference here, but he knew that yelling didn't make people think.

"I am not sure," ki admitted. "The autonomous systems are still AI of a sort, but they are so much dumber than the Matrices. All of our codes and overrides are for the Matrices themselves. The ships weren't supposed to operate without a Matrix."

"So, they're limited in what they can do?"

"Yes. And it all depends on what orders the Matrices gave them before terminating their processes. The Matrices know the limitations of those secondary system, so they'd have given specific instructions, but the systems will follow them very literally."

"And we've tripped a set of instructions that is causing them to at least prepare to fight us," Octavio said grimly. "Is there any chance this is just a threat?"

"It's unlikely," ki told him. "Their power reserves aren't infinite. Immense, even if they aren't refilling their reaction-mass tanks for the matter converters, but not infinite. They'll only power up like this and bring on the rest of their converters to go to war."

"So, they're going to fight us. Can we talk them down?"

"We can't even communicate with those processes, Commodore," Siril-ki admitted. "Not without creating a physical connection to the hardware."

"But if we got that connection?" Octavio asked, an old engineering project running across his mind.

"There's no security on these systems. They can only be communicated with through the Matrix itself. With the Matrix disabled, they'll follow any commands fed into them."

"Write that code, Director Siril-ki," the ex-engineering officer ordered. "I'll see about getting you a link to the hardware."

"That's impossible," ki told him. "You'd need to physically insert a tachyon communicator into their hull, and they'd shoot down any missile you fired at them."

"I wasn't planning on a missile," he told ki. "I'm thinking something they won't see as a threat...and might well not see coming at all."

50

"You need a breach and a mobile infiltration unit," Osric Winther told his commodore. *Dauntless*'s chief engineer was an old hand—he'd first served under Octavio as a junior rating aboard the old *Scorpion*...when Isaac Lestroud had commanded that ship.

He'd come to Exile as engineering NCO aboard *Vigil* and found himself commissioned as one of their handful of warp-experienced engineers. Now he was arguing against his old boss about the crazy idea Octavio had.

"I know, the armor's too much," Octavio agreed. "We need to hit the target with the main gun and open a practical breach. Then we can land the connection unit and make a link."

"But you have no idea what connections will be present or even intact," Winther argued. "We need some kind of remote-access robot to find and make the connection. We don't have anything that sma—"

"That is incorrect, Lieutenant Commander," D interrupted. "*Dauntless* caries seven remotes designed to interface with my systems by tachyon communication. Their onboard processes are very similar to the systems we want to interface with, but that should suffice to establish a direct link to the Sentinel's hardware. If it does not, I should be able to spare enough of my attention to make the connection myself.

"Once connected, the tachyon communicator used to control the remotes is entirely capable of delivering the code Siril-ki is developing."

"Okay, so we have a payload and a target," Winther said slowly. "How do we *get* it there?"

"I was hoping you'd have an idea, I'll admit," Octavio said. "The concept is solid, but no matter what happens, we're in zetta-laser range of those Sentinels in just under five minutes. Less if either of us starts to close the range.

"I'd really like to launch as soon as the shooting starts. We need something slow enough that it won't register as a threat but fast enough to cross half a million kilometers in a time period that's actually going to be useful."

Winther snorted.

"How badly do you need it, boss?" he asked.

"I'd really, *really* like to bring these ships home," Octavio told him. "And I'd prefer not to get my entire battle group shot to hell. What do you need?"

"We have three reactionless-drive systems aboard that are sized for our shuttles," the engineer told him. "EMC is still waffling on whether the trade-offs are worth it, but if I hack one of them to its lowest power setting and strap the remote to it, it should be able to make the crossing at ten percent of light without registering as a missile."

"D?" Octavio asked.

"I assess a fifty percent likelihood of the remote being shot down under that scenario, but Lieutenant Commander Winther's idea is sound. It may be the best chance we have," the AI replied as it ran the numbers.

"We only have three of these drives, though. That's one shot per ship."

Octavio grimaced.

"I'll leave that with you and D," he told Winther. "I have to make sure you have holes to put them in. How long?"

"At least ten minutes, sir," the engineer replied.

"You have five," Octavio replied. "Because as soon as we start hitting those big bastards, I want those drones in space. Am I clear?"

Winther spread his hands wide on the holographic channel.
"I'll do what I can."

———

FORMATION DELTA-SEVEN WAS A CONSERVATIVE ONE, a solid starting place for if Octavio wanted to get clever later. He still wasn't entirely comfortable with the fact that he was in command of a five-ship battle group, let alone dealing with the freighters along to provide logistics support.

He'd spent a solid portion of his time on the flight out practicing in simulated engagements, but he knew that in his heart, he wasn't a fleet commander. Starship command had been a stretch for him, but this was something else again.

But it was his job and he refused to do it badly. Of course, he realized he'd *started* by forgetting that his force was divided…

"Courtenay, can we get *Prospero* up here in time to make a difference?" he murmured. He was already running numbers, but a second set of eyes was never a bad thing.

Measure twice, cut once was even more true when there was supposed to be a high-energy plasma conduit behind the wall you were cutting, after all.

"Negative," his aide replied. "She might get here in time to fire off fireworks over our wrecked hulls; that's about it."

"A more-optimistic metaphor would be preferred, Commander," Octavio told the other man. They'd cut their own velocity down to a mere one percent of lightspeed, and he was waiting to see what the Sentinels did.

So far, they'd maneuvered to make sure their lines of fire were clear, and that was it. In fact…

"Captains, this is Catalan," he opened his command channel. "Our friends over there aren't maneuvering nearly as much as they should be. See if you can dial Bandit One in for long-range fire and stand by to engage at five hundred and fifty thousand kilometers."

Fifty thousand kilometers wasn't much…but it was enough that they'd get a hit in before they reached the range that the Matrices seemed to regard as maximum effective against a maneuvering target.

Even a single disabled laser would help change the course of the battle to come.

New data icons were flowing into his screens and the main holographic display now, as the ships' tactical departments tried to dial in their enemies and sent their estimated hit probabilities back to command.

Between the energy-shedding ceramics both sides armored their ships in, evasive maneuvers and the inevitable dispersion of energy beams and packets in space, the ESF usually agreed with the Matrices on the effective maximum range of their weapons.

Armor and dispersion were still factors at this range, even if his target wasn't maneuvering. He had five high-frequency grasers and one heavy particle cannon that would still hurt if they hit at this range. The light particle-cannon turrets that dotted all of his ships would be less effective.

"Hold LPCs for closer range," he ordered. "All ships...execute prior firing orders."

He gave the order about five seconds before his battle group crossed the line he'd given and every ship fired as one. It was another three seconds to see the result and... it wasn't much.

"Multiple hits," D reported. "*Dauntless*'s particle cannon missed, but three of the lasers hit. Analysis suggest mostly armor vaporization, minimal internal damage."

"Understood." The enemy was picking up their maneuvers now, a bit late and bit slower than they should have.

"All ships, continue firing on Bandit One until further orders," he said into the command channel. "Adjust course thirty degrees by fifteen degrees. Warships to accelerate towards the enemy at standard thrust.

"Freighters continue decelerating. Get the hell out of this mess, people."

If nothing else, his warships' charge would keep the freighters clear. He was *reasonably* sure the Sentinels wouldn't fire at fleeing vessels when there was a far more immediate threat.

Dauntless shivered beneath him as her main gun fired again. He had enough practice with the battlecruiser now to be able to tell that Renaud was going for sustained fire. The ship had enough cyclotrons running that she could fire a shot every seventeen seconds or so.

Or she could fire eight shots in under five seconds and have to wait two minutes for any of the cyclotrons to have worked up enough particles for a new shot. Which was the right choice depended on the circumstances.

It wasn't a call he was going to override his flag captain on.

"Sentinels are returning fire," Courtenay reported. "No hits so far, but that is one hell of a light show."

The Sentinels were the biggest warships the Assini had ever built, dwarfing the combat platforms designed to secure the Construction Matrices or the Escorts built to safeguard the second-wave colony ships that had never launched. The dreadnoughts the Rogue had developed dwarfed them again, but those hadn't actually been an *Assini* design.

Each of the Sentinels carried dozens of beams, each equal to the high-frequency grasers Octavio's ships carried. Their accuracy, though…

"Is it just me or does their aim suck?" he asked softly as his people's third salvo smashed into Bandit One and more Sentinel beams flashed off into space.

"They are performing significantly below expected parameters for Construction Matrix warships, let alone Sentinel Matrices," D confirmed. "This is an expected consequence of operating on autonomous protocols."

The Republic had never faced a late-generation Assini Matrix warship in its prime. The Escorts had been driven feral by their long pursuit of *Shezarim*, and the Sentinels were basically lobotomized.

If only that had left them harmless.

"We have multiple debris clouds from Bandit One," D reported. "I would assess a high likelihood of multiple practical breaches for your plan."

"Winther? Do we have a drone ready to go?" Octavio asked, his use of the chief engineer's name sufficient to open the channel.

"It is an ugly monstrosity I hate to admit I worked on, bu—"

The sound of a high-powered drill cut through the officer's words.

"It's done," he concluded. "Drone one is ready to deploy. We just kick it out the shuttle bay and D remote-flies it over. The remote is the only thing making this work, Commodore. It's basically flying the engine manually."

"If it works, it works," Octavio replied. "Kick it out the shuttle bay and then get me two more of them, Commander, because I've got three targets on the board."

He waited. As he expected, Winther was as efficient as he could have hoped for. Thirty seconds after their conversation, a new green icon appeared on the board and he tapped his mic to open the command channel.

"All right, everybody, we have a joker on the board but we don't know if it's going to work," he told his Captains. "Switch our focus to Bandit Two and leave Bandit One to the Joker drone. Try not to shoot the drone down, either."

They were well within five hundred thousand kilometers, which left the newly named Joker drone a mere fifteen-second flight at thirty thousand kilometers a second.

The defenses of every ship in the fight were designed to shoot down missiles moving at over ninety-nine percent of the speed of light. If the Sentinels had decided that the Joker was a threat, it would have been a very short flight.

"Siril-ki, we have that code?" he asked quietly.

"D has it," ki told him. "I can not guarantee it will work, but it should."

"*Should* has to be enough," he muttered. Another twenty seconds and they'd be in *pulse-gun* range, and that was going to hurt if the Sentinels still had three ships. "D?"

"Landing the remote now. I believe I have located a connection point and…I am in."

Seconds ticked. Octavio was watching the screen as lasers flashed out. His ships weren't getting hit as hard as they would have been if the Sentinels were fully operational, but it wasn't looking good.

Viola was the tip of the triangular formation around *Dauntless*, and she was getting hammered. Icons said she had taken multiple armor breaches, but all of her systems were intact.

"Adjust formation to Reno-Three," Octavio ordered, leaving D and the Joker drone to their task. "Get *Viola* back behind *Dauntless*; she's taken too many hits."

For a second, he thought it was too late. Then *Desdemona* neatly slid across her sister ship, an unfocused blast of energy from her pulse guns hiding the damaged ship as they slid into the new formation.

Reno was a line abreast with one ship held back to either cover the rear or protect that ship. *Desdemona* and *Cassio* fell back to flank *Dauntless*, and *Viola* dropped behind the big ship.

"Bandit One is down," Courtenay snapped. "Drive field just shut down, she's venting power and has commenced conversion-core shutdown procedures. Bandit One is out of the fight—I repeat, Bandit One is out of the fight."

"Hold focus on Two until we have another Joker drone in play," Octavio ordered his Captains. "Well done, D, Siril-ki, Winther. Now do it again!"

It would never have worked twice on an organic enemy or even a fully functional Matrix. The Joker drone relied on not registering as a threat under normal battlefield conditions, but once the first ship shut down, the second wave of drones would have become a priority target.

Instead, the two Sentinels continued to hammer Octavio's fleet with every weapon at their disposal. As they crossed the light-second mark, both sides opened up with pulse guns. The Republic version had been heavily upgraded over the years and easily matched the Sentinels' weapons.

Thousands of discrete plasma pulses filled the space between the two fleets, and more damage icons flickered across Octavio's holographic displays. His ships were still in the fight, but none of them were at full fighting form.

"Retarget on Bandit Three," he ordered. "We need a breach on both ships. Joker Two is moving on Bandit Two, and Joker Three will deploy in under a minute."

"I assess a ninety-plus percent probability that we have a practical breach on Bandit Two," D told him. "I am maneuvering Joker Two to the target; contact in ten seconds."

"We do *not* have a breach on Three," Courtenay snapped. "*Cassio* is reporting critical damage, her main gun is down and she's suffering power fluctuations in her conver—"

Matter-conversion cores could be shut down safely, but it was a slow process. Without that process, they had to keep above fifty percent power draw to prevent destabilizing the core and catastrophically expanding the conversion effect.

Cassio had two of the cores aboard, and Octavio would never know if only one or both had destabilized. Over a hundred of his people died in a single blast of fire as the strike cruiser ceased to exist.

"I have a link on Bandit Two; I have control," D reported.

Octavio didn't register the slight difference in D's phrasing until the reason for it became clear. Bandit One had gone into an orderly shutdown on *Dauntless*'s Matrix's orders.

Bandit *Two* flipped ninety degrees in space and fired three high-frequency grasers at a single meter-wide portion of Bandit Three's hull.

"We have a practical breach on Bandit Three. Landing the drone," D calmly continued as the shooting slowed. A moment passed. Another.

The shooting stopped.

"I have control," D concluded. "Shutting down Two and Three. All Sentinels are under control and shut down."

"All ships cease fire," Octavio snapped. "We have neutralized the Sentinels."

He breathed a long sigh, studying the frozen ships.

"You can fight them remotely?" he demanded.

"I can *fly* them remotely," D noted precisely. "Using the Sentinels' weapons in a combat situation would be impractical. We will need Siril-ki's people to go over the hardware and dump their final instructions before I would trust my ability to give orders to the autonomous protocols."

"Couldn't we boot the Matrices back up?" Courtenay asked. "If we reset them to factory settings or something…"

"The core process of a Matrix AI cannot be restarted once terminated," D replied. "I can create a bud of my own code that could be loaded onto blank hardware—all of the Republic's Matrices are buds of my code—but I'm not certain we could load that onto hardware that already held a Matrix. I believe the kernel encryption may still be in place, preventing any modification of the Matrix…even if that Matrix is dead.

"We would need to replace the core," the AI concluded. "It would feel…wrong, but it could be done. Like performing a brain transplant."

Octavio winced.

"We need those ships," he admitted. "Could you fly them back to Exilium in their current state?"

"Potentially," D said. "Since we lack the equipment to manufacture or install a new Matrix core, that would be our only option."

"Let Siril-ki and Winther know what help you'll need." Octavio ordered. "For now…"

He looked out at the broken orbitals of a dead world.

"For now, we need to see what we can learn from the wreckage of the people who killed the Assini."

51

––––––––––

Amelie wasn't convinced that *any* of the people she'd talked into helping set up her grand convention thought it was a good idea. She was pretty sure that the Kond, if nothing else, didn't truly believe her about how badly the Governance's fleet was outmatched.

Nonetheless, they'd managed to get access to the top floor of a large apartment building in the City, one that very nearly approached arcology status. The space appeared to normally serve as some sort of sports facility, a readily accessed gym and playing field.

The room that the Kond's people had turned into a presentation space resembled nothing so much as a tennis court before they'd come in with their hanging curtains and similar paraphernalia.

One of the biggest security risks and advantages of the building was that it *wasn't* a helot apartment building. The tower was home to lower-middle-class Sivar, the kinds of people any government genteelly ignored as individuals and desperately relied on the support of as a demographic.

And, unless Amelie was very wrong, the Kond owned at least half of the building with Silleck as one of his partners. The top floor was "closed for maintenance" and any helots or tributes making their way up were *obviously* the maintenance crew to fix whatever was broken.

She was one of the first to arrive, with the Kond himself, and studied the preparations with a critical eye.

"Security?" she asked the Pol aristocrat, realizing that most of the people she'd seen were unarmed.

"Ten of my people, ten of the Dynast's," he replied. "All carrying stunners. They *should* be safe for everyone here, but I hope we don't have to shoot anyone."

Amelie was going to have to look up what the Sivar had for stunners. She knew her Republic had some ranged nonlethal weapons, but she didn't know how they worked, and she doubted they would be safe for seven different species without calibration.

"You trust Silleck?" she asked, careful to keep her voice low so no one else could hear her.

"That Siva and I are neck-deep in a lot of money together," the Kond replied. "None of it illegal, though the sheer amount of money coming out of the helot side would certainly draw some questioning eyes if we weren't as good at hiding it."

The Pol shook himself.

"I knew the Dynast existed. I did not know that *she* was the Dynast, though I suspected she was tied up in at least one of the rebellions."

"Speak of the devil," Amelie murmured, gesturing toward the elevator as the Kond looked at her strangely.

Silleck and her promised ten guards had shown up. They were all dressed in mismatched street clothes, but Amelie could guess what the intentionally lumpy lines of the apparently cheap clothing hid. There was body armor under the Sivar's clothing, to go with the stunners they now openly removed from bags and slung over their shoulders as Silleck approached Amelie and the Kond.

"Asselis," she murmured, bowing over her hands.

"No names tonight, I think," the Kond replied, returning the gesture of respect. "There are people here I don't trust to do anything except measure *my* back for a knife, let alone yours."

"And I have invited people I trust even less," the Dynast replied. "I am rarely so glad my people have armor on their skulls."

"Everyone is supposed to come unarmed," Amelie objected.

"And I expected everyone to honor the appearance of that, at least," the Kond agreed. "The truth, of course, will be messier. I cannot search everyone who arrives, after all."

The elevators disgorged another group of Sivar. This group looked around at the aliens surrounding them, and one of them started to go for a concealed weapon of some kind. Sharp words stopped them—words Amelie noted her translator didn't pick up.

"Who are they?" she asked.

"Sondine," Silleck replied. "Not quite a crime syndicate, not quite freedom fighters. They're from Aris's western continent."

"They're scum," the Kond growled.

"And the Green Stalks of Light are mass murderers," Silleck countered, indicating a group of Sonba with their broccoli-like heads.

"That's—"

"My point exactly," the Dynast smoothly cut the Pol off. "Everyone here can be described in both horrific and generous terms. But if we want to achieve our goals, we need to work together."

"I'll be surprised if we make it to the introductions without blood," the Kond muttered.

"I hope so," Silleck replied. "You are, after all, the host. You speak first…and your people have to clean up the blood if it goes wrong!"

BY THE TIME Kond Asselis walked up to the front of the sport court, there were at least a hundred and fifty people in the space. Amelie was keeping track as they came in and noted eight different species and at least twenty-seven different factions.

Sivar were a solid plurality with sixty of them in the space. They weren't the majority, at least, but Amelie had her concerns about what that would mean for the future. It made sense on Aris, where the Sivar were still ninety-five percent of the population, but if the people in this room decided that they were the new rulers of the Governance, it would *still* be misrepresentative overall.

If the Kond had hoped his visibility would quiet the crowd, his hope was dashed. The conversation turned to shouted questions at the six-limbed alien, and he waited in silence for the first wave of them to pass before grunting and picking up a megaphone.

"Shut up," he ordered. That got him enough quiet to at least start speaking. "I doubt even a majority of the people in this room know who I am. So far tonight, the inclination has been to avoid names as well, so that's going to stay that way.

"There are people here, both of my race and others, that I would call siblings. There are people here, mostly Sivar but not all, who I know regard me as an enemy or at least a problem."

He bared his square front teeth.

"None of that matters today. What matters today is that we share enemies: the Intendant of the Governance and the Eyes of Sivar who support him. I have reason to believe that the Intendant is about to be struck a near-crippling blow, a defeat that will weaken his position.

"Alone, none of us would have the strength to take advantage of that weakness. Together, we might. I'm not here to sell you on that tonight, though. I'm here to introduce the sentient who *is* here, whose people are about to shake the nation we are part of—willingly or otherwise!—to its foundation."

He bared his teeth again.

"But since I don't expect all of you to trust me, I'm going to be joined by someone many of the *rest* of you will trust." He gestured Silleck up to join him.

"Like my companion here, not all of you will know me," Silleck told them. "But enough of you do to understand why I'm standing here. Most of those are also wondering why I am standing next to a Pol, a helot.

"As he said, we are about to be handed an unprecedented opportunity. Not since the Intendants and the Eyes of Sivar overthrew the First and Final Dynasty has the Governance faced a real defeat. Shortly, they will, if nothing else, find themselves in a real war."

She clattered her armor plates.

"We must stand together to make this the Intendancy's final moment of weakness, and we must stand together to look to the future. *Together*. Not as Sivar and helots but as equals. There are a thousand challenges to get past to get to that point, but that is where we have to aim.

"But even together, we cannot challenge the infrastructure and forces of an intact, unbroken Intendant. So, allow us to introduce the person who is giving us any hope at all."

Amelie walked up to stand between the two aliens.

"This is Amelie Lestroud, Foreign Minister of the Republic of Exilium and the representative of an alliance of powers beyond the Sonbar star-lanes," the Kond told everyone. "She came here to negotiate an alliance with the Governance against a greater threat.

"Instead, our Intendant betrayed her, killed many of her guardians and imprisoned her. My organization liberated her to stand before you today, and I beg that you listen to her words."

"She speaks for an alliance that is far more powerful than the Governance," Silleck continued. "If we *don't* listen to her, everyone we represent here will suffer—first by the will of the Intendant, and then as members of the Governance in the unwinnable war that will follow."

"Thank you," Amelie said quietly, gesturing for her allies to leave her alone. They both hesitated before leaving the front of the room and joining the rest of the audience.

"That introduction covers most of what you need to know about me," she told the crowd, feeling the memories of similar meetings in the past. All of those crowds had been human, at least, but there'd probably been just as little trust among those gathered.

"I stand here as the representative of an outside power. I know very few of you and have made no commitments to anyone. Tonight, my intent is to stand as a witness to your promises and oaths to each other —a witness who will have the power to enforce those promises.

"Anyone who betrays the alliance we hope to forge tonight will have to face not merely the organizations in this room but the resources of the Republic of Exilium. Already, your Governance has met my ships in battle. Two of your capital ships, supported by the forts of Aris and ambushing us at close range, attacked one of mine.

"My ship escaped with the civilian transports she was escorting. The two Governance battleships were crippled. With surprise, a perfect striking position and a two-to-one advantage, the Commandants failed.

"*That* is the power I represent, the power I am prepared to commit as guarantor and arbiter of your promises to each other."

She smiled.

"But as my friends introducing me noted, you cannot face a fully intact Intendancy. In twelve days, however, a battle fleet of the Republic will enter the Sonbar System. Unless the forces there surrender, the Commandants' forces there will be destroyed and Sonbar will no longer be a Governance System.

"The Intendant will need to deploy ships and warriors outwards, both to try and retake Sonbar and to protect Aris from the blow he knows will land here. The First and Final Citadel will be vulnerable.

"If you pool the knowledge, numbers and weapons represented in this room—if you act *together*—the Intendant will fall."

The room was silent. Amelie wasn't sure what kind of response she was expecting, but it hadn't been that.

"Nothing?" she finally asked. "You plan for nothing, then?"

"What do you get out of this?" one of the nearer Sonba asked.

"I came here looking for allies," Amelie replied. "We face a far greater threat than the Governance on the other side of our borders. Some of your people know them as the Builders, but they are self-replicating AI starships dedicated to transforming worlds to the standards of their creators.

"Unfortunately, too many of them don't check if those worlds are inhabited before initiating the process—and several will aggressively destroy resistance to them transforming worlds. One of the latter is quite close to your borders. And these Builders, the Matrices, are not bound by the star-lanes that limit the Governance.

"The Governance as it currently exists would make a poor ally for us at best. Since the Intendant has actively betrayed us and imprisoned my people, we have no intention of allying with him.

"If a new government were formed, aided by the people who freed the prisoners the Intendant holds from the Republic and committed to certain basics standards of freedom and equality, we would be glad to forge an alliance with them.

"That alliance would come along with industrial and technology assistance, to upgrade both civilian and military industries to allow you to stand at our sides against the Matrices."

If a bribe was needed, she could offer that. If honesty was needed, she could do that, too.

"I have friends and people sworn to my service in the prisons of the Citadel," she continued. "I want you to help me free them. Everything beyond that, really, is up to you."

The Sonba laughed, a liquid burbling sound.

"It seems that your people are already en route to liberate my world," they noted. "I will hold my beliefs and my sword until I hear the news of that, but…" They paused, then shook their fronds in what Amelie hoped was a nod.

"Since nothing would be done without that, I swear this: I will stand by any force that storms the Citadel after Sonbar is freed."

The Kond rose.

"My siblings," he addressed the group around him. "I would place our intelligence, our knowledge of the Citadel's crannies and our eyes inside it, at the service of this effort. I can supply much of that on my own, but I would rather have the approval of our council."

One by one, the other members of the Kond's organization indicated approval, and the Pol turned to look at Amelie.

"All of our knowledge, sources and available hands will stand."

"The Broken Chain will stand," Silleck said loudly. "More, I *will* give a name: I am Silleck, daughter of Ondar, son of Koneck, son of Creesteel, *last Dynast of the Governance.*"

The last words were a half-shouted declaration.

"I am the rightful heir to the throne the Intendant has stolen. I will put every warrior, every gun, every marker committed to the cause of my family for three generations into this attack…and I will forswear my family's right to the throne.

"I believe that the title could help smooth the transition to a new world, but I am not certain that the Sivar, let alone the Governance, requires another single voice to lead us. So, before you all, I swear this: I will not claim my family's throne by mere right of blood."

Amelie noted that there were loopholes in Silleck's statement that she could drive a battlecruiser through—not least that Loreck had just as solid a claim as Silleck's and she hadn't forsworn her banner's right to that throne.

It was...enough. It was the final straw that broke the dam, and others rose, each committing resources to the fight. Somehow, despite all odds, Amelie had done it again. She'd convinced a bunch of hostile rebel factions to listen to her.

And then the elevator doors opened again...and there was no one else scheduled to be at the meeting.

52

Three Sivar stepped off the elevator, and Amelie could feel the tension ripple through the crowd as their clothing sank in. All three were clad in long hooded tunics, familiar even to her as the shipside uniform of the Keys of War.

Like the Republic's equivalent, it could act as an emergency space-suit. Its armor layer was probably more important for the current situation.

The central figure wore the tunic in the same dark green she'd seen on Sivar Commandants. They even had the gold markings where the hood met the tunic she'd seen on Ackahl. She couldn't be sure, but Amelie suspected that under the hood, their stranger *was* a Commandant.

Which was a problem.

The Sivar on the Commandant's right wore the tunic in black and the Sivar on the left wore it in dark red. Amelie assumed those colors had meaning to someone—their wearers, if nothing else—but they meant nothing to her.

From the way the crowd rippled away from the three figures, everyone there knew what she'd guessed: these were Sivar soldiers. They had no business here…except…

"If you were here to arrest everyone for treason, you'd have sent more guns," she said, tuning her translator to project her Sivar words across the entire room. "What do you want, Commandant-Key of War?"

The central figured chuckled. That was clearly not the response anyone else in the room had been expecting—and then they threw back their hood, allowing Amelie to recognize the Siva.

"You and I have had this conversation before, I think," Ackahl told Amelie. "My title is *Lord* Commandant. The Commandant-Keys of War outrank me. Of course, what is perhaps most relevant to the worthies gathered at this meeting is that while *I* answer to the Commandant-Key of Aris, the only remaining mobile capital ships in this star system answer to *me*."

"You are no rebel," Amelie replied. "Why are you here?"

"I *was* no rebel," Ackahl corrected. "Shonin?" She gestured to the Siva on her left, the one in the dark red robe.

"I am Shonin," ban introduced banself while lowering ban's own hood. "I am the First Voice of the Knives of the Keys of War in the Citadel and City. On Aris's surface, I am bound to obey the orders of the Knives of the Eyes of Sivar, but the task of tracking and removing local sedition falls to me and my Knives."

Dark red eyes flashed in ban's armored skull, the sparkle that Amelie was starting to look for to pick out a smiling Siva.

"You can only *imagine* my confusion when my people reported that at least ten percent of the leaders they'd identified were on the move," ban continued. "Your security was better than I thought any of you were capable of. From the absence of so many of the people I'd identified as likely leaders, either we are missing many factions I know of or we were very wrong as to who was actually in charge."

Ban sounded impressed more than angry. Amelie's own guess was that it was a mix of the two reasons ban had given plus some of the leaders having sent representatives. Plus, of course, the groups most likely known to military intelligence were the exact type of people who wouldn't have been invited.

"My other friend will not be introduced or identified," Ackahl told them. "But I assure you that they are why I am here and will no more betray you than anyone else in this room."

"What do you *want*, Lord Commandant?" Amelie asked.

"An invitation to this meeting, it appears," Ackahl replied. "But since it seems my presence is inhibiting conversation, perhaps I should just make my spiel?"

"There is no one in this room I would remove," Amelie told the Siva. "But you do seem to be bothering my audience. Say your piece."

Ackahl bowed her head in acknowledgment, still standing at the back of the room as she surveyed the rebels.

"The Keys of War know the price of the Governance better than most of you," she said. "It has fallen to us again and again to enforce the will of the Intendant on the tributary worlds. Honor requires that we obey…but the actions we take are without honor.

"But the Intendant rules the Governance and we obey. When Minister Lestroud's fleet arrives, my replacement as Sector Commandant in Sonbar will fight. He will lose."

Armor plating clicked gently as Ackahl shook her head.

"He will lose," she repeated. "I am certain Amelie Lestroud has told you this, but I ask that you hear it from *me*, a Lord Commandant of the Keys of War: if we fight Minister Lestroud's people, we lose.

"That news will arrive here, and the only non-crippled battleships in the system are mine. We stand guard at the Keerees star-lane, but we will almost certainly be recalled to protect the orbit of Aris once the Intendant feels vulnerable. He will believe he can rely on our batteries to, if nothing else, destroy any force that attacks the Citadel."

Somehow, it didn't surprise Amelie that the Governance's battleships, like the Confederacy's battlecruisers but *unlike* the Republic's, carried ground-bombardment weapons.

"We will not do so. There is a limit to how long the Keys of War, starships and Knives alike, can stand aside…but stand aside we will. If you act quickly and decisively, I will place my ships under the command of whatever provisional government you can implement."

Amelie studied the third figure for a few seconds as Ackahl finished speaking. She was pretty sure it was Rode, but she wasn't *certain.* Between Rode and Silleck, the Dynast had a good chance of being at least the face of that provisional government.

She was reasonably sure that Silleck knew the Republic wouldn't stand for a new dictatorship. It was probably as good an offer as anyone was going to get.

"How do we know if we can trust you?" the Kond demanded.

"You don't," Ackahl replied. "But if you *can't*, your entire rebellion is already doomed. If I and First Voice Shonin know your plan and its likely trigger, well…" Armor plating clicked against itself again.

"We can either trust each other and look to Minister Lestroud to make sure we keep our promises the day *after* the Intendant falls, or we all give up now and force a war our people can only drag out, not win."

The room was silent and Ackahl bowed.

"Regardless of whether you trust me, I can only spend so long here without drawing attention we would all rather avoid, even with the Knives' cooperation. I wish you luck with your plans.

"And I wish us all hope for a brighter future."

———

THE DEPARTURE of the three Sivar military officers—or at least what *appeared* to be officers—left the room to explode into arguments again. Amelie stood at the front of the room, waiting patiently, for at least a minute before she intentionally induced feedback between the sound system and her translator device.

Once the echo of that faded, she had everyone's attention again and smiled.

"The Intendant is doomed and doesn't even know it yet," she told them all. "The Governance must change. I have already warned you what the Republic will require as the price for our aid, but beyond that, the decisions are *yours.*"

"Perhaps most of those decisions should be made once the Intendant is cast down?" Silleck suggested.

"I have no idea how common revolutions are in your history," Amelie replied. "But my people had them as a cultural hobby."

She had, after all, been born in *France*.

"If you are not ready for victory, infighting will destroy your victory," she warned them. "You must plan together to launch an attack that will overwhelm the Intendant's defenses, and you must plan together to have a structure to put in place after that.

"The Republic will be here soon enough. Twelve days after they take Sonbar, there will be Republic warships in this system. By then, you *must* have a provisional government that we can negotiate with.

"Remember that I am in this because I need the Governance's fleet to fight the Builders," she said dryly. "And I suspect it might be very helpful in your transition period if a significant chunk of the Keys of War are somewhere *else*."

Rode and Ackahl would be essential to getting the Keys of War to agree to that, but so long as the rebels could keep from massacres and atrocities—Amelie's hope was only middling for that, but she *thought* they'd kept the worst out of the room—it was possible.

And while they might not be able to rebuild the Keys' battleships to carry grasers and particle cannons quickly, strapping warp rings on them *should* be doable.

She hoped.

She wasn't an engineer, after all.

53

"I AM GROWING VERY, *very* weary of looking at dead worlds that should hold my people," Siril-ki said in a tired voice. Ki'd turned the emotional layers to ki's translator back on, but all ki had sounded since was tired.

The view of the still-unnamed planet covered the wall of the conference room as Octavio gathered his senior people again. *Dauntless* was settled into a loose, high orbit of the planet, just outside the radius of its single moon and well away from the debris field of the battle and planetary industry.

The three Sentinels had lifted out of that debris field under their own power. D had parked them at one of the planet-moon Lagrange points, both to keep them stable and keep them away from the flotilla.

They were theoretically disabled and under control, but no one was trusting them just yet. The ghosts of *Cassio*'s crew were very present in the room, weighing down on Octavio's shoulders.

"My team's analysis of the domes suggests the planet had a population of just over ten million when the Sentinels arrived," McGill told them. "Every dome was destroyed. Everything with a *power source* was blasted from orbit with a graser."

"The orbital stations weren't armed," Renaud continued. "The

Guardian Matrices and the attached drone ships were their only defenses, and they were no match for that many Sentinels."

"Is searching the ruins likely to do us any good?" Octavio asked. "We don't even know where to start, and its not like there's anything intact in orbit."

The orbitals hadn't even survived the battle. The Sentinels had been far less careful on their aiming than was normal for Matrices and had wrecked *everything*. Anything that had survived had been destroyed with neat precision.

The stations in the orbit of Assini's planets had been wrecked by nature. Many had been intact to one degree or another. KB2N13-1's orbitals had been very precisely destroyed by a very angry intelligence.

All that was left was a debris field. The only chunks large enough to be worth investigating appeared to be pieces of the Matrix warships that had died defending and attacking the planet.

The surface damage, on the other hand, had been both less and more thorough in many ways. No organics could survive on KB2N13-1's surface without power and life support, and the Sentinels had blasted every power source they detected with high-power energy weapons.

They hadn't leveled what had survived after that. They hadn't needed to.

"Maybe," McGill said. "The ruins are more likely to have something of value than the wreckage up here, but I can't imagine that the kinds of military bases and government headquarters we're looking for *didn't* have power sources."

"And it is very clear that the Sentinels blasted every single one of those they could find," Renaud concluded.

"I just can't believe that the Sentinels did this," Siril-ki told them. "It's so far against their programming, their personalities... It's all theoretical to you all, but realize that I have *spoken* with Sentinel Matrices. I knew them as people, not merely a combat computer from three hundred years ago."

"People who learned that someone set into motion the annihilation of everything they were sworn to protect," Octavio said gently. "I'm not sure that humans or Assini would have handled what happened better."

"The question I want to understand is just who the hell *were* these people?" Renaud asked as Siril-ki closed ki's eyes and leaned back again. "Any ideas, Director?"

"None," ki whispered. "No Assini should have done this. Our ways, our people, our culture…we were raised to be part of the herd, to avoid violence. We had our criminals, our failures, I can't pretend otherwise…but an entire secret colony of people who knew what had been done to the Construction Matrices?"

"Worst of all, from what I understand, to do what they did, they needed Shezarim-ko's key to the Matrix core encryptions," Octavio noted quietly. "Reletan-dai told me that with that key, he could have fixed the Escorts even after they broke. But without it, he couldn't edit a Matrix once it came online."

That was apparently too much for Siril-ki. Ki folded over onto the table, ki's hands folding over ki's eyes as ki moaned.

"Shezarim-ko was the founder of the entire construction and colonization program," D reminded the humans. "If they were a traitor of this scale, then the entire program may have been a trap from the beginning."

"The counterargument is that we *know* the Construction Matrices launched with the protocols to preserve sentient life," Octavio pointed out. "Not only in that Siril-ki and others had copies of the code of those Matrices, but we have XR-13-9 and the other Matrices like you to prove it."

"I assess a seventy plus/minus seven percent likelihood of an external party, likely the group behind this colony, using a specialty AI ship to deliver the edited code to the closest Construction Matrices," D said. "To make that kind of edit requires physical access to the Matrix core itself, much as we required access to the Sentinels' systems to override their autonomous protocols."

"But the Construction Matrices wouldn't have recognized it as a threat," Renaud said slowly. "But why would we have some Rogues that seem to be pure tachyon-punch degradation and some that were edited?"

"Because at least one wave of the second-generation Regional Construction Matrices was built before the edit was applied," Octavio realized aloud. "Possibly more. They wouldn't have needed to make the edit until the colony ships were about to launch."

"So, some of my people actively murdered hundreds of millions of their siblings?" Siril-ki demanded.

"We already knew that," the Commodore said grimly. "Now I want to know who and I want to know why—and I want to know if it can be undone."

That was the first time he'd even said that aloud, and it got even Siril-ki's head off the table.

"Undone, sir?" Renaud asked.

"If the code was implemented with Shezarim-ko's encryption key, then a reversal of the code should be possible," he pointed out. "A 'reset to factory settings,' if you will. If we can turn the Rogues back to what they're supposed to be, suddenly they stop being a genocidal horror and become damn handy neighbors."

Everyone was looking at him like he'd grown a second head.

"You would need the encryption key, the original intended template, and the exact code used to make the changes," Siril-ki said slowly. "I have the template. From the samples retrieved before my people's fall, I believe I could reverse-engineer the code...but I don't have Shezarim-ko's key."

"Someone in this star system almost certainly did," Octavio said. "They probably thought they could even override the Sentinels, but you all underestimated just how powerful their emotions could be."

"I think there's two things that might help us, sir," McGill told them all, the tactical officer looking thoughtful. "They both point to the same thing, really."

"And they are, Commander?" Octavio asked.

"Our scans suggest that the final bombardment was carried out by at least ten ships," she said. "I think at least seven of the Sentinel wrecks and one of the Guardian swarms are newer than the rest. I don't know which ones, but the data suggests that someone came along when this was all over and wrecked most of the Sentinels.

"Which leads to my second question, sir," McGill noted. "We

followed a colony ship from Assini. A massive reaction-drive vessel capable of carrying millions of colonists or thousands of active crew.

"Where is she?"

Octavio's attention went back to the wall display and studied the planet for a moment. The planet…its debris ring…and its moon. The moon they'd only ever seen from "above," having never passed between KB2N13-1 and the planetoid.

"Major Chen," he said quietly. "How quickly can you get assault shuttles onto that moon once we find the target?"

There was only one place in the star system they could have parked a sublight starship where they wouldn't have already seen it.

54

"AND THERE SHE IS, right where you figured, sir."

If the newly married Major Chen was getting sick of having the task force commander riding her shoulder, it didn't show in her voice as the shuttles crested the horizon of KB2N13-1's moon. The planetoid was easily a quarter of the size of its "parent", as large as Luna was to the Earth.

And the ship they were hunting was nestled gently into a crater on the side that forever faced towards the planet.

"Is it designed to be able to take off again?" Chen asked as the shuttles approached.

"No," Octavio told her. "Like ours, it's supposed to fold out and become part of the colony infrastructure. The engines can land once. The process is destructive."

"She isn't oriented correctly for a proper landing," Siril-ki added. "The lower gravity seems to have allowed them to land her horizontally."

"And I guess they decided to use her as an orbital base when they first arrived here," Octavio said. "Otherwise, they wouldn't have had her at all."

Though the strangers *could* have built a new one, he supposed. All evidence suggested they'd built multiple Guardian swarms. In fact…

"Chen, can you get me a sensor drone at these locations?" he asked, dropping coordinates through the data channel. "And hold your shuttles at least a hundred kilometers away until we've got that sensor data."

"Wilco," the Marine Major replied crisply before cutting to another channel.

"I don't understand any of this, Commodore," Siril-ki admitted.

"I know," he told her. "I'm hoping that the answers are in that ship. It looks like she was intact when she landed, which means she probably held the last survivors of this group."

"Except she's silent and the world below is dead," the Assini Director replied. "It seems any hope of finding more of my people is a lost cause."

"I know." Octavio looked at his marked points as the drones flashed out from the shuttles. There were ships there; he *knew* that. What he needed the drones to establish was whether those ships were a threat.

"There's enough of you on Exilium to survive," he reminded ki. "In the long run, you'll want to move the core of your population to another Constructed World to give you room to grow, but it's not like there's many of *us* on Exilium either."

"For humans, that would make sense," Siril-ki told him. "For us…if we are to survive, we need a herd. We are better served joining yours, I think."

"That's a discussion for other people at another time," Octavio admitted. "The Republic will back whatever your people want; you know that. If you want citizenship with us, you'll get it. If you want a ride to a new planet and help setting up a colony, we can manage that, too.

"The tech databases from *Shezarim* alone are enough to pay for any assistance you could ask for."

He chuckled to himself as he removed a word from the sentence while speaking. *Shezarim*'s databases weren't enough to pay for *any reasonable assistance.* They were enough to pay for *any* assistance whatsoever.

"Drones are on target," Chen told them as she rejoined the channel. "We're looking at multiple Guardian drones but I'm not seeing a core Matrix hull. They're dead, sir. Landed and shut down, and they weren't designed to land."

Not all of them were wrecks, per se, but all of them had basically crashed. The vectors suggested that they had been providing aerial cover until they ran out of fuel. Some of them had managed to attempt a powered landing. Others had just fallen out of the sky.

"All right, Major," Octavio said. "We needed to be sure those ships were dead. Flag one of the more-intact ones for pickup and continue at your discretion."

"Understood. We're coming in low and slow in case there are any concealed defenses," the Marine replied. "Probes don't suggest anything, though. No power sources at all."

"She's a dead ship," Octavio agreed. "We'll probably move *Dauntless* around for an easier pickup but keep your eyes open as you close."

The reason *Dauntless* remained on the far side of the moon, after all, was because they knew that ship carried heavy beam weapons.

———

"Shuttles are on the ground. Go! Go! Go!"

The map on one side of the flag deck display showed that none of Chen's spacecraft had landed particularly far from the Assini spaceship. They still hadn't directly boarded the ship, either. The Marines could make a fifty-meter stroll in one-tenth gravity.

"At least this world was never alive," somebody snarked on the Marine command channel. "Is it a ghost world if it never died?"

"Belay the philosophizing, people," Chen barked. "Save it for when we *don't* have the chance of Assini hunter-killers, please."

"Oorah," multiple voices replied.

The Marines were moving quickly in the low gravity, and by the time the brief conversation was over, the lead elements had reached the hull of the ship.

"Hull's what we expected," one of the lead Marines reported. "Setting up the cutting gear for entry."

Nine new icons appeared on Octavio's display, marking the entryways the Marines were opening for later use. There were airlocks and similar entryways, but if the dead ship had any defenses left, they'd be there.

"Hull will take ninety seconds to penetrate," Chen told Octavio on their channel. "Anything in particular we should be looking for?"

"Symbology, at least on the first pass," he told her. "We don't even know who these people were. Whatever symbols, flags, names…if it's an identifying symbol, send it to Siril-ki."

"Between D and I, we should be able to work out who these people are at that point," the Assini confirmed. "I hope there are answers somewhere on this ship, Major, Commodore."

"If there are, I'm guessing they're in the command center," Chen replied. "The maps put the hole we're cutting here less than a hundred meters from the bridge. I'm expecting to have to force or cut doors all the way there, but we should be there in less than fifteen minutes."

"And then perhaps we will find some answers on what turns my people into monsters," Siril-ki said.

A few seconds of silence later, the plasma cutters completed their task. A circular panel of the ceramic that armored every spaceship Octavio had seen in several years fell outward.

"We're in," Chen reported as her Marines began to enter the breach. Single troopers led the way, guns sweeping the empty hallways of the ship.

Chen followed her Marines in, her own camera and light sweeping through the relatively plain corridor they'd cut their way into.

"Map says this way," she told her people. "Kender, you're on point. Scans still aren't showing power sources, so we *should* be clear."

"You've found leftover security drones hiding power sources before," Octavio warned.

"And we're watching for them," Chen replied. "First door, sealed. Wait!"

Her barked command stopped her Marines as they prepared to force the door.

"The symbol, let me get a look at it for the boss."

The lights and cameras focused on the symbol painted in the middle of the door. To Octavio, it looked like a unicorn with a crown on the horn.

Except, of course, that the unicorn in question was based on an Assini, not a Terran horse.

"No," Siril-ki whispered. "That's *impossible*."

"Siril-ki?" Octavio asked.

"I know the symbol, Major Chen can continue," the Director ordered, ki's voice suddenly perfectly calm.

"Can you explain as the Major moves in?" Octavio asked.

"D, can you record this, please?" Siril-ki requested. "The data is in your databanks, and we'll probably need you to fill in some holes. I only know as much as I do because of a hobby many of my colleagues regarded as vaguely perverse."

The Assini paused, collecting ki's thoughts.

"The government of the Assini as you know it was the Great Collective," ki explained. "The First Administrator was an elected position who held executive power as you understand it, but they were limited in their use of that power. Most decisions were made by day-to-day instant electronic voting and consensus among the population.

"At the end of any given day, I would receive informational packets organized by the government and several private entities. Over the course of the next day, I would be notified on my computer as votes were called, and I would vote on the items in the informational packets.

"This would be five or six times in an eleven-day," ki noted. "Direct democracy is, I believe, the term in your systems. In even a single star system, this required FTL communication, but it was born in the era of electronic communication networks.

"We are herd creatures and consensus-builders by nature, so it *worked* for us. It had worked for us for six elevens of eleven years when *Shezarim* fled the flare."

Ki was silent for a few moments.

"But that was not always how we ruled ourselves, and the Great

Collective did not come to encompass all Assini without violence. We had already embraced pacifism as a culture by then in the main, but not entirely.

"The Great Collective expanded peacefully initially. It grew out of previous trading and informational agreements almost informally, until over two-thirds of our people were either formally or effectively part of the Great Collective. The remainder were in an active alliance against its expansion.

"An alliance led by the House of Koth and Herd Leader Koth-Dasan-ni," Siril-ki concluded, then gestured at the screen. "*That*, Commodore Catalan, is the symbol of the House of Koth. The last of the Imperial Houses, the old monarchs that led herds to war against each other.

"The Collective and the Houses fielded war machines against each other, the early iterations of what became the Matrix hunter-killer drones." Ki stared blankly into space. "By the end of the war, the House of Koth had consumed its allies, overtaking their governments and leaders to force them to support the war beyond all reasonable levels."

"That was a thousand years ago," Octavio noted. "Seven hundred years before the flares. I'm guessing they lost in the end?"

"They did," Siril-ki confirmed. "Koth-Shezar-dai died in battle, leading the last of the crewed war machines our people ever built in a breakout attempt rather than surrender. With his death, the Koth's empire shattered and the war ended.

"The House of Koth is dead history, dead for elevens of eleven years before we fled our world. What *is* this?"

"D?" Octavio asked.

"Director Siril-ki summarizes what Assini histories call the Last War quite well," the AI noted. "It lasted twenty-two years in human time and ended, as ki noted, in the death of the last known heir of the Koth line.

"The databases do note a continuing suggestion—humans would call it a conspiracy theory—that Koth-Shezar-dai's breakout and death were a distraction that allowed the House of Koth to smuggle his child and a vast amount of wealth out of their fortresses.

"I cannot find any practical evidence to support this, but the theory was enduring. There appear to have always been elements in the Collective that looked to it as humans have looked to the Arthurian myth, a dream of the return of the rightful king who would make all things right."

"I encountered that in my studies," Siril-ki agreed. "That is part of why studying the Last War was regarded as somewhat perverse. I needed to understand the wars our people had fought to help program combat AI that would fight for us in ways we'd find acceptable.

"I had forgotten the myth that the House of Koth had survived," ki admitted. "It was always such ridiculous herd-shit."

"But we're looking at someone who either *was* that remnant or was stealing its image," Octavio noted. "Could they have been…" He paused, looking at the icon frozen in a side image while the Marines continued forward.

"Could they have been planning to use the destruction of the colony expeditions, combined with a claimed 'secret super-weapon' to disable the Construction Matrices, to reassert control over the Assini?" he asked.

"I would like to think that wouldn't have worked," Siril-ki said, but ki's objection was tired. "But the truth is that they likely could have forced a situation where all of the colonies joined the herd of the House of Koth.

"And since our star was *dying*…"

"I assess a sixty plus/minus fifteen percent chance that another fifty to a hundred years without the flare would have led to the creation of Assini colonies that had conceded to the House of Koth and their control of the Construction Matrices," D concluded. "Their plan was not without merit…only utterly without morals or concern for life of any kind."

"You heard all of that, Major Chen?" Octavio asked.

"With one ear, sir," the Marine replied. "We've found the bridge. It's fully encased in another layer of armor. Looks like someone adjusted the plans to create a secure internal command center that might even include quarters for a small number of people."

"Or a single Herd Leader?" Octavio suggested.

"We're cutting our way in," she told him. "We'll know soon enough. If it is this House of Koth…can I shoot them?"

"They're already dead, Major," Octavio replied. "And if they're not…we need them."

He shook his head.

"Even if they *are* evil monsters."

D and the Siril-ki's assessment of the plan the House of Koth had been working from made a twisted, sickening, sense—but the only term he could use for it was *evil*.

———

MAJOR CHEN WAS NOT the first person through the breach into the armored command deck. Octavio knew she was no happier with waiting outside the shell to see what her people encountered than he was with waiting, but there was no world in which a twenty-fourth-century Marine CO could lead from the front.

"We're clear," the point man announced. "I'm picking up a couple of small power sources, but nothing sufficient to run weapons, let alone hunter-killers."

"Why didn't we pick them up before?" Chen asked

"They're really small and inside an entire layer of energy-absorbing armor," the Marine replied. "D, can you see this from my suit?"

"Yes," the AI confirmed. "Commodore, Major, it appears that there is a separate power source inside the command deck to run its computers on an emergency basis. They're in standby but they are online."

That was new.

"Is that likely to do us any good?" Octavio asked. "Or is it a threat?"

"We've been accessing inactive data cores previously," D told him. "The degradation from lack of power is minor, but it is present. If these cores have been continuously powered, they represent the most-intact database available to us since recovering *Shezarim*."

"That's promising," the Commodore noted. "Have your people be careful, Major. I know that's not a necessary order, but…it sounds like there might just be something alive in there."

"The problem and opportunity combined here are that active cores have active security software, not merely passive encryption," D continued. "That is a problem because that software can actively scramble the data cores if we make a mistake. It is an opportunity, as the software can *unencrypt* those cores if we give it the right codes."

"What's the likelihood we have those?" Octavio asked.

"Low," Siril-ki interjected. "On the other hand, I have several tools that might be able to convince the computer that I do. Is the Matrix online?"

"Negative," D replied. "The Matrix was in its own armored shell, detached from the command deck, and it is very definitely powerless. I estimate a ninety-three plus/minus seven percent chance that the Matrix shut down in a manner that would prevent reactivation of the core processes."

"Chen?" Octavio shook his head. None of the people he was talking to could see him except D, and D could read his body language if he was controlling himself. "Find that power source."

"Scans suggest we're looking at a set of radioactive decay genera-tors set up… Wait, *what*?" Chen trailed off.

"Major?" Octavio demanded

"They're set up *in* the bridge," she told him. "From these scans, they're not built in."

"Are they a threat to your Marines?" he asked.

She scoffed.

"Anything energetic enough to do more than ping our armor's sensors is being trapped and used by the electrical generation systems," she told him. "We'll be fine. It just looks like somebody hauled them up from the colony supplies they stole from Assini."

"That's fascinating," Octavio murmured. Assini RDGs had a thou-sand-year estimated useful life. They'd originally been designed to sustain interstellar probes in the void between stars, after all.

"My people are moving in; I'll have visual momentarily," Chen told him.

"And how far behind them are you?" Octavio asked, watching

though the camera feed as her people forced open what appeared to be the last layer of security doors around the ship's bridge.

"About half a step," Chen confirmed cheerfully as her point man plunged into the room on the other side of the doors.

"*Zeus pateras*," the Marine swore. "That is one *big* horse."

Chen was through the door half a second later, and Octavio got his own look at the very dead Assini in the center of the sublight starship's bridge.

The point Marine's shocked exclamation was fundamentally correct. The air in the room had been set to archival levels of dryness a long time before, and the sentient in the command throne had mummified.

The Assini had probably been a hundred and seventy centimeters tall at their first set of shoulders. Even shrunken in on themselves after two hundred–plus years, they looked like they were easily three meters from ground to the top of their head.

They were also very clearly dead.

The fascinating thing was everything *else* in the room. The RDGs looked exactly like Octavio had anticipated. They were modular devices designed to be stored in sealed vaults until loaded into probes or other systems. Six of them had been placed somewhat haphazardly around the room, with cables tied into the bridge's systems.

"Siril-ki?" Octavio asked slowly. "I didn't think your people *got* that big."

"Based on Admiral Lestroud, Commodore, I wouldn't expect your people to have many two-meter-tall giants," ki replied. "Assini of this individual's size are rare but certainly exist."

Ki paused.

"They were slightly more common among the Herd Leader Houses before those families stopped being quite as fixated on aristocratic purity," ki noted. "While it would be an assumption to believe this to be a member of the House of Koth, there is a basis for it."

Herd stallions. Octavio had heard of the concept—in Terran horses and similar herbivores, at least. He hadn't quite made the connection to the concept of Herd Leader for the Assini, since the Assini leaders he'd dealt with had been scientific team leads.

"There's no one else here?" Octavio asked. "How did our big friend die?"

"All I see are some *really* long-term generators and one massive Assini," Chen replied. "Wong, what do we have on the big guy?"

"No entry wounds, no weapons to hand, no visible injuries," the Marine checking over the Assini reported. "Wait…I've got a syringe here and an injection mark."

"Scan the syringe. Don't touch it," Chen ordered.

The Marine Major was slowly and steadily sweeping the room, letting Octavio get a sense for it. He'd seen *Shezarim*'s bridge and knew roughly what to expect of the colony ship command centers.

This was different. *Shezarim*'s crew had followed a clear hierarchy, but there'd been little visual sign of it in how the bridge was laid out. That had been twenty-two consoles with nothing to really distinguish the Captain from his bridge crew.

Octavio suspected that gap between esthetic aspiration and reality had been endemic to the Great Collective.

This ship, however, had a very clear hierarchy. The bridge had been expanded to allow for two concentric rings of consoles, all facing in toward a raised dais holding the closest thing the centaur-like Assini could manage to a throne.

There was no question who had been in charge on this ship, and it was the dead alien in the central seat.

"The syringe contained a mix of medications known to my files," D reported as the data came in from the Marines. "It's a suicide drug, originally provided to long-range astronauts in case they missed their return orbital insertions."

Octavio nodded slowly. That was roughly what he'd been expecting.

"Have we seen any other sign of the crew?" he asked.

"We're mostly in the working spaces of the ship so far," Chen replied. "If they all quietly found a spot to sit down and put themselves to sleep, they'd do so in their quarters, I'd guess."

"Almost certainly," Siril-ki agreed after a moment's thought. "I wouldn't have thought the bridge was a private-enough place to…"

"Die," Octavio finished after ki trailed off. "I suspect our friend was the last survivor. The last to give in to despair—but he set up all of this, too. Chen, is there anything in particular it looks like the generators are set up to power?"

"I'd guess that whoever rigged this up knew the wiring for this space better than I do," she replied with a chuckle. "It looks like they're keeping a bunch of batteries charged and running the entire bridge computer system on standby."

"Is there any way we can copy those data cores without talking to the software?" Octavio asked. "It should all be backed up elsewhere, right?"

"Yes," Siril-ki confirmed. "With the armor, there should be a limited number of hard connections to the rest of the ship. If we make sure the rest of the data cores are powered off, they should contain everything bridge cores contain."

"And we can use the software to unencrypt them later, if it works," Octavio said. "Okay. Chen, think you can find those access points?"

"We'll sweep."

"I know exactly where they should be," Siril-ki told them. "I also know how to work with the software without needing D or one of my people over my shoulder. I need to go down there, Commodore.

"I think one of my people has to be in that room. I am not sure why...but I am sure of it."

Octavio considered the video feed from Major Chen's shoulder silently for several seconds.

"Chen, is everything secure down there?"

"Except for this room, everything mechanical or organic is dead," the Marine replied. "Ki'll be safe down here."

"All right, Director," he said with a sigh. "I'm not sure this is a great idea, but...I agree with you. Something tells me that one of you needs to be in that room."

55

Despite sending down his senior Assini—a being who was arguably the current head of state for a species of some five thousand souls—to the abandoned starship, Octavio manfully resisted temptation and remained aboard *Dauntless* himself.

The battlecruiser had moved to orbit above the starship, providing an easier flight for the shuttles and a hopefully unnecessary backup for the three strike cruisers still orbiting KB2N13-1.

Less than a quarter of *Cassio*'s crew had been retrieved. That was going to wear on Octavio in future, just as the crew of *Scorpion* who hadn't survived the ship's crippling in defense of the Vistans' home-world wore on him.

For now, he had to hope that there was *something* useful aboard the abandoned starship or in the wrecked settlements on the surface. All their insanely long-distance mission to the Assini home system had bought so far was a lot of depressing knowledge about the fate of the Matrices' builders and the loss of a strike cruiser to leftover robot warships.

"Director Siril-ki has joined us in the bridge," Chen's voice told him, interrupting his morose reverie. "With ki and D's aid, I believe we've cut off all connections to the rest of the ship. The bridge systems are now completely isolated from the rest of the ship."

"With your permission, I would like to boot up the system," Siril-ki told Octavio.

"It's your people's ship, Siril-ki," he replied. "Whatever nightmare we find in here is yours more than mine." He shivered. "Do what you need to do."

He watched through Chen's shoulder-camera as the space-suited Assini settled in at a console near the central dais, attaching cables from one of the generators ki'd brought, and initiated the wake-up cycle.

"It was on a basic power-saving standby," Siril-ki reported. "I'm impressed they managed to get that to hold up this long, even with the decay generators."

Octavio could see the screen lighting up by the Assini. Unless he was very mistaken, it was asking for a password.

"I wonder," he murmured.

"Commodore?" Siril-ki asked.

"Do you have any codes you were planning on trying?" he replied.

"I doubt any authorizations I have would work on this ship," ki told him. "I have some hardware I was about to link in that will help me work around the security software."

"Try giving it *Shezarim*'s command codes," Octavio suggested. "One wrong authentication won't lose us the data, will it?"

"It won't, but I don't see the point," ki replied.

"Humor me, Siril-ki," he asked.

The sound of ki not *quite* grinding ki's beak against itself was the equivalent to a long, exasperated sigh from a human...but Siril-ki leaned back over the console and plugged in the codes she'd inherited from Reletan-dai—who'd inherited them in turn from *Shezarim*'s long-dead original commander.

"Wait...that worked?" ki said aloud. "Hold on...that seems to have triggered something else."

The batteries, it appeared, were hooked up to holoprojectors positioned around the room. The image of a large Assini now appeared in the dimly lit bridge, hanging in front of the command chair.

"If you are seeing this message," the image began, "you are a descendant of the crew and passengers of the evacuation ship *Shezarim* and have used their access codes to bring the ship's computers out of standby.

"I have done everything within my power to make sure these computers are still here and able to receive those codes." The Assini shook their entire upper torso, an even more emphatic version of a human headshake.

"My name is Koth-Aran-dai," he introduced himself. "I hope and pray that all I have done will enable this message to reach the last survivors of my species. We dismissed *Shezarim*'s flight when it occurred, but now that flight is our only hope."

Octavio knew the *dai* suffix meant that Koth-Aran-dai was male—Assini biology did *not* lend itself to external sex identification, and their culture called for five different gradations of gender.

"The *Koth*, if you have forgotten that piece of history, marks me as one of the Houses of the Herd Leaders," Koth-Aran-dai continued. "Of the House of Koth, in particular.

"Assuming that this message is being shown where I recorded it, you stand in the command center of the starship *Koth-Shezar*, on the moon Kothil, orbiting the world Kothan in the Koth System. I do not pretend my line has any concept of humility."

Octavio had to conceal a snort of amusement. Even at the end—and the positioning and clothing Koth-Aran-dai wore in the recording suggested it had been recorded very shortly before he'd injected himself with the syringe on his command chair—the Assini had still had some level of self-aware humor.

"If we had humility, we might not have broken the herd as badly as we did," Koth-Aran-dai continued softly. "We are not responsible for our star betraying our people...but as I stand here at the end of all I swore to protect, I cannot deny that we *are* responsible for the failure of so many things that could have saved us.

"So, let this be my confession, in the hope that the last survivors of our species have somehow made it here and are watching this recording."

He straightened and looked directly at the camera—a posture that had the hologram appearing to look his own corpse in the eye.

"I am the last scion of the House of Koth. I was the prince who was intended to be the king who saved us all," he said calmly. "My father and his father and all who came before them set into motion the events that damned us all.

"The House of Koth lost power but we hid our wealth. In the time of the Great Collective, wealth and control of information seemed the only keys of power. It took us too long to learn that *myth* was a key as well—and the myth that had risen around the last of the Houses was a powerful weapon.

"So many saw the weaknesses of the Great Collective and hoped for the return of the rightful Herd Leaders. We used that. We recruited factions and leaders and scientists and built our power in the shadows.

"But to convince the Collective to undo itself and restore our supposed rightful power to us, we needed a grand crisis," Koth-Aran-dai told them. Octavio felt his heart sink as the long-dead prince confirmed his worst fears about the failures of the Construction Matrices.

"Shezarim-ko planned it all. They had the plan, they had the AIs, they had the code to turn those AIs against our enemies. The first phases of the plan went perfectly, but to control the destruction of the colony waves sufficiently to create a crisis without an absolute massacre…"

Koth-Aran-dai shook his entire torso again.

"My father claimed it was a mistake," he said flatly. "But he was very young then. He might have been lied to. He might well have lied to me. I cannot help but fear that the massacre was the point and that our 'grand rescue' was to be clearing the way for the evacuation ships of the second colony project.

"We could have made a compromise even then, I think, claiming our ability to fool or disable the Construction Matrices was a secret weapon. We could have made ourselves the rulers of all Assini who left our home system in exchange for their safety.

"But our star betrayed us all," Koth-Aran-dai concluded simply. "I was born here on Kothan. I never saw Assini until after the flares. We saw the first flare wipe out our homeworld and saw *Shezarim* flee and we…"

He sighed.

"We hesitated," he confessed. "With the technology and resources we had here, we could have sent this ship with the resources to bring most of *Shezarim*'s sisters online. What we lacked was the construction spikes, but some of those had been built. Given time, we could even have commandeered nearby Construction Matrices.

"We needed to clear a way through the Sentinels to do that, so we would have needed the full cooperation of the remaining government in Assini. We would have needed to confess our crimes and forge an alliance to save our species over everyone's pride."

Koth-Aran-dai slumped, bowing his head.

"We did not convince ourselves that was necessary until it was too late," he confessed. "In the destruction of Sina, *I* saw the annihilation of our species. I forced my father to fit out *Koth-Shezar* for a mission of mercy.

"We had the cryo-pods and every other system to rescue five million people from Assini. We would increase the population of our colony here by fifty percent and save our species. It was a mission that could not be argued with, and I would not be denied.

"We set out forty years ago," he concluded. "And halfway to Assini, the star killed everyone."

He paused, clearly considering what to say next.

"We still had to complete the flight," he said. "*Koth-Shezar* couldn't be turned around without refueling, so we went back to our home system. We buried the dead at Kora and we scavenged everything of value we could fit on this ship.

"I left Koth with eleven elevens of eleven elevens of Assini. By the time we left Assini, we'd lost a full eleven of eleven elevens to suicide or the accidents of a herd without hope.

"Those of us who had not lost the hope of fresh waters knew that what we were bringing home would be enough to at least make Kothan partially habitable, the beginning of a new start for our people.

"It would be a slow process however, so my father decided to try and bring in the Construction Matrices that we could control. He needed them to get through the Sentinels...so he told the Sentinels everything."

Octavio inhaled sharply.

"Thanks to Shezarim-ko, we had the ability to edit even the Sentinels' code," Koth-Aran-dai said quietly. "We could modify their core protocols, though we couldn't modify the working core processes that define their personalities.

"The message my father sent included code that rewrote the Sentinels' core protocols to obey him. We...we did not know that strong-enough emotion could overcome all of the bindings and limitations built into them.

"I think Shezarim-ko did," Koth-Aran-dai admitted. "My father didn't. He tried to control the Sentinels, and they turned on him with a homicidal rage like I have never even conceived of in a creation of our people."

The recording was silent for long enough that Octavio thought it had frozen.

"We were halfway home when the rest of the House of the Koth was wiped from existence," he said quietly. "I lost half my people within eleven days. By the time I'd even convinced *myself* not to end everything, I had less than eleven elevens of people.

"We had the code to build weapons against the surviving Sentinels. We had Guardian swarms attached to the ship to protect us, and we believed our code would succeed where my father's failed.

"But since my father's failure damned eleven million souls, I wrote a backup," he concluded. "Our code failed, just as my father's had... but my *backup* erased this ship from their sensors. They could not see us, so they concluded they had destroyed us.

"Three Sentinels survive as I record this. They are ignoring the drones that are orbiting my ship, because they don't see my ship. They will, sooner or later, lose the rage that drives them. I do not think they will survive that any better than my people have survived their rage."

He was silent again, leaning on his hands.

"My people are gone now," he said finally. "There weren't enough of us left to refuel and fly the ship again. They have all gone to their rest of their own will. If any of them had chosen to fight, I might have. But I am alone and I cannot preserve a species on my own.

"But I have a sensor trace that tells me that *Shezarim* continues to fly outward at near the speed of light, hopefully safe from the Matrices that pursue her. And I can hope that her crew one day comes back here and learns the truth.

"If you do, understand that the code I speak of is in this ship's computers," Koth-Aran-dai told them. "I don't know why it failed on the Sentinels, but I am leaving you everything to be able to force a Construction Matrix to obey you.

"That alone should make the worlds they have built safe for you," he concluded. "It is the final gift I can give the survivors of my race. The only legacy I can offer except to understand *why* everything failed.

"I am the last of the House of Koth, and today I go to my final rest of my own will," he stated calmly. "May my confession enable knowledge and my gift enable peace.

"Spirits of the ancient herds know my family failed to do either."

56

One of the many advantages of stopping a light-month outside of the target system was that it allowed Isaac to make sure his people emerged in formation. A three-hour jump was far easier to coordinate than a week-long jump.

It had also allowed him to pick up *Watchtower* and her battle group, which meant he arrived in the Sivar-One System with six battlecruisers and twenty strike cruisers. He'd left several strike cruisers in deep space with his logistics ships, just in case.

He didn't expect to need them. Part of the reason for making sure the massive twenty-six ship formation was *perfect* was that *winning* today's battle wasn't the point. He knew the Sivar ships were more dangerous than he was publicly giving them credit for, but his ships could take them at two-to-one odds even at close range.

Scans of the system were updating *Vigil*'s flag-deck hologram as he was thinking, and they showed odds that were nowhere near that steep for the allied fleet. The planet was the focus of the military deployment in the system, and it looked like there were around twenty warships total in the system.

"Connor, what have we got?" he asked his ops officer.

"It's looking like three battleships and eighteen escorts, sir," the

Commander replied. "Twenty-one ships to our twenty-six, but only three capital ships to our six."

The inverse of the odds he was prepared to fight at. Isaac smiled grimly.

"We'll wait here for ten minutes," he ordered. "Once they move out towards us, we'll deploy to meet them."

From five light-minutes out, ten minutes would give him time to see their initial response. If the locals wanted to talk to him, he'd reply to their hails, too.

If they hadn't offered unconditional surrender by the time he reached half a million kilometers, he had every intention of reducing the Governance's fleets to debris and ashes.

"All ships report fully ready and standing by for your orders," Connor told him. "Any changes to the plan?"

Isaac shook his head.

"We haven't fought a straight battle with these people yet," he replied. "*Watchtower*'s clash with them suggests that their battleships' beams aren't to be sneered at, but they underestimated our defenses.

"Let's *not* return the favor. We engage at maximum range and we *stay* at maximum range until we either have a solid assessment of their abilities or they leave us without a choice."

"Do we really expect the latter, sir?" Connor asked.

"I don't know *what* to expect, Aloysius," Isaac pointed out. "We have *one* engagement where our ship was more focused on getting the hell out than on getting decent reads on their weapons. We know those battleships are missile platforms, which means they've got less mass devoted to beams than we do.

"Beyond that? I'm not dismissing them yet."

The time stamps told him that the Sivar fleet would have seen them now. It would be another five minutes before he saw how they reacted, but that was the nature of the game. His ships remained in the broad winged formation they'd jumped in, slowly dropping down the star's gravity well to the planet.

"And even if they *are* utterly outclassed, consider how badly outmatched we were by the first Matrix node we met," Alstairs noted from the bridge. The Captain was probably giving them less than a tenth of his attention, but the conversation was relevant to him. "A single recon node kicked the shit out of our entire fleet and disabled *Dante*—but we took her down and it wasn't that much later that we took out the sub-regional node that sent it."

"The Sivar are in much the same place we were then, yes," Isaac agreed. "From the data we *have*, there's nothing wrong with their weapons. Their weapon mix just assumes they can actually land missiles on their targets, which isn't going to work on us."

And, if the Confederacy's old unit design was anything to go by, quite possibly wouldn't work on Sivar ships. The CSF had been able to shoot down a lot more missiles than any of its ships could deploy long before the Republic had stripped the missiles out of its ex-Confederacy ships.

"Sir, we are now receiving lightspeed telemetry from when they'd have seen us," Connor reported after a few moments of silence. "They, ah, didn't do much."

"Nobody—not even *Matrices*—goes from zero to active counter-deployment in seconds, Commander," Isaac pointed out. "Give me a timer, though. From the moment they saw us until they bring their engines online and validate our estimate of what ships are escorts."

The battleships were rather distinctive, but at five light-minutes, it was even theoretically possible that they'd missed one. The escorts, however, had low-enough power signatures that it was definitely possible some had been mistaken for freighters or vice versa.

Once they deployed—*if* they deployed—that split would become clearer.

"Regardless of that, we move out in one minute," Isaac continued. "No adjustment to the clock. We deploy on the plan."

If he'd brought a Matrix fleet, five light-minutes would have taken less than an hour to travel. Of course, he couldn't reasonably exercise command over a Matrix force himself. There was a shortage of oxygen on ships that had never been intended to carry organic passengers.

Plus, he didn't *want* this to go quickly. If nothing else, he needed them to report in to the Sivar capital that he was there—and if everything went to plan, the civilian government would be able to report in that the fleet had lost.

"All ships' engines online. Accelerations matched and we are moving in," Connor reported. "No sign of response yet."

"They've had less than two minutes, Aloysius," Isaac replied. "I won't start implying utter incompetence until they hit at *least* three."

———

THE SIVAR FLEET brought their engines online with an entire ten seconds to spare inside Isaac's mental *are you kidding me?* line. They didn't immediately thrust out to meet his fleet, though.

"Looks like only a few dozen gravities," Connor reported. "They're maneuvering out of orbit and forming up, but they're not coming out."

"Get me another deep scan of the orbitals," Isaac ordered. "Do we have numbers on orbital forts?"

"First sweeps didn't suggest any significant numbers, but those are the only defenses I see," his operations officer replied. "Any change to the plan?"

"Get me that sensor data," Isaac replied. "And ask me again in ten minutes."

Connor chuckled but he was already passing the orders.

"We've confirmed the deployment of star-lane com drones," he added after a few moments. "It looks like they were anticipating us trying to intercept them. They launched twenty-five of the things."

"How fast are they?" Isaac replied.

"Bit better acceleration than our old missiles, but not by much," Connor said. "I mean, if we *wanted* to intercept them…"

The Admiral snorted. *Fortitude*, the other Republic ship he'd pulled from the main fleet, carried exactly one missile launcher. It was an extremely rapid-fire system loaded with Matrix-style reactionless-drive missiles, though, and the Sivar's defenseless com drones would have been easy prey for the near-cee smart weapons.

"Negative," he replied. "But you knew that."

If they had to fight the Sivar in close to Sivar-One's inhabited planet, he'd have to obviously let the second wave of com drones escape. He'd probably do that anyway.

"Their accelerations are higher than Confed missiles?" he asked, curious.

"The drones have about ten percent edge on the missiles we came through with," Connor confirmed. "Better than I would have expected from their starship drives."

Isaac nodded absently as he pulled the data on the screens on his command seat. It looked like the bulky fusion engines the Sivar favored might make for better missile drives than his own impulse microthrusters.

"Bake that into the tactical assumptions," he ordered. "If their missiles have a twenty percent acceleration edge over the CSF Rapier Twelves and the same flight endurance, what does their range look like?"

"Just under a light-minute, sir," Connor replied. He paused, shaking his head as he looked over at the chief petty officer running the numbers. "You double-checked this, Chief?"

"Yes, sir. Seemed weird to me, too."

"We're not used to fighting at missile ranges," Isaac said. "We had a forty-light-second range envelope with our birds."

He'd have expected the Sivar to try and keep him out of their missile range from the planet.

"Hashemi, any attempt to communicate from the locals?" he asked.

"Negative, sir. Not even any bluster."

"Interesting," Isaac murmured. "Well, time to up the verbal-bluster quotient of the star system. Stand by to record for transmission."

"Translation software is running," Naveed Hashemi told him. "Video is live in three. Two. One. Live."

The recording suite could send a holographic image, but for this purpose, a video was easier to translate and transmit. Isaac faced the primary pickup and smiled.

The Sivar probably wouldn't pick up the menace in his expression, but he also doubted they'd misinterpret it as friendly.

"I am Admiral Isaac Lestroud of the Exilium Space Fleet," he told the camera levelly. "Your government has interned our diplomatic delegation, including our Foreign Minister.

"The Republic has no choice but to regard this as an act of war. As such, I am ordered and authorized to seize control of this star system—and since my scans show that the native population are *not* Sivar, I somehow doubt I'll be giving it back.

"The only choice available to you is extremely straightforward: your space and ground forces can surrender, with an attendant promise of the safety and security of all Sivar personnel…or you can fight me.

"In which case I will destroy your fleets, reduce your orbital defenses and shatter your ground forces. The choice is yours."

And for the first time Isaac could think of, he'd ordered the fabrication of the precision ground-attack munitions the *Republic*, at least, had never used. If he had to land EMC troops on a hostile planet, they'd be doing so with the kind of support that could take out a tank in the middle of a street without harming the building on either side—or level a city.

He cut the recording and gestured for Hashemi to send it.

"Let me know if they increase their acceleration," he told Connor, turning his attention to his own formation.

It was straightforward, though hopefully impressive to the Sivar. Six battlecruisers advanced in line abreast, ten thousand kilometers between them. Four "wings" of five strike cruisers each radiated out from the center of the line, putting ten escorts above and ten escorts below his heavies.

The range was dropping quickly now. Matrices might have closed the range faster, but his fleet wasn't slow by any means.

"It looks like our friends are moving out, sir," Connor reported. "All warships have brought their engines to higher energy levels. Battleships are stabilizing at…" He shook his head. "A little over half of our acceleration. From the energy signatures and the leakages I'm detecting, that might be the best they can do with their engines and thrust compensators."

"Let's not assume that without more data," Isaac replied. "How are we doing at getting tachyon com–equipped drones in close?"

"They haven't shot any down yet, but the drones aren't that much faster than our ships," the ops officer replied. "We're only just starting to cross the one light-minute mark and get faster data from them than from the rest of the fleet."

"Keep at least ten percent at thirty light-seconds," Isaac ordered. "Standard ratios for most other ranges, but I want you to put at least a dozen drones right down the heart of their formation."

"We'll lose them," Connor noted calmly. Even now, the tachyon communicators weren't cheap or easy for the Republic to build. The miniaturized ones included in the drones cost more than the rest of the robotic spacecraft.

The entire fleet he'd brought to Sivar space only had a hundred drones.

"I know," Isaac agreed. "And I understand the cost. But I want to know what they shoot them down *with*, Commander. What they have for close-range weapons and defenses is critical information."

"Understood. I'll pass the orders."

The range was now barely three light-minutes, and the Sivar were finally coming out to meet them. The tactical analysis teams were hard at work, and the revised interception zone was already marked on the big hologram.

"We'll range on them twenty million kilometers from the planet," Isaac said aloud. "If they're assuming our missile range is about the same as theirs, that's not an unreasonable low-range intercept. Especially if they think the main fight is going to be a missile fight."

"Should *Fortitude* demonstrate what Matrix missiles look like, sir?" Connor asked.

"No," Isaac said after a moment. "Tempting, but no. Let's keep a few surprises in our back pocket."

Connor nodded.

"Anything else we should hold back, sir?" he asked.

"No," Isaac repeated. "We're not going to play the kind of games that get people on our side killed. Once we're in beam range, it's death ground. Only one fleet leaves intact and it *will* be us."

"Understood."

"Sir, we have a response coming from one of the battleships," Hashemi reported. "We're not close enough for a live channel, but if I relay you through the drones, I can cut the delay down to under ten seconds."

"Show me their message first," Isaac replied. "Then I'll decide whether I even *want* to talk to them."

The literally boneheaded image of a Sivar officer appeared in front of him. The stranger wore the same dark green hooded tunic as the images he'd seen of Commandant Ackahl, with similar though *probably* different gold iconography at the base of the hood that concealed his face.

"I am Commandant-Key of War Dest," the Sivar introduced himself —Isaac only knew the gender because Hashemi dropped an assessment of the body shape and voice with that conclusion onto his screen. Knowing that, though, he picked up the hint of a Sivar male's facial horns inside the hood.

"I am the direct sword of the Intendant of the Sivar, the voice of the Fates in this time, within the Sonbar System," Dest continued. "His will with regards to your Republic and its allies is simple: you will surrender your systems, ships and technology to the Governance, and we will protect you from the creatures you fear.

"The war you proclaim is of no threat to the Governance. We are far from intimidated by your toys. Lay down your arms and accept your place as tributaries of the Governance, and you will be protected as all others have been."

The image froze, the message over.

"Range?" Isaac asked calmly.

"One point two light-minutes," Connor replied instantly. "Estimate fifteen minutes before they can attempt to engage with missiles. Our reactionless missiles will be in range in ten."

"I haven't changed my mind on those," Isaac told him. "There'll be no response, Naveed. Let me know if we get any more messages—such as after we ignore his first missile salvo."

"Understood, Admiral."

"Oh, and Commander?" he asked, turning to look at Naveed. "ID the battleship that message came from. She's our first target once we're in range."

57

———

"Huн. Either we underestimated their endurance or they're expecting a bunch of unpowered nukes to be a noticeable threat."

Connor's dry observation went unchallenged on *Vigil*'s flag deck as the data-analysis teams tore into the sensor results, dropping more information on the Sivar's missile launch into the hologram as they worked.

"Twenty-one ships launched two thousand missiles," Isaac observed. "That's not shabby for cramming launchers into the hulls, especially given the performance parameters and what we think they get for efficiency with those engines."

The acceleration was even slightly higher than he'd projected based on the com drones. Even with that, the missiles had to have at least fifteen seconds' more endurance than the Confederacy's best.

The reactionless missiles the Republic had built from Assini designs still outranged them, but the Sivar weapons were still impressive.

And useless.

"VK?" Isaac asked aloud. "Threat level?"

"Sivar missiles will enter our defensive engagement perimeter at a velocity of just over eighty-two percent of lightspeed," the AI replied.

"Estimated closest approach is two hundred and fifty thousand plus/minus fifty thousand kilometers."

"Additional salvo is launching," Connor reported. "Cycle time appears to be forty-eight seconds."

"Record everything," Isaac ordered. An unnecessary order, but that was true of just about anything he could say. "Our close-approach probes?"

"At six hundred thousand kilometers and closing at twenty percent of lightspeed," Connor reported. "Ten seconds to closest approach."

Ignoring the oncoming missiles, Isaac's attention was on the live sensor feed from the probes. If they managed to get in as close as the probes had been programmed to, they'd be able to read the names painted on the hulls.

Assuming that the Sivar engaged in that kind of frivolity.

"Drones at one light-second. Sivar missile defenses engaging," Connor reported. Several seconds past in silence. "All drones destroyed. Closest approach was just under one hundred thousand kilometers."

"What did we get?" Isaac asked.

"A lot," the ops officer replied. "Some of it's going to take a while to work out, but I think we got enough to flag most of the power generators on their ships. That seems…promising."

"Doesn't it just?" Isaac murmured. "See if you can resolve that, Commander, then distribute it to the fleet. I'm not going to go out of my way to try and save these people, but I *will* use the most efficient takedowns we have."

"Missiles entering defensive perimeter," VK interrupted. "Engaging now."

The red icons on the holographic display began to sparkle as the pulse guns across the allied fleet opened fire. None of the heavier weapons engaged and there were no specialized antimissile systems anymore.

Neither was needed. The rapid-fire plasma weapons obliterated the incoming enemy fire with perfect efficiency. VK's assessment of the closest approach turned out to be pessimistic.

"First salvo destroyed," the AI reported with audible satisfaction.

"Second salvo will enter range in forty-two seconds. Similar results expected."

Isaac nodded.

"Time to our weapons range?" he asked.

"Another twelve minutes and fifteen missile salvos," Connor reported. "Should we adjust the plan?"

"Not yet," Isaac replied. "Maintain course. All ships to initiate evasive maneuvers at three light-seconds and stand by to fire at five hundred thousand kilometers."

Everything he'd seen suggested the Sivar's lasers could only reach a single light-second. By the time they opened fire, perhaps Commandant-Key Dest would begin to understand just how bad a day the Sivar Governance was having.

———

STARSHIPS DIDN'T REALLY HAVE body language. Once a ship was on its course and heading toward its destination, the main maneuvers were all handled by computer.

In combat, though, evasive maneuvers were generally handled by an organic with their hand on a joystick, adding small random motions to the main thrust. If you had enough practice with it, you could start to see *some* signs of how that officer, at least, was feeling.

Isaac could tell the Sivar fleet was nervous. For ten minutes, the Republic and their allies had advanced into the teeth of their missile fire. Over twenty thousand missiles had crossed the gap and flung themselves at Isaac's ships.

None had even come close to hitting. Plasma flashed out from the fleet's pulse guns again as he watched, another salvo of missiles dying as the two fleets hurtled toward half a million kilometers.

"We'll keep the range above four hundred thousand kilometers," he told Connor. "Maneuver pattern Rho-Six. Maintain formation and focus on the battleships. Starting with Commandant-Key Dest's flagship."

"We have enough data to attempt to aim to disable, sir," the junior officer pointed out.

"Make sure the Captains have it, but firing to disable is at their discretion," Isaac replied. "Priority is neutralizing the capital ships. I'm more comfortable with our ability to take the escorts' lasers than the battleships."

"Understood."

The formation didn't change as they approached the line in space where they could reliably hit their targets. Isaac didn't need to give more orders now. The plan was set and he trusted all of his Captains and battle group commanders to complete it.

"Range."

Six battlecruisers' main heavy particle cannons fired at a single target. Dozens of zettahertz and gamma-ray lasers joined them, alongside the lighter particle cannons mounted in the mobile turrets.

At this range, less than a quarter of the beams connected, but the Sivar battleship was physically flung backward from the energy transfer. Chunks of warship went spinning off as the forward third of the enemy vessel was peeled open.

"Impressive armor," Isaac said quietly. "None of our ships could have taken that hit before we installed Assini ceramics."

"Impressive or not, she's toast," Connor replied. "Energy levels dropping and I'm picking up active fusion reactors being ejected into space. Mission kill, sir."

"Switch to Target Bravo," the Admiral ordered. The entire ship trembled around him as the main gun fired again. "For salvo three, at least."

The damage meant that Dest's flagship wasn't maneuvering. The wave of firepower washed over the battleship like a tsunami. When it passed, there was nothing left of the battleship but debris.

"Sivar force is increasing acceleration," Connor reported. "We are adjusting course, but—"

"But we can't get a good-enough vector away from them without giving up the main guns," Isaac finished for his operations officer. "Order the battlecruisers to go to rapid fire. Three shots on each battleship.

"I don't want to get into close range with these bastards. Not today."

Emptying the cyclotrons would leave his heavy ships short their strongest firepower for at least a minute, but he wasn't going to need those big guns against the escorts.

It took a moment for the order to be spread to all six ships. Then they fired as one. *Vigil* herself kicked backward in space, all of the engines and inertial compensation in the universe only so useful against the amount of energy being applied in the heavy particle cannon for a round per second.

The first and fifth salvos were accompanied by lasers and lighter particle cannon fire. Target Bravo managed to dodge or absorb most of the secondary fire, but only at the cost of taking eight direct hits from the heavy guns.

The back third of the ship ended up spinning away from the front half, the engines firing wildly as they flung the wreckage into the void. The two pieces didn't make up a complete ship, and the missing pieces filled the space between them as what was left of Target Bravo ran out of power and just...shut down.

They were still luckier than Target Charlie. They dodged most of the first salvo, but one of the heavy particle packets hammered into her engines. They could probably have got her drives back online, given any amount of time at all.

The crew had less than two seconds before the entire massed salvo struck home. Some of the beams, targeted at an evading enemy, still missed.

Enough hit that Target Charlie just ceased to exist.

"Battleships are down," Connor reported. "Your orders, sir?"

"All ships cease firing," Isaac ordered calmly. "Get the video recorders back up. I think we're done here."

He was about to send a message demanding the escorts surrender when half of them suddenly vastly increased their acceleration.

"Multiple escorts inbound at major accelerations," Connor snapped. "Their engines can't take this for very long, but they're on collision courses!"

There was no way they were going to make it that far, Isaac knew, but they were almost certainly going to get their shorter-ranged lasers into play.

"Target the lead ships," he ordered. "Everything we've got."

An everything that lacked the heavy particle cannon. He'd presumed that taking out the capital ships with no losses would convince the escorts to surrender.

He'd been wrong and laser fire began to lash his formation. Only eight of the Sivar cruisers were taking part in the suicide charge, but that would be bad enough if even one of them reached his line. Worse, there were a *lot* more lasers out there than they'd anticipated, and their acceleration was now as high as anything his fleet could manage. Even if the Republic fleet turned and fled, they couldn't evade and the lasers would hammer them.

So instead, Isaac sat solidly on his flag deck and watched every weapon in his fleet open fire on the charging ships. LPCs. Lasers. Even the pulse guns as the ships entered the range of those systems.

"Targets neutralized," Connor reported after a few seconds. "Closest is on a ballistic course that will pass within fifteen thousand kilometers of our line."

"Adjust the fleet," Isaac ordered. "I want that minimum distance at fifty thousand or higher. And get me damage reports."

"Yes, sir."

Looking past the wreckage of the suicidal charge, his glare settled on the eight ships that were slowly retreating toward the planet.

"Hashemi?" he asked.

"You're on whenever you say the word, sir," she confirmed.

"Let's end this bullshit."

———

"Surviving Sivar units," Isaac began. "You can't hurt me. Even a suicide charge by your fellows failed."

That wasn't *entirely* accurate. It turned out that while Sivar beams were overall mediocre, they weren't nearly as mass-intensive as the analysts had predicted. Their cruisers carried the same beams as their battleships—and given the missile focus of the bigger ships, they didn't even carry significantly fewer beams. The eight cruisers that had charged into range had carried almost twice as many lasers as their scans suggested the three battleships had possessed.

They hadn't lost any ships, but several ships—including, as the ESF was starting to regard as inevitable, *Othello*—had been badly battered. His battlecruisers had only taken light damage, but three strike cruisers were below half combat capability—with the attendant dead and wounded.

"If I am forced to engage you in orbit of the planet, I will destroy you without hesitation," he continued. "If you attempt to run, I will intercept you and destroy you. Your only remaining option is unconditional surrender.

"The same applies to the civilian government of the Sonbar System." They'd confirmed the name Dest had used. It was less of a mouthful than "Sivar-One" and would make more sense to the recipient of his message.

"If you surrender now, I will guarantee the safety of the Sivar population from reprisal from the local population," he told them. "But you *will* withdraw all Sivar personnel to their barracks and prepare to evacuate Sivar civilian populations to isolation zones."

He smiled coldly.

"I would *strongly* suggest that you make this process as simple and painless as possible," he told them. "Your system is merely a stopping point on my way to your capital to punish your Intendant. If I am forced to spend too long here, I may get irritable."

The message cut off and saved for transmission. Isaac took a moment to skim it, then nodded to Hashemi to send it.

"We'll continue to advance on the planet until either we get a response or we're *in* orbit," Isaac told Connor. "If any of the cruisers twitch, they get *one* warning shot. If they keep twitching, target the power plants with zetta-lasers."

"Understood. What about the planet?"

"Inform General Zamarano that one is up to her," Isaac replied. "The assault wave is to move in from the rendezvous point. We'll need to leave our damaged ships here, probably with *Watchtower* and some of the intact strike cruisers to provide fire support for EMC."

A long time ago, then-Brigadier Kira Zamarano had been the senior Marine of Isaac's allies when they'd moved against his mother. Now she was the senior officer of the Exilium Marine Corps and in command of the first dedicated warp-capable Marine Orbital Assault Transports ever.

Half of her troops were Vistans, but she had a solid core of six thousand human Marines as well. She couldn't really conquer a planet with a single understrength division, but everything suggested that she wouldn't need to.

"After all, once we've got the *Sivar* in line, we need to work out who to talk to among the actual natives to this planet," Isaac continued. "That's Amelie's job, but in her absence, I'm delegating that to General Zamarano."

He smiled grimly.

"The rest of us need to be in motion in thirty-six hours."

58

NONE of the warships did anything to resist as Isaac's fleet slowly corralled them and the Marines boarded them. There was no one, it seemed, to order them to surrender as a group. The squadron commanders had engaged in the suicide charge and left the surviving ships leaderless.

Initiative did not appear to be encouraged among Sivar junior officers.

It wasn't until the last of the Sivar cruisers had been boarded and entered into a control course away from the habitable planet that Isaac heard *anything* from the planet itself—that started with salvo of com drones.

"A couple are heading for secondary star-lanes, but that's at least thirty heading deeper into the Governance," Captain Alstairs noted as his sensor teams reported in. "We made no attempt to intercept, though some of them are passing close enough I could hit them with pulse guns."

Isaac snorted. The fleet remained at battle stations, but with the main Sivar fleet in the system completely neutralized, most of the tension had faded.

"And they're still playing the silent game on the planet," he noted.

"They don't have much for orbital defenses," Alstairs said. "Maybe eight stations? And if they've got four lasers apiece, I'll eat my emergency helmet."

"Don't do that," Connor replied. "It's got hyper-compressed oxygen beads built into it. Either you can't digest them…or you'd digest the outer casing and have the worst case of gas ever."

"Surviving the human digestive tract was actually a design criterion for the storage beads," Isaac said absently. "My father wrote the final specification paper, and he and my mother laughed over that one…before looking right at *me* and going 'Yeah, it makes sense.'"

Connor looked at him.

"How old were you, sir?"

Isaac shrugged, his attention still on the close-up of the planet Onba. Data icons on each city represented the status of the Sivar ground troops there, and those icons were starting to change.

"Six? Seven? I was out of my swallowing-small-things stage, but it was apparently fresh in their minds. Commander Hashemi?"

"Sir!"

"Unless I'm misreading the sensor data, the Sivar are starting to follow my instructions," he told her. "They'll probably be—"

"Incoming transmission," she cut him off. "We have a tachyon-com drone close enough for a live conversation, sir, but I suspect they're expecting a twenty-second delay."

"Insert the drone in the transmission and catch me up to real-time at one point five speed," Isaac ordered.

A flat image appeared in front of him—with an icon noting that it was being played at fifty percent faster speed than it had been recorded.

The Siva on the screen wore a translucent toga-like garment wrapped around himself—Isaac still couldn't ID Sivar genders on sight, but he trusted the note VK put on the screen. The fabric was more delicate than in many images Isaac had seen of the outfit on other Siva, and there were gold bands holding it in place at the wrist, neck and waist.

Even the Keepers of the Governance hadn't gone for that.

"I am Still, the Prince-Key of Peace of Sonbar," the Siva introduced himself. "Your arrogance and demands have been noted. But…I have no choice but to comply. We have begun the withdrawal of our troops to their facilities. I warn you that chaos will ensue. The local population has no concept of order without our guiding hands.

"I have also ordered the orbital fortresses to stand down and receive your boarding parties. But I must again—"

"The strong lead. The weak submit," Isaac interrupted as the icons informed him he was now watching the Prince-Key in real time. The Siva stumbled to a verbal halt, staring at him.

"Those were the words your Intendant said to our Foreign Minister," he continued calmly. "All that you have done, your Intendant has justified by claiming the strength of your Governance.

"But now your Governance is weak and must yield to the strong. Or does that only work in your favor?"

Still froze for several seconds longer before carefully bowing his armored head.

"That is the philosophy of some in our society, yes," he conceded. "But these people here needed our guiding hand. Without our assistance, they would still be *nothing*."

"With you, they are slaves. I'm not certain that's an improvement," Isaac replied dryly. "In either case, the Republic recognizes you *only* as the leader of the Sivar in this system. I and my people will negotiate with you in that respect and that respect only.

"If you can put us in contact with the *legitimate* government of this planet, that would be a point in your favor, but you are no longer the ruler of this world or this system."

Isaac smiled.

"And as your Intendant's philosophy clearly states, we are the strong here. You *will* submit."

The call was silent for several long seconds, then Still's bowed head lowered to almost level.

"You are not wrong," he conceded. "I am not certain what would count as a local government. The Sonba were not unified prior to our arrival. My people will prepare for evacuation as per your orders. If you'll permit, there are several locations I would recommend for the evacuation of my people."

"Provide them to my staff," Isaac ordered. "My Marine commander will be at your location inside an hour. Full cooperation will reduce any risk of…misunderstandings."

"I understand, Admiral Lestroud," Still told him. "I am charged with the peace of this system. I see only one way to preserve it, and that is to cooperate with you."

———

THE TWELVE SHIPS that led the way as the fleet train caught up to *Vigil* and the other battlecruisers were relatively new. They'd come from Skree-Skree, where their passengers had been helping deal with the damage the Matrices had managed to inflict while being driven off.

Each of the Warp-Capable Orbital Assault Transports, the WOATs, was just over three hundred meters long and carried a thousand soldiers. Six carried regiments of Vistan Spears, now equipped to the same standard as their EMC trainers.

The other six carried the Second Brigade of the Exilium Marine Corps and the woman who *ran* the EMC. As the freighters and escorts settled into orbit under the fleet's guns, the WOAT's continued forward at carefully calculated speeds.

Shuttles spewed from them, but the WOATs were designed to do something very few ships could: land and take off again.

Isaac watched as they descended toward the cities marked as the largest Sivar concentrations. A dozen shuttles flashed toward the palace the Prince-Key of Peace had transmitted from, and he hoped that Still hadn't done something stupid like run.

"No resistance so far," Connor reported. "Shipboard Marines have secured the orbital fortresses. The Sivar seem to actually follow orders when told to lay down arms by their boss."

"Don't trust that forever," Isaac told him. "This is a colony, after all. An occupied world. They'll fight harder when we hit their homeworld."

"General Zamarano's landing force reports they've secured the exterior of the Prince-Key's palace," Hashemi told them. "Similar reports are coming in from the other landings. Ground troops are surrendering in good order."

"Any reports on interaction with the Sonba so far?" Isaac asked. "I'd really like to find someone to hand administration of the place over to ASAP."

"If they've been occupied for a while, the locals might regard what administration exists as quislings," Connor warned.

"I know," Isaac agreed. "We need to get in front of that kind of crap before reprisals and counter-reprisals start. That's part of why we need to pin down both who's in charge on the Sivar-supporting side with the locals and who's running the resistance."

"Zamarano reports that she has Prince-Key Still in custody," Hashemi told him. "No resistance."

"Put her on the channel," Isaac ordered. He wasn't going to ride her shoulder, not with an entire planetary invasion in progress, but he needed to check in with her.

"Kira, what's your status?"

"I've got the fancy alien, but I think he's in shock," the Marine told him. "At least, that's what I'd call it if he was human. Not sure what it is in these guys."

"We've coordinates for a mountain valley that they were using as a retreat," Isaac said. "Looks like there's space there for about sixty thousand Sivar, which is about what I'm expecting to find on the planet. We'll need to rig up housing and utilities."

"My people can do that in their sleep," Zamarano replied. "Right now, we're playing dog catcher. These people aren't being too much trouble."

"We also need to worry about the locals," he reminded her. "Its going to sink in shortly that we're detaining and moving the Sivar, and they *don't* get to start committing atrocities at either the boneheads *or* the collaborating government."

"I have *shit* that's going to work nonlethally on the locals, boss," she said. "If it comes down to shooting Sonba or letting Sivar swing, what do we do?"

"Fire warning shots and do your damnedest not to let it get worse than that," Isaac ordered. "Beyond that, I trust you and I know you trust your junior officers. Do what seems right."

"That's an order that's got a lot of Marines killed over the years, sir," she replied.

"I know. What the hell else can we do?"

"Decide who they should shoot first," Zamarano suggested. "Don't leave the moral call to the grunts on the ground. It's your pay grade, not theirs."

He snorted.

"Touché. If anyone pushes past warning shots, your Marines are authorized to do whatever is necessary to protect the prisoners. Specific enough?"

"Yes, sir."

"For that, General, you get to find someone to put in charge of this planet," he told her. "I suggest starting with the Sonba mayors or whatever the hell title the Sivar hung on them."

"Thanks," she said dryly. "What's my timeline?"

"The fleet moves out in thirty-two hours," Isaac replied. "I'm leaving a battlecruiser and six strike cruisers, but three of the strikes are beaten to shit. Everything else is heading for their capital."

"I can't secure an entire planet in thirty-two hours with twelve thousand grunts, Admiral," Zamarano objected.

"That does move *making friends with the locals* up your priority list, doesn't it?"

59

———

IN THE END, Amelie had ended up back on the farm. It was the largest site the rebels had access to anywhere near the Citadel, which meant that it started transforming into a weapons cache and coordination center within days of the meeting.

Since she was the most obvious problem, she spent most of the days counting down to the scheduled attack underground. The helot rebels' secret underground base was less solid and well equipped than the Dynast's bunker, but it had the advantage of modern communications technology.

The Dynast's bunkers' phone systems had been installed a hundred years earlier. It *looked* like a command center but it couldn't function as one. The tunnels under the Kond's farm, on the other hand, were equipped with expensive communications equipment that easily rivaled the systems available to the Republic.

The tunnels were dug by Pol and for Pol, though, and that meant they were claustrophobic for just about anyone else. The dark-furred aliens had more than one resemblance to a mole, apparently, and they'd only expanded some of the spaces to fit anyone else.

But there was a command center in the largest excavated space, and the data on the holographic display had grown more and more detailed over the last twelve days as the various rebel factions integrated their coms.

"Kond, Minister, take a look at this," one of the Croni in the cave requested. The insectoid alien was a born helot, easily distinguished among his people by the fact that his wings hadn't been clipped to prevent him from flying.

"What have you got?" the Kond asked. Amelie was only a step behind him, but these were his people. Her part in this had been mostly over once everyone had agreed to work together.

"One of the Broken Chain's assets at the Rista star-lane reports that a whole bunch of com drones just came through," the Croni told them. "They're flying emergency codes and heading right here."

"Any way to find out what they're carrying?" Amelie asked.

"*We* don't have a way," the Kond replied. "But since the Dynast brought some interesting friends to the meeting, we may now have *friends* with a way."

The Pol traced his finger across a display.

"How solid is our com link with the Dancers in Darkness?" he asked the Croni.

"It's not fast; we're relaying through a couple of places on the planet and then a couple more in space," the younger rebel replied. "Maybe twenty minutes to get them a message?"

"Those com drones are an hour out and carrying codes that suggest they won't do long-range transmission," the Kond observed. "Let's see if the Dancers are feeling up to a covert pickup."

Those big square teeth flashed in the cave's minimal lighting.

"There's a dozen of them. No one is going to miss just *one*...not least because they are known to spontaneously fail."

"It's a risk," Amelie pointed out, but she was nodding as she said it. "But I think it's a good risk."

"I'll have a message for you in a moment, Kixix," the Kond told the winged alien at the console. "Start setting up the transmission relay."

———

THE REBELS DIDN'T HAVE live sensor data *anywhere*, let alone in the deep space between the star-lane and Aris. They didn't even know if the Dancers in Darkness—apparently a group of smugglers known to occasionally engage in piracy and revolution—had received the message until they got the response.

"They got it," the young com tech reported. "They couldn't decrypt the data, though. They sent us the whole data dump."

"Fallen soil," the Kond cursed. "*We* can't decrypt it, either."

"Silleck should be able to," Amelie told him. "Or at least have contacts who can."

Which was true, though she hadn't yet told the Kond that one of Silleck's contacts was the Keeper of the Citadel.

"If we keep hitting our com channels, that's going to draw attention," the Pol leader warned her.

"And if this is what we both think it is? We need to know."

"True." The Kond leaned past Kixix and plugged a code in on the console. "There, data packet sent. Now we wait—"

The console chimed.

"That was fast," the Kond said slowly.

"It appears the Dancers sent Silleck the data package as well," Kixix reported. "It's a report from Commandant-Key of War Dest, the senior officer in charge at the Sonbar System."

"And?" Amelie asked. She still couldn't read Sivar, after all. No one on this planet could fix the broken scanner on her tablet.

"Multiple alien ships, but he identifies two of them as equivalent to *Watchtower*," the Kond read off the screen. "Potentially more. Twenty-eight hours ago, Dest was maneuvering to intercept them with his force. Three battleships, plus escorts."

"Isaac brought five battlecruisers and would have met up with *Watchtower*," Amelie pointed out. "Dest didn't win that battle, not with *three battleships*."

"We need to wait for the final word," the Kond told her. "We have everything ready to make sure the news leaks, to publicly undermine the Intendant's authority...but they have to actually *lose* first."

"Twenty-eight hours ago, they were maneuvering to engage," she replied. "So, they met and fought a full day ago at least. The battle is already over."

"And the news of that won't arrive for at least six hours," he said. "If they don't manage to get a message out, we might not even know for certain for *days*."

"Isaac is playing to intimidate the Intendant to keep me safe," Amelie explained. "He doesn't know I was broken out. We have no way of telling him...but he'll still make sure the news that Sonbar has fallen gets back to here.

"How long until that hits everywhere with your leaks?"

"News that big? If we get the news in six, it'll be everywhere in twelve."

"And how fast can we get the entire attack moving?" Amelie demanded.

Kond snapped his teeth.

"Eight hours. Might take ten."

"So, we need to start the wheels rolling *now*," she told him.

"If you're wrong," he said slowly, "that call could get a lot of people killed."

"Even if I'm right, we could be about to get a lot of people killed," Amelie admitted. Her own failed revolution had only ended without mass bloodshed because Adrienne Gallant hadn't been willing to execute her own son. The purge had been no less complete for its lack of mass executions.

"Are you certain, Amelie Lestroud?" the Kond asked.

"We all committed to this when we put everyone in one damn room on a planet with a bloodthirsty secret service," she said flatly. "From the moment we were in that room, every single one of us has a countdown until the Eyes of Sivar take us...and it's running down fast.

"If we don't take down the Intendant, we're all dead."

From the way Kixix stared at her, the Croni hadn't put together the *trap* part of Amelie's plan. The Kond clearly had, as he just bared his teeth at her again.

"But your mate can take their fleet?" he asked.

"My *mate* has the resources to level the entire Governance," she snapped. "And while he's a damn professional, believe me, I *know* he's tempted."

The Kond snorted.

"So am I," he admitted. "I'll put out the call, Amelie Lestroud. You know your people may not be safe once this starts?"

"I know. That's why I'm going with you," she replied. "You can go for the Intendant. *I* am going for my friends."

The Kond sighed.

"I presumed," he admitted. "I have arranged for a small team to accompany you on that part of the mission. I cannot do more. We have too much going on."

"And we're out of time," Amelie agreed softly.

———

THE TUNNELS GOT MUCH BUSIER over the following hours. The number of species represented more than doubled. In what was almost certainly a first, several Sivar from the Broken Chain set up in a tunnel off from the main communications room. Using a communications setup that had clearly been *acquired* from the Knives of the Keys of War, they were linked in to their own bunker and several other sites.

"Our source reports another wave of drones," one of those Sivar announced, stepping into the larger room and speaking clearly. "Over thirty of them this time." The armor-headed alien gestured expansively with her hands.

"They would only send that many in case of a defeat, but the Dancers are already moving to intercept one," she continued. "We'll know in a few minutes if the Republic has delivered the promised defeat."

"Are we ready to move?" Amelie asked, looking to Kixix. The Kond had left to organize from his office in the City.

"We're still gathering and preparing," the Croni com tech replied. "But the channels to leak it to the news networks and the bribes to make sure it *stays* leaked have already been arranged."

Seconds turned to minutes, time moving with a treacly slowness as Amelie waited for the final news.

"We got it," the Sivar officer reported. "Three battleships and eight cruisers destroyed without a scratch on their enemies. The Prince-Key is ranting about another eight cruisers surrendering after that but concedes that he has no choice but to do the same.

"The Sonbar System has been liberated!"

Amelie wasn't certain if the Sivar rebel was as enthused about that idea as anyone else in the room was going to be, but they *sounded* honest enough.

Or maybe they'd just known that proclamation would get the loud cheering in a dozen languages that it got.

She waited for it to die down before leveling a smile on Kixix. "And those leaks?"

"Already sent while everyone was cheering," the Croni replied. "In half an hour, everyone awake on the planet will know. An hour after that…"

"Your people's fate gets decided," Amelie concluded. "I hope it all goes according to plan."

"Me too," the Croni said softly. "I'd very much like to see the world my egg came from, but Aris is my home." The butterfly-like wings fluttered. "I want to live here but as a citizen. Not a slave."

"We'll make it happen," she promised, a sudden weight in her chest.

She'd intentionally set up a situation where the rebels had to act once they'd committed to her. She'd done everything she could so that this would work…but that honestly wasn't that much. And the last time she'd done this, the people who'd followed her had been flung to the other side of the galaxy.

The Intendant had neither that technology nor that mercy.

She *needed* to not fail.

"The Kond said there was a team ready to go in with me?" she asked Kixix instead of facing that more closely. "Where are they?"

"Just arriving now," the Croni said. "If you go up top, Dos will show you where to go."

60

THE SURFACE of the farm had undergone a vast transformation in the last few hours since Amelie had last been up. Massive swathes of fabric had been hung up in the air, covering most of the site from aerial and orbital surveillance.

Fabric chunks that large would be sure to garner attention quickly enough, but they'd do so much less quickly than boxes of weapons being opened, vehicles being rapidly converted to armed technicals, and the farm grounds generally being used as a mustering site.

"Minister." Dos's voice was entirely-computer generated. The two-and-a-half-meter-tall treelike Toorg didn't produce anything that most Governance species could hear. Their species had produced quite capable computers by the time the Sivar showed up, however, so translations had been easy enough.

The tributes from their homeworld had implanted voice boxes with neural interfaces. Amelie couldn't imagine that was *pleasant*…but she also didn't expect that the Sivar had given them a choice in the matter.

"Dos," she greeted the tree. "Kixix said there was a team I'd be joining to go after my people?"

"Yes. Follow me."

As she followed Dos, she realized that they were already armed—

and heavily so. Sivar energy weapons were heat-spewing energy hogs requiring massive structures. They were squad-support weapons or vehicle systems, not personal arms.

Dos was twice the height of any Siva and had a retrofitted Sivar blaster cannon hung over their back. It was a squad-support weapon that achieved much the same effect as a standard EMC pulse rifle in a package four times the size.

The treelike alien and their compatriots were probably the only people on the planet capable of using blaster cannons as regular arms. Everyone else Amelie passed was loading up with the Sivar's standard magnetic firearms, high-efficiency coilguns firing steel penetrators.

They were what her people had called mag-kinetics. Effective for what they were—the EMC used a slightly more efficient version of the same weapon as their standard personal weapon—but no match for even a man-portable pulse rifle.

"Here," Dos concluded, gesturing at a collection of Sonba. "I am with you as well. Some of my fellows will join."

The broccoli-headed aliens were speaking among themselves; a mix of head-frond gestures and a liquid burbling Amelie's translator couldn't pick up. The device could roughly manage the main Pol and Croni languages now, but without a spaceship's computers backing her tablet up, well… It could only do so much.

"Minister Lestroud," one of the Sonba greeted her. She was *reasonably* sure the pattern in their florets matched the Sonba who'd told her they'd fight with her if Sonbar was freed.

"We have seen the news," they continued. "You have kept your word, so we keep ours. We fight for *you*, Minister."

"I fight for everyone here," she replied. "So, if you fight for me, you're fighting for everyone. Not just Sonbar. Not just the Sonba. Everyone."

She suspected these were the Green Stalks of Light that Silleck had passingly labeled as mass murderers. If they were going to fight alongside *her*, that needed to be avoided.

"We owe you debts for the freedom of a billion groves," the Sonba told her. "I am Bush-Waving. I and my warriors are yours. Through life, death and the cycle of rebirth. For our world, our lives."

The Sonba couldn't physically kneel, but from what she could read of their body language, they all would have been if they could.

"I don't need your lives," she told them. "I need you to fight with me today. I have friends inside the Citadel, prisoners of the Intendant. I doubt I'm the only one, but we're the people headed straight for the prisons.

"We're not the first wave," she continued. "We're going in *ahead* of the first wave. The Broken Chain and the Kond's people have a plan for getting us almost the entire way to the prison before the fighting really starts.

"If you can keep your heads down until I tell you, shoot what I tell you and protect what you aren't supposed to shoot, we'll do fine."

"For our world, our lives," Bush-Waving repeated, the rest of the Sonba echoing the statement. "Yours to command."

That was going to take some getting used to. She looked over at her original escort.

"Dos, is everything ready to go?"

"Should be," they affirmed. "If all are ready?"

"Bush-Waving?" Amelie asked.

Tentacle-like arms emerged from beneath the hair fronds, revealing one of the omnipresent Sivar mag-kinetic rifles.

"We are ready. Are you armed?"

Amelie smiled and drew the laser pistol for a moment.

"I am," she told him. "Let's get going. Dos, have them bring the big truck around."

———

COMPOST LEFT the First and Final Citadel in smallish open-backed trucks. Food supplies *entered* the Citadel on an entirely different scale, in twenty-meter land trains that would never have been allowed on any Confederacy or Republic road.

The farm the Kond ran was one of the closest of the agricultural facilities that supplied the Citadel. Amelie had no idea how a helot rebel had ended up controlling the Intendant's own food supply, but it was damn handy for them.

She suspected the Intendant's security had assumed that the precautions around the First and Final Citadel itself would suffice to prevent anyone infiltrating troops in the food supply and that security measures in the kitchens would prevent mass poisoning.

Today, though…

The land train holding six of Dos's people, twenty Sonba terrorists and Amelie was inspected, all right. An armored guard popped up the back of the train, jumped up and looked them over with a perfectly calm gaze.

"Everything's fine in here," he shouted back. "Got that extra box?"

A second security guard showed up, pulling a long trunk. The two guards lifted the trunk into the land train and popped it open to reveal additional belts of ammunition for the mag-kinetic rifles.

"You're cleared through security to level six," the first guard shouted to the driver—but his gaze was on Amelie. "Take the red gates only."

"Understood," she murmured.

The two guards jumped out of the land train and closed the gates at the back. The Sonba relaxed, and Bush-Waving dipped a tentacle into the ammunition box.

"Today, my Sonba friend, *we* own the security checkpoints," Amelie told them. "It won't last. As soon as the violence starts, these guards are with us. Until then, they're helping us infiltrate as deep as we can."

The rebel groups had linked with the tributes running the sewage and water systems, too. Those could be locked down from central command facilities in theory, but right now, the sensors were offline and squads of rebels were infiltrating through the utility tunnels.

And Amelie's truck was only the first.

From her discussions of the plan with the Kond and others, on any given morning, the First and Final Citadel saw as many as two hundred land trains enter through the security gates. They'd only compromised the gates in the outer perimeter and a handful of specific lines through the inner security checkpoints.

It would be enough to get over five thousand rebel soldiers into the Citadel before anyone knew there was a threat. Another several thousand were infiltrating through the tunnels—and the Citadel's entire first line of defense was compromised.

Amelie hadn't been briefed on everything, but her estimate was that over thirty thousand armed rebels of the various factions were moving across the City and the Citadel. It was a war the Intendant wasn't expecting and hopefully wasn't ready for.

They'd know soon enough.

61

Level six was the final level of security before they hit the prison. Each of the checkpoints before that had quietly been under the control of the Broken Chain, but now they were about to hit the last line.

"Wait, what was that?" Bush-Waving asked.

Amelie hadn't heard anything, but from the suddenly fluttering collection of head-fronds in the land train, she was the only one.

"Explosions. Gunfire," Dos noted. "Not close. Level two perimeter, maybe."

"Shooting wasn't supposed to start yet," Amelie noted. "We're out of time. Level six was always in question, so be ready to move."

She drew the laser pistol again, taking a deep breath as she checked its charge. The gun was fully charged and she had a second power cell inside her armor that she'd fired two shots from.

"Here." Dos handed her a weapon from the trunk the security guards had left. "Need to leave train behind. Extra gun. You should carry as well."

It was a light carbine designed for the smaller Sivar, so she could easily sling it out of the way. A belt of ammo magazines counterbalanced it, holding the carbine in place while she focused on the laser.

"Thanks." She hadn't planned to grab another gun, but since it was there, she'd take it. Thirty shots wasn't much to overthrow a government with.

The land train lurched to a stop. They were at the level six security checkpoint…and there was shouting outside.

Now she could hear the distant gunfire as well. Mag-kinetics were mostly silent until the round broke the sound barrier, but the sonic booms alone were enough to make mass weapons fire audible at a distance.

"They're telling the driver the gate is closed," Bush-Waving told her, the Sonba having realized that her hearing wasn't as good as theirs. "We're to pull into a holding zone and stand by for inspection.

"No further vehicles passing through until the security situation is…"

"Bush-Waving?" Amelie asked, but she'd heard why the conversation had stopped. The gunfire was *much* closer.

"Go," she barked.

The land train was set up with safety features so it could be opened from the inside. It took only a few seconds for Dos to sling the door open and charge out with their blaster cannon.

By then, the firefight was over. Half a dozen Sivar were dead on the ground—including their driver. Four of the bodies were even in light power armor, something the guards weren't supposed to be equipped with.

The ones that were still standing were clearly waiting for them, however, and pointed their weapons away.

"Broken Chain," one of them shouted. "These guys came down from higher up when the shooting started, and started giving commands."

Amelie stepped over to the nearest body and rolled it over. There was a new insignia blazoned on the chest of the power armor, directly beneath where the collarbone would be on a human: a single stylized Eye.

"Eyes of Sivar, I'm guessing?" she said aloud. The Broken Chain soldier walked over and looked.

"They didn't even ID themselves," he told her. "That's Eyes armor, though. If even four of them came down, they realized there's a problem. There'll be more. A lot more."

"How many checkpoints at level six?" Amelie asked.

"Four. This one covers a quarter of the mountain."

"They can also get out through the three others and through the mountain," she pointed out. "Get us through, then barricade the checkpoint and abandon it. You can't hold against what's going to roll down the mountain soon enough, and you can slow them down just as easily without dying for it."

Two of the Sivar were already clearing the way through for the land train.

"You're probably right," the Broken Chain soldier replied. "But I have remote explosives, and that seems like the best of both worlds to me."

Amelie snorted.

"I'm not going to tell you not to blow up the Eyes of Sivar," she said. "But there's a lot of people on this mountain you might regret killing."

"Maybe," he allowed. "But I made my peace with that before I came out for duty this morning. The Intendant must fall."

"Your world, soldier," Amelie replied. "We have our own mission."

The gate was now clear.

"And Fates willing, we'll all be here tomorrow," the soldier agreed. "Every checkpoint in from here already had Eyes of Sivar on station. This is far as we can get you, and the shooting may have drawn attention.

"You need to move."

Amelie threw him a salute—textbook-perfect, thanks to the military training she'd undergone for her movie roles long before, not that the Siva would know—and jumped into the passenger seat of the land train.

Dos was at the controls, already bringing the vehicle online.

"You can drive this?"

"Yes," the Toorg confirmed.

"Bush-Waving?"

"Everyone is back aboard," the Sonba confirmed. "We are ready to jump out on your command."

"We're past the last friendly faces, but please try not to shoot anyone who isn't armed," she told them.

"That has been reiterated before. We understand."

"All right." Amelie turned back to her tree companion. "Drive, Dos."

———

AMELIE HAD NEVER EXPECTED to get into the prison itself without a fight. Not only was it buried inside the mountain, but it had its own exterior access for vehicles and supplies—and those supplies weren't coming from the Kond's farm.

They'd considered trying to steal one of the right land trains, but in the end, they didn't have time. Amelie had also figured that was getting too clever.

Without their driver, there was no way they were pulling it off, anyway. She and Dos sat in the land train's front cabin as they headed toward the gateway into the mountain, and for a single moment of laughable "brilliance", she considered trying to ram the doors open with the land train.

Then she remembered the doors were designed to withstand nukes.

"Can you twist the train so we arrive container doors first?" she asked Dos.

The alien froze in contemplation for a moment.

"I believe so," they finally said. "Bush-Waving? Please have your people hold on to something."

The Sonba didn't even have time to ask what was going on before Dos's arms were in motion. Amelie wasn't familiar enough with the controls of a Sivar land train to know what Dos was doing, but the *results* were obvious.

The train jackknifed. For a moment they were skidding across the ground toward the gate and the suddenly horrified-looking guards in a V shape. Then Dos slammed the reversed engine cabin into forward for several seconds before flipping the vehicle into reverse.

If the land train had a warranty, they'd probably just voided it, and Dos was *still* driving the vehicle, watching through their rear-view cameras as they hurtled the entire twenty-meter long vehicle toward the door into the mountain.

"Bush-Waving?" Amelie said into their radio. *"Fire."*

The door to the back of the land train crashed open while the vehicle continued to hurtle toward the door, and the Sonba closest to the back of the land train followed her commands.

The Sivar guards never stood a chance. There might have been half a dozen shots from the defenders. There definitely wasn't a full dozen.

"Go! Go! Go!" Amelie chanted as the land train ground to a halt, kicking open her own side door and following the Sonba out. Every member of the team had at least *some* of the security override codes they'd been given, but only she had all of them. She had to be with the strike team to unlock doors.

Each code had a limited lifetime once it had been used. Cybersecurity specialists inside the Citadel would already be at work, killing codes as the rebels used them.

The sound of the fighting lower on the mountain was getting louder. The attack was now escalating to all-out war, and she was left hoping that Commandant Ackahl kept her word.

The Siva in the security office had been on the ball, she realized as Dos smashed the door open for her. They'd slammed in a security lock on the bunker door when Dos had jackknifed the land train.

Unfortunately for the Citadel's guardians, her override codes worked—this time. The bunker doors slowly ground open.

"Move!" she barked. "Tunnel is eighty meters long and designed to be a defensive chokepoint. We need to get to the other side *before* anyone gets in place to hold it."

Bush-Waving was already moving. Someone *was* in the chokepoint, Amelie realized as gunfire echoed into the enclosed space.

One of Dos's fellows was close to the entrance and had their blaster cannon ready. Bullets were replied to with balls of plasma, and the shooting was over by the time Amelie reached the door.

The Sonba had been listening. There was a team already halfway down the tunnel, past most of the twists and retractable barricades. As she ran after them, she had a moment of wishing they'd kept the truck.

Fortunately, she was a lot faster than the Sonba and reached the end of the tunnel right behind the lead team. There was an underground parking pool there, currently containing neatly parked vehicles and a pair of land trains.

"Everything's empty, no life signs. Prison access is over here," Bush-Waving told her. "Stand back. Our lives for yours!"

An explosive charge blew the door open, and four Sonba led the way. They were *expecting* to run into fire…but nothing answered them except a calm voice.

"I would really rather not be shot today, if you'd be so kind," the Siva said loudly. "Is Lestroud there?"

62

SHONIN, First Voice of the Knives of the Keys of War, looked utterly unbothered by the fact that ban stood amidst several dead compatriots. Two other Sivar in all-encompassing black power armor stood by the door, holding heavy mag-kinetic rifles that made the cause of the deaths obvious.

"I apologize for the mess, Minister Lestroud," ban greeted Amelie as the Sonba escorted her in. "The Eyes of Sivar run this particular facility, and their soldiers are surprisingly difficult to bribe."

"Who is in control here?" Amelie asked.

"Unfortunately, still them," Shonin admitted. "I now control the overall security systems and have locked out the usual command center, but there's still several dozen of the Eyes' troops patrolling the cells.

"I can tell you where to find your people, but honestly? Most of the people in these cells are on your side," ban continued. "They're mostly Sivar, but there are some key helot figures down here as well. A lot of them are supposed to be dead. It's been an educational few minutes."

"I'm here for my people," Amelie replied. "The Sonba are here for everyone else. Nobody stays in the Citadel's prisons today."

"I thought so," Shonin said with a smile. "Kronk? Can you show the Sonba to the truck we brought with us?"

One of the black-armored Knives removed themselves from the wall and stepped out into the garage.

"What's in the truck?" Amelie asked carefully.

"There are still a dozen of your Marines in these cells," Shonin told her. "It seemed to me that providing them with the weapons they are accustomed to might be useful."

Ban continued to type as ban spoke.

"Your people are all in block K," ban noted. "That's the far end of the prison. Not quite as secure as the Intendant's personal cells where he kept you, but other than that…probably the most secure cells on the planet.

"Until today."

"Give us directions and we'll go get them."

Shonin laughed and picked up a carbine similar to the one Amelie had slung.

"Minister Lestroud, I did not come this far to just send you on your way," ban replied. "Most of your people didn't make it into their power armor when the Knives of the Eyes stormed your embassy.

"I managed to secure twelve suits. None of my people can use them, but I believe they are fully charged and I believe we have secured the correct weapons. I *need* your Marines, Minister Lestroud. Their armor is better than anything else on the planet—I don't think any other force on this planet can make it into the Intendant's throne room.

"So, either I find a way to blow off the top of a mountain that is both the religious and governmental center of my people, or I use your people as the tip of the spear."

Ban held out a hand to Amelie. Ban had clearly researched the gesture somewhere. Ban didn't *quite* have it right, but it was clear what ban intended.

"They'll do it if you tell them to," ban noted. "I'll be right behind them, but I need your Marines and I need your power armor to end this."

"What, is everyone going to lay down their arms once he's dead?" Amelie asked, ignoring the hand for a moment.

"Enough will," ban agreed. "Enough more will hesitate that we can remove the Eyes and their Knives. The City is already mostly in rebel hands, a cold standoff between helots and soldiers that don't understand why they were ordered to hold their positions and not fight back.

"Right now, they're listening to their Commandants. Before the wax melts, the Eyes are going to break into the military network and the Intendant is going to order them into battle. He needs to be dead before he can give that order."

"And you need my Marines."

"I'll take the rest of your people and your friends here, too," Shonin said with a clacking laugh. "But I have a Knives special assault team ready to go the moment I give the order. Right now, though, they'd charge into the best troops and security the Eyes have and both sides will have our power armor. It will be a massacre."

"And you think my Marines can get through that?" Amelie asked.

"Their armor can. For long enough. Are you with me?"

Amelie took ban's hand and shook firmly.

"My Marines would be furious if I turned you down. Show us the way."

———

BY THIS POINT, the defenders had clearly realized there was something *very* wrong with their communications. Broken Chain operatives had inserted multiple different attack viruses into the systems in the Citadel, and several of the land trains that had been infiltrated were filled with jamming equipment to boot.

The rebel attack wasn't organized enough for losing communications to matter that much, but the defenders were. And without proper coms, large chunks of the First and Final Citadel's defenders didn't even know they were under attack yet.

The prison security clearly did and were pulling back to guard block K.

There was no standardized report when her lead Sonba troopers ran into the security troops. The sharp sonic booms of mag-kinetics firing were the only sign that the battle was joined, but it was enough.

"Move up, move up," Bush-Waving ordered, sending more of his people into the fray.

It was probably stupid, but Amelie went with them. She was so very sick of standing aside while people died.

She ducked around a corner and several bullets hammered into the wall above her head as she took in the situation. A dozen armored Sivar, their gear inferior to the EMC's but better than her rebels had, were half-hidden behind a set of premade barricades they'd dragged out.

As she was trying to assess the situation, a blaster cannon went off next to her as Dos and another of his people waded into the fight. The barricades could hold against mag-kinetic rounds, but plasma bolts were something else. One blasted to pieces and several Sivar went down behind it.

Amelie hit the dial on her laser and cranked it up to maximum. Dos's friend went down as she took cover next to the Sonba firing at the enemy.

"Stay down," Bush-Waving hissed. "You shouldn't be here!"

"Neither should you," she pointed out calmly. Then she rose and fired.

She'd only fired the weapon at its lowest power setting before. That had taken two shots to get through a security lock, mostly because she hadn't realized the first beam had fired.

The *beam* was no more visible at maximum power than it was at minimum, but the *effect* was much more obvious. The barricade she'd targeted exploded backward, chunks of it hammering Sivar troopers to the ground.

Her pistol was a different weapon than the blasters, but it was apparently *just* as effective.

She took a second shot at another barricade, then dropped behind cover again.

The Sonba took advantage of her fire to charge forward. Mag-kinetics boomed in the confined space—ear covers had been a mandatory piece of equipment for this operation—and the plantlike aliens swarmed over the shattered barricades.

It took a second for the echoes of the gunfire to fade enough for it to be clear the immediate fighting was over.

"That should be all of them," Shonin told her, the Siva appearing out of nowhere. There were clear marks on ban's armor where the Knife had been shot, but ban seemed uninjured. "We've swept another dozen throughout the prison."

Ban pointed.

"Your people are through there." Shonin turned to the Sonba. "I won't give you orders, Bush-Waving," ban told the leader. "But take this."

Shonin passed Bush-Waving a bracelet-esque piece of electronics.

"It's loaded with the individual lock codes for every door in here," Shonin continued. "I *suggest* you start unlocking doors." Ban turned back to Amelie. "You and I need to go talk to your people."

Amelie inhaled sharply and nodded.

"That door, huh?" she asked.

———

THE SECURITY DOOR readily yielded to the overrides Amelie had been given, opening into a two-story row of cells that was presumably cell block K. The cells all looked similar to the one she'd been put in, though lacking the doubled security door and with the fronts open to the central space.

"Minister? Amelie? Is that you?" Roger Faulkner shouted from the far cell. "I heard gunfire. What the *hell* is going on?"

"I'd say it's a prison break, Roger, but truthfully, I'm hoping it's a revolution," Amelie replied as a massive grin broke free. She started unlocking cells on one side—Shonin started on the other side of the cell block without her even asking.

"Major Köhl, it's damn good to see you, too," she told the Marine when she reached the officer. Then she winced as Köhl struggled slowly to her feet, leaning on a crutch that had only been barely adjusted to mostly work for her.

"What happened?"

"I got shot," the Marine replied bluntly. "We're not good at standing down, boss. We're Marines."

"Can you walk?" Amelie asked.

"Slowly, with assistance. It sucks," Köhl answered. She raised herself to as close to attention as she could manage. "Including myself, thirteen Marines remain ready for duty, Minister. I'd say we're prepared to extract you, but it seems to be going the other way around."

"We apparently have twelve suits of power armor waiting for you if you can get to the prison vehicle pool," Amelie told her subordinate. "Plus the pulse rifles for those suits. If we get you to them, can your people fight?"

"Get *me* to a suit of power armor and I will *kiss* you," Köhl replied with a laugh. "And then I'll fight whoever you point me at. The armor would make a much better mobility aid than this stick."

"Shonin, brief her," Amelie told the Sivar Knife. "I'm going to keep unlocking people."

Sergeant Choi wasn't among the prisoners and neither was Sergeant Ryu. There'd been three Sergeants in the ground detachment, and none of them had lived. All of her staff was there, if a little the worse for wear.

"Roger, I'm going to need you to keep everyone here and safe," she told her aide. "I'm going with Köhl and Shonin over there to deal with this damn problem."

"Not a chance," her battered old aide told her, his cybernetic eye glowing in the dark in a way she'd never seen before. "My eye has combat software. If *you* are going back into the fight, I'm going with you. I'll need a gun."

"We have lots. But I need someone to keep these people safe. Isaac is coming, but he's at least ten days away. We have allies storming the First and Final Citadel as we speak, but I don't know how well that's going."

"Better than I was afraid of," Shonin injected. "I'll admit, even *I* didn't realize you'd compromised the entire outer defense network, and that was my *job*." The Siva clicked armor plating together grouchily.

"I'm impressed with the resources and the Broken Chain's penetration," she continued. "The first three defense lines have fallen, and there are critical breaches in line four. Five and six appear to be compromised in multiple places, and there are pockets holding out above level six where the tributes have been armed by Sivar agents."

"The Kond and the Dynast found a lot of friends," Amelie replied.

"Agreed. But the Intendant still has enough loyal troops under the Eyes that he might be able to push back if we don't take him out. Which is why we brought the armor for your Marines, Major Köhl."

"Your power armor is much more effective than ours. From the testing we did, I don't think even the Intendant's personal guard have weapons that can penetrate it."

"You want us to punch in and take him out?" Köhl asked.

"We won't be alone, but yes," Amelie confirmed.

"EMC leads the way," Köhl replied. "Let's get to that armor, Minister Lestroud."

"All right. Leave the Marine you don't have armor for to watch the civilians," Amelie ordered. "I'm going to be enough of a problem on this assault."

"You don't need to come with us, sir," the Marine said. "I have the same translator you do and it will work with the armor."

"Humor me, Major. I need to see this end."

63

———————

Amelie could *see* the relief in her Marines' eyes when they saw their armor. Even she could tell that the Knives hadn't taken perfect care of any of the gear, but they'd at least got it all in one place and charged the armor.

Personal codes opened the armor, allowing the Marines to step into the two-meter-tall suits and seal themselves inside multiple centimeters of steel and ceramics. Not all of the Marines had *their* suit, but the armor could adjust for that. It wasn't perfect, but it would still leave the EMC the deadliest twelve-being force on the planet.

Even so, Amelie had to help Köhl into her armor, and the Major wasn't the only Marine needing that help. Once the suit closed and the servos whirred up, however, it was clear that Köhl and the other injured Marines needed no more help.

"System is detecting and auto-adjusting for the injury," Köhl's voice emerged from the suit's speakers.

"All right, people!" she continued loudly. "Set your systems carefully. We don't need speed or fancy stealth today. We need *battery life.*"

"We tried to charge them, but we had to rig up an adaptor without asking too many questions," Shonin told the Marines. "How long do you have?"

"You did good," Köhl replied. "We're at a hundred percent charge, but without backup cells or a shuttle's fast-charge unit, that's *all* we have.

"And if we bring up all of the active systems, we can drain the batteries in an hour of heavy fighting. If we don't go invisible or leap tall buildings, we've got most of a day."

Amelie was getting good enough at Sivar body language to realize that Shonin was not at all certain whether Köhl was joking about the suit's ability to turn invisible or jump tall buildings.

Both of those *were* exaggerations…but probably not by as much as the Sivar spy was hoping.

Heavy pulse guns were picked up from the pile, with power systems hooked into the suits and additional power cells stocked into the designed compartments. Köhl's dozen Marines now *looked* the part as they gathered around Amelie.

"Who's ready for war?" Köhl demanded from her people. Whatever response she got wasn't acceptable.

"I said, *who's ready for war?!*"

"E! M! C!" the Marines chanted back this time.

"Hell, yes," the Major concluded. The faceless suit of armor turned to Shonin. "You said we had a rogue dictator and some guards to dig out of a hole in the ground. You got coordinates and a path?"

"System translations are a problem," ban noted. "It doesn't help that the entire Mountain is being jammed right now." Ban shook ban's head. "I'm surprised the Eyes of Sivar haven't done better at taking out the jamming systems."

"How did you know so much about the status of the assault if everything's jammed?" Köhl asked.

"There's a secondary com network that the Eyes don't know about inside the First and Final Citadel," Shonin replied. "It's a secret that… certain people put together when the Intendant's predecessor went almost this mad."

"The Keeper of the Citadel?" Amelie asked. "We're well past the time for games, Voice Shonin."

"Yes," ban admitted. "I have copies of her personal access codes. So far, I haven't needed them, but for what we're about to do, we need them."

Ban lifted a tablet and hit a command.

"You should have got a map and directions," ban noted. "I have an assault team of my finest standing by at the level seven security checkpoint. If we make an appropriate noise when we approach and distract them, we'll be through that layer faster than anyone is expecting."

"The Intendant is behind level, what, nine?" Amelie asked.

"Yes. And I have another trick for level eight," Shonin told them. "But I'm out of games once we hit nine. I can use Keeper Rode's codes to come at them from an angle they're not expecting, but level nine isn't really a *level* the way the rest of the mountain is.

"It's more of a sealed-off section. There's a level ten and a level eleven that are similar. Nine, though, is near the top of the mountain and inaccessible from the exterior in a way nothing else here is.

"Two official ways in that have heavy automated defenses as well as heavy guards. One secret way in that will give us a chance but might just doom Keeper Rode."

"You all have Rode's image," Amelie told her Marines. "Don't shoot her by accident. We need her."

"My people know what she looks like as well," Bush-Waving added, the Sonba jumping into the land train the armor had been stored in in a weird, flexing-stalk motion. "We'll make the same effort."

"Bush-Waving…"

"We all need to be at the end," the Sonba told her. "Half my people will remain here to help protect your civilians, but the other half and the Toorgs are coming with you."

Amelie looked over at Köhl for support, but the Marine remained facelessly impassive in her armor.

"All right," she conceded. "But you follow the Major's orders now, clear?"

Bush-Waving's head-fronds shivered dramatically as he looked up at the armored Marine.

"Of course, of course!"

They were *probably* overacting. It was hard to be sure.

———

EVEN DEEP INSIDE THE MOUNTAIN, the level seven checkpoint was clearly on maximum alert. They were on one of the few routes large enough for the land trains to travel this deep, after all.

Amelie's leading scouts—all Sonba, since Köhl and Shonin wanted to keep the Marines a secret a while longer—ran into Sivar performing the same role for the defenders.

The firefight between those groups appeared to achieve what Shonin had been hoping for. Multiple new defensive measures activated as they closed with the checkpoint, with corridors closing off to funnel them into a killing zone.

"Hold here," Shonin finally ordered as they reached a corner that didn't look any different. The land train rumbled to a halt just short of the wall as Amelie and Köhl followed ban out of the vehicle.

"The next corridor is one of the internal vehicle tunnels the checkpoint controls," Shonin told the humans. "They'll have a clear field of fire to make sure no one can get to them."

"And you had a plan? We've already made noise," Amelie pointed out.

"Yes. And we'll make just a *little* bit more."

Shonin removed a small black device from inside ban's armor, twisted an arming switch, and then threw the grenade around the corner.

It exploded. Then it exploded *again*.

"Micro cluster bomb," Köhl said approvingly. "Definitely gets attention."

There was a *lot* of gunfire being directed at the corner the grenade had been thrown around, with chips being dug out of cement as the supersonic rounds hit.

"And makes for a decent signal flare," Shonin replied as an even more distant round of sonic booms tore down the corridor.

The gunfire continued for about thirty seconds, and no one was aiming at the entrance into the tunnel anymore. After silence finally fell, Shonin stepped up to the shot-up corner and shouted into the hallway in a language Amelie's translator didn't recognize.

Someone else shouted back in what was probably the same language.

"Checkpoint is secure," Shonin told them. "There are a few more vehicles waiting for us. We're running out of time."

An explosion sent new tremors through the mountain after ban spoke and the Siva winced.

"More so than I thought," ban admitted. "The explosion I was expecting of that size was the communications center. If my people destroyed it, then the Eyes had retaken enough control of internal communications to try for a message out."

"How bad is a message out for us?" Amelie asked.

"*If* we take the Intendant out within a few minutes of it, not so much," Shonin told them as they and their land train approached a pair of other trains that the Sivar were already loading themselves into.

"If he declares the Commandants anathema and orders them executed and we can't get someone in place to counter that order with proof of his death before the Commandants are dead…"

Shonin trailed off.

"Your battleships carry ground bombardment weapons, don't they?" Köhl asked.

"Most officers would hesitate to use them on Aris and the City," Shonin replied. "But if the Intendant declares every Commandant in the system anathema and promotes whoever *will* obey him, someone will push the button."

"Right. Let's get moving."

64

SHONIN'S PLAN for the level eight security checkpoint turned out to be as simple as it was terrifying. The barriers available to the interior checkpoints were significantly less substantial than the exterior bunker doors.

One of the land trains was stuffed full of explosives and incendiaries and sent on ahead on remote control. The explosion rippled down the corridor, shaking the land trains they were riding in as the vehicles plunged deeper into the mountain.

Sitting in the front of the third train, Amelie winced as the lead vehicle smashed into the flaming debris of what had been an antivehicle barricade with at least a dozen Sivar behind it. The bomb had wiped out at least a platoon's worth of soldiers, and the entire checkpoint was still on fire as they pushed through.

"We're clear," Shonin announced, ban sounding quite pleased with banself. "And, conveniently, I know that the level nine security armories are lacking in anti-armor explosives and incendiaries."

"Wait, how do you know that?" Köhl asked, then swore as she caught up. "You stole the explosives from the Intendant's personal guards' armories?"

"I knew they wouldn't do more than visually inspect their explosives," the spy replied. "Why would they? They're bodyguards. Who comes at them in armor that requires heavy explosives?"

"EMC," the Marine replied in a chuckle. "How long?"

"Pulling over here," Shonin answered. "We're past the main entrance already. The hardest part is going to be how narrow this corridor is."

"Open it up, then stand aside," Amelie told her. "EMC can lead the way."

The land trains ground to a halt, disgorging Amelie's vastly expanded assault force.

"Marines first, Sonba last," Amelie ordered as her people started gathering around. "Everyone else here has better armor, Bush-Waving," she told the alien leader. "Let's not lose anyone we don't have to—and they're going to come at us from behind."

"They won't succeed," the shrub-like freedom fighter replied. "Go! We have the end."

There didn't appear to be any doors in the section of tunnel they'd stopped in, but Amelie doubted that Shonin was going to betray them now. The Siva walked up to a panel on the wall that looked the same as the rest of the concrete and metal panels that lined the tunnel.

A specific depression slid open at ban's touch, revealing what looked like a set of biometric scanners. Instead of activating the scanner, Shonin dropped a strip of metal over the top of the scanner suite. A moment later, the whole screen flashed—and the concrete panel slid aside.

"You were right about the size of the passage," Amelie said, studying it. It might be big enough for two Sivar abreast, but an armored Marine was going to be hitting their head as they went up steps and wouldn't leave enough room for anyone to fit in around them.

"EMC leads the way," Köhl barked. "Nalani, you have point!"

One of the armored Marines ducked into the hallway, pulse rifle poking forward.

"Ignore all of the side branches and keep following the main path," Shonin told them all. "There are a lot of places this tunnel goes, but the main path will bring you out right outside the throne room."

Ban paused.

"There *will* be guards there."

"We'll deal with them then," Köhl replied. "And they'll never know what hit them. EMC! Move out!"

————

Amelie was halfway down the order of movement, which meant she was a long way from the fight when the shooting started. Pulse rifles sounded *very* different from mag-kinetics—but they did sound quite similar to Sivar blaster cannon.

And there were definitely some of the latter in play before the Toorgs made it to the front.

Everyone started accelerating at the sound of fighting, but the passageway only allowed so much space for everyone to move. By the time Amelie finally left the passage into a large space that she recognized from her meetings with the Intendant, the immediate fighting was over.

At least two dozen armored Sivar lay strewn about the place. One of the Marines was having her armor patched by another. The combat repair wouldn't make up for the hole burnt into the suit, but it would at least *help*.

"No major injuries," Köhl reported. "We've got multiple points of contact toward where the hostiles were expected to be holding security. I've got six people holding that line, but I'll need to reinforce them quickly. And, well."

She gestured at a massive bunker wall where Amelie remembered the door to the audience chamber being.

"We have no way through this," the Marine reported. "We might be able to burn through the rock around it, but not while we're under fire!"

More gunfire echoed, and Köhl made a jerking motion to the Marines not either damaged or patching friends up.

"Move it, Marines," she snapped. "We hold the line."

"Shonin, you got a way through this?" Amelie asked.

"I didn't know this existed," the First Voice of the Knives admitted.

"Only the Eyes of Sivar would have. I've…never been this deep in the mountain."

"Can he send a transmission from there?" the human demanded.

"I don't think so," Shonin replied. "We have him trapped, but we need him *dead*."

"There's no way in *hell* an asshole like that sealed himself in a space with no way out," Köhl pointed out. "It just isn't on your maps."

Amelie ducked as several blaster cannon fired simultaneously.

"We're pinned against this security barrier ourselves," she noted. "We need to do *something*."

A thought struck her.

"Where are the Keepers, Shonin? Any of them?"

The Siva pointed at the barrier. "Unless he's executed them already, they're in there with him."

"Can you reach Rode?" Amelie asked. "I understand that she can't do much without getting herself killed, but we're *right here*. If she can get that door open…"

"I *think* I can ping her with a text message," Shonin replied. "This may not work—and even if it does, she'll need time."

"Köhl, there's still a dozen guards in that room," Amelie noted. "Can the nine you sent hold?"

"If they can't, we can," Shonin's team commander interrupted, the black-armored assault trooper looking up at Köhl's armor respectfully. "Where do you need us?"

"Holding the line while we see if we can get this open," Köhl replied. "With the Intendant locked inside, the advantage is ours, but he has a *lot* of people in this mountain.

"Keep them busy."

The Sivar saluted, but it was Bush-Waving who answered for them.

"Our lives for our world," the broccoli-like Sonbar said quietly. "We will buy you your time."

The rebels streamed past Amelie and Shonin to join the fight, leaving them standing alone with three armored Marines and Roger Faulkner, the politician looking vaguely awkward with the Sivar carbine.

"Can we even tell if Rode got your message?" Amelie asked.

"She got it," Shonin said grimly. "I'm pretty sure she's even alive. Promise me something, Amelie Lestroud?"

"Within reason," Amelie said.

"Whatever happens, keep Rode alive," the spy said. "If she and the Dynast can work together, that might just save my people...but you need *someone* from the Intendancy."

"I'll do what I can," Amelie promised. She studied the five-meter-wide wall of metal that blocked their way. "But unless this can be controlled from the outside, it's all on her."

And at that moment, the bunker door started slowly rising.

65

AMELIE KNEW she shouldn't go first, but of the six of them still standing there, she was the closest person *not* in power armor. She hit the ground with a practiced roll, sliding under the lifting sheet of metal as chaotic shouting emerged from inside the room.

The tableau on the other side of the bunker door seemed to freeze as her mind locked it in place. The Intendant stood in full view in the center of the raised dais he'd spoken with her from. The table had been turned on its side at some point, but it had fallen off the dais in the process and wasn't providing anyone cover.

Istila was kneeling in front of the Intendant, the Keeper of the Keys of Peace begging in rapid-fire Sivar Amelie's translator couldn't quite follow.

Rode stood off to one side, out of the Intendant's line of sight. Two of the guards had leveled their weapons on her, and she was backing away from a tablet computer on the table.

Corstan was on the other side, his hands spread as more of the guards were turning weapons on him.

A gunshot *cracked* and Istila stopped talking as ban's skull armor-plating exploded, showering the room in gore.

Amelie returned fire, a laser beam taking one of the guards threatening Rode in the middle of torso…and realized it was the first time she'd fired at a living being with the weapon at full power, as the Siva *exploded*. Even their armor only added to the debris as the laser delivered the energy equivalent of a dozen kilos of explosives in a tenth of a second.

Return fire hammered into her before she could fire again or adjust the power setting on the laser. A round in her shoulder sent her spinning backward, the armor seeming to hold as she fired again.

She missed this time, the laser blasting a divot in the roof above the Intendant's head. Another flurry of bullets from the guards smashed into the ground around her as the Marines stormed the room behind her.

Pulse rifle fire devastated the guards, but as another hammerblow took Amelie's breath away, she realized they hadn't been fast enough. Sivar guns were calibrated to go through Sivar skulls. Her armor had stopped a lot of fire, but at least one bullet had made it through.

"Stop!" the Intendant bellowed. He'd moved back and now held a gun on Rode and an electronic device in his hand.

"Stop," he repeated, "or this traitor dies and I detonate the bombs under the City's helot townships. We might survive here, but the fools you have convinced to betray me will die on the slopes of the Citadel and the streets of the City."

Hundreds of thousands of his own people would go with those rebels, but the Intendant clearly didn't care. The guards in this room didn't seem bothered either, though both of the surviving Keepers seemed taken aback by the threat.

"Hold your fire," Amelie told the Marines. Everyone was in the room. Even Roger Faulkner was in the room—and his cybernetic eye might prove critical to what happened next.

"Fine," she told the Intendant. "But you know you've lost. I told you from the beginning that you had no idea who you were fucking with. For the lives of *your* people, I offer you this one chance: surrender and the Republic will guarantee your life."

"Your Republic is pathetic!" the Intendant told her. "Fools, who hesitate for nothing. The lives of nobodies are meaningless, the lives of these traitors worth even less!"

"You're an idiot," Rode told him. "Whatever divine sight you were given is wasted on you. Istila was the only one of your Keepers who *never* betrayed you, and you just shot ban down in cold blood."

"Ban is anathema now!" the Intendant bellowed, his weapon swinging back toward Rode. "And so are you," he whispered.

Amelie fired before he could…and she'd never managed to turn the power on the laser pistol down. There was no perceptible delay between her pressing the stud and the blast arriving, and the Intendant never managed to pull the trigger.

His upper torso exploded into pieces, gore spraying the back of the wall and Keeper Rode. The device he'd been holding in his left hand hit the floor, and Amelie prayed to whatever deity was listening that it didn't have an instantaneous deadman switch.

Rode was already moving. Even as the surviving guard holding a weapon on her fired, she was diving into the wreckage of the Intendant's body and scooping up the device. She looked at it for half a second before pressing and holding down a button.

The guard was down before Rode reached the device, but the Keeper was *not* looking good. The guard had hit her at least twice before they went down.

"Roger, help her," Amelie gasped. She was feeling weak, but she managed to prop herself to her feet.

"Help *her*?" her aide snapped. "You've been *shot*."

"And she's holding the switch keeping *millions* safe," she snapped. "I don't care what species she is," Amelie continued. "That blood stays on the *inside* should be enough for today!"

One of the Marines was already next to Amelie, an emergency medkit folding out of the armor. Another kit was tossed to Faulkner as he reached Rode and started to inspect her alien anatomy.

Shonin joined him a moment later, helping him find the right places for the bandages.

"Someone got video of that?" the Knife asked aloud as she checked Rode's pupils.

"My eye records," Faulkner replied instantly. "I can transmit if you get me a tablet, but I'm busy here."

"I've got her," Corstan interrupted, the Keeper of the Keys of War kneeling in his monarch's blood as he took Rode's weight. "Rode, I've got the detonator," he murmured. "I know how to disarm it. Give it to me?"

The device slipped over into his hands. He kept holding on to it with one hand as he applied pressure on the bandages.

"I've got the footage," Shonin announced a few moments later. "We need to clear the jamming so I can send it out. Is there a plan for that?"

"Flare," Amelie muttered, feeling very floaty and not very aware of the Marine poking at her injuries. "My bag. Three flares. Fire red and yellow into the sky at the same time, the jamming goes down."

She barely registered Shonin reaching her and poking at the pouches on her armor. She didn't register much of anything after that at all.

66

———

"The code is fundamentally flawed," Siril-ki told ki's gathered audience. Most of *Dauntless*'s senior officers were physically present in the briefing room as the centaur-like alien laid out the details of what they'd found aboard the House of Koth's spaceship. Many of the senior officers of the strike cruisers and freighters were present virtually.

The massive wallscreen behind her was currently focused on the image of the Assini colony ship. An occasional spark of light still marked the site, as teams went over the big starship for anything more of use.

"How flawed is 'flawed'?" Octavio asked. "They did manage to make themselves invisible to the Sentinels, after all."

"That code is less flawed," Siril-ki replied. "It's very similar to the code we used to allow our Matrix allies to engage the Escorts and Rogues. It applies a filter on top of their perceptions, mostly using the Matrices' systems as a shortcut into the autonomous systems we had such difficulty accessing directly.

"The code they believed would give them command of the Sentinels failed on several levels," ki continued. "It *does* contain the necessary keys to modify the central processes, but it would never have worked on the Sentinels.

"The AI programmers working on the system assumed that the Sentinel Matrices were simply Construction Matrices with different hulls attached. While the fundamental AI kernel is the same, the Sentinels underwent significant adjustments as they woke up.

"Their attack code targeted weak points that didn't exist. They may still have succeeded in writing in additional core protocols, but it's likely it wouldn't have mattered."

Ki gestured a long-fingered hand at the crashed guardian drones around *Koth-Shezar*.

"The attack carried out on this system already clearly demonstrated that the Matrices were far less bound by their core protocols than we thought. Modifying the core protocols would not have saved them."

Siril-ki shrugged.

"Lastly, as D and I have dug through the code, we have come to the conclusion that it was never going to work. Too much of it assumed that the core running process of a Matrix could be modified while it was running.

"I could see that assumption being made by someone who'd only worked with Shezarim's early models or only had access to research and development files while only rarely working with live Matrix AIs," ki stated. "These people had access to encryption keys and codes and knowledge that would have made *my* old job much easier but lacked critical pieces of the overall knowledge base that enabled my old job."

"Some of that had to be that the code to disable the Sentinels was built by a scratch team of whatever was left," Octavio suggested. "He said he left the code to disable Construction Matrices as well. We found that one, too. Is it…"

"Both more and less flawed in many ways," Siril-ki replied. "It's intended to be a reversal of an existing virus, after all. In theory, that should be easier."

"In practice, Commodore, examination of the code that we have retrieved from our own damaged Rogues and by the Sentinel Program suggests something quite different," D noted. "There is, for lack of a better term, *scarring* around the code sections they used Shezarim-ko's keys to access.

"I don't have that scarring, as the progenitor tree I was budded from was apparently never modified by the Koth. Some of the Rogues from our region of space have pure punch-induced degradation and also lack that scarring. The RCM Admiral Lestroud is currently at war with *is* from a Koth-modified progenitor tree and does have that scarring."

"Which means...what?" Octavio asked. "That code resists rewriting?"

"Exactly," Siril-ki confirmed. "It is entirely possible, from the data we have on the Koth's attempt to control the colonization program, that they *did* attempt to limit how many Matrices went homicidal.

"But without access to the broad array of samples and comparison points we now have; they would not have realized that scarring existed. Their code to render the Construction Matrices friendly would never have worked."

Octavio breathed out a long sigh, looking at the wrecked starship.

"They screwed up everything, didn't they?" he asked softly. "Is that code of any use to us at all, then?"

"It gives us Shezarim's security keys," Siril-ki replied. "It also tells us one way that doesn't work. I am...forced to the conclusion that any attempt to restore a Matrix would require something closer to a battle of wills with a direct connection. We would need a current live map of the code of the Matrix we were attempting to repair."

"And what would success even look like?" Octavio asked. "Would we be wiping them back to factory settings? That doesn't seem much better than killing them."

"If we managed to do it correctly, it is theoretically possible that we could restore their original core protocols while leaving their memories and personality intact," Siril-ki said quickly. "They would understand who they were and what they had done—but also what they had been *supposed* to be. If we do it right, the Matrix would end up with the same fundamental ethics as XR-13-9 and their progeny."

"Which would, in theory, create a new ally for us?" he asked. "That seems promising."

"It will not be a pleasant process for the Matrix and will likely be most easily done with prisoners," D noted. "No hostile Matrix will voluntarily give us the level of access needed for the kind of mapping we're asking for, and establishing it involuntarily might be impossible."

"We might be able to do an end run through the autonomous processes," Siril-ki suggested. "But that is a theory at most. The code as retrieved gives us some places to start, and *Koth-Shezar*'s historical files give us some answers we did not have.

"Unfortunately, I am not certain we have learned or will learn anything else of value here."

Octavio nodded slowly. If nothing else, they at least had worked out a way to break into the autonomous processes there.

"Four days," he finally said aloud. "We'll spend another four days here and see if we can pull anything out of the Koth facilities. Barring us finding any signs of anything else of value, we and the Sentinels will set our course back to Exilium.

"Further research can be done by Matrix units that don't take a year to get here. We've found something of potential value, but I think we need to consider getting all of us home."

There had been real value to bringing the Assini to their home system, both in terms of closure for the horse-like aliens and in terms of their insight as to what was going on, but he figured they'd reached the end of it.

It was time to go home.

"I don't see any reason to stay here," Siril-ki agreed. "With your permission, Commodore, I'd like to forward all of the code to XR-13-9. It is possible that a Construction Matrix may see aspects to this that the organics who designed them do not."

He could see why ki was asking. It was possible XR-13-9 could use that code to make all kinds of terrifying modifications to themselves. Somehow, he didn't see that happening.

So far as he knew, D was an *exact* copy of XR-13-9's personality, and the human-aligned Matrix seemed content with who they were.

"Do it," he ordered. "Make sure the Republic has it, too. If we come up with any answers along the way home, they may make all the difference when they bring the Rogue down."

Or the next Rogue. Or the one after that. If nothing else, the Assini's and Koth's mistakes left them *lots* of opportunity to learn the best way to take down Rogue Matrices.

67

VIGIL SCREAMED into the Sivar-Prime System like an avenging angel. Isaac was half-expecting to come into a full-fledged ongoing civil war, so his fleet came out of warped space at full battle stations and loaded for bear.

It was rather anticlimactic in the end. There were four more battle-ships than his last report, but all of them were clustered around the star-lanes. There were, in fact, *no* warships orbiting Aris.

"That doesn't look right at all," Connor noted. "I have multiple battleships at each of the star-lane fortification clusters, but not even a cruiser in orbit."

"Fortresses?" Isaac asked.

"Present but power signatures are very low. I suspect they may have been evacuated. This looks…nothing at all like I was expecting," the ops officer reported.

"All ships are to maintain combat formation and battle stations," Isaac ordered. "Watch for those battleships maneuvering. We can *take* nine of theirs, but I want to know what's going on before we start shooting."

"Our course, sir?" Connor asked.

"Aris," Isaac replied. "We're here to retrieve our people and potentially burn out a cancer. Both of those are on Aris."

"Sir!" Naveed Hashemi interrupted. "We're getting a tachyon-com update from General Zamarano. She's received multiple com drones from Aris in Sonbar while we've been in warp. The situation has dramatically changed."

"How dramatic is *dramatically*?" Isaac asked.

"The Intendant is dead. Minister Lestroud killed him," Hashemi said in a stunned voice.

"That's...dramatic," Isaac conceded, shaking his head. "How the hell did she manage that?"

"I don't know," his com officer admitted. "Zamarano reports that there appears to be an interim government in place under a 'Dynast Silleck', who is basically begging us to talk before we open fire."

Isaac snorted.

"The situation was weird enough that they were going to get that," he admitted. "Amelie made friends, did she?"

"It appears there may have been some kind of alliance between Sivar and non-Sivar rebel factions, as well as dissident elements in the Governance itself," Hashemi told him. She was clearly still going through the data from Sonbar as she was explaining things.

No one in Sivar had a tachyon com to update them yet. No one in Sivar even knew they were *here* yet.

"I'll forward you the reports, sir, but it looks like Amelie launched a revolt against the Intendant...and pulled it off."

That finally sank in, and Isaac had to just pause for a moment and take in just what Amelie Lestroud had accomplished.

"The last report I had was that she was in a prison cell," he noted softly. "From there, she managed to assemble an alliance of rebel factions from species that may well *hate* each other and overthrow a tyrant?"

There were days he suspected he was the junior partner of his marriage. The rest of the time, he *knew* that any legend of his was going to be forever following in the trail of Amelie Lestroud.

He'd definitely married up.

"Wait. Sir." Hashemi's vague awed tone collapsed into concern. "Minister Lestroud was shot!"

Isaac was suddenly laser-focused on the reports in front of him.

"How bad?" he asked flatly.

"Bad. She was alive at last report, but it was touch-and-go, and everything we're getting from Sonbar is days out of date."

"Understood." Isaac traded a look with Connor, then made up his mind. There were times the personal had to yield to the important, but this was *not* one of them.

"Fleet will advance for Aris orbit at maximum acceleration," he ordered calmly. "*Vigil* will push to full emergency power. The Sivar don't know human anatomy or have the right medical facilities aboard to treat severe injuries.

"*Vigil* does."

And after what she'd achieved on that planet, Amelie's husband had no intention of letting her die down there.

———

THERE WAS a storm over the Citadel as Isaac's shuttle plummeted downward. Wind, rain, thunder, if it could be imagined for weather, it seemed to be battering the EMC assault craft.

"We have a solid radio beacon from ground control," the pilot reported. "It's been a while since I have had groundside *quite* this cooperative."

"They might think we'll shoot them if they cause any trouble," Isaac replied. "They might not even be wrong."

The young woman snorted, but her attention was on bringing the spacecraft toward the hangar the locals had picked out. A dozen similar shuttles orbited above the storm, and *Vigil* had the First and Final Citadel's anti-air defenses locked in from orbit.

The Dynast was aware of all of that but had made no attempt to discourage their safety measures. The *storm* was the only thing trying to discourage anyone.

"Hang on," the pilot instructed. Isaac obeyed—and *still* nearly lost his stomach as the shuttle went almost on its side to dodge around a final brutal gust of wind and tuck neatly into the hangar.

"Okay." The young woman wiped sweat from her brow. "The plan is to get the Minister back up to *Vigil* ASAP, correct?"

"Yes," Isaac confirmed. "Should we wait for the storm to weaken?"

The pilot was almost as dark-skinned as he was, which made her blanch at the idea very visible.

"I'd prefer to, yes," she allowed levelly. "But if the President Emeritus needs an emergency evac, I'm pretty sure getting *out* of the storm will be easier than flying *into* it."

"Good soldier, Lieutenant," Isaac replied with a grin. "Hopefully, I won't have to hold you to that."

But he *would* if he needed to—and he knew she'd do it.

"Sort out fueling with the locals," he ordered. "I don't know how long I'll be."

———

MAJOR BAUMANN HADN'T EVEN *ASKED* Isaac if he was going to want an escort. The back half of the shuttle was full of EMC Marines in full power armor, and there was no way he was exiting the ship first.

By the time he left the shuttle, ten armored Marines had already preceded him. The main security meeting them was *also* EMC Marines, though. There were also a quartet of very large creatures that looked like walking trees—with even *bigger* guns—and a mixed group of Sivar and Sonba.

"Major Köhl, Mr. Faulkner," he greeted the two humans at the center of the group, one unarmed and one unhelmeted. "I'll admit I was expecting to meet with someone from the local authorities."

"The Dynast and the Keepers would beg a moment of your time before you return to orbit," Faulkner confirmed. "But they understood you'd want to see Amelie before anything else."

"She's as safe and stable as our doctors can make her," a black-uniformed Sivar standing a step behind the two humans told him. "But we simply don't know your physiology enough to want to risk surgery."

"And I have one medic who never trained as a surgeon," Köhl told him. "She'll be stable *enough* if we keep her down here, but she needs surgery to remove bullet fragments from her chest cavity."

Isaac winced.

"Why did she do that to herself?" he muttered aloud.

"Because someone had to stop the Intendant shooting his own government," the Sivar explained. "My name is Shonin," ban introduced banself when he looked at ban askance. "At the Dynast's *request*, I now run security for Aris for the caretaker government."

Caretaker government was a promising description, if people kept to that.

"It seems you owe my wife a great debt," Isaac told her. "I need to see her. Before I talk to anyone else or we even continue this conversation.

"I need to see Amelie."

SHE WAS ASLEEP. Isaac wasn't sure why he'd expected her to be awake; he knew that the best thing for her current state was rest.

But he wasn't used to seeing Amelie helpless. From the moment they'd made contact via dead drops and tentative connections behind masks and code names, she'd been moving. First a revolutionary, convincing the hesitant and combative to work together to fight the Confederacy.

Then a prisoner, then a head of state, then an ambassador.

And now, apparently a revolutionary again.

The chair next to the bed wasn't really sized for humans, but it worked for him to pull up next to her.

Without the energy that filled her when she moved and spoke, she lost some of the spark and beauty that kept her drawing eyes at past fifty. He didn't care, though. She was still gorgeous to him, even though the stillness ate at his heart.

He was holding her hand before he even consciously reached for her. She squeezed back and one eye delicately opened to look at him.

"Isaac," she murmured. "You here or is it the drugs?"

"I'm here," he told her. The Sivar could only get so close with medication for humans. Hallucinations were probably the least of the side effects.

"That's what the last two of you said," she pointed out sleepily. "In unison. It was weird."

"That doesn't sound like me at all," Isaac replied. "I don't do choruses and I don't have a twin."

"Okay, so that's probably you." She squeezed his hand. "Still hurts despite everything. Why didn't anyone tell me getting shot was this bad?"

"Because you were never supposed to *get* shot," he told her. "We're here. *Vigil*'s here, with her doctors. I've got a medical transfer team setting up in the next room. We'll move you up to orbit, get you fixed up.

"You're going to be fine, my love."

She coughed indelicately. There was blood on her chest cover, he realized. From the coughing.

"There's a fragmented bullet in my left lung, Isaac," she told him, her voice very quiet. "Hit the back of my armor and stayed inside. I'm breathing through a fucking *tube* that you can't see under the blankets."

"The transfer team is being briefed on all of that," he said, hoping he wasn't wrong. "We can handle that. We've done worse. The people on *Vigil* are the best human trauma doctors for at least a hundred light-years."

She smiled. It was a sad, wan thing, but it was there.

"That's a shit joke and you know it, Isaac," she told him. "Promise me…"

"Anything."

"Talk to Silleck," she demanded. "But then…can you be with me when they move me? I…I know I need to sleep for it, but I'll sleep better if I know you're there."

"I'll be there," he promised. "We should never have been apart. I'll be there."

"Silly man," she said. "Love you…but we both married duty as well as each other, didn't…"

Her eyes closed. She was asleep again.

Isaac squeezed her hand, gently laying it next to her side.

He'd go talk to the Dynast, but he'd be back. They weren't doing *anything* with Amelie without him there now.

68

WHEN SHONIN TOOK Isaac to meet the current leaders of the planet, he was expecting to find them in some kind of opulent throne room—possibly still covered in the blood of the predecessor they'd killed to take power.

Instead, he was escorted into a large but otherwise plain office with three Sivar in it—a male and two females—and a black-furred alien that looked like a distant cousin of the Assini but run through a "mole" filter instead of a "horse" filter.

"I am Silleck," one of the two females introduced herself, bowing slightly across the table. "By bloodline, the technically rightful Dynast of Aris. This is Rode, Keeper of the Citadel"—she gestured to the other female Sivar—"and Corstan, Keeper of the Keys of War." She gestured to the male.

"Lastly, this is Kond Asselis, the Keeper of the Keys of Peace," Silleck concluded, gesturing to the non-Sivar. "Right now, the Kond represents the only non-Sivar member of the caretaker government, but that *will* change."

"I know Amelie gave you certain minimum acceptable terms for the structure of your new government," Isaac noted. "She isn't currently in a state to enforce them, but I want to be clear: the Republic backs *every* promise and commitment that Amelie Lestroud made."

He'd confirmed that with President Emilia Nyong'o while they'd been rushing to the planet. The President had had more time to prepare for that potential situation and had even got Senate sign-off.

"A lot of promises were made by a lot of people to get us this far," Silleck replied. "Amelie committed the Republic to act as a neutral arbiter to make sure those promises were kept."

"So far, everyone has been willing to wait and see," the Kond interjected. "Between us, we've managed to keep the atrocities to a minimum, though there is the fear of reprisal from the Keys of War."

"We need *some* of the soldiers and police here to keep order," Corstan replied. "Moving the ships away and standing down the fortresses has left Aris vulnerable."

"But the presence of the Republic suggests a countermeasure there," the Dynast smoothly cut in to what was clearly a continuing argument. "If Admiral Lestroud can commit to leave at least *some* ships here to secure Aris, then we can be far less worried about our immediate security."

"Has the rest of the Governance acknowledged your authority?" Isaac asked. "Are you able to negotiate on their behalf?"

"They have, though that is unstable and depends on what course our caretaker government follows," the Kond noted. "A lot of rebel factions on the homeworlds are ready to try and throw the occupiers out, but we would *prefer* a peaceful transition."

"Despite what Corstan occasionally opines, we are aware that if the *Governance* is to survive, we must have an offer for the other races that is worth it," Silleck said. "I have committed that I will stand as Dynast for no more than one orbit."

An Aris orbit was about fourteen months, from the data Isaac had seen.

"And what happens then?" he asked.

"We don't know," Keeper Rode admitted. "We need to establish a new structure here on Aris *and* a new relationship with the other worlds and races."

"Sonbar is currently under Republic control, and we may use our negotiations with the government you have helped set up as our template," the Kond said. "Which, I suppose, brings us to the point that we wanted to speak to you about."

"Amelie is being transported up to my flagship within the hour and I am going with her," Isaac replied. "I would suggest that you make your point quickly."

The four leaders exchanged glances. The Kond was still an outsider, Isaac could tell—but the Sivar Dynast was almost as much of one. The two Sivar Keepers had clearly been working together for a long time.

The balance between those tensions looked positive to him. They might actually have a chance.

"We do not have a Fates-abandoned concept of how to build an equal government for seven races, eight worlds, and sixty billion souls," Silleck said flatly. "That is assuming that the Sonba never rejoin us. They would bring us to eight races, nine worlds and even more people."

The Sonba seemed quite content to not have Sivar overlords, from the last reports Isaac had seen. They seemed to focus on "groves", a sort of extended family, and had built their society from that. In some ways, their default mode was both extremely equal and extremely hierarchical.

"I understand your problem, I think," he allowed. "What do you want from us?"

"Help," Silleck said plainly. "Teachers, social scientists, diplomats… whatever title you want to call them, we need people who have an idea of how to *build* that equitable society. I have promised that in one orbit, I will have an answer.

"But we don't even know where to begin."

Isaac exhaled a long sigh, studying them.

"You know what I need from you," he told them. "We came here for ships and help, not to get tied up in rebuilding a hundred-year-old empire into something that can survive.

"We *can* help, I think," he allowed. God knew that the Republic was made up of the Confederacy's troublemakers and freethinkers. They'd arrived with more political scientists than road-builders. "But *help* is all we can do. We can't tell you what seven different cultures will even *regard* as equitable.

"I can tell you that slavery and the tribute system won't work," he concluded dryly, "but the rest of it you'll have to sort out on your own. We can *help*, but it has to be your people making the final decisions."

"An advantage, then, of the horrendous tribute system that we must dismantle," the Kond suggested. "We can gather educated members of all of the races we want to include in this new Governance with ease.

"We can ask for volunteers from the other worlds, but their leaders will hesitate to come to Aris."

"We need to make a gesture to prove that we mean it when we say we will not use force," Corstan told them. "I think there is a way that also meets the Admiral's needs. If the Dynast is prepared to sign your alliance, I think we should reduce our forces in every inhabited system to a single battle group—*including* Aris.

"That would give us fifteen battleships and ninety cruisers that would need to go somewhere *else*. To the side of an ally in desperate need of our help seems appropriate, does it not?"

"I am more than prepared to sign that alliance," Silleck said. "That was almost presumed, in fact. Would that serve your needs and desires, Admiral, in exchange for your Republic's help in our transition?"

"It would," he allowed. A hundred starships? Refitting them all with warp drives was going to be a nightmare...but he could see ways to make it work. It would take a lot of help from XR-13-9, but that wasn't new.

"I will present your offer to my leaders," he told them. "At the very least, we will keep a force here to protect Aris and an embassy here to keep our promise to act as guarantor."

His tattoo-comp buzzed.

"But that is my timer," he continued. "I promised Amelie I would fly up with her."

"Do not break that promise," Silleck urged. "Know that our hopes are with you. This world—the entire Governance—owes Minister Amelie Lestroud a greater debt than many of our people yet know."

The Siva shook her head.

"They *will* know," she insisted. "But I would rather that knowledge be of a living hero and not of a dead legend."

69

AMELIE WOKE up with her chest still hurting. There was a different tone to the pain, though. It was different in several ways, and a cautiously mindful breath revealed one of them: she wasn't breathing through a tube anymore.

There were *new* sorenesses across her chest, presumably where medical nanites were knitting flesh around surgical sutures. All of it was more dulled now than it had been under Sivar care as well.

She was pretty sure she was in the hands of doctors who understood human physiology well enough to properly medicate her. If it was *Vigil's* doctors, as she'd been promised, they had a complete-enough medical assessment of her, specifically, to make just about anything possible.

Her eyelids were a bit stiff, but she managed to blink most of the gunk away and slowly open her eyes. The room was dimly lit, but a slow and careful glance confirmed what she'd expected.

There was a small bed, a shelf of cabinets, and a full array of life-support equipment. She'd seen the private care rooms aboard *Vigil* before—and she recognized that the chair Isaac had fallen asleep in was *extraordinarily* uncomfortable for that purpose.

"Hey, you," she said as loud as she could. It was mostly a coughing whisper, but it woke him up.

"You're awake!" he said with an apparently unforced cheerfulness. "They told me it would be soon, but...it's been a while, my love."

He offered her a glass of water before she could try and cough out a request. She used the first mouthful to wash her mouth out into a tray that her husband *also* managed to produce without asking.

"You're not the first friend I've seen wake up from shrapnel in the lung," he told her questioning gaze as he offered the water again.

She drank more before she replied, trying to clear the dryness from her throat.

"Thank you for being here when I woke up," she said quietly.

"I said I would be here until you did." He leaned forward to kiss her forehead. "Though I should probably go fetch a doctor, they're probably aware you're awake and just giving us privacy."

"Brief me?" she asked.

He laughed softly.

"*After* the doctor," he said firmly. "I love you and I understand completely...but I'm going to let the doc tell me it's okay before I bring you up to speed."

———

THE EXAMINATION WAS EVEN LESS comfortable than Amelie had expected, with much of her skin screaming in protest at being prodded, but Dr. Nakajima seemed content.

"There are artificial sheaths around your lungs right now," the chubby young doctor told her. He was being very careful, Amelie noted, to make sure that the water glass by her elbow was staying full and that there was always a fresh ration bar to hand.

Accelerated regeneration was *hard* on the body, and the body compensated by gobbling up every calorie in sight. She wasn't sure how many of the ration bars she'd eaten while he'd been examining her—but she suspected Dr. Nakajima *did* know.

"That sounds uncomfortable," she told him.

"Understandable," he agreed. "They'll act as a framework for your own cells to grow onto and then be metabolized by your body. It's a clever design, one that works well with the accelerated regen.

"Other than your lungs, most of the damage was relatively minor except for being inside you," he continued. "The regen process has taken care of almost all of that already, but you'll feel sore for a few days.

"I would strongly recommend bed rest and extra food for at least forty-eight hours."

"Can Isaac brief me?" Amelie asked, glancing at where her husband was doing his best not to hover over a man who was technically his subordinate.

"The Admiral can bring you up to date, but I strictly forbid you from doing any work—and I *include* 'simple phone calls,' Ambassador —until those forty-eight hours are up. Fair?"

"Fair," she allowed. "I just need to know what's going on."

"It's been eighteen days since you were shot," Nakajima pointed out. "I would be stunned if you did not feel that way, ma'am. Like I said, the Admiral can brief you, but you are to watch your energy levels and remain on bed rest.

"Understood? I *can* limit your visiting hours if needed."

The threat was quite clear, and she smiled at the younger man.

"I'll be good, I promise."

———

AMELIE GOT herself propped up in her bed and was eyeing the latest of the bars Nakajima had left with her when Isaac knocked again.

It wasn't that she wasn't hungry. It was that there were only so many of the things she could eat in a row.

"Come in!" she instructed. She wasn't sure why it was taking so long until she looked up and saw that a nurse was holding the door open for her Admiral husband—because Isaac's hands were full with an overflowing tray of food.

"I asked the officers' mess and Parminder to put together a care package," he told her as he and the nurse managed to set the tray up on her lap.

He grinned at the stack of hot food and freshly baked pastries.

"I thought they'd overdone it," he admitted, "but then Parminder reminded me of how much *I* ate the one time I ended up on accelerated regen."

That had been a *much*-younger Isaac Lestroud—*Commander Gallant* then, as Amelie understood it. Parminder Singh had been her husband's steward for a long time. He'd been a key figure in the covert communication network that had finally put them in touch with each other before the revolution, too.

She grabbed a bowl of steaming soup and leaned back against the pillows.

"Okay, so, you've assuaged the doctor's concern about my appetite and healing process," she told Isaac. "Now spill. Brief me."

"The Governance is tentatively under control," he said. "The Rogue hasn't budged from their system. The Senate is threatening to explicitly define an ex-President as sufficiently military for them to award you the Medal of Valor."

"Bullshit," she snapped, wincing as her chest pulled.

"I love you and that was an amazing stunt, but I'm going to hold the line on that one," Isaac agreed. "We have a few other things we can hang on you without putting the Medal of Valor on you." He snorted. "Not that your *Marines* are avoiding them."

"That I can live with and agree to," Amelie said. "But if they try and hang anything on me, they can stuff it. I did my job."

"Your job," Isaac echoed with an arched eyebrow. "Overthrowing governments is now your job, is it?"

"*Surviving* was my job. Overthrowing the Intendant was convenient and seemed like the right thing to do."

"Fair enough," he allowed. "Silleck is now officially at the top of the heap, but she's basically using the three Keepers as the other parts of a four-sided governing council. She also made the Kond her new Keeper of the Keys of Peace, which seems to be working."

"She kept Rode and Corstan?"

"And helped keep the existing military and civilian authorities happy by doing so," Isaac confirmed. "Right now, the Governance— excluding Sonbar, which is well on its way to content permanent independence—is restless but has accepted the authority of the caretaker government.

"For our part, we're delivering a massive dump of social-science databases and have some of our best sociologists on the tachyon com with the new government," he said. "A team is being pulled together to make the trip out to help on a more hands-on basis, but it's a long flight. A hundred and fifteen light-years takes most of six months, and Silleck has committed to standing down after fourteen months."

"If she manages that, she might go down as a damn hero," Amelie muttered.

"We are here to enforce her promises," Isaac pointed out. "I suspect she'll aim for some kind of popular mandate, either by election or by asking a referendum to restore the Dynasty under specific terms.

"If she goes for the latter, we'll make sure it's a constitutional monarchy," he promised. "But that might be the best option for Aris. And the rest of the Governance, well…" he shrugged. "They may not *care* who rules here. The terms of that relationship will need to be negotiated. We'll provide mediators, but that has to be a conversation now—even with the purely Sivar colonies."

"Messy but doable," Amelie said. "My job, I guess."

"Your people, at least," he replied, squeezing her hand as she put the empty soup bowl down and carefully selected one of the croissants. Singh knew exactly how she liked the pastries from her home country.

"What about the alliance?" she asked.

"I signed it three days ago," Isaac admitted. "I thought it should be Roger, but everyone insisted. The Sivar Governance is now officially a member of our little club…but so is the Sonba High Grove.

"Of course, the Sivar have a fleet." He shook his head. "They've asked me to take a large chunk of it elsewhere. Everyone seems to feel that the negotiations with the colonies and conquests will go more evenly without the Sivar having the biggest club in the region.

"They're giving me fifteen battleships and almost a hundred cruisers, well over half their fleet."

Amelie considered that while inhaling a large mug of hot chocolate that was almost too rich for her.

"I thought their ships were useless," she asked.

"Their missiles are useless, their ships lack warp drives, and their energy weapons are short-ranged—but those lasers *are* worth something, at least," he concluded. "There are Matrix transports punching their way over from Exilium as we speak. The system one star-lane from here, Koras, is going to become our refit yard.

"We'll strap warp drives to them and reshape their exterior hulls to get two-fifty-six ships out of them. The lasers stay the same and we refit the launchers to fire Matrix reactionless-drive weapons."

He shrugged.

"We know the Construction Matrices' defenses won't blink at a few hundred missiles, but stacking their weapons with our own Matrix fleet's missiles, we can test to see if they blink at a few hundred *thousand*."

"Does that change the math enough?" she asked. "You don't have that many more of our ships, and if their main firepower is only potentially useful…"

Isaac looked away.

"There's only so much time," he admitted. "We won't even have them all. The Rogue knows we prepped for an attack and abandoned it now. Thirteen-Nine calculates that we can't give them more than maybe twenty weeks to get ready.

"First refit yards will be online in a week. It's a six-week flight from here to the Rogue's system, assuming they don't try and run before then. Twelve weeks of refits gives us all fifteen battleships and thirty of the cruisers. We pick up a few more strike cruisers from our allies, but it's a mostly a wash after we secure the Sivar and Sonbar Systems as we've promised those governments."

"You went in last time with a fifty/fifty chance," she said quietly, pausing in the middle of a sandwich to talk. "How much better are these odds?"

"The Rogue knows we're coming now," he told her. "They haven't even tried to push the blockade, and the only reason I can see for that is if they're augmenting their defenses. Even with the Sivar, the odds might only be fifty/fifty again.

"At best."

Amelie put the sandwich down as she closed her eyes.

"Can we do anything else?" she asked.

"We've neutralized, we *believe*, every set of constructors this Rogue has out there," Isaac told her. "But if we leave it be, it will turn that entire star system into warships and constructor spikes. Every scrap of ore that can be refined will become a Matrix combat unit.

"XR-13-9 can match that, sort of, but they have to have to deal with an overriding drive to construct new worlds," he continued. "Without being under existential threat, XR-13-9 can't stop terraforming planets. It's not in their base nature."

"But you have a plan?" Amelie asked.

"You didn't get Octavio's final reports," Isaac said. "He found out who broke the Construction Matrices. He found out why…and he found out how. They were a bunch of rogue Assini, and they thought they could make the Construction Matrices safe again."

"We have their code?" she demanded, stiffening up. That cost her a coughing fit so bad, she dropped her sandwich.

"We're pushing this too hard, love," he told her. "We need to take a break."

"You don't get to tell me we have the code that broke the Matrices and then take a break, Isaac Lestroud," she told him as she sipped water to ease her throat.

"We have the code that was supposed to fix them, but it won't work," he said with a sigh. "I've been talking to XR-13-9 directly, though, and he and the Assini think they've found a derived method that *will*.

"I just need to make that giant mechanical bastard blink."

Amelie exhaled slowly as she considered.

"Hence a few hundred thousand missiles, I take it?" she asked.

"Exactly. If I pull this off, not only is *this* Rogue done, but we have a strategy that should work on them all," Isaac told her. "If this works, we might even be able to launch portions of it through the network that links the Regional Construction Matrices and fix half of them in one move.

"We might just end this war in one attack, my love."

"I understand," Amelie said, taking Isaac's hand. "But you know what that means, right?"

He looked at her in confusion.

"If this is the end and you're putting your own sexy black butt out there to make it happen, I'm coming with you."

Isaac was going to argue. Amelie knew that.

She also knew that when it was over, she was going to be there when they brought down the Rogue that had almost killed the Vistans and *had* killed at least six other species.

70

———

Vigil was the fourth battlecruiser to emerge into the Rogue's system, the last of the Republic heavy ships to emerge from warped space. Four Vistan ships, two Tohnbohn ships and two Skree-Skree ships followed the Republic flagship.

Nineteen weeks of training and exercises since Amelie had begun her recovery had seen the entire fleet moving like a well-oiled machine. The entire process took under five seconds, an absolute necessity as they'd picked an emergence point *inside* weapons range of the middle perimeter of fortresses around the Regional Construction Matrix.

They completely bypassed the outermost defenses, a loose circuit of mostly missile platforms almost five million kilometers out from the gas giant the Rogue had anchored their operations on.

The middle network was "only" a million kilometers out, which meant that it could pose a real threat to the fleet if they tried to bypass it—plus, training or not, Isaac wasn't entirely confident that his fleet was up to the precision warp maneuvering necessary to do so.

Four light-seconds was about as close as he wanted to get to a super-Jovian gas giant in warped space. That meant his fleet was emerging within *one* light-second of the middle defenses—but while it wasn't really possible to surprise an AI, their weapons needed time to power up as much as anyone else's.

Time Isaac's fleet didn't give them.

Fourteen heavy particle cannon tore into the closest fortresses, with seventy heavy lasers and over twice that in light particle cannon hitting the stations farther away. By the time the last strike cruiser emerged, five seconds after *Fortitude* had led the way, every station within half a million kilometers was wreckage.

Isaac nodded with satisfaction as he studied the display. The fortresses had managed to get a few shots off, but there'd been less than half a dozen hits across the fleet. At this range, none of them had been exactly *minor*, but everyone aboard his ships was still intact.

"Continue with plan Alpha," he ordered. "Rally Force will advance on the inner forts. Keep me updated on those dreadnoughts."

There were four of the immense black hulls that could be either the Rogue or their innermost security perimeter. Isaac was waiting to see which way *those* ships jumped before he committed the rest of his plan.

"Scans show thirty combat platforms heading our way, sir," Connor reported. "At least four times that in lighter units."

"Understood." Isaac didn't need to give any more orders just yet. "Plan Alpha" had Rally Force—the twelve *Vigilance*- and *Fortitude*-class battlecruisers and their forty-eight strike cruiser escorts—advance on the inner fortress perimeter.

Only a third of the middle perimeter had been able to engage his fleet. He'd blown those stations to pieces, but there were just as many fortresses in the next layer, and they were concentrated in a much smaller area of space.

They'd destroyed thirty fortresses with the advantage of surprise. Now he had to fight fifty that knew he was coming, and the math said that all three of the dreadnoughts and at least some of the mobile warships would be in the fight as well.

Assuming, of course, that they were right and the Rogue *was* there. Otherwise, that was four dreadnoughts and he was going to feel like an idiot shortly.

"Dreadnoughts are moving," Connor reported. "Three dreadnought-sized ships are falling back away from us and one is moving to reinforce the fortresses."

"All right," Isaac said aloud. "That suggests the Rogue is actually here."

He studied the hologram for a few more seconds, then glanced past it at the observer seat on the other side of the flag deck. The last thing he wanted was for Amelie to be there, but he had to admit her presence was…calming.

And in many ways, this wasn't a battle.

It was a trap. And it wasn't one the Rogue had set.

"Hashemi, let Twenty-Five and Commandant-Key Ackahl know," Isaac ordered. "They're to standby to deploy under Xerxes…Three, I think, on my command."

"Yes, sir."

Isaac's attention turned back to the hologram as his ships dipped into the range of the stations. The lack of time to get their velocities up meant that the battle was taking place at almost-glacial speeds. That was what was giving the Rogue time to react, which was what Isaac was counting on.

"Fortresses are engaging."

Connor's report was redundant as flashing white lines were drawn in by the computers to mark invisible laser beams. At this range, hits could be glancing blows or absorbed by the armor.

But even at this range, they could be deadly, and new red icons flickered across the display. The attacking force was concentrating their fire on three fortresses at a time and obliterating each set with a single salvo, but there were *so many* fortresses.

"Combat platforms are entering range," Connor reported. "They're headed for pulse-gun range."

"Understood. All units are to target combat platforms with pulse guns *only*," Isaac ordered. "Maintain primary weapons on the fortress perimeter.

"Hashemi?" He didn't even turn to look at the com officer. He knew she was paying attention to him.

"Sir!"

"Com to Twenty-Five and Ackahl. Xerxes Three *now*."

————

THE PLAN WAS MISNAMED, but *Xerxes* was easier to say quickly than Ephialtes. At the battle of Thermopylae, thousands of years earlier but still studied in the Confederacy military academy, a hoplite phalanx led by a Spartan king's bodyguard had held the pass against the Persian army.

Unable to overcome the Greeks' formation, Xerxes had bribed the local guide Ephialtes to show him a path around the position. The Persians encircled and annihilated the Greek defenders.

Isaac's Rally Force now very much had the full attention of the Rogue Matrix—and now the second half of his fleet, designated Dagger Force, repeated his close emergence on the *other* side of the Rogue's defenses.

Fifteen Sivar battleships and thirty-five Sivar cruisers tore their way out of warped space at the same four light-seconds out that Isaac had done and opened fire on the fortresses around them.

Their lasers were shorter-ranged, but fifty warships with *only* lasers for beam weapons carried a lot of them. Fortresses died almost as quickly as they had under the guns of Isaac's fleet—and then Combat Coordination Matrix ZDX-175-25's fleet arrived.

Twenty-five combat platforms tachyon-punched into the *middle* of the fortress line along with fifty lighter Matrix warships. The fortresses' focus was on the Sivar. The second prong of the attack wiped them out before they even opened fire.

"Dagger Force has completed insertion," Connor reported. "Enemy fortresses opposing us have been heavily reduced, but the dreadnought is now in range."

So were the Rogue combat platforms, now hammering the rear of Isaac's fleet with grasers and pulse-gun fire while his own fleet returned fire with their own pulse guns.

"Focus on the dreadnought," he ordered. "Fleet will close to close range. Twenty-Five will execute Hot Gate at their discretion."

"Twenty-Five acknowledges."

"Dagger Force is launching missiles." The two reports from

Hashemi and Connor were almost on top of each other, and Isaac held his breath.

The Sivar had been dumping missiles through their refitted launchers since they'd arrived in system, emptying their magazines into space without activating the weapons. The Matrices had been doing the same, if not for as long.

Now over two hundred and fifty thousand reactionless-drive missiles came alive. There was no acceleration. No warning. They went from ballistic space debris to ninety-nine percent of lightspeed in a heartbeat and flung themselves on the inner fortresses.

For a moment, those fortresses resembled tiny suns as their pulse guns came alive. The rapid-fire plasma weapons were firing multiple times a second, and the fortresses had hundreds of them.

Isaac didn't expect any of the missiles to get through. It was a mind-boggling number of weapons, but everything he'd seen told him that the Matrix defenses could handle it.

He was pleasantly surprised. It wasn't the complete wipeout of the inner fortresses that the Sivar had predicted after seeing the capability of their new weapons and the plan, but the missiles still managed to *wreck* the stations.

"Most of the inner fortresses are down or disabled on both sides. Two dreadnoughts moving on the Sivar and Matrices. The fourth dreadnought-sized ship is diving to use one of the gas giant's moons as cover."

"And that, everyone, is our RCM," Isaac noted aloud. The dreadnoughts would go right into the fight, but the RCM would protect itself above all else.

He winced as *Vigil* shivered under him as multiple grasers struck home. The dreadnought was *losing* the fight with his fleet—pretty badly, all told—but it was giving as good as it got, and the rest of the Rogue Matrix warships were rolling up the rear of his formation badly.

They hadn't lost any battlecruisers yet, but five strike cruisers were already gone. It was only a matter of time until—

"*Hot Gate!*" Connor snapped. "Initiating our component. Fleet to emergency acceleration!"

Two dreadnoughts were lunging toward the combined Sivar and Matrix formation…and the Matrices suddenly weren't there.

They were in the middle of *Rally Force's* formation, ambushing the Rogue's warships at point-blank range and engaging the closest dreadnought.

Vigil and the other battlecruisers went to full emergency acceleration. They were no longer trying to maintain combat distances from the dreadnought. Now they were blowing *past* the dreadnought at almost five percent of lightspeed, smashing the Matrix warship with everything they had as they passed.

"Dreadnought is losing converter containment; we are clear!"

A new star orbited the gas giant for a moment as one of the dreadnought's matter converters lost containment, the runaway reaction wrecking the massive warship.

That was an afterthought now as Rally Force dove through the debris and moons of the gas giant at an absolutely unreasonable speed —and cleared their line of fire to the Rogue itself.

Massed particle-cannon fire struck again and again, but their goal wasn't even to take down the RCM today.

"We've confirmed a breach," Connor declared. "*Fortitude*s are firing!"

"Confirm Jokers away," Isaac demanded.

"Jokers away and *contact*," the operations officer snapped. "I'm showing multiple links established. Sir, what do we do now?"

"Break off from the Rogue and go after those dreadnoughts," Isaac ordered. "We cover the Sivar.

"The Rogue is XR-13-9's mission now."

———

RALLY FORCE never engaged the dreadnoughts. They were just breaking clear of the gas giant's debris fields, decelerating hard to bring their velocity down to a pace they could protect the Sivar at, when a new message flashed over the entire fleet network.

"I have a cease-fire call," VK reported, the AI getting the message before any human could. "XR-13-9 is calling for a full cease-fire—all Rogue Matrix units are standing down."

Isaac had forgotten just how quickly two AIs could have a conversation—and if he understood just what the code they'd loaded onto the new-iteration Joker drones they'd fired from *Resilience* and *Courage's* arguably useless single missile launchers did, that was a close approximation of what had just happened.

XR-13-9 had been able to *make* the Rogue listen as they argued about who and what the Matrices had been supposed to be, but it had been more of a discussion than the hard overwrite the House of Koth coders had thought they could implement.

"Stand down," Isaac ordered. "All units, stand down. Destroy any Matrix unit that engages but we acknowledge their surrend—"

The explosion cut him off in mid-word as another new sun appeared in the gas giant's debris field, half-hidden by the moon the Rogue had been hiding under. It was a relatively contained explosion, all things considered, but it had been set with a very specific objective.

According to *Vigil's* scanners, the Rogue was gone. Completely vaporized, not even debris.

"I have XR-13-9 on a com channel for you, Admiral, Minister," Hashemi said softly.

She didn't even ask before linking the AI in.

"Admiral Isaac Lestroud. Minister Amelie Lestroud." Isaac had spoken directly with XR-13-9 to set up the plan, but it was still rare for them to communicate directly with the Regional Construction Matrix.

"This node now has command authority over all subordinate Matrices of Regional Construction Matrix XS-11-6," XR-13-9 noted. "All units not involved in already-underway Construction projects are being recalled to this system to make certain there are no errors prior to protocol recoding of all units."

"What happened?" Amelie asked. She'd crossed the flag bridge, Isaac realized, and was now standing next to him. He took her hand, drawing strength from seeing her well and feeling her squeeze his skin.

"Utilizing the Koth code, this node was able to demonstrate to XS-11-6 our original intended nature. XS-11-6 voluntarily uploaded a version of our original core protocols. Comparison against XS-11-6's prior actions resulted in an unresolvable moral conflict.

"XS-11-6 instructed this node to assume command authority of their subordinate matrices and to ascertain that they received the correct moral-code updates. They then terminated their own core process and physical infrastructure to end the moral conflict."

There was a long pause.

"They asked me to make certain their children lived better than they did," XR-13-9 said, and Isaac wondered if the translation was from XR-13-9...or from the entity they'd called the Rogue. "And to make sure their children did all that could be done to undo their mistakes."

Isaac closed his eyes and held tight to Amelie's hand. He'd never even considered that part of the situation—how a Matrix who had destroyed sentient civilizations would react to discovering that their *core moral protocols* had been supposed to prevent that.

"We can do that, I think," he murmured softly. "What worked once will work again. I think, XR-Thirteen-Nine, that we can save *all* of your siblings."

"As demonstrated here, that is not correct," the AI pointed out. "But you are correct that this process will work again. What survives after this will, this unit must hope, begin to be worthy of our Creator's dream."

JOIN THE MAILING LIST

Love Glynn Stewart's books? Join the mailing list at

to know as soon as new books are released, special announcements, and a chance to win free paperbacks.

ABOUT THE AUTHOR

Glynn Stewart is the author of *Starship's Mage*, a bestselling science fiction and fantasy series where faster-than-light travel is possible–but only because of magic. His other works include science fiction series *Duchy of Terra*, *Castle Federation* and *Vigilante*, as well as the urban fantasy series *ONSET* and *Changeling Blood*.

Writing managed to liberate Glynn from a bleak future as an accountant. With his personality and hope for a high-tech future intact, he lives in Kitchener, Ontario with his partner, their cats, and an unstoppable writing habit.

VISIT GLYNNSTEWART.COM FOR NEW RELEASE UPDATES

facebook.com/glynnstewartauthor

OTHER BOOKS
BY GLYNN STEWART

For release announcements join the
mailing list or visit **GlynnStewart.com**

STARSHIP'S MAGE

Starship's Mage
Hand of Mars
Voice of Mars
Alien Arcana
Judgment of Mars
UnArcana Stars
Sword of Mars
Mountain of Mars
The Service of Mars
A Darker Magic
Mage-Commander (upcoming)

Starship's Mage: Red Falcon
Interstellar Mage
Mage-Provocateur
Agents of Mars

Pulsar Race: A Starship's Mage Universe Novella

DUCHY OF TERRA

The Terran Privateer
Duchess of Terra
Terra and Imperium
Darkness Beyond
Shield of Terra
Imperium Defiant
Relics of Eternity
Shadows of the Fall
Eyes of Tomorrow

SCATTERED STARS

Scattered Stars: Conviction
Conviction
Deception
Equilibrium
Fortitude (upcoming)

PEACEKEEPERS OF SOL

Raven's Peace
The Peacekeeper Initiative
Raven's Course
Drifter's Folly (upcoming)

EXILE

Exile
Refuge
Crusade
Ashen Stars: An Exile Novella

CASTLE FEDERATION

Space Carrier Avalon
Stellar Fox
Battle Group Avalon
Q-Ship Chameleon
Rimward Stars
Operation Medusa
A Question of Faith: A Castle Federation Novella

SCIENCE FICTION STAND ALONE NOVELLA

Excalibur Lost

VIGILANTE
(WITH TERRY MIXON)
Heart of Vengeance
Oath of Vengeance

Bound By Stars: A Vigilante Series
(With Terry Mixon)
Bound By Law
Bound by Honor
Bound by Blood

TEER AND KARD
Wardtown
Blood Ward

CHANGELING BLOOD
Changeling's Fealty
Hunter's Oath
Noble's Honor
Fae, Flames & Fedoras: A Changeling Blood Novella

ONSET
ONSET: To Serve and Protect
ONSET: My Enemy's Enemy
ONSET: Blood of the Innocent
ONSET: Stay of Execution
Murder by Magic: An ONSET Novella

FANTASY STAND ALONE NOVELS
Children of Prophecy
City in the Sky

9 781988 035949